CONGO
SHADOWS

First Edition Design Publishing
Sarasota, Florida USA

Congo Shadows
Copyright ©2016 John B. Franz

ISBN 978-1506-909-34-9 AMZ TRADE
ISBN 978-1506-903-40-8 PRINT
ISBN 978-1506-903-41-5 EBOOK

LCCN 2016958394

November 2016

Published and Distributed by
First Edition Design Publishing, Inc.
P.O. Box 20217, Sarasota, FL 34276-3217
www.firsteditiondesignpublishing.com

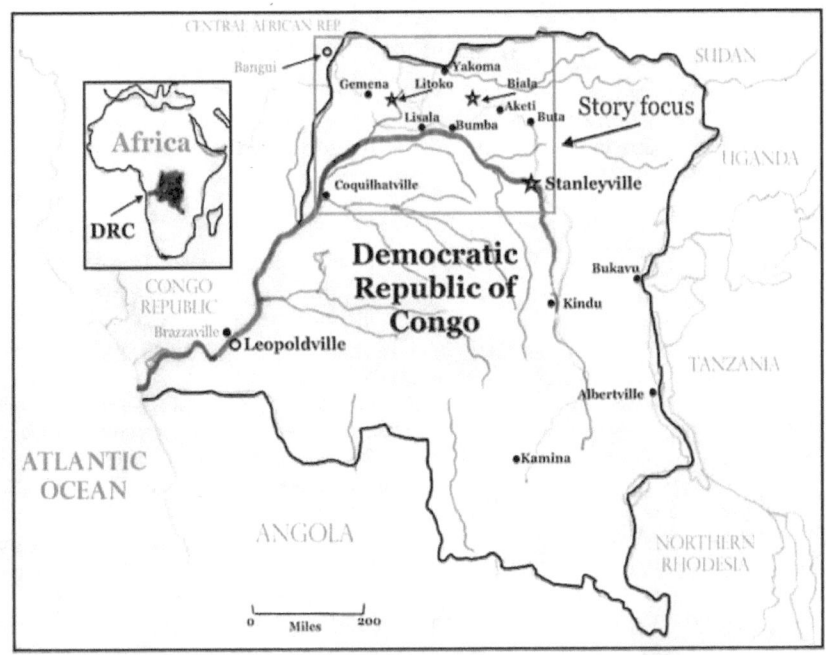

MAP 1 - DRC & Story Focus Area

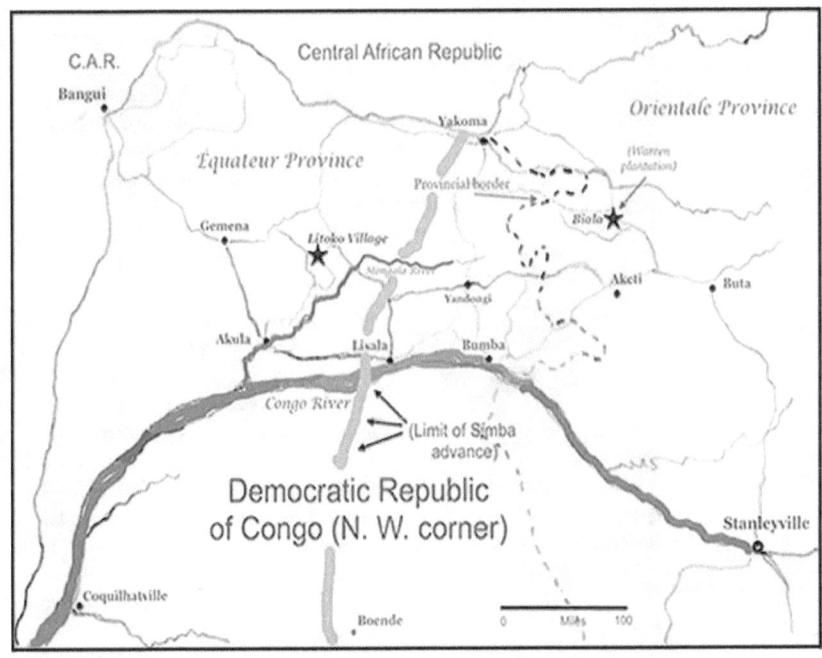

MAP 2 - DRC NW Corner

Congo Crisis Timeline
(1960 – 1964)

1960	June 30	• **Independence Day in DR Congo;**
		• Kasavubu is named President; Lumumba, named Prime Minister
	July	• DRC army (Force Publique) mutinies
		• Katanga Province secedes, Tshombe, hires white mercenaries, Belgium supports the decision
		• UN peacekeepers & mercenaries replace Belgian troops to restore order, safety for whites
	August	• Kasai Province secedes
	September	• Pres. Kasavubu fires Prime Minister Lumumba & Lumumba fires Kasavubu: government standoff
		• Col. Mobutu overthrows Congo government, arrests Lumumba with US & CIA support
1961	February	• Lumumba is killed, with US/Belgian compliance?
	March	• Orientale Province (Stanleyville) briefly secedes, Gizenga named Head of State
	August	• Adoula becomes DRC's PM
1963	December	• Riots take place in Albertville, discontent flares
		• Col. Olenga creates Simbas, recruits his army
1964	January	• Kwilu rebellion grows, Idiofa, Gungu are occupied, Mulele & jeunesse lead
	June	• Albertville is occupied by Olenga's Simbas, slaughter of the educated & leaders begins
	July	• Simba forces advance, occupy Port-Empain, Paulis, Bumba, Lisala; slaughter local leaders occurs
	August	• Olenga's Simbas occupy Stanleyville; Kinghis is appointed President, then Gbenye, Soumialot is named Prime Minister of People's Republic of Congo
		• Tshombe is named PM of DRC, hires mercenaries
		• 500 of Congolese Stanleyville elite are slaughtered
		• Bukavu is retaken by US supplied ANC, Simbas are defeated
		• Albertville is retaken by US-supplied ANC, plus Katanga reinforcements, 400 Simbas are slaughtered
	September	• Lisala is retaken from Simbas by a small mercenary force & ANC; 400+ Simbas killed
	October	• Bunia is recaptured by ANC from Simbas
	November	• Whites in Stanleyville are rounded up & brought to Hotel Victoria;
		• Lima One force (mercenaries) heads for Stanleyville
	November 24	**Operation Dragon Rouge –**
		• Belgian Paratroopers, dropped by US planes, liberate 1,600 expatriates from Simbas in Stanleyville; mercenaries & ANC retake the city & region

Prologue

Early afternoons are hot and humid during Congo's rainy season. The air feels heavy, dense. It's hard to breathe. Rising above, swirling plumes of white clouds fill an azure sky like steam escaping from some gigantic pipe. They morph into anvil shapes and begin to darken. Here and there, sunbeam shafts spike through the billowing mass, celestial spotlights that briefly illuminate people or objects below.

Shortly, the afternoon's brightness fades, and darkness spreads across the land, like some unseen hand has turned the dimmer switch. Drama is in the works. The first rumblings of distant thunder confirm it. Soon, the sky explodes. Thunder crashes, and lightning cracks: one, two, three times in succession. The heavens open with a roar. Rain arrives in pulsating sheets, assailing every living and moving thing beneath. Nothing, no one is untouched.

And then it is over.

Steam rises in hazy, shimmering billows and the thunder drifts off. Broken branches, sodden ground and dripping leaves bear witness to the power of the passing storm. Wet dogs emerge from beneath bushes to shake dry. Lingering trickles anoint the heads of people who reappear from dark doorways and scurry back to life.

The events surrounding the birth of the Democratic Republic of Congo, in many ways mirror this rainy season ritual. Some said independence was inevitable, as predictable as the p.m. showers. To many Belgians, however, it was only hypothetical, something belonging to an uncertain future. It's leaders and citizens living a privileged life in Congo did not see the storm coming. Perhaps they didn't want to. Colonial practices barred Congolese from management roles. It was the *Belgian* Congo, after all! At Independence few new citizens could be found with *any* leadership aptitude and experience.

But ready or not, independence arrived in the Congo. It came suddenly. Drama was in the works. Riots in Léopoldville and Stanleyville in 1959 prompted a hastily organized constitutional convention. Independence was granted the following June, 1960. Leaders were appointed. They were, however, woefully ill prepared to govern the continent's second largest country.

Almost from the onset of Independence, darkness set in. National army troops mutinied within days. In the southwest, the country's richest mining region, Katanga Province, seceded. The diamond-rich central Kasai Province quickly followed. With uranium, copper, cobalt and coltan deposits at stake, like vultures on a floundering prey, outsiders swooped in. Belgian business interests, white mercenaries, UN peacekeeping forces and finally America's CIA and the Soviet Union's agents all entered the unfolding African drama.

Independence was a confusing time for average Congolese as well. Unrealistic promises had been made; expectations of new wealth and power were introduced. As the country's whites exited, however, commerce ground to a halt. The hopes of common people were dashed. Disillusionment turned into widespread anger. Order broke down. Old rivalries and jealousies surfaced. It became unsafe for expatriates and nationals alike. Business owners fled by the score, and Western missionaries were evacuated.

A deadly game of musical chairs occupied Congo's leadership ranks during the early years. President Kasavubu fired Prime Minister Lumumba. Not to be outdone, Lumumba, in turn, fired Kasavubu. Top military commander, Joseph Mobutu then removed both. After the charismatic Lumumba was killed, a succession of leaders followed, but none were able to successfully fill the vacuum. Rebellion flourished.

The most significant early insurgent movement was the so-called Simba Rebellion, led by the infamous Lt. General Nicolas Olenga. It forms the backdrop for this novel's story. Birthed in the disaffected eastern side of the country, it was defined by its use of witchcraft combined with brutal violence and torture of victims. The Simbas eventually controlled nearly half of Congo, presenting an ominous threat to the young, faltering central government. The Soviet Union joined with other interests hostile to the West in supporting these rebels.

US and Belgian intervention was finally triggered by a major strategic miscalculation of the Simbas: they occupied Stanleyville (present-day Kisangani) on August 5, 1964 holding 1,600 expatriates hostage for 111 days. This exploit focused international attention on the rebellion and its horrors, prompting widespread condemnation. White mercenaries from South and East Africa were once again employed to shore up Congo's national army. Belgian and US resources joined to overthrow the rebels and rescue the hostages.

This novel's story is embedded in the actual events leading up to and including the historic Stanleyville rescue. Part I describes the growing pre-Independence storm. The separations and evacuations that followed brought about changes in the social order that divided clans and families and encouraged rebellion. They also motivated attempts to restore and reconcile broken relationships. In Part II the spotlight focuses in to illuminate the story's central characters as they navigate the shadows and darkness of an expanding Simba Rebellion. Nothing, no one is left untouched. Finally, Part III introduces efforts extended to rescue, release and redeem the brokenness that impacted the lives and futures of all concerned.

The specter of violence and its containment inevitably spawns moral dilemmas, effects that must be addressed once the storm has passed. As history once again confirms, only the presence of light dispels the shadows.

CONGO SHADOWS

John B. Franz

Table of Contents

PART III The Aftermath

PART I

The Gathering Storm

CHAPTER 1
Litoko, June 1957

Deep in conversation, the mismatched pair made their way down the quarter mile path to the river. Surrounding the two missionary mothers and their children were a dozen lively African youngsters, prancing, skipping, giggling and chattering away with one another and their white playmates. Parrots in the high canopy overhead screeched in protest at the invasion of their domain.

The shorter of the two women, Patty, wore a lemon yellow muumuu with dark red flowers and carried a large cloth bag slung over one shoulder. Heavy-set, her round cheeks shone a rosy pink, more from the warmth of the day than from exertion for they were walking slowly. She held the hand of her youngest, nine-year-old Lizzie, as they made their way along the sun-mottled path.

Nathalie, her neighbor, walked alongside. She was half a head taller and slender, appearing almost gaunt in her loose-fitting powder blue cotton dress. Her dishwater blonde hair was tied in a bun at the back. She also carried a cotton bag over her shoulder filled with snacks, water and extra towels for an afternoon at the beach.

"After more than a decade here, you'd think I could speak decent Lingala or French. I still get the words all mixed up, Nattie. When Doug's gone I seem to always end up having trouble getting through to Tata Rafael. Last night he burned our dinner, claiming I told him 'cenquante' not 'quarante' for the cooking time." She sighed. "Perhaps he was right. I wish I didn't have to *have* house workers."

"Does it help to write the words down, Patty?" Nattie slapped at a fly on her neck. "That's what I've had to do to learn vocabulary."

"Nothing seems to help. Some days I get so tired of *everything* we have to do just to *try* to live a normal life. Killing giant cockroaches, sifting weevils from the flour, boiling drinking water, taking luke-warm baths, you name it. I confess it wears on me."

Nattie smiled, unruffled. She had heard all of this and more many times before. "Well, Patty, I guess that's what we signed on for when we came to Africa. Daily living is full of challenges, for sure."

Nathalie slowed to remove a small stick from her sandal, hopping on the opposite foot. "But this life also comes with its rewards. Warm afternoons by the river are one of them. Like today." She chuckled. "Forget the cockroaches for a little while, okay, Patty?"

"Oh, Nattie, you're always so positive. I don't know how you do it. I suppose the difference is that you *wanted* to come here. I didn't."

Patty gestured as the path opened to a clearing next to the river. "Well, here we are." They entered the open area. It was an inviting grassy spot, shaded by large trees. A narrow sandy beach and shallow inlet provided a perfect place to wade and paddle about in the cool water.

As the children raced for the inlet, Patty called out, "Ah-ah! We don't go in the water without adult supervision. You know the rules, kids." The menacing presence of the dark green river flowed deep and fast just yards off shore.

The escort of Congolese children raced on ahead, unrestrained, laughing and splashing into the water. Six white faces – the missionary kids – all wore sour expressions. The boys picked through fallen mangos to find some keepers while the two mothers spread blankets on the grass.

Their task completed, Patty and Nathalie followed their smiling children as they sprinted ahead of them into the water to join their friends. Patty observed fourteen-year-old Nick and his best friend Masemba moving off to her right, in the direction of marshy weeds at the end of the beach.

"Where are you going, Nicky?"

"Frog hunting. We'll stay in sight."

"Well...okay," she said hesitantly, frowning. "But do keep a careful watch for snakes."

"Don't worry, Mama. I've got my hunting knife," he called over his shoulder, hurrying to catch up with Masemba.

"Honestly, Nattie, I *do* worry about that kid. He is fearless. That's Doug's doing. Frankly, I'd prefer he didn't get too used to this country."

"Really? I think it's a *wonderful* place to grow up." Nathalie smiled and pointed. "Look at all the fun the kids are having."

Thirteen-year-old Ellie Ellis was cheering a friend in a hopscotch game at the river's edge. She had followed the older boys for a time, but lost interest when they ignored her. *"Frogs are a dumb boy thing,"* she concluded and turned back to join the girls. They clearly adored her.

Ellie's two younger brothers, Kyle and Kevin, were engaged in a splashing contest. Squealing in delight, they churned the knee-deep water into each other's faces, scattering the others nearby. The laughter ended when eight-year-old Kevin took in a mouthful of water, coughing and crying.

"Okay, boys. That's enough." Patty was standing a few yards away holding onto Lizzie's outstretched arms while she practiced her kick.

The words had no sooner left her mouth then Patty gasped and pointed, releasing her daughter. Lizzie dropped face-first. *Ka-splosh!* She came up sputtering in protest, just in time to hear her mother emit a blood-curdling scream: *"Eeyeek! Ngando! Crocodile!"*

Startled by the shrieks, the other children froze in place. Then, as if on signal, they turned and raced for the riverbank, screaming in panic. To Patty's right, Nick and Masemba straightened up from their frog stalking, heads and eyes turned to the screams. Lizzie struggled to her feet, reaching for her mother. Beyond them, the two Ellis boys stood in place. As Kyle, the older of the two, glanced about in alarm, a dark shape with two eyes at the surface, glided toward him from the deep water.

The five-foot crocodile dove as it attacked. Clamping on to its victim's leg, it twisted in a death roll. Ten-year-old Kyle screamed as he fell and flailed in the water, a huge frothing splash. After pushing Lizzie toward the shore, it took Patty three lunging steps to reach the struggling child. Grasping Kyle's flailing arms, she pulled, tugging backwards. *"Someone...help!"* Patty's efforts dragged the croc a foot closer to shore, but its deadly grip held onto the screaming, sputtering child.

Nick and Masemba plunged across the shallows in giant steps. "I'm going for the eyes, like Dad said," Nick called to his friend as he pulled his knife from its sheath. *"Kanga ye na nsima! Grab his backside."*

"Ehh!" Masemba replied, taking a quick breath as he dove, hugging the back legs and tail of the writhing animal with all his strength. Nick grasped his prized knife in both hands. Swinging it above his head to use his body weight, he plunged it into the animal's eyes; first into one, then even harder into the other. On the second stab, the croc released its grip on the child. It rolled and twisted away from Masemba's grip. Nick's knife remained sticking out of its eye.

"Grab him boys!" Patty directed as she, Nick and Masemba half floated and half carried the sobbing, injured Kyle toward shore and into the arms of his frantic mother, wading toward them. The lower part of his calf and foot were shredded, bleeding profusely. Chunks of flesh hung loose.

"Run to the mission. Get help! *Noki! Hurry!*" Nathalie screamed, while tearing strips of her dress to wrap around Kyle's leg. "We'll have to make a tourniquet. Someone give me a belt." Ellie rushed up crying, tore the belt off her shorts and handed it to her mother.

Masemba, dripping wet, took off at a sprint, heading back up the river path and on toward the Catholic mission.

Patty saw that the young boy was lying very still by then. "He's fainted. We should keep him warm." She retrieved a blanket. Once Nathalie had stopped the worst of the bleeding she carefully wrapped the blanket around her unconscious son.

Patty rounded up the other hysterical children who had gathered in a tight group, crying and holding onto one another. *"Bana, tika makalele wana. Banga te! Ngando akufi. Stop the noise, children. Don't be afraid, the crock is dead."* Her attempt to quell the noise and reassure the distraught children changed little. Patty stroked and hugged Lizzie who was sobbing uncontrollably and would not let go. She was still shaking, herself.

Nick looked back to the river. He noticed that the croc was now floating, white belly-up, unmoving. It wasn't a huge animal, but plenty big enough to cause serious harm. Wading over to the carcass, he dragged it onto shore. Then, using both hands, he pulled his hunting knife out of the animal's eye. After wiping the blood off on some grass, he returned the knife to its leather sheath. Nick's heart was still racing, but he felt good that he had known what to do and did it. *Dad will like this*, he thought.

Patty called out, "Nicky, leave that horrid beast alone and come here. You're bleeding." A trickle of blood from a long scratch ran down the back of his leg.

"It must have been the croc's claw when I jumped him. It's not deep, Momma." She walked him over to their blanket and found a cloth to clean his leg. Lizzie and eleven-year-old brother Todd stuck to her like shadows. "Whatever possessed you to do this, son?" Patty muttered, shaking her head.

"Wow, Nick. That was neat!" Todd said with big eyes. Nick returned a slight smile. His leg was starting to hurt.

It took a half hour for the helpers to show up. Sarah Nkumu was the first to arrive, breathless from her run. A former member of the Ellis household as a foster child, her face displayed alarm. Rushing up to Nathalie, she wrapped her arms tightly about her.

"Oh, I'm so sorry this happened, Mme. Nathalie. How is Kyle?" Sarah released her grip and dropped to her knees, gently brushing the hair back from his closed eyes.

"Yaka komema mwana oyo, Come, carry the child." she called out, directing the panting male nurses to load Kyle on the litter they

carried. She continued in English, this time to Nathalie. "Before I left the mission, I placed a radio call to the doctor. He will meet us at the clinic. He should be waiting by the time we get Kyle there."

Nathalie nodded, tears streaming down her cheeks. "Thank you. Thank you so much, Sarah. I'm grateful."

"You see, Nattie? I told you this is no place to raise a family!" Patty finished wiping the blood from Nick's leg. She seemed determined to have the last word.

Nathalie let her. Her attention was all on Kyle.

CHAPTER 2
Litoko, June 1957

The small group of hunters emerged from a dark forest path that opened to one side of the well-groomed Litoko mission compound. Even in the long shadows of the late afternoon it was easy to tell they were hunters. The white man in the lead, wearing a floppy hat, carried a rifle over his shoulder. Bows and arrows were slung from the shoulders of the four African men who followed. Sections of freshly killed antelope were lashed to the center of a pole balanced between each pair. The men walked in a weary, even pace.

Two small figures burst from the porch of one of the four residences. "Daddy! Nick killed a croc!"

"It almost ate Kyle. He's at the clinic! Mama saved me and Kyle."

The two breathless children hugged their father's legs, bouncing and jumping with excitement.

"What? Wait. Start again. Not at the same time, kids. What happened?" Doug Warren set his rifle down and knelt to hug the children and talk at eye level. His hunting companions lowered their poles and looked on with puzzled interest.

Doug smiled as the two youngsters breathlessly recounted the afternoon's drama. "Swimming at the river, a whole bunch of us. Mamma saw it. She screamed. The croc chomped Kyle's leg. Blood all over the place. Mama tried to pull him away but he went under. Then, Nick and Masemba came. Nick stabbed the *ngando*. Yeah. With the knife you gave him. He killed it. Masemba tackled it. Kyle's hurt bad. The doctor had to operate."

Doug looked up to notice that Patty, Nick and Masemba had descended from the porch of their house and were approaching. Nick ran the last few steps and hugged his father around the neck. Doug ruffled his hair, patted Masemba's shoulder and smiled at Patty, reaching to give her a hug and greeting.

"Some afternoon at the river, you had today!" Patty did not smile back. She stood stiffly and did not return his embrace.

"It was just awful, Doug. Kyle barely escaped with his life. Nick took a foolish risk and all of the children are afraid to close their eyes. I don't see how we can ever go to the river again."

"But, it sounds like you, Nick and Masemba, here, were the heroes of the day. Isn't that true?" Doug's smile had been replaced with a puzzled expression. Nick, still hugging, looked up and nodded. Patty continued to frown.

"It's dangerous here, Doug. Today proves it. It's no place to raise a family. Nicky took a foolish risk. Your giving him that knife made him think he was some kind of super kid. The croc could have turned on him. If it had, *then* what would you say? He *did* get hurt, by the way." She pointed to a bandage on Nick's leg.

Patty crossed her arms. "I think we should leave *now* before one of our children is injured like Kyle. He may lose his foot."

Nick started to protest, but his father signaled him with a shake of his head and a partially raised hand. "Not now, son. We'll talk later."

Doug turned to his Congolese companions and offered a brief explanation in Lingala of the family's animated report before giving them directions as to where to take the meat from their hunt.

"Ye, abomi ngando? He killed a croc?" One asked, pointing at Nick. *"Ye wana, mwana makasi! That one's a strong child!"* he declared with an admiring look.

"I don't think Nick should be praised as some kind of 'tough kid'" interjected Patty. "He was lucky this time, but he *is* only a child. You make him think he can do far more than he should. He takes risks he has no business taking."

Doug released Nick, and grasping Patty by the arm started off toward their house. "Let's discuss this in private, Patty. Not here. Not now. You've all been through a lot, today."

Nick turned to Masemba. "Come on, *ndeko*, let's go see if Ellie has any more news about her brother.

"Yes, if there *is* news, *Ayeba-trop* will know." A quick smile of recognition passed between the two friends as they headed off.

CHAPTER 3
Litoko, June 30, 1960

Three Years Later – Depanda

The early morning air was already warm, humid and full of familiar daylight sounds from the surrounding jungle. Monkeys chattered, sunbirds and cuckoos called and chirped to one another, insects whined, trilled and made sounds like sawing wood.

Nick laid still, eyes closed, listening intently to the familiar morning chorus as consciousness slowly settled in. *Depanda. Today is the day. It doesn't sound any different. Maybe quieter?*

He wasn't sure what to expect from this day. For the last several months while away at the MK school in Karawa, he and his classmates had heard troubling reports of violent protests ranging from Léopoldville 600 miles distant to Gemena, the district capital only 75 miles to the west. Having just finished his junior year, Nick and his siblings were home at Litoko station for the summer. And *Depanda* had finally arrived.

Nick sat up on his bed, swung his feet to the cement floor and rubbed the sleep out of his eyes. The bright, crisscross pattern of morning light lit the opposite wall through open barred windows. "Hey sleepy head. Wake up!" he called to Todd across the room. The younger teen was tangled in sheets, unmoving, drooling mouth open in his bed.

The words had barely left his lips when, right behind him came a loud animal noise. "*Roar!*" Nick jumped. "Whaaa...?" Todd sprang upright, eyes wide open.

"*Mboté, Kiuta. Sango nini? Hello. What's happening?*" The laughing greeting came from just outside the open window.

Smiling, he recognized his soccer nickname, *Kiuta*, Gaboon viper, reflecting his reputation as a deadly forward striker. Nick looked out through the bars. "Hey, Masemba. You made me jump like a *niao, cat.* C'mon in. We're just getting up. What're you doing out so early?"

"Attende. Nakoya na ndako. Wait. I'm coming in the house."

As Masemba circled around to enter the house, both boys jumped out of bed and into motion. Nick pulled on the cut-offs and blue tee shirt he had flung on a corner chair the night before. Todd removed his carefully folded shorts and polo shirt from the dresser drawer and put them on.

"Likambo nini na mama na bino? What's with your mother?" Masemba, flicked a glance back toward the living room as he entered.

"I don't know. Is something wrong with Mama?" Nick and Todd looked at each other before heading for the door and on into the front room.

In the rocker by the window sat their mother. She was softly humming "It is well with my soul," as she rocked, eyes closed, bible open on her lap. Right away Nick noticed her tear-stained cheeks.

"What's wrong, Mama?" He and Todd stopped short. "Where's Tata Rafael...and the workers? Is today a holiday for *everyone*?"

His mother did not answer the questions. "It's just too much, too much."

"What do you mean, Mama?" Nick knelt beside her rocker. She placed her hand on his arm and looked up.

"Tata Rafael told me he is no longer working for *mundeles* now that Independence has arrived. He also said that we'd better plan to leave in a hurry since people in the village are already talking about coming here to take our things."

Her voice was shaking and the tears had begun to flow again. "Why did your father choose *now* to go on a hunting trip? It's just like him to ignore trouble and leave us in the lurch. I just know he won't want to leave. It's too much – I...I don't know how to deal with it."

Nick didn't know what to do either, or what to *say* for that matter. Fourteen-year-old Todd just stood, wide-eyed, staring at his tearful mother, rocking slowly. Masemba looked on in silence.

For several extended moments no one moved, until the spell was broken by a noise outside. Someone came bounding up the steps to the open front door. *"Coa-Coa-Coa!"* The young voice called out in the African version of a doorbell.

It was the Warren's 16-year-old next-door neighbor: perky, self-assured Ellie. Her father, Brandon Ellis, was the head of the mission station. The Ellis's possessed the station's only short-wave radio, the sole contact with the outside world for the four American families that lived there. Ellie loved being "in the know," serving as the station's principal source of information, and truth-be-told, rumor. She loved it way too much in Nick's opinion.

"CEM headquarters in Léopoldville has just gotten word from the U.S. Embassy that Americans in outlying areas should be on the alert. Trouble is expected. Belgians are leaving Congo by the score. The Embassy has placed us all on notice." This troubling information spilled out in an almost gleeful tone by the slender blonde teen.

"Me, too? Am I on notice?" asked Masemba, with a chuckle. Ellie just rolled her eyes.

Nick frowned. "Thanks *a lot* for the info, Eleanor," He stared down at her cheery face. "'On notice?' What are we supposed to do –Worry? Break out in a sweat?"

"That shouldn't be hard for you, Nicholas Warren," she sneered. "I just thought you should know. By the way, where's your dad? Gone hunting again?" Ellie drew out the word, *hunting.*

Nick read the shaded contempt in her question. *Of course she knows Dad has gone hunting. He would have had to clear that with her father.* While it was no secret in the tiny community that tension existed between his parents, he found Ellie's awareness and disapproval annoying.

"You know very well he's hunting. I haven't seen *you* or any of your family passing up an antelope meal Dad provided, Miss *Ayeba-trop.*" Her immediate scowl showed that he scored on that exchange. She hated the Lingala/French nickname he and Masemba had given her: Miss Know-it-all.

"I'll let you know if anything further develops," quipped Ellie over her shoulder as she dashed out the door and across the lawn towards her next stop.

Softly moaning, Patty continued to rock. *She's really depressed this time*, Nick thought. Her gloom had settled in like a paralyzing fog; it seemed to immobilize her. Clicking into his take-charge mode, he turned to his younger brother. "Go wake Lizzie, while I find something for breakfast." Todd headed to the bedroom to rouse their 12-year-old sister while Nick dug out some bread and jam from the propane fridge.

As he set out their breakfast, Nick reflected. *Dad's frequent absences don't help things. He doesn't seem to know what to do about Mom's moods other than to yell and take off. Without Tata Rafael, we might have starved by now, and now...no Tata Rafael.*

After they had eaten, Masemba led Nick, Todd and Lizzie down the path toward the village cemetery. "I have something I want to show you," he told them, somewhat mysteriously.

Recent work crews had widened the cemetery path in anticipation of *Depanda*. Some believed that dead ancestors would return with truckloads of wealth. It was widely rumored in the village that the country's black-white roles would be magically reversed and shops, houses, vehicles and prized goods presently held by whites would somehow revert to Africans. *How* was unclear, but there were rumors that raffle tickets were quietly being sold to determine the redistribution of white wives.

When the path opened up to the cemetery clearing, Masemba stopped and gestured with a sweeping motion. *"Tala. Yongo ezali lokuta monene. Look. Before us is a huge lie."* The open gravesite area was littered with scores of containers, metal and bamboo. Many were broken, all were open, and some were still stuffed with grass and leaves.

"Yes, it *was* a big lie all right," commented Nick. Local Shamans had convinced village folk that when *Depanda* arrived, if they placed leaf and grass filled boxes over the graves, ancestors would transform the greenery into money.

A handful of sad-faced people wandered among the graves and clutter, kicking at broken containers, here and there, retrieving metal boxes that could be reused.

"How awful," Lizzie said with a sigh.

"The people are not happy. It is a bad start to *Depanda*." Masemba's English words had a prophetic sound.

CHAPTER 4
Litoko, June 30, 1960

The chiming of church bells broke the quiet of the early afternoon. It was a call for the community to gather for the Independence Day celebration.

Nick, Todd and Lizzie along with the Ellis family, the Larsons and the Brannons – the entire station except for Nick's parents – heeded the call. The small group walked together down the shady quarter-mile dirt road that led to the MAF airstrip. The younger kids chased each other in high spirits. Kyle Ellis was impressively agile with his latest prosthetic foot, just arrived from the States.

The airstrip doubled as a site for holiday celebrations. The community's Protestant church stood to one side of the grassy strip, a brick tin-roofed building with open arched windows.

"Wow, look at the crowd," Todd's eyes widened as they approached. "I didn't know that many people even lived around here." Hundreds had gathered in the hot afternoon sun.

"Independence is a big deal. Everyone is here...everyone who is anyone." Nick pointed to a stage of sorts, standing at one end of the field. It was framed with palm branches. All eight of the local village chiefs were seated on the platform on white plastic chairs. They had on a curious combination of clothes. Each *nfumu* wore an ill-fitting Western coat over a colorful ankle-length cloth wrap, and each wore a fancy hat with a matching cane in hand. The horns, nobs and colored beads that covered hats and canes were symbols of their authority.

Lizzie picked out the only non-missionary white faces to be seen anywhere in the crowd. "There are those Belgian men. I don't think Daddy likes that palm oil guy."

Shaking hands and working the crowd were the regional Belgian Magistrate, Mr. Van den Bergh, and the local Belgian palm oil plantation manager, Mr. Vermeulen. His assistant, Pierre and the perpetually red face of the stocky, diminutive French priest, Father DuBois could be seen nearby. Fr. DuBois served the Catholic mission, five kilometers down the road. Nick was never sure if the priest's distinctive coloration was from the sun, his drinking, or both. Noticeably absent were any of the Belgian men's family members. They had been safely dispatched back to Europe within the last few days.

The drums, singing and dancing had already begun in earnest by the time Nick and his companions arrived. A long row of food stalls stood to one side, palm branches shading the vendors. The wafting smoke from palm oil, fried peanuts, plantain chips and the sour scent of *fufu* and *chikwanga* filled the air, making Nick's mouth water. He noticed that the booth selling palm wine and Primus beer at the far end had attracted the biggest circle of noisy customers.

Nick and his two siblings, plus the three Ellis children left the Litoko missionaries and drifted into the crowd. They were at once surrounded by an exuberant group of young, smiling Congolese faces.

"*Masemba!*" The two best friends exchanged their soccer team's insider greeting: hand slide, finger snap, double fist thump and hip bump.

"*Mboté, ndecko! Greetings, brother.* A good day to be happy, yes?" The bright-eyed, full-lipped soccer player spoke in heavily accented English, learned while dribbling soccer balls and hanging out at the Warren house. He was almost as fluent in English as Nick was in Lingala.

The teenagers, black and white, circulated together, snap-thumping soccer greetings with teammates, greeting elders and sharing news. They walked about arm in arm, or lightly holding hands as was the Congolese custom among good friends.

The Warren kids bought Fanta soda and oil-fried plantain chips for themselves and their friends. The group took in the colors, sounds and smells of the memorable African celebration. They were varied and intense, filling their senses: charcoal smoke, fragrant blooms, sour sweat and *mwamba* stew. Spirited dancers, bare upper bodies glistening with perspiration, twisted and jumped before them to chanting music and rhythmic drumbeats. The mood was upbeat and celebratory.

Later in the afternoon, a local Congolese official took the stage. He began the formal ceremonies with a greeting and then turned to introduce Magistrate Van den Bergh. The drumming stopped and an angry murmur arose. As the community's familiar Belgian official rose to express his Independence Day regards, grumbles turned to shouts and soon it became impossible to hear a word he said.

"Away with him!" The crowd yelled in several languages. "*Sale flamand!*" Someone threw a rock at the stage, narrowly missing the startled white man. Soon, rocks, mangos, dirt chunks, even bananas were flying at the stage.

The crowd surged toward the platform as the officials scrambled to get off of it. In their haste, two village chiefs fell backwards in their plastic chairs. Like the sudden chill of a tropical shower, *Depanda* good will had shifted to anger and fear.

Before they could fully absorb this, Nick and his startled siblings were summoned. "Now, kids! Come at once. Follow me." Rev. Ellis rounded up the Litoko missionaries and trotted the group back down the road toward their homes.

Along the way, once friendly Congolese neighbors scowled and shouted phrases Nick had never before heard. "Return to your own village!" – *"Zunga na mboka na bino!"*

Nick realized the disappointment of failed expectations was sinking in. No money-stuffed grave boxes, no truckloads of ancestor gifts, no transfer of *mundele* goods had taken place. There had been no appreciable change at all! The hopes of *Depanda* had shattered like a palm wine gourd on river rocks.

As the scurrying missionaries approached their homes, Rev. Ellis barked out, "Lock your doors and start packing. Men, meet at our place in an hour. I'm going to radio headquarters for advice. My best guess is that we'll be leaving shortly."

As the others scurried off, Rev. Ellis turned to the three wide-eyed Warren children. "Nick, in the absence of your father, plan to join us men at my place."

CHAPTER 5
Litoko, July 3, 1960

A tattered brown suitcase sat open on the bed in front of Nick. In it, he had already placed jeans, shorts, soccer jersey, his favorite tee shirts and swimming trunks. Sighing, he reluctantly added his Sunday slacks and dress shirt. Socks and underpants were stuffed into the corners.

This is one time I wish I was as organized as Todd, he thought as he looked at the gray duffel bag neatly packed and waiting by the door. *He's already done.*

Looking around the room in the afternoon light, he spied his favorite collection of tiny, bamboo-sculpted cars on the shelf. *They won't survive this journey,* Nick decided. Bouncing a soccer ball, he realized it would never fit in the suitcase either...*something else I have to leave behind, like my entire life so far!*

Nick pulled the Academy photo album out of the top drawer and piled it on his clothes. *That's going for sure!* Then he spied his favorite photo on the dresser top. It was a picture of him and Dad with a bushbuck taken on his very first hunting trip at age 10. Dad's arm was around his shoulders and he looked so proud. He had nailed that deer!

Where is Dad and what's going to happen to him? Nick's face clouded as he carefully slid the framed picture between layers of tee shirts.

Leaving his open suitcase, Nick turned to check on his mother in the next room. She was busily packing her clothes, soaps and favorite linens, humming "Peace like a river."

She glanced up, meeting Nick's frown.

"It's going to be okay, honey. Check on the others, will you?"

At the meeting with the men, Rev. Ellis had insisted that aside from passport, cash, a small suitcase with clothes and a few keepsakes, everything else would be left behind. Bedding, quilts, instruments, dishes, books, tools, records. All would remain. The worst part was leaving Dad behind. The timing of Congo's Independence was lousy. *Lousy.*

The call to Congo Evangelical Mission headquarters had urged the Litoko missionaries to evacuate as soon as possible. However, it took the families almost two days to prepare, moving trunks of bedding, china, tools and canned food to their attics. Everything went into storage: sewing machines, typewriters, rocking chairs, rugs, record albums and bicycles. They hoped for a prompt return to their preaching, teaching and medical assignments. All indicators pointed in a different direction, however.

At times, rocks hit the doors or clattered off the tin roofs onto the missionaries' porches. Children with toys in hand were directed back into dark, empty rooms; windows and doors were closed to the shouts and taunts of visitors outside. *This can't be happening*, Nick thought.

At one point, church leaders showed up to advise Ellis and the others that their safety could no longer be guaranteed. On the second evening, shouting men gathered in front of the Ellis's house demanding the *mundeles* leave and hand over keys to houses, cars and cash boxes. Nick was greatly relieved when local church elders arrived to calm the protesters, assuring them the missionaries were already packing to leave. They left, yelling for the whites to go home.

A three-car caravan of missionary families headed out in the darkest hours before dawn, traveling light. Rev. Ellis insisted on the one bag limit. The packed Land Rovers headed for Bangui in the Central African Republic (CAR) across the Ubangi River.

Some time later they found out that shortly after first light, a mob had returned to Litoko station. The missionaries' houses were broken into and looted before they were burned. Only the Warren home was not razed and torched, a fact that gave Nick some private satisfaction. His father was well regarded by the locals. Unfortunately, the same was not true of Doug Warren's other CEM colleagues.

The tiny Litoko Station caravan linked up along the way with other evacuating missionaries. Their daylong journey to the CAR was not an easy one. Roadblocks, military shakedowns, stream crossings, vehicle breakdowns and a constant cloud of sadness and fear accompanied the group throughout their evacuation drive to the border.

The Warren children and their mother rode with the Brannon's and their two small children. The others in the vehicle - and in the caravan - were anxious and tearful, especially the other missionary women.

"Everything we've worked so hard for. How can we just leave? God has called us here, what can He be doing?"

"What's going to happen to our church friends? What about the school and clinic?"

In sharp contrast, Patty seemed happy, even cheerful. When others expressed concerns about deep sandpits, blazing sun, over-heated engines or rickety ferries, she'd sit taller, lift her chin and voice platitudes. "The Lord is with us. He will keep us safe. It's all for the best."

"What about Dad, Mama? What's going to happen to him?" Lizzie and Todd repeated the question, concern clouding their eyes as they stared at empty jungle and grasslands, mile after mile.

The question filled Nick's mind as well. *Will Dad be okay? Will he find his way back to us?* His mother, however, her previous alarm reversed, now seemed unperturbed by her husband's absence.

"He's very resourceful. I'm sure he'll be OK."

"But how will Daddy find us?" Lizzie's face wrinkled with worry.

Her mother repeated the same response. "I don't know, but I'm sure he'll be okay. Don't worry about him, dear."

The kids finally stopped asking, but the question never left their minds.

CHAPTER 6
Lombard, September 1960

The evacuation process – Africa to Europe to the U.S. – was taxing and traumatic. Strange uncomfortable lodgings, endless boring delays, paperwork screenings by officials, and long plane flights in noisy military aircraft all left the Warren children and their mother exhausted and disoriented.

"Why do we have to do this, mama? I just want to go home," whined Lizzie.

"We *are* headed home, dear." Patty flashed a reassuring smile. The children were not reassured.

Finally, the four Warrens arrived in the U.S. They settled in with Patty's parents in Lombard, a quiet tree-lined village on the DuPage River, twenty miles west of Chicago.

One day shortly after their arrival, a telegram was delivered to the house. It was a message from Doug to Patty. It was both welcome and disheartening, at least to Nick and his siblings.

> DEAR PATTY
> MADE IT SAFELY TO LEO VIA CONGO RIVER BARGE –(STOP)- WILL RIDE OUT DEPENDA CHAOS HERE –(STOP)- PLANNING TO STAY ON EVEN IF CEM SAYS NO –(STOP)- DONT WORRY I HAVE LOCAL RESOURCES –(STOP)- I AM NOT YET DONE WITH CONGO –(STOP)- KEEP THE KIDS SAFE –(STOP)-
> LOVE DOUG

"I can't believe Dad is not joining us. Why not, Momma? What did he mean, 'Even if CEM says no?'" Nick paced back and forth, scowling, trying to make sense of things. "When *will* we see him?"

Todd slumped into a chair with his head between his hands and stared at the floor. "Phooey! We should've stayed too."

Lizzie ran over to Patty in tears, hugging her.

Patty's only comment was, "Well, I can't say I'm surprised."

In the days that followed, whenever Nick referred to his dad's telegram, Patty's dismissive comments made it clear to him that she viewed their family's separation quite differently than did he, Todd and Lizzie. *Mom doesn't miss Congo at all. She doesn't seem to miss Dad, either.*

When Patty called the family together for a meeting a few weeks later, Nick could tell from her strained expression and stern directive, that something bad was about to go down.

"Kids, I have decided to file for divorce. It's for the best." Patty's blunt declaration sent a shock wave. Her parents, their eyes welling, hugged the children. Todd and Lizzie burst into tears. Nick swallowed a lump that felt like a baseball.

"I never wanted to go to Congo in the first place. I followed your father because I thought I had to, but I was miserable there. Your father was not. He wouldn't hear of us leaving Congo. The evacuation, however, took care of that question. Doug...Dad, is determined to stay there in spite of everything and against my express wishes. So now he *will* stay...but without me, without *us*."

A deep ache gripped the pit of Nick's stomach, as he stood, speechless. After a strained silence, he spoke up. "How can you do this, Mama? It's not right. It's against our beliefs!"

Face flushing, Patty's eyes narrowed. "Some things that are broken just can't be fixed. Don't you start judging matters you don't understand, Nicholas."

Nick hooked an arm around each of the younger kids and guided them down the hall toward their bedroom. Both Todd and Lizzie leaned into him, shaking with sobs as he stroked their backs. How could he find words of comfort in this disaster?

"It hurts like crazy losing Dad this way. But I saw it coming. Just know, guys, I'll always be here for you."

A response from Doug came in a short letter Patty received and read aloud to the children soon afterwards.

> *Dear Patty,*
> *A messenger from the Embassy brought your registered letter to me today with the divorce papers enclosed. I do not agree with this action you have taken but I will not contest it since you are determined to end our marriage. I regret that it was a failure and that you were so unhappy in Congo. I have signed the papers.*
> *I am now formally separated from CEM, too. I plan to start a business here, up-country. Our joint stateside savings account will*

*have to serve as my contribution to child support since I don't
expect to have a regular income for some time to come.*

Please tell the children I love them and will miss them.

Doug

A few days later, the three Warren kids sat together in the front
room watching a TV special entitled *World Refugee Year, 1960.*
Halfway through the program, Lizzie jumped up. Heading for her
room, she paused in the doorway with her hands on her hips. "I don't
want to see this. We're refugees too! I *hate* being a refugee." With that,
she rushed down the hall and slammed her bedroom door.

Nick and Todd looked at each other. "She's got a point," Todd said
as he got up and changed the channel. "We *are* losers – we've lost our
home, school, friends, and now our family. Everything is so different,
all messed up. We *are* sort of like refugees."

Nick sighed. "I don't know what bugs me more, Todd -- being mad
or feeling sad all the time. I can't figure out what's going to happen
next."

For virtually his entire grade twelve year Nick sent off weekly
letters to his father, pouring out his misery.

November 1960

Dear Dad,

*We miss you. Please come get us. We want to be with
you and we want to go back home to Congo. It's always
been better when you're around and worse when you
aren't, but now it's gotten really bad for us. Lizzie cries
all the time and all of us hate it here, except Mom, of
course. I know Mom doesn't like it that we are unhappy
but that's just Mom. She's always been negative about
stuff and still gets upset with us when we don't agree
with her, especially with me. We miss you. You always
made us feel OK, cared for. Now there's no one watching
out for us. Grandma and Grandpa just leave the room
whenever Mom gets in one of her moods.*

*Dad, you can't let Mom do this – file for divorce.
Didn't you and Mom always teach us that marriage is for
life and divorce is wrong? Now that she's filed the papers*

you're just going to go along with it? She read us your letter, that you are staying in Congo and not going to fight it. Please don't give up. We're a family. All families have struggles, don't they? If you and Mom divorce we're not a family any more. If you stay in Congo what will happen to us? We don't want to be here, we want to be with you, Dad. Please, come see us. Or at least write.

Love, Nick

*****

December 1960

Dear Dad,
I've been missing you a LOT lately. I keep thinking about Africa, dreaming about Congo all the time. I remember our hunting trips with Masemba and his dad, camping in the jungle. All the things you taught me – how to hunt a duiker, getting them to freeze in the light at night, how to skin a bushbuck, what kind of forest mushrooms are safe. All the stuff the kids in my school can't even imagine. They call me "Tarzan" and "Bongo Boy" and laugh when I don't know about TV programs or music. Most of them have never been anywhere but here. I don't belong here.

I'm trying to be strong for Todd and Lizzie, like you taught me to do when you were away at Litoko, but these days Mom is just impossible. She gets an idea – like not letting us go to the movies with friends – and she won't budge. When I object she tells me "You're just like your father." Well, I think that's a complement.

Please let me come live with you, Dad. I won't be any trouble, promise. At least answer my letters, no matter how busy you are. I miss you. Someday I'm going to return to Congo and be with you. That's where I belong.

Love, Nick

*****

February 1961

Dear Dad,
High school in the states is double awful. No one is interested in me. I can't even talk about Africa. It's all about TV programs, movies, music and cars none of which I know or care squat about. I feel like a fish out of water here. I just exist. I'm not really living.

The last three letters I sent to you just came back unopened, along with a note from CEM that they are no longer forwarding mail to you since you are not with them now. I have been writing to you every week and it's been seven months now and no reply. Why won't you write back to me? I don't understand. Did I do something that made you mad? Did Mom make up something bad about me?

I always thought that we were close. Masemba used to tell me how lucky I was to have a father like you who taught me things. So it really hurts not to hear from you. What has happened? I have to know that you're OK. Someday I'm going to figure out how to get back to Congo and find you.

Love, Nick

*****

There was no response from Dad for months. Finally, one day when Nick chanced to be home for the mail delivery, an aerogram affixed with Congolese stamps arrived at his grandparents' home. It was addressed to Nick and it was from...Dad!

Nick opened the aerogram, careful not to tear any part of the message inside. As he scanned the familiar handwriting, his heart sank.

March 1961

Dear Nick,
It's been a while since I last wrote to you and I'd still like to find out how school is going and how you, Todd and Lizzie are doing. I've been working on acquiring a

coffee plantation from a Belgian friend who is leaving Congo. Actually, he's already left. It's located in a remote area well over 200 miles NE of Litoko, in the rainforest. I'm buying it on speculation – I will pay for it by selling future crops.

I returned to Litoko station a couple months back and sad to say there's not much left. Our old house is the only one still standing. The others were burned at Independence. I managed to find a few of our things – some tools, my boots, our fishing gear and some kitchen things. Most everything else was taken or destroyed. There's nothing there for me now. I did see Masemba's father, Nzuzi and a few others.

I'm sorry our circumstances make it impossible to see one another. I miss you, son. Due to the remoteness of my plantation and the present chaos in Congo, mail service is infrequent at best. Corresponding will be difficult. Don't expect to receive regular letters from me. Hopefully, things will change sometime soon. Watch out for your younger brother and sister and do your best in school. Show me you're still my mwana makasi.

Love, Dad

There was no return postal address on the aerogram.

What's wrong with Dad? Doesn't he love his family? Can't he do any better than that at expressing his emotions? Why does he need to stay in Congo, anyhow? What is he trying to accomplish? Is there something wrong with me?

Angrily wadding Dad's letter into a ball, Nick threw it across the room. Tears burned his eyes and soaked his shirt. Only later, he retrieved the balled up aerogram and carefully straightened its thin skin. He would study its message repeatedly over time.

English, Physics and Calculus homework proved to be able distractions for Nick, as did running his guts out on the soccer field. In June, he graduated from Glenbard East High School and was accepted at nearby Wheaton College. Solid in scholastics and officially considered a child of missionaries, he scored with both academic and MK scholarships. He also scored on the playing field, as a skilled soccer player.

Nick was naturally drawn to the other MKs attending Wheaton. Some wore Brazilian soccer jerseys; others sported wax prints from Africa or beads from Central America. As fellow internationals with expanded worldviews, they seemed potential allies in the unfamiliar land of his passport. In the end, however, Nick still felt like an outsider. Most of the other MKs had solid families, mission connections and glowing stories of adopted homelands. Nick's parents' divorce, dis-affiliation from the mission, and untimely evacuation were not typical MK credentials.

Meanwhile, much to his disgust and bitter protest, Nick's mother warmed to the attentions of Harold Smalley, a widowed CPA at the large fundamentalist church she attended. Harold and Patty married during Nick's freshman year at Wheaton. The Warren children entered the world of blended families. Harold had a son from his first marriage; 12-year-old Harry Jr. aka "Junior" enjoyed special treatment from his father. The Warren children, however, enjoyed nothing about this new development.

Nick mostly stayed away from his mother's place. In no way did he identify with it as "home." Occasionally, he stopped by from his dorm to pick up Todd and Lizzie for a ball game or hamburgers, but life in that household was alien to him. Arbitrary rules and countless restrictions, lack of affection, favoritism toward Junior – it all seemed toxic, weird, something to be avoided.

Whenever Nick, Todd and Lizzie got together they reminisced about Litoko. Speculating about their father's life, they spun out fantasy scenarios of how they might arrange a return to Congo.

"Will we *ever* see Congo again? Will we ever see Dad?"

CHAPTER 7
Coquilhatville, March 1961

Wispy white clouds flicked by beneath the small Cessna aircraft providing the only clue that they were traveling at 120 mph. Otherwise, a green blanket of vegetation spread from one end of the horizon to the other, seeming to suspend them in air, virtually motionless.

Next to Brandon Ellis, the pilot, Wally Anderson, kept up an incessant monologue about flying, weather, Congo politics, religion and well…he wasn't really sure what else. Brandon had long since disengaged from the conversation. His contributions were limited to an occasional grunt or "hmmm."

It was March, 1961, the warmest month of the year in Coquilhatville, the MAF plane's destination, but Ellis was not sweating from the heat, not yet anyhow. The drops of sweat that ran down his sideburns were from nerves. *What have I gotten myself into?* Off to the left was the wide brown swatch of Congo River. *We should be arriving soon.*

He was about to meet with Zubusa Pierre, the regional CEM Bishop and also with the Governor of Équateur Province, Mossai Numanda. These were two of the most influential leaders of the huge region that comprised the entire northwest Congo. It bordered the Central African Republic to the north and the former French colony, the Republic of Congo, to the west. The mighty Congo River was the boundary. This was his mission's first post-Independence meeting with the region's top officials. Ellis was carrying a briefcase full of cash for each official. And sweating.

Ellis, a balding man of 46 years, bore a ruddy complexion on his medium frame. He was not the kind of man who naturally drew attention to himself by either appearance or personality, tending by nature to be serious-minded and soft-spoken. Perhaps seminary had contributed to this; he possessed a doctorate of theology. Ellis's bright mind and quick, dry sense of humor, however, marked him as no one to be taken for granted. Nothing got past his radar.

Rev. Ellis, his usual title, had mastered several languages. That fact, combined with a pragmatic and progressive approach to mission work had moved him early on into leadership roles on the Congo field. Presently, he served as the Field Director of CEM, a position he had assumed just six months ago. It had been conferred on his return from evacuation following the country's post-Independence chaos.

On this particular occasion, Rev. Ellis's mission fell much more solidly into the pragmatic rather than the spiritual realm. Wally's commentary droned above the Cessna's engine as Ellis pondered his decision to meet with the two Congolese leaders.

Congo's post-Independence political scene had become frighteningly unpredictable. Changes in top leadership had shifted like musical chairs, and the succession movements in various parts of the country were emerging as real and growing threats in spite of the government's efforts to quell them. The stability and future of mission work in that great land was at stake. It didn't take a doctor's degree to figure that out.

Ellis had received a surprising lunch invitation shortly after his return to Congo in October. He was invited to meet a U. S. Embassy consul at the fancy Memling Hotel in downtown Léopoldville. The consul, Loren Durban, said he had a business matter to discuss with him, "one that has significant potential to influence U. S. interests in the Congo for decades to come." That statement captured Ellis's attention and he consented to the meeting.

Heavy silver clinked on bone china and the crystal chandeliers radiated shafts and glimmers of light around the room as the two men sat and spread crisp linen napkins on their slacks. They ordered steak and lobster from the menu. That meal had been elegant, far above what Ellis had ever imagined, let alone experienced in Congo.

Loren Durban was a solidly built, dark haired, square-jawed man in his early 30s. He did not fit Ellis's stereotype of the diplomatic corps. He seemed more agile, more reflective and conveyed a quiet confidence unlike the chain-smoking extroverts the Reverend had met at occasional embassy events.

After small talk of family, weather and CEM's work in Northeast Congo, Durban got to the point: "Congo is in grave danger of falling into the Communist circle of influence and with it, all of Africa. Vital natural resources the country possesses are at stake: copper and uranium, chief among them. Evidence has confirmed that the Soviet Union and China are behind the current succession movements, supplying arms, personnel and money to promote their goals. The U.S. is being forced to take strategic action."

"What sort of strategic action?" Ellis set his fork down on the plate and looked squarely at Durban.

"Well, for one thing Lumumba is no longer a threat." Durban continued without explanation, "For another, we are intent on establishing a network of sympathizers and informants across the country so that we can track any movement of opposition forces by Lumumba's followers, repel their advance, and prop up the central government."

He dropped his voice and leaning forward, elbow on the table, eyes locked on Brandon's. "That's why we need you."

"I...I don't understand." Ellis stammered, puzzlement creasing his face. "I'm a religious person, not a politician or diplomat. Why should I be of any interest to you? And why should your 'strategies' be any concern of mine?"

After a pause, Loren Durban slowly sat back in his chair, took a deep breath, exhaled and replied with a question. "How long do you think Protestant missions – *American* missionaries – will be allowed to continue if the opposition overthrows Congo's central government?"

Without waiting for a reply, he continued. "Your interests and ours are fully in alignment here, Reverend. Our analysts predict immediate expulsion of expatriates or worse: *harm* for westerners if the Léopoldville regime falls. Precisely because of your experience in this land, because of your contacts and because of your reputation in Équateur Province, we are seeking your help."

Consul Durban had elaborated. They wanted Brandon Ellis to facilitate the recruitment of key leaders in the region with whom they could collaborate in establishing "listening or observation posts" to track movement of opposition forces in the province.

"Whoa. Not so fast, Mr. Durban." Rev. Ellis' face became flushed.

"I have an entirely different point of view on this matter. We Protestants need to keep our distance from Congo politics. It's only because we've insisted on maintaining our neutrality that we have avoided past trouble. True, possessions have been taken or destroyed but no lives have been lost. That could change were I to accept your invitation. If we are in any way perceived as providing support to one side or another, both our parishioners and mission personnel could find themselves in harm's way."

"I think you have it exactly backwards, Reverend. You need our help. We could use yours. I think you should definitely reconsider your position."

"Not at all." Ellis pushed back from the table. "Besides, this all sounds a lot more like CIA activity than normal embassy business."

Loren Durban waited and looked him straight in the eye. "I can't confirm my reporting line, but I can tell you this as a "heads up" courtesy. If you choose *not* to help us directly we will be forced to proceed on our own. Doing so is not our first choice, however. Expect to hear in the coming days that our people have approached many of your contacts in the region. We monitor all short wave radio traffic so we are aware who they are. We *will* create a network with or without your help. Some assets are, in fact, already in place."

"The time may well come when you will want to know what's happening – such as whether or not your people are safe – and you will contact the embassy for that purpose. We simply have a similar need. We want to promote stability, not chaos. Let's at least agree to help one another informally, off the record. What do you say?"

Thinking about it now as the aircraft began its final approach to Coquilhatville, Ellis was satisfied that he had officially rejected Durban's invitation to become an agent of the U.S. government. He had, however, permitted Durban to convince him that "unofficial" cooperation was the patriotic and practical thing to do. He was either a pawn or a pragmatist. *Consul Durban will want to debrief this visit...can I keep others from finding out? Can I maintain neutrality? Haven't I already crossed the line?*

Ellis' mind was spinning. Follow-up meetings with Durban had clarified what was needed and CEM's Field Director found himself identifying reliable contacts in Équateur Province, both Congolese and expatriate. He was then given strategic resources to distribute: short wave radios with codes for communication and money to solidify the cooperation and commitment of his collaborators. That was what had prompted the present trip.

Rev. Ellis had been advised by Durban not to disclose their relationship to his mission superiors, but rather, whenever possible to expand his CEM travel agenda to include "embassy business." Thus, while public education comprised the *official* agenda for this meeting with Bishop Zubusa and Governor Numanda, *unofficially* they had been notified that he would be bringing gifts from the U.S. government to reward their favor of American interests in the region.

After circling the confluence of the Congo and Ruki Rivers, the small Cessna made a northwest approach to Coquilhatville airport. Wally called out a genial conclusion to his monologue. "Here we are!"

Rev. Brandon Ellis wiped the sweat from his face with a handkerchief. *What a strange way to advance the gospel.* He then unbuckled and crawled from the plane before planting his feet firmly on the ground.

CHAPTER 8
Kindu, December 1963

Though it was only midafternoon, the sky was dark, lit by sporadic lightning flashes and loud crashes of thunder. Sheets of driving rain whipped and slashed against mud-splattered buildings, a typical December day in eastern Congo.

The main street of Kindu, *Avenue Lumumba Libérateur*, unpaved and stretching along the western bank of the Lualaba River, was deeply rutted, an uneven row of gray buildings bordering a quagmire. It was the height of the rainy season and this isolated railhead linking Albertville on Lake Tanganyika, Congo's eastern frontier with the Maniema mining region, was receiving the full annual December deluge: nearly 21 inches of concentrated rain.

Through the torrent one could make out swaying groves of banana and palm trees behind the tin-roofed, single story buildings. The streets were deserted with only an occasional resident slogging quickly from one small shop to another.

In one of the dark doorways, just out of the whipping rain sat a handsome man in his early 30s smoking a cigarette at a rickety table. Tall and ebony-skinned, Nicolas Olenga glowered into the storm. He was large-framed for a Congolese, at six feet. His hard muscles, chiseled features and dark, intent eyes made him a striking figure.

Olenga sat, long legs crossed, brooding over his circumstances. Fate had not been kind to him in recent times. But he was determined. *I will not be stuck in this backwater village for the rest of my days. I have a destiny to fulfill, to lead my people.* An exhale of thick smoke punctuated his thoughts.

Pierre Lutete, the shop's owner and cousin to the brooding smoker, came up behind him. Slapping a callused hand on his shoulder, he inquired *"Likambo nini, motema moto? What's up, impatient one?* Why are you scowling at the storm? Do you have something better to do than enjoy a quiet smoke on a rainy day?"

Olenga sighed and flicked his cigarette out into the rain. "I was just remembering my former Belgian employer, the one who threw me in jail for taking a bar of soap from the kitchen."

Pierre laughed. "That was years ago. If I recall, your jail time didn't last long, cousin. It helped that both your jailor and the local magistrate were fellow Batetela. You were out in no time at all. Am I remembering that right?"

"True. But the shame I felt and the arrogance of the *mundeles* left a mark on my soul. *Les sale flamand* are still in our land. *Les Belge* and their Léopoldville *domestiques* are still in control. *Dependa* did not change things, not nearly enough. But that *will* change sometime soon. It *must* change. They need to go, all of them! Lumumba was right, Congo for Congolese!"

Pierre pulled a chair over, straddled it, laying a calming hand on his agitated cousin's arm. "You tried that already, Nicolas. Forcing things. You were among the first to join up with Gizenga Antoine's movement in Stanleyville three years ago and look what happened. That whole dream was crushed by the ANC like a ripe papaya. You were fortunate to escape back here with your life."

"Gizenga carried Lumumba's truth, but he did not have an army. He did not have weapons. He lacked the support necessary to defeat Léopoldville and their *mundele* masters. That mistake won't be made again. More time has passed. People are angrier now, more ready to defy Congo's puppet leaders."

Olenga stood and began to pace, clenched fist in hand. "Perhaps the spirit of Kindu will once again find its voice, like it did with the Italians during Gizenga's time. That move made the *mundele* world take note. We were given respect."

Olenga's reference was to the 1961 incident in which thirteen hapless Italian pilots who were part of the United Nations peacekeeping force were slaughtered and dismembered in Kindu by Gizenga's troops. They were, at the time, presumed to be in league with the enemy -- Moise Tshombe's Katanga military. The bloody incident, even now known as the *"Kindu Massacre"* was a good representation of the brooding man's sentiments: *rid Africa of external influence just as the martyred Lumumba taught.*

A welcome but discordant sound interrupted the two men's gloomy reflections. A whistle announced the arrival of the 4 o'clock train. Pierre again patted his cousin's shoulder. "These are difficult times. Who knows what it will take to change. Patience." They both sat quietly, pondering the thought.

At last, Lutete rose and heading for the back room, called over his shoulder. "I'm expecting a shipment from Albertville. Send Wemba to get it."

Olenga rose to dispatch Wemba, curled in a ball, dozing on crates in the corner. He pulled the startled young man to his feet and with a wry smile, shoved him out the door, stumbling into the driving rain to retrieve the supplies. *At least I don't have to get wet and muddy.*

When Wemba returned a short time later, soaked to the skin, he brought with him not only the ordered goods from the train station but also news of dramatic developments taking place in Albertville.

Wemba lowered the dripping crate from his head. With water puddling and eyes sparkling, he reported the freshly arrived gossip. "Schools and shops are closed. No work, no money, only promises. Albertville now is filled with angry people. They sacked the government offices. They control the town."

The 6 p.m. report on the radio confirmed Wemba's words.

Olenga's eyes sparkled. He rubbed his hands together at this welcome news. *Things are looking up!*

The next morning, conspicuous among the passengers on the return train to Albertville was Nicolas Olenga, a man on a mission.

*****

A natural leader, Olenga quickly co-opted the fledgling Albertville insurrection. Bestowing on himself the military rank of "Lieutenant Colonel," he conceived and recruited an army. Those joining his movement identified themselves as *"Simba"* warriors, employing the Swahili term for lion.

Simba recruits were motivated to join up by two factors. The main one was the widespread and obvious deterioration of their daily lives since Independence. There also existed a residue of deep bitterness from the assassination of venerated and charismatic tribesman-turned-prime minister, Patrice Lumumba. His philosophy of ridding Congo of external influence combined with ironic, enthusiastic offers of support from Communist Chinese and Soviet sources to position Olenga's rag-tag army as anti-West, anti-American.

Olenga's initiation methods proved to be both ingenious and effective. Recruits, many of them teenagers, were marked with tattoo-like welts on their foreheads and chests made by rubbing charcoal into small cuts. The witchcraft notion of *"dawa,"* a form of magical power was evoked. If recruits carefully followed a series of specific taboos, they were told they would be bulletproof in battle: the bullets would magically turn to water. They were not to have sex in daylight hours, not to wear Western attire, and to look neither to the left nor right when going into battle, but to stare straight ahead.

The protection of *dawa* gave Olenga's recruits a boldness and fearlessness they would not otherwise have. It also imposed a measure of discipline: battlefield deaths were interpreted as a failure to respect the rules of *dawa*. A shrewd organizer, he even acquired the services of a well-known, aged sorceress from the area, Mama Onema. She was famous, widely feared throughout the region for her powers. She added to the Simba leader's perceived credibility and reputation.

Designated subordinates with leadership promise were dispersed to rural villages across the region. Just as courtyard embers were stirred to fire at night, the Simba recruiters stirred the resentment and animosity of common folk towards the central government, posing questions that fanned the flames of discontent: "How long since you have had new pots, salt for your greens, cloth for a shirt or wrap around? Are the roads smoother, jobs plentiful, is health care improved? Are you better off since Independence?"

Olenga's recruiters earned a hearing for their appeals in the villages, particularly among the youth. Soon, on certain days and evenings, young men of the village were missing. Dodging possible opposition by elders, in secluded forest centers nearby they were trained, indoctrinated and initiated into the new *Simba* army.

By July, 1964, when sufficient numbers had accumulated, Olenga marched his teenage warriors West from Albertville. Led by a line of sorcerers waving palm fronds, they entered first one small town and then another. Central government soldiers assigned to each location fled in panic before their lightly armed and strangely clad adversaries.

The *Simba* army met virtually no resistance in these initial forays. In each instance, after taking control, they rounded up government functionaries along with any educated citizens they could locate, brought them to the town center and beat or hacked them to death. Over 200 were reported killed in the eastern Congo town of Kasongo, alone. The *Simbas'* fearsome reputation began to spread far and wide.

Within a matter of weeks rebel forces made their way north to Kindu. Once again the army fled without offering any resistance. *Simbas* rounded up the local leaders and government sympathizers and publicly executed them in the town center. The slaughter of collaborators and the educated was becoming a ritual.

By the time Olenga arrived back in his hometown, he had conferred upon himself the rank of "Lieutenant *General*." His army had acquired a growing cache of abandoned government weapons and vehicles to facilitate their advance.

Olenga was pleased. His Simbas' notoriety grew, along with the perception that they were indeed invulnerable. As they marched into each new town, the rebel force adopted the chant, *"Mai, Mai,"* the Swahili/Lingala word for water. The pattern was repeated: government soldiers panicked, resistance evaporated, executions followed.

Lieutenant General Nicolas Olenga's creation had become a force on the move, *A People's Army.*

CHAPTER 9
Wheaton, July 1964

Four Years after Independence

By mid-July, summer had already passed its apex. Nick's brow furrowed beneath his thick, dark brown hair. His hazel eyes glazed over. In only six more weeks the fall semester would start again and he would head into his senior year at Wheaton College. But what was he heading for?

After changing majors several times, Nick had finally settled on Political Science. He wasn't all that excited about politics or government. Mostly, he just wanted to graduate in four years. What one might do with a degree in that major was a puzzle without a solution. *Maybe things just eventually fall into place.* Someone told him that once. *Career, love, spirituality, and direction in life – what if a person is clueless on all counts?*

As Nick contemplated, around him swirled a very different tenor of subject and sound. He and his two painting crew buddies, Ryan and David, fellow Wheaton College students, sat in a neighborhood bar enjoying post workday beers. It was a college guy thing to do, but not one that was sanctioned by either their conservative parents or school officials.

All Wheaton College students had to annually sign *The Pledge.* Also known as the "Statement of Student Responsibilities," this formal, mandatory, annually renewed declaration forbade drinking, smoking, dancing, gambling and attendance at movies and theater productions among other proscriptions. It symbolized the college's conservative values.

In Nick's experience, *The Pledge* produced far more rebellion than compliance among Wheaton's students. As a 21-year-old newly legal drinker, adventure thoroughly trumped guilt when it came to respecting or breaking *The Pledge.* Both Ryan and David agreed.

As the latter poured a pitcher of brew, he declared it to be "such a stupid rule -- no one takes seriously." *They* didn't, anyhow.

The three college friends had been earning good summer money the last two months, repainting houses in the Western Chicago suburbs. They were one of several crews working for *Midwest College Painters (MCP)*, a company that employed teams of college students and public school teachers. It was decent summer employment but held no future career possibilities.

This was Nick's second summer with MCP and it had been solely through his efforts that his college buddies were able to get in on the well-paying gig. They owed him big time.

The table conversation that evening centered on the Rolling Stone's concert in Chicago, a summer highlight the three had attended together. Their ride home in the car had witnessed all three singing at the top of their voices to *"Time is on my side,"* playing on the radio.

But was it really? Nick wondered. The Stones had made a recording stop at the famous Chess Studio and rocked out with Muddy Waters, Chuck Berry, Buddy Guy and other rock and blues idols. As the three friends pondered this rock summit encounter, the group's latest hit, *"It's All Over Now,"* thundered away in the background, drowning their words.

Nick drew deeply on his frosty brew, watching colored images from the TV flicker on the bar mirrors. The words *Rebellion in Congo* blazed across the screen.

Nick jumped up, knocking over a chair. He pointed to the TV over the bar. *"Wait, stop!"* He dashed to the bar, his athletic six-foot stride closing the distance in an instant. "Turn up the sound on the TV!" he shouted to the bartender, *"Turn it up!"* The startled man reached up and gave the knob a twist.

The headline read: *"U.S. Cautions on Rebellion in Congo."* When the sound finally came on, a TV reporter announced... "Washington officials have been watching conditions deteriorate due to a Communist-backed rebellion in the southeastern part of the conflict-plagued, four-year-old democracy. U. S. citizens have been advised to evacuate from troubled areas, but the State Department has no clear recommendation as to what to do to help restore stability. Military intervention has been ruled out. Nobody controls anything in the Congo," the exasperated official concluded.

"Hey, that's where you're from, isn't it?" quizzed David, refilling his mug as Nick finally slumped back down into his chair. Nick just nodded. But he was somewhere on the other side of the world.

Ryan made a try at drawing him back. "So, what does this mean? Is your father anywhere near the action?"

Without answering, Nick rose. "I've got to go, guys. It looks bad. I need to find my Dad. He often goes to Stanleyville, exactly where the rebels are headed."

"You're leaving now?" Ryan called out as Nick headed to the door. "See you tomorrow?"

"If it doesn't rain." Painting was cancelled on days it rained and dark clouds had rolled in as they finished work that afternoon. Nick dashed away leaving his friends looking at one another and shaking their heads.

When he reached his apartment, Nick dialed up Todd, a freshman attending nearby Elmhurst College, and still living at home.

"Have you seen the news about Congo?" Nick blurted.

"Yes. It doesn't sound good, does it?"

"I think Dad is right smack in the path of the rebels, Todd. *Now* is the time to find him." An urgency that surprised him animated his voice.

"Find him? We don't know for sure where he is. And what do you think you could *possibly* do in all that chaos besides get into trouble, yourself?" Todd sounded stressed. "Are you seriously thinking of just bailing on your senior year of college to find Dad? And how, pray tell, would you manage to get there anyway? Do you even have the money or contacts you'd need? That's nuts!"

Todd had always been a practical, down-to-earth fellow and he was asking the right questions. "Look, man, I haven't got all the details worked out. I wanted to start by talking with you. If anyone on the planet might understand *why* I want to go, why I've *got* to find Dad, I figured it would be you."

Nick's vote of confidence seemed to melt Todd's resistance. In a softened tone he replied. "You know I'm in your corner, big brother. Let's talk."

The next day began with a bang. Lightning flashed, thunder clapped and broiling gray skies sent sheets of rain down the streets and gutters of the West Chicago suburbs. No house painting was going to happen that day.

Nick arranged to meet his brother at a coffee shop across from the Elmhurst campus. He was not surprised at his brother's questions or skepticism. In fact, they were just the kind of thing he needed to think through and flesh out a do-able plan.

"You're not going to get *any* encouragement at all from Mom, you know." It was typical of Todd to offer no greeting but just dive into a topic. He wrestled off his wet coat and slid into the booth with raised eyebrows.

"Nor from Lizzie." Nick sipped his coffee while the waitress stopped by to fill Todd's cup. "But for very different reasons."

"Yeah, like genuine concern for you and Dad, you mean?" countered Todd. "I think Mom still resents our years in Congo. She never did take to Africa, not like the rest of us. She blames Dad for wrecking her life."

"Exactly!" Nick paused while the waitress took Todd's order for eggs and a short stack. Breakfast did not interest him. "It's for that reason I'd like to request that you not say anything about this to either Mom or Lizzie any time soon. Can I count on it?" Nick studied Todd carefully, looking for reassurance.

"I suppose so." Todd poured more sugar in his coffee, "But this seems like such a stretch, a huge over-reaction to bad news. I think you should just chill. Give it more time before you do anything as crazy as pulling out of Wheaton right before your final year."

"I promise I'll give it more thought. I can't *not* think about it now, for cripes' sake. But it's not like this is the first time I've considered going back to Congo or reconnecting with Dad. It just seems much more urgent right now. He could be in serious trouble. I want to be with him, to help in some way if I can…I'm not sure in *what* way, but I've got to do *something*."

Nick stirred his coffee, staring into the cup. In a more subdued tone he added, "I also want to see if I can feel normal again by returning to Africa…yeah, normal."

Nick's sentiments spilled out freely. They emerged in such a natural way, however, that he found himself strangely comforted in a new resolve: *I'm going home, to Africa and Dad.*

CHAPTER 10
Wheaton, July 1964

The idea of returning to Congo, as many-layered as it might be, was simple compared to the *reality* of arranging such a voyage. This fact became clear in Nick's phone call to CEM's headquarters in Bloomington, Indiana the next morning.

Fortunately, this was a rainy week in the upper Midwest and Nick caught a break in being able to escape from house painting for several days in a row. Figuring out his Congo interests occupied every waking thought. Having never made travel arrangements himself, Nick reasoned, *"I'd better start by seeing what kind of help I can glean from the folks' former mission agency."*

He made the call to the CEM office. Two awkward explanations and a like number of transfers later, Nick was finally connected with the staff member in charge of travel and logistics. His reception was far from warm or encouraging, however.

"This is *not* a good time for a former MK, or *anyone else* for that matter, to visit the Congo."

Nick persisted. "Okay, but can you just tell me what official papers or visas a person must have to enter Congo?"

"Yellow fever, tetanus and other vaccinations have to be up to date. Tourist visas to Congo are essentially non-existent. I am unaware of ever *hearing* of anyone traveling there on one. If you were to visit the Congo you would need a letter of invitation from the national church to obtain a visa."

Pausing, she added cynically, "You would surely need a *much* better reason for entering the country than just 'checking on your ex-missionary father.'"

Ignoring the clerk's jibe, Nick continued, "So my visit needs to somehow assist the national church? What kind of assistance might that be?"

"I have no idea. Sorry, young man. I cannot help you any further with this fantasy of yours."

The annoyed clerk flatly refused his request to furnish contact information with Congolese church officials. At his persistent probing, however, she admitted that CEM *did* have a checklist for Africa travel. She agreed to send him a copy.

Nick set the receiver down and slapped his open hand on the table as he rose. "Ha. Not a bad start. I can work with this." He resolved to make as many travel arrangements as possible and to wait until the last minute to notify Wheaton College of his intent to withdraw.

When the College informs Mom and her husband – he couldn't bring himself to call Harold "stepfather" – *all hell will break loose. The two of them might not be able to stop me, but they could probably slow me down.* At a minimum, he figured their objections were going to be a major stressor.

Nick's next step was crucial. He thought long and hard about his options. The crisis in Congo meant he could not just sit around for weeks waiting for a visa. *Who knows what might happen if the rebels continue their success?* His passport was up to date: he had just renewed it a year ago, always hoping…

One possibility was to book flights and take a chance at entering Congo without a visa. *I could take extra money to grease the palms of immigration officials at the airport. That might work. But how much would it take? What if I'm turned away?*

Then, perhaps he could contact someone in Congo. *Maybe someone from CEM still remembers me, someone who might help me get a letter of invitation from church officials and a visa.*

The long delays and uncertainties of the Congo mail system made this a dubious option. He decided to sleep on it.

The following morning it was raining once again. *Thank you God*, Nick grinned.

He awakened with a plan. Shuffling through the papers on his desk, Nick finally pulled out a recent CEM Mission newsletter, *The Congo Chronicle*. In it was a list of current missionaries and their contact information. The present Field Chair was listed as none other than former Litoko Station Chief and neighbor, Rev. Brandon Ellis. Even better, it listed his Léopoldville address and telephone number!

What a break.

Nick's nighttime epiphany had given him the idea to somehow make an international phone call. Wishful thinking for sure, he reasoned, *perhaps I can contact and persuade a sympathetic CEM official to help me. And now, I know which official to call.* He smiled.

By Nick's reckoning if it was 9 a.m. in Illinois it would be 3 p.m. in Léopoldville. He scanned the directions in the phone book for international calls and dialed the long string of numbers from the newsletter. After a short delay, the phone rang on the other end. It rang and rang.

He was about to hang up when a familiar voice came on the line. *"Bon jour, ici CEM."* Nick just about swallowed his tongue.

"Rev. Ellis," he blurted, "It's Nick Warren calling from Illinois."

"What a surprise to hear from you, Nick," There was an awkward pause before Ellis voiced a cautious question. "Has some emergency happened in your family? What prompts your call?"

Nick hesitated and then poured out his story. He told of his parents' divorce, his longing to see his father, his alarm at the news of rebel successes and his determination to come to Congo...now. He ended his monologue with an impassioned plea.

"I was told that to get an entry visa I'd need a letter of invitation from the national church. Can you help me? *Will you* help me? I really want to see Dad. It's been such a long time. Of course I miss Congo a lot, too."

Nick waited, anxious. There was a long, crackling delay. Finally, Rev. Ellis spoke.

"You know, I think I'm going to do something I'll probably regret. I'm going to help you, Nick. I've always thought you were a levelheaded and courageous kid. Ever since you saved our Kyle. It goes without saying that our family owes you a debt of gratitude. Frankly, I'm touched by your determination to see your father once again. Your family has been a casualty of Congo's Independence. I'm genuinely sorry for how things have unfolded. There are important facts about your father's situation you can only learn if you come here. If you've got the means and the courage to come on your own, I think I will see if I can help make that reunion of yours possible."

Ellis detailed various documents and information Nick needed to FAX and what he should expect when he arrived in Léopoldville. "You can stay with us while you're in the city. We'll figure out travel plans for heading up country once you arrive, hopefully within the next few weeks."

Rev. Ellis offered one last comment before signing off. "You might be interested to know that Ellie is here. She's been volunteering with the mission this summer while on break from Gordon College."

Nick gave a matter-of-fact response. "Oh. It will be nice to see her again." Then he thanked Rev. Ellis once again and hung up.

As he flopped back in bed, Nick smiled and let out a whoop that rattled the windows. It was *real* after all: he was headed for Africa, headed for *home.*

Even at this joyous thought, a chill went down his spine. *What am I actually headed for?* This trip would be a huge risk. He'd be leaving school, draining his savings, possibly traveling into harm's way. Even reuniting with Dad would be without his awareness or permission. *What am I thinking?*

As quickly as it came, Nick shook off the chill and sighed deeply. "Now, life is finally starting to get interesting again."

He closed his eyes, hands behind his head, took a deep breath and jockeyed a soccer ball around Masemba against a jungle background fragrant with frangipani blossoms and ripe mangos.

CHAPTER 11
Léopoldville, June 1964

A white van dodged its way through the noisy chaos of afternoon traffic in downtown Léopoldville, June, 1964. Its driver, a white man in his mid-20s, seemed unaffected by the wild and erratic, swerving, honking lane changes around him. Taxis, vans, overloaded buses and trucks carrying huge piles of sacks filled the broad *Trente Juin Boulevard*, named for Congo's Independence Day. The dry season air was hazy with the acrid smell of diesel fuel and burning garbage.

Alert, with impressively quick reflexes, the young driver's mind was not focused on the traffic; it was centered on the striking young woman he had just met.

A mundane delivery of supplies to the CEM orphanage across town had turned out to be anything but a routine stop for Aaron Krehbiel. *Wow, that new summer intern was something else: beautiful, articulate, self-assured and popular. She could speak both French and Lingala like a native. In fact, she was practically a native...an MK just back from college.* He was impressed. She seemed to belong here a lot more than he did.

Aaron's service with the Mennonite Central Committee (MCC), a relief organization, had just begun year two. His assignment: warehouse deliveries of relief goods in the capital city, Léopoldville. This project fulfilled his Selective Service obligation: the Vietnam draft was in force.

A Pennsylvania farm boy, Aaron did not initially like urban Africa. It seemed way too intense and stressful for him. One could never for even a single minute, let down one's guard. It seemed that there was always someone or something hovering in wait, poised to pounce. Beggars, pickpockets, police, wild drivers, government officials, and merchants: all seemed to be on the alert to exploit any sign of weakness or inattention.

But that girl, now *there* was a worthy distraction! As he deftly dodged a careening Toyota taxi he chided himself, *What's the matter with me? I must be losing my grip; I'm not here to find romance, I'm here to serve the Lord and to fulfill my draft obligation. Focus, Krehbiel!"* But the vision planted in his brain was too vivid to dismiss so easily.

Suddenly, the street ahead closed with vehicles and he came to a screeching halt, facing an irregular collection of glowing red taillights. People jumped out of their cars and vans. A crowd collected on the street. Since there was no moving either forward or backward, Aaron also left his van and slowly made his way toward the onlookers. A cloud of dust was rising, along with a growing din of loud shouts and screams.

Using his height to advantage, Aaron peered over the heads of the agitated onlookers to see a clutch of arms and legs pummeling two people. They had each attempted to curl into a ball to avoid the wildly thrown punches and kicks of the mob.

"Likambo nini?" Aaron asked the wide-eyed man at his shoulder, employing his novice Lingala to find out what was happening.

"La voiture ezoki motambola." came the explanation of a pedestrian having been hit by a car. *"Les chauffeurs...bakokufa!"*

The drivers will die? Aaron was both shocked and alarmed. It appeared that the mob was about to perform brutal and violent street justice right before his eyes.

Without thinking he charged through the milling onlookers. Stiff-arming one assailant, he pulled another back by the waist. He hoisted the man off the ground and flung him into the throng with the same ease he'd toss a bale of hay onto a wagon at home.

"Stop!" He screamed at the top of his voice as he stood over the two crumpled victims.

The crowd seemed startled by his intervention and stepped back. He pushed the nearest attackers hard enough that they stumbled backward into the masses surrounding the two bleeding and moaning victims.

"Police!" Aaron bellowed at full volume.

His surprise intrusion disrupted the angry mood of the crowd. Some shouted for the *mundele* to leave, but most just milled about. Several women in brightly printed wraparounds knelt over the motionless body of a stricken pedestrian, weeping and wailing. Two scowling Congolese policemen pushed through their midst.

The policemen dragged the two bloody and swollen-faced casualties to their feet. Loud voices from all directions described the traffic incident to the officers. Some screamed threats to the drivers. Several slapped or punched the barely conscious captives, now held upright by the police.

In the absence of an official police vehicle, (there were few to be found anywhere in the city), the officers dragged the two battered detainees toward the nearest taxi. They roughly pushed them in and sped off. The mob dispersed and slowly the traffic jam began to clear.

Driving back to the warehouse, Aaron rubbed his shoulders and arms, aching from his efforts with the vigilantes. His legs felt shaky from his charge through the crowd, but even more so from the excitement of the incident.

He was a pacifist, yet violence and retribution were all about. They seemed ingrained in Congolese culture. Congo was, of course, not really unique in that regard: American culture – movies, TV, music – glorified violence and revenge too. *Take the Vietnam War, for crying out loud! But here, in Léopoldville violence seems so tangible, immediate and unforgiving. Life seems cheap and expendable.* Was this a legacy of Belgian cruelty in Congo? The stories of Congo history were incredible: chopping off hands in the rubber harvest if quotas weren't met. *This place has a brutal legacy.*

Aaron's reflections continued, turning inward, deeper. *How should a person respond in the presence of violence? What is an appropriate response for a Christian, a pacifist like me?* The idea that pacifists should be *passive*, just "trusting God" and taking no action did not make sense. He had no doubt that had he done *nothing* the two chauffeurs would have met their end right in the street.

But didn't my intervention use violence, too? And where is God, protector of the innocent, when all this was taking place? Where does one draw the line between trusting God for the outcome and taking the initiative to act?

It was all so confusing. *I wish that I could just sit down with Father and ask him to explain.* Not that he had done much of that in recent years, but it dawned on him that his father had often spoken wisely and clearly about the foundations of their Mennonite faith in the past. *I had just not been ready to listen. I am now.*

Aaron was nearing the warehouse when a lovely vision returned to his consciousness: *Ellie.* Now *there* was a pleasant thought. He wondered if she would be attending any of the church functions that filled his evenings. *Does she have a brain to match the rest of her obvious attributes? Her parents are missionaries, but does she possess a personal faith?*

Aaron decided he'd just have to check her out. Something in the back of his mind, however, told him he'd better keep his guard up. *She is probably a heart breaker*

CHAPTER 12
Lombard, July 1964

"He did *what?*" she screamed at full voice. Patty Smalley threw the dishtowel to the floor as she spun to face her 16-year-old daughter, Lizzie.

"He dropped out of Wheaton" came Lizzie's soft, cowering reply.

"When did he tell you this? You aren't messing with me are you, young lady? Well, *are* you? Why did he do it? What *exactly* did Nick tell you?" The questions came fast and furious. By then, tears were streaming down the remorseful teenager's face as she sobbed, eyes downcast.

Todd, hearing the racket, came running into the kitchen. "Oh no, Lizzie...you didn't tell her did you?" he said as he took in the scene. This only made his younger sister cry harder.

"I'm sorry, Todd. I didn't mean to – it...it just slipped out." She gasped between sobs.

"Why are you two trying to keep something *that* important from me?" their mother demanded, flashing eyes darting from first one to the other of her children.

"Because of this, exactly *this!*" Todd threw back at her. "We knew you'd freak out and create major drama. Nick was right to keep it from you."

By then Harold Smalley had appeared in the kitchen. He put a protective arm around Patty. Wide-eyed young Junior peaked carefully around the corner.

Patty pushed her spouse away as she continued her tirade. "You kids are all against me. Nick is about to do something that will ruin his life and you three all planned to keep it from me! Did you imagine I wouldn't find out? Do you think that I'm supposed to *approve* of Nick running off to Africa to find his no-count father? He has gone native. He can *stay* lost. Good riddance, I say."

By then, Todd had his arm around Lizzie and was guiding her toward the door. "That's enough, Mom. Actually, that's *more* than enough. C'mon Lizzie, we're outa here."

The two of them passed through the kitchen door and headed down the back steps toward the garage. They could still hear their mom's unrelenting rant along with Harold's attempts at placating her, as they descended the steps.

"It's OK, Lizzie," Todd said in a soothing tone. "She had to find out sometime. I'm partially to blame since I told you about it after Nick asked me not to. Nick leaves tomorrow from ORD. What do you say about driving him there with me and seeing him off?"

Lizzie brightened, "Could I *really* come with you? I'd like that a lot. I'm going to miss him so much." After a pause she added, "I just wish we could go along."

"Not this trip, Lizzie," said Todd with his hand on her shoulder. "He's on a special mission of his own. Besides, it sounds pretty unsettled. Congo is a dangerous place right now." They arrived at his car. "Let's get some distance from this, OK? I say it's cokes at the Corner Café. My treat."

The next morning Lizzie and Todd slipped out of the house before breakfast to avoid any further exchanges with their mother and drove to Nick's apartment. He greeted them at the door with a big smile and ushered them in. Hugs all around.

"Todd, I've got to thank you for all your help in the last few days: boxing and storing my stuff, doing a last-minute yard sale, and finding a place to garage my car. And now, a ride to the airport, Thanks. Those are fine gifts." Nick had purchased sweet rolls and coffee from the deli down the street so the three siblings enjoyed a last meal together as Nick briefed them on his travel plans.

"My flights will take me to Brussels, Belgium, from Chicago and then on to Lagos, Nigeria and finally to Léopoldville. I'll be on Sabena Airlines. I'll arrive late tomorrow night...27 hours straight. Whew! When I get to Léopoldville I'll be looking for an airport "facilitator" Rev. Ellis has arranged to help me navigate Congo customs. Supposedly, that guy will deliver my fast-tracked entry visa."

It was obvious that there were plenty of unknowns and anxieties to face down just in this arrival.

The three headed for O'Hare airport, talking about locating their father, finding out about his life and greeting friends at their former mission station.

Todd and Lizzie walked Nick up to his gate. The three Warren siblings exchanged hugs and tears as the line of passengers slowly moved toward the gate and the Brussels-bound plane.

In that final moment, a shriek rang out across the departure waiting area.

"Nick!"

All heads turned and all eyes followed the small middle-aged woman, red-faced, arms outstretched, running toward the gate.

"Stop, Nick...stop!" Patty called out again.

Nick froze. Todd murmured, "Oh, bloody no!" Lizzie gasped. Breathless, Nick's mother rushed up to him, clutching his sleeve and shirtfront.

"You can't do this. I forbid it," she shouted into his face. Silent, Nick just looked down at her with a pained expression.

An airline steward stepped up, addressing Patty Smalley quietly, but sternly: "Please, madam, don't make a scene. This young man has every right to fly with us. Do not disrupt the boarding process."

The agitated mother tried to shake off the agent's hand hooked under her arm. She continued repeating in a loud voice, "I forbid it. Stop this, Nick. I insist."

Nick slowly stepped back out of her grasp. Turning, he headed through the doorway and down the ramp to the plane. He stopped briefly, to wave to his brother and sister and then without a single word walked toward his future.

Behind him, chaos reigned. The agent had summoned airport police and together they restrained the protesting Mrs. Smalley. Harold had arrived by that time and was attempting to calm his wife. In the confusion, Todd and Lizzie slipped away, heading for their car.

For Nick, it was an ominous exit...or was it a beginning?

CHAPTER 13
Léopoldville, July 1964

A shaft of morning light sliced through the room, illuminating the far wall. Congo dawns were more like incidents than events, after all. The abrupt brightening of the room acted as a wake-up alarm.

Ellie sat up rubbing the sleep from her eyes. In that first moment of consciousness she was flooded with a sense of well-being. *It is so good to be back.* The familiar sights, sounds and feel of Africa were comforting. Even the Congo smells, from sweet Jasmine blossoms and mango blooms to the mixed aroma of charcoal fires and diesel fumes touched something at her core. She smiled.

And on top of all this there was Aaron. She smiled again.

If Ellie's first thought on waking was pleasure at being back in her beloved Congo, her second was of the young man who had captured her heart in the past few weeks, Aaron Krehbiel. She first met him in June at the orphanage when he made a delivery of food and equipment from the Protestant Relief Center's warehouse where he worked. Aaron: the Mennonite, the conscientious objector half way through a two-year assignment, the dream guy.

Ellie had been assigned to the CEM orphanage for a summer of volunteer work between her sophomore and junior years at Gordon College in Massachusetts. A write up of her summer experiences would earn her academic credits.

How handy that this assignment also provides an opportunity to live at home with my folks and to return to my roots, to Africa. At home! The thought prompted yet another smile.

Ellie enjoyed a delightful degree of acceptance from the orphanage staff, both missionary and Congolese. Most short-term volunteers were more trouble than help. Their lack of language skills and intense culture adjustments made them high maintenance challenges for full timers. Not so, Ellie Ellis. She had both children and adults adoring her from day one. Her language proficiencies were engaging; her up-beat enthusiasm and energy were infectious.

Thinking about it now, it seemed that Aaron's attraction to her had been slow in blooming. *Perhaps this is what caught my attention*, she mused. Ellie didn't try to turn heads, it just happened. Strikingly attractive, her slight but curvaceous figure, long blonde hair and pale blue eyes begged a second look and young men especially, gave her a second glance.

Ellie was used to being noticed. From a childhood spent with dark-skinned friends on a mission station, to her recent strolls across the college campus, her presence attracted attention. In truth, she had come to expect it, though she would never admit this.

Aaron was friendly in their first encounters, cordial but not instantly charmed and impressed, at least not that she could tell. *I guess it was Aaron's reserve that first appealed to me. He has his own mind. He's different than most guys.*

Aaron Krehbiel cut quite a figure, himself. At six foot three, muscular shoulders and arms, thick wavy brown hair and a quiet confidence, he had no trouble attracting girls. He had recently graduated from Bluffton College in Ohio. Possessing a bright, quick smile, he was soft-spoken and reflective by nature, deeply spiritual. If opposites truly attract then Aaron's contemplative qualities served as a powerful magnet to extroverted Ellie. She shared his spiritual interests though clearly not his reserved personality.

Ellie found additional points of contact with Aaron in her first weeks back home. They both ended up attending a mid-week Bible study sponsored by the English language Protestant church in Léopoldville. Initially founded by the British Baptists in 1915, the Kalina church had become an interdenominational fellowship for the entire English speaking expatriate community in Congo's capital city.

Mid-week Bible study stretched both young adults since diverse spiritual and denominational perspectives were represented. Questions and issues extended past each session. These loose ends provided a good opportunity for follow up discussions between the two.

Their interaction was stimulating. "So what do you think, Ellie? Is that guy right about the role of women in church – that they should remain silent? He quoted the Apostle Paul in I Corinthians 14, '...it's disgraceful for a woman to speak in church.' Disgraceful? Really?"

Aaron asked the question with a twinkle in his eye. A sly smile played at the corners of his mouth.

"What? No way!" Ellie snapped with a frown that dissolved into a grin once she detected Aaron was just testing her.

"It may have made some sense in first century Israel, but it sure doesn't now. I'd *never* make it in that fellow's church."

She shifted in her seat for better eye contact. "But don't Mennonite churches have strict rules for women? I've heard that men and women have to sit in separate sections and such?"

Aaron slowed down as they turned down the quiet tree-lined street leading to Ellie's home. "Yes, some churches are very literal in their interpretation of the Bible, but not all. Women are very active participants in our fellowship at home. According to our pastors, Jesus forbid any hierarchy in Christian relationships, the 'lording it over one another' and 'exercising authority' over each other as noted in all three synoptic gospels. We were taught that that perspective applies to men and women relationships as well. That's what I believe, anyhow."

"What a relief," Ellie quipped, still smiling as they turned into her yard.

Ellie's parents took note of the budding relationship. "Ellie, we were beginning to get worried. You are later getting home from Bible study each week. Is it a such great study or is it Aaron?"

Ellie just smiled.

Finally, one warm Saturday in July Aaron invited Ellie to picnic with him at a scenic waterfall location just outside the city. That was a turning point in their relationship.

The afternoon was perfect. Lazy clouds billowed overhead and the dull roar of the long, low waterfall was soothing. It provided a kind of privacy to their interaction, welcome in the company of a score of Congolese children and several Belgian families sharing the site. The temperature was balmy near the flowing water, degrees cooler than their drive from the city. Some of the young couple's best features were revealed and mutually admired as they splashed, laughed and swam in the refreshing river and later lounged on the blanket to enjoy their picnic.

"It" had been on both of their minds for some time already, but had not been realized. In Ellie's mind, the culmination of that picnic was even sweeter than the French pastry they brought for dessert: "it" was a first warm embrace. The afternoon had ended with Aaron's well-muscled arms wrapped around Ellie and hers about him as their lips met...and lingered.

Virtually dancing into her parents' living room later that evening when she returned home, Ellie's only declaration to their question of how the day went, was: "What a perfectly dreamy, guy!"

Grinning ear-to-ear, she floated off to her room as the elder Ellis's exchanged knowing glances.

CHAPTER 14
Léopoldville, July 1964

Curry dominated the intense aroma of spices filling the dining room. In the background an Indian woman's lilting, wailing song danced and wound above the accompanying sounds of sitar, wind instruments, drums and cymbals. Beaded curtains separated the kitchen from the dining area. The walls were painted a deep red with gold trim, bearing shelves on which rested ornate vases and shiny metal plates, engraved with exotic designs. A large embroidered tapestry hung on one wall, filled with images of elephants and tigers aligned in some sort of caravan.

Ellie and Aaron sat at a small table near the front window. Their attention was on one another, not their surroundings. Before them were sweating glasses of iced coke and a plate of warm samosas with lemon slices. Ellie squeezed juice over a half-eaten morsel.

"This place makes the best samosas on the planet," she managed just before popping the next bite into her mouth with thumb and forefinger. "When I was growing up we used to come here for a treat whenever we traveled to Léo."

"These are great! I think I like the meat ones better than the vegetarian kind." Aaron reached for a fresh triangle-shaped roll. "I'm glad you located this place again and shared it with me." The 'shared it with me' part he said looking deep into Ellie's eyes. They sparkled with an acknowledging smile.

"So tell me how you decided to become a conscientious objector, Aaron." Ellie shifted the topic. She had been hoping to find out more about what made him tick. "Did your parents or your church somehow require you to? Did your father do CO service?"

"Yes, and a qualified yes to your questions," he managed, swallowing his mouthful.

"Dad served as a CO in a mental hospital in Utah during the Korean War. I suppose it *is* an expectation of sorts that the young men in our faith tradition do alternative service. However, the Selective Service has a detailed CO application and Dad made sure I filled it out in my own words. He helped me answer some of the questions, but in the end it was my words."

As an afterthought he added, "I now wish, though, that I had paid closer attention to Dad's counsel."

"What do you mean?"

"Well, a couple of weeks ago I came upon an accident on *Trente Juin*. The crowd was beating up two chauffeurs who had hit a pedestrian with their car. I think I told you about it at the time."

"Yes, go on...what does that have to do with this topic?"

"Well, I've had some second thoughts about my reaction to that incident. There's just so much violence everywhere. We see it here in Léo almost daily. I struggle with what my response should be as a CO."

He leaned forward, concern creasing his face. "I do believe in trusting God and following Jesus' example, but I wonder where is the line with taking action to stop harm? 'Trusting God' can't mean just standing by. I can't buy that."

"I'm not sure I get it, Aaron. What's wrong with confronting wrong-doing with force? What about all the wars and violence throughout the Old Testament, Aaron? God approved war in those stories. Doesn't that imply that it's OK for Christians to use guns and even to kill evil people if they have to, to keep the peace today? It's biblical, isn't it?"

Ellie had not really thought much about this whole issue before. *All the Christians I know believe military service is a good thing. After all, we need armies, police and guns to protect our freedom to worship.* This was all a little puzzling.

"In our Mennonite tradition, Ellie, Jesus' example and teachings are first and foremost. We believe Jesus is the fullest revelation of God. His teachings to love enemies and do good to those who harm us, are what we try to follow. But as the saying goes, 'the devil's in the details.' At least it is for me."

"All this spiritual talk is making me hungry. How about a second order of samosas?"

This was way more serious a conversation than Ellie had intended when she first asked about Aaron's beliefs. Her conclusions were more personal than spiritual, however: *I'm not sure what I expected, but Aaron is sure not like anyone I have ever dated before.*

She next voiced a different line of questions. "Once you were drafted, how did you end up here in Congo, Aaron?

Aaron laughed. "You wouldn't believe me if I told you."

"Try me."

He paused, as if debating whether to proceed before finally answering. "A dream. I came here because of a dream."

"Dream? What sort of dream? What do you mean?"

"Well, once I had received my draft notice I began to explore where I should serve. One night I had this vivid dream. It was dark all around and I was frightened. Danger surrounded me. Someone handed me a match and this voice commanded: "Light the lantern!"

I struck the match and lit the lantern sitting before me. The surrounding area became brightly lit. When I looked around there were palm trees and African people around me. At that point I woke up. Somehow, from that moment I just knew that I was supposed to go to Congo. I was aware MCC had work here. The rest is, as the expression goes...history."

"Wow. Some story! I don't think I have ever heard anyone report that dramatic a sense of direction or calling." Her tone lacked conviction.

"I told you that you'd not believe me."

"I'll bet *you'd* have trouble believing you, if you heard it for the first time," she smiled.

"I suppose you're right. I'll say this, however: recalling that dream has been a comfort to me when the going has gotten tough here, even though its reality might be a stretch for you to believe."

The discussion then drifted from family to school to their separate volunteer assignments. Finally the couple's conversation reached a natural break. Both sat in comfortable silence before Ellie volunteered a comment that invited a new level of intimacy.

"Aaron, I haven't been back to my former mission station of Litoko since we were evacuated four years ago at Independence. I've hoped all along to return there this summer, to see what it looks like now, to remember. I'd really like you to see it too, to see it *with* me."

Aaron smiled. His response was immediate. "What a great idea, Ellie. I do have some vacation time coming and even before you came on the scene I had planned to get out of the big city into the interior. This would be a great opportunity to see rural Congo."

Ellie's face lit up. "Really? Do you *really* think that might be possible?" She grasped both of his hands across the table. "Dad could arrange it with MAF and he could also set things up with local contacts in the Litoko area."

Aaron chuckled at Ellie's excitement. "I'd love to see those places you have talked about. Perhaps we could even meet some of the people who were part of your life as a child. Former friends. Let's do it."

With that, Ellie flung her arms around his neck: another excuse for an animated kiss. Aaron's reserve had by that time melted in her presence.

Things were heating up in the Congo.

*****

It was the first of August, 1964. Still in the midst of the dry season, the afternoon was warm and hazy. Trees and bushes were brown and dry, covered with fine dust. The distinctive chugging of a VW Beatle signaled Ellie's return from a busy day at the orphanage.

"Nick Warren is coming. He'll be here in a matter of days." With these words, Rev. Ellis greeted his daughter as she entered the house and headed across the living room.

"What?" Ellie exclaimed. She stopped dead in her tracks with an astonished expression. "Why? What in the world would bring him back to Congo?" In the same breath, she quickly answered her own question. "Ah, I suppose it must be his father, right?"

"That's correct." Rev. Ellis set down his book. "He hasn't seen Doug for over four years and with the tension building in the east, he is determined to find him. It's sort of an overdue reconciliation, I suspect."

"Well, there's *a lot* of explaining to be done, it seems to me," said Ellie, sourly. "I just don't get it. How could Doug Warren abandon his family, divorce his wife, virtually disappear into the bush for several years and still claim to be a Christian? And what about his new life? It sounds like Nick and the kids don't even know about it.

Rev. Ellis started to speak and then caught himself. After a brief pause he commented quietly, "Ellie, sometimes things are more complicated than they seem on the surface. I'd withhold judgment if I were you until you have all the facts."

"I have no idea what you're referring to, Daddy, but I'm just thankful *you* didn't pull something like that on *us*. To change the subject, Nick has been at Wheaton, hasn't he? It'll be interesting to see him again."

With that, she headed off for her room.

Brandon Ellis glanced at the ceiling and slowly shook his head. "She's one of a kind all right," he said to no one.

CHAPTER 15
Brussels/Léopoldville, August 1964

Nick sighed as he settled into his seat, folding his legs and tucking in his feet for the 9-hour flight to Brussels. He ducked as passengers filed past, staring at him. *Mom's screaming fit isn't necessarily my worst nightmare; she wasn't able to stop me, after all. However, her big scene definitely ranks up there. Major embarrassment.*

He cringed at leaving his siblings to deal with Mom's hot-tempered emotions in the aftermath of his departure. *There will surely be more drama to come,* Nick thought. *Fortunately, I won't be there to witness it.*

The flight crossed the great lakes glinting at sunrise and rose over cities, fields and the vast Atlantic with its distant white caps. Nick stretched his legs and spread his elbows, thankful no one sat next to him. He needed time to sort through his swirling thoughts and emotions, to calm his nerves and prepare for the unknown.

Will my French and Lingala come back to me after four years in the States? Will Rev. Ellis' promised facilitator show up with critical paperwork and a visa in hand? Will I be able to arrange travel up country without a long delay? Can I somehow get word to Dad that I'm in the Congo looking for him? What's happening with the rebellion? Is trouble being managed by now or is danger growing?

As if in response, a blanket of clouds obscured his view out the window and Nick dozed off. He woke as a food cart rolled by, asked for a turkey sandwich and coffee, black. He then dozed again, pleased to be snatching some sleep to shorten the flight and rest up for whatever lay ahead.

However, after lunch, the stench of cigarette smoke filled the cabin and circulated through the air vents giving him a headache. *I wonder if airlines will eventually ban smoking on flights to attract customers?* Instead, this airline offered complementary four-packs of cigarettes with their meals. *Ugh.*

The layover in Brussels was only two hours and Nick spent it standing, strolling, stretching his legs and avoiding the passengers who smoked.

When he boarded his Africa-bound Sabena flight for the next two legs, he discovered that this time he had a seatmate. It was a handsome, brown-skinned young man from South Asia. He appeared to be nearly the same age – perhaps in his mid-20s.

Nick greeted his seatmate in French, receiving a friendly *"Bon jour."* But in his next breath the young man addressed Nick in accented English, "Aren't you American?"

Nick nodded, surprised to be so easily identified.

"Are you headed for Legos or Léopoldville?" asked the fellow.

"Léopoldville...you?"

The man smiled and nodded. "Same. So what is an American doing traveling to the Congo...now? Americans aren't very popular there these days." The young man's tone was pleasant and inquisitive.

"I grew up in Congo – Équateur Province. My parents were Protestant missionaries. My dad still lives there – he's a plantation owner now – and I'm going to see him, or actually to find him since he is somewhere near the rebel activity in the northeast."

"I also grew up in Congo – in Stanleyville." The young man held out his hand. "I'm Amin...Amin Rahman. My parents were originally from Pakistan. They own a couple of shops in the city. I've been away studying at the University of Antwerp."

Nick shook his hand. "Hi Amin, I'm Nick Warren. Nice to meet you."

The two young men continued talking right through preflight announcements, lift off and well over the Sahara.

"I was ready to start a new semester at the university but I kept reading reports in the Belgian press of the advance and success of the rebels. They call themselves *Simbas*, lions. Just days ago I read that they had marched unopposed into Stanleyville, my home city."

"Yes. I heard that report as well. I'm wondering what that means for all the expatriates who live there. I wonder if my Dad is in the city. Have you heard anything from your family?"

"Not since the rebels arrived. The latest word from my parents – last week – was very sad. Marauding *Simbas* killed my uncle who owned a small shop east of the city. His business was looted. The rebels hadn't yet reached the city when I last heard from Mother and Father. They were worried. I'd say the rebellion has become personal. Personal for both of us."

"What do you know about the *Simbas*?" Nick's face was creased with alarm.

With increasing intensity, Amin explained what he knew about the rebel movement. "New recruits are initiated with magic potions, called *dawas* to make them invincible, supposedly turning their enemies' bullets into water. This is the meaning of their *"Mai-Mai"* chants as they head into combat. They reject most Western ways to keep their magic spells potent. *Simbas* are feared by both the common people and the army (the ANC or Armée National Congolaise) because of their brutal and violent ways."

Amin's eyes widened and his voice rose as he poured out his anxious descriptions of Congo's turmoil. "Captured enemies are routinely tortured, then killed and disposed of. Some even claim *Simbas* eat body parts to acquire their power – hearts and livers mostly."

Amin distained the "inept and cowardly ANC, who are more likely to flee than fight. Underpaid and ill equipped, they often rape, rob and brutalize the people they were sent to protect. They're almost as bad as the *Simbas.*"

Nick sat motionless, barely breathing, as Amin peeled back the layers of Congo's rebellion. Some of it he had already heard, read about or suspected, but he had not grasped the scope of it with such clarity and from such a personal perspective.

When Amin finally took a breath, Nick asked for more. "So, why *are* you traveling to Congo *now*?"

"My family," Amin's lips were drawn, his jaw set firmly. "I've got to be with them, to help them, to do whatever I can to get them out of harm's way."

Nick nodded. "Yes…yes. I understand." A common purpose drew them forward like a magnet.

The hours disappeared unnoticed by the two intense young men locked in deep conversation. Each described their family members, shared bits of their Congo childhoods and discussed recent academic pursuits.

Amin identified with Nick's expression of feeling marginal in college. "I also could not fit in, no matter how hard I tried. In my case, having Pakistani roots made me even more of an outsider with my Belgian classmates."

Both young men found themselves drawn to return to the Congo. And now, it seemed, they had a good reason to do so.

The conversation finally turned to "What happens next?" Nick and Amin shared their travel plans and hopes of reaching northeast Congo. Amin intended to fly to Elizabethville in the southeast and to either link up with a commercial truck heading north or to arrange transport with UN personnel still posted in the area. He expected family members living in Elizabethville to assist him.

"Amin, you appear to have strong support network. You can count on help from Pakistanis spread all over rural Congo. That's a huge advantage over my situation." His seatmate just shrugged and nodded. *With only the friendship of Rev. Ellis plus some childhood friends near my former mission station*, Nick thought to himself, *I am not holding a good playing hand in this high-stakes game.*

Nick shared his idea of starting a search for his father near his former home area, Litoko. He planned to reach that location via MAF. Their small planes transported missionaries to remote locations in Congo and many other countries.

"I suppose that's as good a place to start." Amin cleared his dry throat, asked for 7 up from the passing drink cart and handed one to Nick. "Missionary Aviation Fellowship is a handy way to move in Congo; you're fortunate to be able to use them."

Nick hoped he was right and that his MK status would still give him access to MAF. He finished his drink and expounded on his thinking. "If the *Simbas* are invading from the east, I figure that Dad might very well head west where he is known and has friends. Perhaps if things continue to deteriorate I will meet him as he heads for safety. He's not one to be easily intimidated, however, so I doubt he'll leave his plantation until he absolutely has to."

The more they spoke of their plans the clearer it became to both young men that what lay ahead of them was daunting, dangerous and uncertain. As this realization sunk in both fell into deep thought. Finally, Nick pulled up a bottle of water, gulped it and cleared his throat.

"Do you believe in God, Amin?" His voice was low and uncertain.

"I suppose so. My family is technically Christian but we were not very religious growing up. Why do you ask?"

"Well, with all the danger and life threatening things going on I find myself wondering where God is in all this. I guess it's my missionary upbringing."

"Are you a religious person, Nick?"

"I used to think so. These days I don't even know how or what to pray. Ever since my parents' divorce my interest in spiritual things evaporated. Now...." Nick's voice trailed off.

Amin nodded, then brightened. "Well, I've always been told that there's nothing like adversity to bring a person to their knees."

Nick managed a brief flicker of a smile. *I'm not sure what I was expecting by raising that topic.*

The Sabina aircraft descended to Lagos, Nigeria and the two new friends disembarked to wait in the humid transition area. Beads of sweat had formed in the short walk from the plane. Rusted air conditioners sat idle under the windows to one side of the room. Nick noted the familiar acrid odor of urine inside the airport. *"Just like Congo,"* he thought as they sat on cracked vinyl seat cushions waiting for their plane to be serviced.

It took a lot longer than expected to re-board their aircraft. Some unexplained delay in cleaning or restocking the plane? "We get to practice patience. It appears we have indeed made it to Africa." Amin grimaced a cynical half smile.

Finally they lifted off on their last leg to Léopoldville.

It was nearly midnight when the aircraft landed two hours later but the night offered little relief from the humid heat wave that engulfed them as they stepped out of the air-conditioned Sabena cabin and descended the portable stairs to the tarmac. It seemed difficult to breathe. The warm, dense air carried the co-mingled scents of garbage, charcoal fires, diesel fuel and body wastes to the passengers.

"Ah," Amin took a deep, smiling breath. "The familiar scent of Congo, of home...nothing like it anywhere."

Nick was less impressed.

As they followed the passengers to the terminal, Amin asked, "Do you have a *'Laissez-passer'* document for your travels up country?"

"I'm not sure what that is. Can you explain?"

"It's an official document, signed and stamped that says you have permission to move about the region. The Congolese are touchy about foreigners traveling though their land without documentation. They check often. My parents sent me a couple of the signed forms for our region, Orientale. Both have all the required signatures and stamps but one does not have the name filled in. You could use it. Here...I'd like you to have it." Amin reached in his pocket for a folded piece of paper. "If you eventually make it to our area, it may come in handy."

Nick took the paper and stuffed it in his carry-on bag. "I'm not planning to go that far, but thanks, Amin. That's thoughtful of you."

He had no way of knowing that this last minute gesture of friendship would save his life.

CHAPTER 16
Léopoldville, August 1964

Nick and his new friend joined a slow-moving line of twenty passengers from their flight. Sleepy agents and airport staff roused themselves, drawn like a pack of hunting animals to the gathered queue. Their primary objective was revenue, not service, or so concluded Nick as he tensed for the infamous and well-practiced shakedown of arriving travelers.

Amin preceded Nick in line. By the time he made it to the immigration desk with his passport and papers in hand, a middle-aged Congolese man was standing beside the official, leaning over him and speaking quietly in his ear. The agent turned, and looking up, nodded and shook the man's hand, and then placed something in his pocket. Returning to his duties, the agent took a perfunctory glance at Amin's papers, stamped them several times and motioned him on, all without even glancing up at the young man.

Nick's experience with the immigration official could not have been more different. As soon as the man spied his U. S. passport, he came to life. Looking carefully from Nick's papers to his worried face, the Congolese agent slowly leafed page by page through first his vaccination booklet and then his passport. After a short delay, he looked up and frowned.

"Vous ne disposez pas d'un visa pour ce pays, monsieur."

No visa for Congo? What do I do now? Nick swallowed hard and thoroughly scanned the area. Amin had already left to retrieve his baggage and there was no one in sight who looked like a facilitator. No facilitator, no help, no visa equaled big trouble.

After several futile attempts to explain to the official that he had been told a visa would be waiting for him, the scowling agent beckoned to another uniformed man. A policeman carrying a rifle joined this second official.

"Suivez l'officier!" the man directed Nick in a commanding tone pointing with his extended chin.

Nick did as he was told and was led to a windowless side room in the airport terminal. In a loud, annoyed voice Agent Number Two then delivered a long and agitated tirade about the *"grave infraction"* that had occurred via Nick's attempt to enter the Congo without permission. He would be fined, held overnight and put on the return flight to Brussels the next day, the official declared.

The policeman stood by, looking bored.

Nick's stomach tightened and his hopes sank. For a fleeting moment, returning to his screaming mother and Wheaton College seemed an almost welcome alternative. *What a disaster! If I ever do get out of here, it is going to be an expensive escape, I'll bet.*

Nick was just about to try negotiating in his hesitant, stale French when a knock sounded at the door. The same middle-aged Congolese man, who had been present at the immigration desk when Amin sailed through, stuck his head around the door, addressing Number Two in Lingala. The agent rose and left the room. A few minutes later he returned with Nick's papers in one hand.

"Vous pouvez passer," He said simply, pointing to the door. Without a further word he strode away.

The Congolese rescuer took Nick by the arm. *"Come. We go now."*

They hurried out a side door into the dimly lit airport lobby. As they passed through the doorway, Nick and his new escort came upon three men: Rev. Brandon Ellis, and two distinguished looking Congolese dressed in dark slacks, white shirts and ties. Amin was there as well, along with two Pakistani companions. Nick's bags stood beside Amin's, each bearing a large chalk customs check mark.

Nick rushed up to embrace Amin with a moan of relief.

"I thought you might need a little help." Amin's face wore a huge grin, delight danced in his eyes.

Nick turned, receiving an unexpected hug from Rev. Ellis that caused him to stumble. *"Mboté!* Welcome to Congo, Nick. Welcome back."

Nick was overwhelmed. "Have you two met?" he asked motioning to Amin. Both men nodded. Nick was then introduced to the two church officials standing behind Rev. Ellis and also to the two Léopoldville relatives of Amin.

Rev. Ellis offered an explanation and an apology. "I'm so sorry you were delayed. Our airport facilitator was prevented from entering the immigration area with your visa. He and your friend Amin's facilitator, however, are well acquainted from past airport visits. Amin arranged for his man to fill in for ours. Fees were paid; your visa was paired with your passport and all your paperwork was stamped. You are now 'official.'"

With repeated thanks and well wishes, Nick and Amin said their goodbyes and each departed with their respective escorts into the black, muggy Léopoldville night.

They had barely headed out in the VW Kombie on the drive to Rev. Ellis' house in the city, when the two church officials started telling stories about Nick's father. They were tales he'd never heard before, mythical anecdotes. Mr. Ellis translated, explaining quietly in English that the two men would decide whether they could support his trip to Équateur Province.

The taller man reflected that the senior Mr. Warren was a very skilled and brave hunter. "'Ye Mukolo,' the 'skilled elder,' is how he is remembered in Litoko village. Mukolo knew that lions sometimes circle tracking hunters and attack from behind. On one occasion, he hid behind a tree and shot a stalking male, just as it charged his companions."

"And, Nick, are you still killing crocodiles and scoring goals?" The younger, shorter man asked, smiling. "I recall that you saved the life of Rev. Ellis' son when you were a youngster. You became a star forward on Litoko's football team. They still call you *Kiuta*, Gaboon viper, for your deadly strikes."

Nick grinned. The man was correct on both counts, but he had no idea anyone remembered these facts, other than the Ellis's, of course. Perhaps evenings around village fires were full of retold tales. *Now I'm home. Fully known again.* He could not hide his smile.

Much to Nick's relief, his grilling by the church leaders turned into a home-coming reunion, assisted by Rev. Ellis' fluent restatements and translations when Nick's language skills faltered. In the end, the church officials promised to sign off on a *laissez-passer* for Nick's travels up country.

Rev. Ellis added, "Ellie had wanted to come along to the airport to welcome you, but since your flight arrived so late, I thought it would not be safe for her."

Nick could hardly imagine the danger Ellis alluded to. *Could white women really be kidnapped or harmed on a nighttime drive to the airport? Is Ellie really that vulnerable?* Nick wondered what his childhood nemesis, was like by now. *Will she be any easier to get along with?*

CHAPTER 17
Léopoldville, August 1964

The 14-mile drive to the Ellis's took nearly an hour and a half, as Rev. Ellis dodged craters, selecting shallow potholes instead in pitch-dark conditions – no streetlights. Some appeared to be fissures, their depth barely illuminated by the headlights; others, just teeth-rattling cracks and holes.

Their progress slowed even further as they turned off the main road and headed into the *cité* to drop off the church officials. The headlights cast eerie shadows on the closely packed shanties. The four men bounced and swayed along a rutted, unpaved maze of pathways that passed for streets in this all-African section of the city.

Nick noted the cement block construction and corrugated tin roofs. They identified this as a better section in the city of ten million. Thatched roofs with stick and dried mud siding filled Léopoldville's true slums. Still, the aroma of charcoal cooking fires, rancid, rotting garbage and open sewage wafted from the ditches that lined the dusty undulating streets.

Occasionally, Nick could make out a person sitting on a low reclining chair beside a small fire.

"Sentries?" he asked Rev. Ellis.

"No – More likely just someone keeping warm. Have you forgotten? It's dry season, the coolest time of year."

"Bonne nuit – Tikala malamu!" Rev. Ellis bid his two colleagues a familiar bilingual parting for the evening. He and Nick then slowly bounced and jostled their way back to the main road. A few minutes later they turned into the commune occupied by Europeans or *mundeles,* both common Congolese catch-alls for white people. The streets were paved; the neatly landscaped, whitewashed residences were walled and gated; electric lights illuminated doors and driveways in the upscale neighborhood. *What a contrast to the crowded and dismal cité,* thought Nick.

A sentry in khaki pants, warm shirt and jacket, machete in hand, rushed to open the gate as their VW Kombie approached.

"Home at last." Rev. Ellis parked and went around to fetch Nick's bags. "We have a bed made up for you in one of the boy's rooms. You can wash up if you wish. You must be exhausted. Sleep in as long as you like in the morning. You must be jet-lagged."

Nick thanked him, dropped his bags and after a quick trip to the modern bathroom – running water, flush toilets and lights – he collapsed on the bed and was instantly out.

Despite the short night, Nick was too excited to sleep-in the next morning. Bright light streamed in the windows and voices from other parts of the house brought him fully to his senses.

As he dug out shorts, tee shirt and sandals, Nick noted the high ceilings, cement floors and open screened windows with crisscrossing security bars: all, familiar Belgian construction. Even two small geckos traversing the walls were a familiar sight. It all felt so...well, *familiar*.

He headed down the hall and toward the sound of voices in the dining room. The family of five turned his way as he entered the room. *"Hey, Nick...you're up! Welcome. Good morning. Mbote!"* came a chorus of friendly greetings.

The Ellis's, their two sons, Kevin and Kyle, 14 and 17, and 20-year-old Ellie rose and shook Nick's hands. Mrs. Ellis hugged him. Ellie had become a striking young woman. Lean and tanned, her fetching white-toothed smile was framed by long, honey blonde hair. Her flawless face was animated with sparkling blue eyes.

Nick was startled by the dissonance of the current Ellie compared to the gawky teenage Litoko version in his head. All he could muster by way of a greeting in reply was a stammered, "Uh, good morning all..." He stared at Ellie, mesmerized, until Kyle jumped up to give him a bear hug. "Hey, Kyle, look at you, all grown up. And your foot!" Nick smiled at the young man's impulsive show of affection.

Kyle lifted his prosthetic foot so Nick could get a better look. "You sure took care of that *ngando*, Nick. But thanks to you, he only got a small taste. This new one works well. I can do most everything." Nick examined Kyle's foot carefully, then sat down, focusing on the other Ellis family members.

Breakfast was papaya and pancakes, coffee and bananas. Nick and the Ellis's soon caught up on their respective lives since they were last together at evacuation.

Mrs. Ellis asked about Nick's mother with such concern that he felt free to be candid with his response. "Sadly, Mom is still pretty negative about Congo. She holds a very different opinion of our years here than we kids do. She's always telling us that she hated living in Africa and was unhappy being married to Dad. It's hard to listen to. Frankly,

Todd, Lizzie and I were disappointed that she gave up on Dad and even more upset that she married Harold Smalley so soon after her divorce."

He brushed off questions about his college experience with a succinct summary: "Sure, I landed academic and MK scholarships but it was hard to settle on a major. It was a lot more difficult than I thought to fit in."

Ellie listened carefully. She finally entered the conversation with a series of questions that Nick found troubling.

"Why hasn't your father returned to the States? Don't you blame him *at all* for your parents' break-up? So why are you here looking for him, *now*?"

Nick bristled at these personal probes. They carried a familiar critical edge to them. No matter how good-looking Ellie might be, she was still a pain-in-the-backside busybody. He flicked an annoyed glance at her and looked over at Rev. Ellis in reply.

"I have a lot of unanswered questions about Dad and so do Todd and Lizzie. Frankly, we miss Dad. We miss him a lot. If he is unwilling or unable to come to us then I figured I'd better go to him."

Nick reached for his cup as Mrs. Ellis poured him another round of coffee. "Dad's separation from us is a puzzle. The news of trouble up country made me decide I needed to do something now. If anything were to happen to Dad we could miss out forever – not knowing him and his side of things. I need answers; *we* need answers."

Quick glances were exchanged between Ellie and her parents. Ellie opened her mouth to reply to Nick, but her father caught her eye, frowned and subtly shook his head. His clear "No!" signal was not witnessed by Nick. Ellie sat back confused, and did not voice her question.

Nick's monologue seemed to satisfy Ellie's curiosity and her inquisition. Nick smiled to himself. *Well, at least I accomplished one thing today.*

CHAPTER 18
Léopoldville, August 1964

Nick had no sooner finished his *"Why I'm here"* statement than a loud knock rattled the front door. Ellie leaped up, calling out as she dashed off, "I'll get it! That's Aaron. I told him to stop by and meet Nick."

"Aaron?" Nick frowned. "Who's that?"

Rev. and Mrs. Ellis exchanged knowing glances. "Aaron is a Mennonite Voluntary Service worker. He and Ellie...well, they have become good friends this summer." Mrs. Ellis said this quietly, almost apologetically. Through the dining room door Nick glimpsed the young couple greeting each other in a lingering embrace at the front door.

Ellie came floating into the room smiling broadly as she clung to the arm of a tall, handsome young man. He exceeded Nick's six-feet by at least three inches and bore the square shoulders and solid build of a farm boy. Looking directly at Nick with friendly wide-set brown eyes, he smiled and held out his hand. "I'm Aaron Krehbiel, from Pennsylvania. Ellie tells me the two of you grew up together on the same mission station."

"Nick Warren, from Illinois. Nice to meet you, Aaron. Yeah, we knew each other pre-Independence in Litoko."

"Aaron and I plan to visit Litoko next week." Ellie's eyes sparkled. "He's using a couple of weeks' vacation so I can show him where I grew up and have him meet some of my childhood friends."

Nick perked up at this. "You two are headed for Litoko? Next week? By MAF?"

Ellie nodded.

"What are the chances of my tagging along?" Nick could not restrain himself. "I've been hoping to start my search for Dad from the Litoko area."

"Actually, Nick, Daddy already spoke with us about that. He's cleared it with MAF as well." Ellie spoke in a condescending tone. "So it looks like it will be the three of us making the trip together."

Nick nodded, attempting to mask his surprise at this announcement. His raised eyebrows and open mouth gave him away.

Aaron and Ellie pulled up chairs and sat close to each other at the table. The younger Ellis boys used the interruption for a quick exit. The three young adults discussed the day and time of departure, people they hoped to see, the post-Independence condition of the station and other details.

Finally, Aaron stood to leave. "I've got to get to work at the Ag Center downtown before I'm late. Sorry to leave in such a hurry. I'll see you after work, Ellie." A solicitous Ellie escorted him to the door, sending him off with yet another kiss.

Nick looked on sourly. *Love is not a great spectator sport,* he mused to himself.

"Can I speak with you privately?" Rev. Ellis lowered his tone as his wife and their cook began to clear the breakfast dishes. Nick nodded, wondering what was about to come his way.

"This is a little awkward." Rev. Ellis drew Nick into the next room. "And I need to count on your complete confidentiality...that you will not reveal what I am about to tell you to *anyone* else. It is my judgment that you can be trusted."

Nick raised an eyebrow. "I...I guess so...what's going on?"

"First, I must confess to you that I have reasons of my own for bringing you to Congo and for arranging for your travel to Équateur."

"There's no easy way to say this so I'll just jump right in. For some time I have been working with the U.S. government, supplying information and identifying local Congolese contacts, individuals who secretly report in from Équateur Province – from the CEM field. My field leadership and years with the mission have provided excellent 'cover' for these discreet actions. My help was first sought by the American embassy several years ago when rebel threats began in the region."

"By the CIA, you mean." Nick frowned, full of skepticism.

Rev. Ellis just shrugged. "Some of our informants have apparently defected to the rebels. Others have just disappeared. Your visit and quest to find your father seemed a serendipitous opportunity to get some first-hand observations and intelligence about the extent of rebel influence in the region."

"You've been away since Independence and have a legitimate motivation to travel through the area. That's a good cover. Your MK experience and language skills are also an asset. It's an innocent quest for *you* but a unique opportunity for *us*. Going there now is admittedly risky, but hopefully not especially so. The present danger is well to the east."

Nick sat stunned, not knowing what to do or say.

"Can I count on your help?"

Nick shifted in his seat, crossed and uncrossed his legs. "What exactly are you asking of me?"

"Only that you keep your eyes and ears open. And we expect you to periodically report back by short wave radio. I'll furnish you with code words and phrases and identify locations and people in the area that have radios you can access." Rev. Ellis continued with more details for nearly an hour.

"Does Mrs. Ellis know about this?"

"Yes, yes, but only she. Not the children or anyone else in the mission." He rose and offered Nick his hand. Hesitantly, he reached out and shook it.

Some sort of bargain had been struck.

Nick retreated to his borrowed bedroom. *What have I just agreed to? Am I now a pawn of the U.S. government or an agent in Ellis's spy ring? What of those who had disappeared...have the rebels cracked the code words? Just how dangerous is this becoming? Who could ever dream up something as bizarre as this?*

Still, he owed Rev. Ellis. He had provided a visa, travel papers, MAF flight and a place to stay. *I'll likely need a good deal more assistance in the days ahead, especially if I run into trouble.*

In Congo, it seemed like trouble was a constant companion. No...not exactly a companion, more like a prowling leopard looking for an opportunity to take down its prey. *Survival here requires a person to be constantly alert, vigilant, now more than ever,* or so it seemed.

A new and ominous shadow had just fallen across this journey. Still, Nick felt more alive than he had for years...for *four* years to be exact.

CHAPTER 19
Litoko, August 1964

Mottled midafternoon sun filtered through the jungle canopy as the agile young Congolese teacher made his way carefully down the narrow path through dense vegetation. His light steps and gliding movements were quiet, barely moving the foliage. His senses were alert: without extra care, one could easily trip on roots and vines in the dim light or even step on deadly vipers. His alertness was also prompted by a forbidden destination. He needed to be attentive should anyone else be moving through the forest.

So far, so good: the normal chirps and chatters of the rainforest were undisturbed. Even the heavy, humid aroma of damp earth and green vegetation was reassuring, normal and familiar.

Masemba was not actually a teacher...yet. He was currently the official teacher's assistant in his village, being groomed to eventually assume the top role. He had finished his secondary level studies a year ago, graduating at the top of his class. In August of 1964, the career path to becoming a village teacher was to serve an internship. This functioned as the Congolese version of teacher education. Such was his apparent bright future.

Masemba's internal appraisal of his circumstances, however, was surprisingly mixed. Instead of feeling proud and hopeful of his future prospects – regular employment, income and status – he found himself deeply conflicted.

Does being educated mean being sold out to a corrupt regime? How can I plan to work for a government that I don't believe in, that I wish to see defeated? Will my internship cause me to lose the support of my comrades? Or worse, will it place me in danger from jealous or radical peers? Elsewhere it is the educated ones who are being executed. It could easily happen to me.

The path improved and Masemba picked up his pace, moving through the dense foliage with quick stealthy animal-like strides developed over years of navigating the rainforest.

While instincts guided his steps, his mind was focused elsewhere. *Hiding my support of the rebellion is a wise move, even though it requires an extra measure of secrecy. I will have to make sure my fellow comrades understand that my school and village leader roles provide useful 'insider' information for our cause.*

Masemba's father, Nzuzi, a village elder and church leader, recently became aware of his clandestine forest meetings with the small group of angry young men plotting insurrection. He had expressly forbidden him to participate. Zabusu, head teacher and his school supervisor, was also firmly opposed to the strong anti-government rhetoric of the area's young men. Remaining alert to surrounding dangers applied to more than navigating the jungle.

Masemba hadn't always felt so strongly negative toward the powers-that-be and their *mundele* collaborators. By virtue of his father's position in the village and church he had had a good deal of contact with important people during his childhood: local Belgian administrators, missionaries, village and area leaders.

He considered Nick Warren a close friend and the Warren family had practically adopted him as a child. Masemba enjoyed his friend's books, toys, food and even the *mundele* language, all of which were huge advantages. *They, as well as my school success, mark me as a leader in our small community,* Masemba reluctantly acknowledged. *These are dangerous privileges, however, especially now.*

As Masemba and Nick grew into young adulthood, it had become increasingly clear to the perceptive young Congolese that their futures would be very different. Nick would return to a land of unimaginable wealth and be educated for a life of abundance and success. *I, on the other hand, am destined to remain in poverty surrounded by so-called leaders who lie, are controlled by outsiders and will take for themselves whatever they can of our assets, however meager or precious they might be. God is unfair.*

Independence had seemed to offer hope – at first. Sure, rural villagers expected unrealistic abundance, but Masemba'a expectations were more concrete: autonomy and opportunity. *Finally we Congolese will be in charge of our own country, our own destiny.*

Prime Minister Pierre Lumumba's bold affront to visiting King Baudouin in his unscheduled Independence Day speech was a proud moment, a symbol of defiance. Just three months later, however, the fragile alliance between him and President Kasavubu had shattered; deadly battle lines were drawn.

By January, 1961, Lumumba was dead, killed in a mysterious assassination some thought to have been arranged by the American

CIA. For Masemba, his death and the conspiracy of *mundeles* –Belgians in the army, and Americans in politics – revealed Congo's true state of affairs: corruption, dependence and deceit. *Lumumba was right: Congo for and by Congolese; all others should leave.* Congo's distressing circumstances had created dark shadows on his heart.

"Brrreeet," "brreeet!" The sharp bird sounds signaled that Masemba's approach had been witnessed by a posted lookout. He had finally arrived at the designated rendezvous.

Masemba stepped from the dense forest into a small clearing no more than twenty yards across. Seated on fallen logs in a semi-circle were a dozen alert young men, mostly barefoot, clad in shorts and tee shirts. A few were shirtless. In his white shirt and slacks, Masemba was the most formally dressed of the group. He had come directly from school. Following his arrival, two other youth emerged from different sides of the clearing, the last of the expected attendees.

A lean, wiry man of medium height, in his mid-30s, stood. Placing one foot on a mossy log, elbow resting on his knee, he looked around as he addressed the gathered group. Kasongo was his name and he was an outsider, a *Simba* organizer and rebel. A Batetela sent by Colonel Olenga to recruit for The People's Army, he spoke limited Lingala, preferring to address the group in a combination of Swahili and French. Masemba translated for the group.

"Mboté na bino, nyonso! Greetings to all." His sparkling eyes danced from one side of the group to the other. He continued in French. *"You who have gathered here have chosen to become a part of the true Congo, a movement begun by our brave and martyred leader, Patrice Lumumba. Together, we will overthrow our oppressors, cast off the corruption and influence of* les Belges, les Américains *and establish a proud, independent Congo. For too long we have been a passive, fearful people. Others have dominated, controlled and enslaved us. No more! The time has arrived for us to take back what belongs to us. Congo for and by Congolese!"*

The group cheered as Masemba finished his translation of Kasongo's words. A pleased smile spread over the speaker's face.

He then updated the group on recent successes in rounding up similar groups in the region. He inspired them with news from the East: *"Like our namesake, we* Simbas *are a force to be reckoned with. Protected by powerful* dawa, *our warriors are even now moving rapidly across Maniema Province toward Stanleyville with no opposition. The ANC and Léopoldville government are filled with fear and dread; their days are numbered."*

In a similar vein, he rambled on for nearly an hour as the group listened, spellbound, asking few questions.

Kasongo then focused on the next objective in the Litoko region: to undermine the influence of local leaders who were in league with Léopoldville and to demonstrate the power of the *Simba*-led rebellion to the local people. "Villagers need to see that it is in their interests to support the rebellion, not the present government." He asked for ideas to accomplish these goals.

Various suggestions were put forth, both modest and dramatic.

"We could slash tires on government vehicles."

"I say let's burn the Catholic mission." Kasongo let them brainstorm without comment.

At one point, Mboka, a short, stocky young man, interjected a comment. Fr. DuBois employed him as a yard worker at the mission.

"I just overheard a radio message that in two weeks MAF is flying here to Litoko with the daughter of Rev. Ellis, the former Protestant Chief. She wants to visit her childhood home. We could dig a trap for the plane. If it falls into our pit it would be a warning to *mundeles* to stay away. They are no longer welcome here. It will show our people there is local support for Olenga's cause."

Mboka's creative suggestion captured the imagination and enthusiasm of his peers. In an animated fashion, they began to discuss when and how this could be done without the knowledge of outsiders.

Masemba remained silent throughout the exchanges. He didn't particularly like the Ellis girl. His childhood experiences had left him with the impression that she thought she was better than others – both missionaries and Congolese. He was reasonably certain that Nick Warren shared this view of his former neighbor.

Mlle. Ellis has personally done me no wrong, Masemba reflected to himself. *She is no longer a resident of Litoko and her scheduled visit is only a friendly stopover. She could be harmed or killed by our act of sabotage. It could turn sentiments in the wrong direction.*

The plan being discussed was unsettling to Masemba. Fearful of appearing to be sympathetic to *mundeles*, however, he kept his reservations to himself.

The group plotted several other minor disruptions before they gathered in the center of the clearing to follow Kasongo's lead in performing calisthenics. As the shadows lengthened across the small clearing and the group prepared to disband, the *Simba* recruiter offered one last challenge.

"This is not a time for sympathy, but courage. You must be strong and ruthless like a lion after his prey. Keep training. Carry out your plans. We will meet again in a month."

With that, the band of new recruits to the People's Army faded back into the forest with its discordant cacophony of birds and insects. But the peace and serenity of the Litoko community was about to be shattered.

CHAPTER 20
Johannesburg, August 1964

The blurry-eyed barfly leaned forward, twisting on his stool to glance at a trim, crew cut young man sitting next to him at the counter. "Well? What 'bout you?" He slurred and spilled his friend's drink as he leaned towards him. "You interested? Huh?

It was the last week of July, 1964 and three young men in their mid-20s were drinking at the Red Dragon bar in Johannesburg, South Africa. The questioner awkwardly stabbed his finger toward *The Rand Daily Mail* lying open on the bar. It announced, in the "Situations Vacant" section:

> "Any fit young man looking for employment with a difference at a salary well in excel of £ 100 per month should telephone 838-5203 during business hours. Employment initially offered for six months. Immediate start."

"I called the bloke. It's Patrick O'Malley, the radio guy what got fired for decking some stupid clerk. He's recruiting for Mad Mike in the Congo. They're putting together a fighting force once again. That's right up your alley, Crash, ain't it?"

Gary Wilson was a wiry man of 28 years, with deep-set eyes that revealed an intelligent, perceptive mind. Soft-spoken and reflective, he came across as quietly self-assured and in-control regardless of what might be happening around him. His smooth cat-like movements, impressive core strength and straight-backed posture reflected his years of military training. Wilson took his time in responding to the drunken query, staring deeply into his beer.

"Well...I don't seem to be making it as a racer. Maybe this is an omen for change," he finally observed, more to himself than to his companions.

Things had not exactly worked out as he expected since his discharge from *The Blues*, the elite British regiment. A graduate of the Royal Military Academy Sandhurst, the British officer training center, Wilson served two years in Cyprus before posting to South Africa.

The past nine months had been a roller coaster of hope and disappointment. After his discharge, Gary Wilson had formally immigrated to South Africa. That part was just fine; he liked Africa. Figuring out the next chapter of his life was something else, however.

Pursuing a dream of racing sports cars, the agile ex-Army officer quickly achieved a series of impressive victories. Thanks to fearless, risk-taking driving strategies he worked his way up through amateur ranks in record time, finally earning an invitation to join a professional racing team. Two consecutive crashes, however, including an end-over-end spectacle he walked away from, reversed Wilson's good fortune.

Those mishaps cost his employers their expensive racing machines and earned him a new nickname: *"Crash."* His accidents ultimately cost him his new career as well. *What next?* That was the heavy question that accompanied him to the Jo-burg bar that cool July afternoon.

By the end of the week, after further research, the foot-loose veteran came to a decision. Together with his drinking partners, he sought out the up-beat recruiter Patrick O'Malley and all three signed papers and began packing their bags. They were told to report in just two days to the Johannesburg airport where a chartered DC-4 would be waiting to fly them to a former Belgian airbase, a location called Kamina, in southeastern Congo, 650 air miles from Léopoldville.

Military life was not new to Crash Wilson; it was all he knew well. Frankly, he missed it. Camaraderie, challenge, adventure, risk-taking, these were the attractive elements of a manly lifestyle adding luster to an otherwise vague job description. They were also a convenient answer to 'what next?'

There was, however, another surprising element that factored into Crash Wilson's decision to serve with famous Congo mercenary Mike Hoare: *idealism.*

Researching Congo, Crash discovered that its chaotic political scene had recently become even more dangerous. UN forces that had quelled the secession of the rich mining province of Katanga were about to leave. Two new rebellions were growing in strength: one in the central Kasai region and a second in the northeast.

Congo's President Kasavubu had just done a remarkable thing: he dismissed his bland prime minister, Cyrille Adoulla and appointed his former enemy, Moise Tshombe, ex-leader of the Katanga rebellion. Tshombe's response was equally surprising. He set about visiting each of the recalcitrant outlying provinces intending to bring all dissident parties to the conference table to form "a government of reconciliation."

Predictably, the prime minister's efforts were unsuccessful; the central government's enemies were determined in their opposition, fueled by surging military successes and the near collapse of the ANC from mutinies and mounting losses.

Tshombe concluded that the Congo government's only hope was to once again employ the services of white mercenaries. It was an unpopular decision, though his experience in Katanga convinced him it was a necessary one.

What attracted Crash to join up with this controversial fighting force was his understanding that Tshombe was sincerely attempting to form a multiracial society in Congo.

Later, the *N.Y. Times* would report his answer to Mike Hoare's 'Why are you here?' question. "I figured I could help this creation. The Congo might thus offer the world some hope, some symbol in contrast to the separation of the races in my country."

Youthful idealism.

CHAPTER 21
Litoko, August 1964

The perpetual dry-season haze of cooking fires and burning garbage hung low over sprawling Léopoldville in the early August morning as Nick, Ellie and Aaron, departed. Their MAF flight to Litoko involved a refueling stop at Coquilhatville, a trading station on the Congo River, near its tributary, the Tshuapa River. It took the tiny MAF Cessna just over three hours to cover the 360-miles.

Originally founded and named "Équateurville" by famous explorer, Henry Morton Stanley, Coquilhatville sat directly on the Equator. The Belgians, at the beginning of their colonial rule, changed its name and it served as the capitol of the northern Équateur Province.

Norm Bowerman, their MAF pilot, pointed out an ashen shell near the town center as they descended. For two decades an elaborate city hall, and once the tallest building in the (former) Belgian Congo, the entire building was torched to destroy the statue of Belgian King Leopold II that stood on top.

The young travellers strolled the airport grounds while the single engine plane was refueled, then folded back into their seats for the last 250-mile segment to Litoko. Since he had the longest legs, Aaron got the front passenger seat, leaving Ellie and Nick crammed into the two back seats.

Above the engine roar, the two childhood neighbors sustained a constant stream of shouted memories, familiar landmarks and speculations about what lay ahead. Nick found himself unexpectedly energized. *How amazing to be able to speak freely with someone who completely understands.*

The small plane floated rapidly downward across the thick jungle canopy, then dropped sharply into a straw-colored clearing. Litoko's landing strip looked like a giant cookie cutter had sliced it from the forest. The aircraft came to a bouncing landing along the rough dirt and hand-cut grass surface. A small cluster of people was gathered at one side of the field to greet them.

But, as the Cessna turned back from the far end it *crashed* nose-down into a deep hole. The pit had been camouflaged, invisible during their landing and as they taxied.

The plane's single propeller dug deep into the earth and stuck, its engine frozen and smoking as the aircraft shook to a stop, tail pointing upwards at a forty-five degree angle.

Ellie's brief scream on impact was cut off by the collision of her head with the pilot's seat. Aaron lay slumped in the front seat, unconscious and bleeding from his head, the windshield cracked from his cranial impact. Norm groaned as he half stepped and half fell out the door. He had a bloody nose and held his left arm tightly against his body as he slumped to the ground.

Nick was shaken and dazed but had reacted quickly enough to brace himself and keep from crashing into the seat in front. *"Ellie! Ellie, are you OK? Say something."* He unbuckled first his and then her seat belt.

She moaned and stammered as consciousness returned: "Whaa... what happened?"

"We hit something. Crashed," was all Nick got out before the first helpers reached the plane. Loud voices shouted directions in several languages and many hands helped remove Ellie, Nick and Aaron from the plane.

The passengers were safely pulled out, Aaron placed on the ground. A Land Rover roared up in a cloud of dust. Diminutive, red-faced Father DuBois had been in the crowd when the plane crashed and had dashed for his vehicle. Nick was relieved to see his familiar face.

Speaking in rapid and fluent Lingala, the stocky priest directed the bystanders to load Aaron, still unconscious, into the back of his vehicle. He then gently guided the other three into his four-wheel drive before heading across the landing strip and down a bumpy dirt road to the nearby Catholic mission.

Later that evening Nick sat before a meal of bread, stew and fruit, recapping with Fr. DuBois the dramatic and troubling events of the day. Ellie was camped at Aaron's bedside as he regained consciousness in the mission's infirmary. She held an ice pack to his head and, occasionally, up to her swollen face. Norm, who had a mild concussion and a broken arm, was spending the night in the infirmary as well. Attentive nuns were treating their patients like celebrities.

"Someone, somehow learned of today's MAF arrival and set a trap. That much seems clear. But who and why?" Nick frowned and spoke up in between spoonfuls of stew.

Fr. DuBois shook his head in vexation, "It must have been a member of my mission community, though I suppose it's always possible someone might have intercepted our short wave transmissions. I am very sorry for such a terrible homecoming."

DuBois added an ominous observation. "There still seems to be a good deal of resentment toward whites around here. Rebel sympathizers are rumored to be particularly opposed to Americans, although their stated goal is a country free of foreigners of any stripe. Today's plane accident was carefully planned. It is both a gesture and a warning."

It was a sobering realization to Nick. *My return home is not welcomed by all.*

As they concluded their conversation, Fr. DuBois had a couple of further surprises. "Nick, I have already been in touch with Rev. Ellis via radio to report this day's events. He let me know that you are aware that he has a network of informants in this area. I, in fact, am one of them!"

Speechless, Nick stared mid-bite and dropped his spoon. "The Reverend Ellis expects to speak to you on the radio this evening. He wants a first-hand report."

A few minutes later, Nick and Fr. DuBois sat behind closed doors, listening to a familiar voice crackling on the mission's radio. After greetings were exchanged, Rev. Ellis quickly inquired about Ellie and Aaron's injuries.

Nick leaned forward into the microphone. "Ellie's face is swollen but she is packing it with ice. Aaron is now conscious and recovering but he will probably need a day or two to be 100%. We're shaken but doing okay."

"Those are reassuring words. We've been so worried since Fr. DuBois called us this afternoon. Nick, you must use great caution in informing *anyone* of your travel plans. The sabotaged plane is an indicator of how dangerous things could easily become...how dangerous things have *already* become! Stick close to Ellie and Aaron. An MAF flight will be arriving in two or three days to bring a repair team, a new plane propeller and to return Norm and you kids back to Léopoldville."

Shaking his head, Nick's retort came quickly. "I understand the urgency of returning Mr. Bowerman to Léo, but as I said, the rest of us are okay, or we will be in a couple of days. We don't want to rush back. We haven't even seen Litoko yet."

"The latest reports of Simba activity are not encouraging, Nick. ANC troops are reported to be fleeing west from Stanleyville. The rebels are on the move in the same direction. They seem to be enjoying little opposition from local villagers who are glad to see an oppressive occupying army leave. They are hoping that the pursuers will treat them better. It's a false hope."

When Nick didn't reply, Ellis continued. "So let me get this straight. In the light of this new information, are you still determined to head out after your father?"

Nick's reply was immediate. "More than ever! I heard today that there are still commercial vehicles traveling east. I intend to be on one as soon as I'm sure Ellie and Aaron are okay."

"I'd advise against it, Nick."

"Thanks for your concern, Rev. Ellis, but as you pointed out, the rebels are a very long ways off. I haven't come all this way just to turn around because there *may* be trouble. I knew that much before I left home."

Rev. Ellis was silent for a time before replying. "I'm sorry I am not there to talk this over with you in person. Please discuss it further with Fr. DuBois before you make a final decision."

"I appreciate your caution, but as I said, I'm determined to follow through on finding Dad. Now, please, if you have contacts for me, can you share them now? I may need to leave quite soon."

"If you do end up heading east, against my better judgment I might add, I have three contacts for you." Ellis' voice was somber. "The first is a Swedish Baptist couple serving in a mission about two day's journey away, near the tiny hamlet of Ngale on the main road to Lisala. The second is a Pakistani national who runs a small general store at the Yandongi crossroads about a day's drive north of Lisala. The third is a Belgian plantation owner close to your father's location near the village of Biala in Orientale Province. Assuming that all three contacts are still on site, you can stay with them. You can also report your observations. Each has a radio."

With that last bit of crucial information and with a final request to send his love to Ellie and best wishes to Aaron, Brandon Ellis signed off. Nick slowly made his way, lantern in hand, across the mission grounds from the church offices to his room in the guesthouse.

This was not the welcoming, open-armed, singing, chanting, return to home he had envisioned. The dense night swallowed the feeble lantern glow, lighting only his next step.

How fitting, Nick mused.

CHAPTER 22
Biala, August 1964

The late morning tropical sun glistened on rivulets of sweat that coursed down the bear arms and back of the laboring man. He was short and lean, wiry and muscular with scarcely an ounce of body fat. Deeply tanned, with thick, black, close-cropped hair, he resembled a mulatto more than a Midwestern Caucasian American, his actual roots. He had spent nearly half of his 45 years in the Congo and it showed: he looked, talked and moved like an African.

Doug Warren was in a hurry. He needed to finish pruning this last row of coffee trees before threatening afternoon showers drove him to shelter. It was year four in the young life of his plantation and the first harvesting of the coffee crop had already been successful. If the next two rounds of this year's crop were as bountiful, he could pay off half his debt to Pierre Wouters who had fled to his Belgian home during Congo's Independence chaos.

"Come eat, Douglas...Yaka kolea" It was a familiar call to lunch by a bright-eyed ebony woman in a green and yellow pagne with matching headscarf. She stood near the coffee trees, smiling as she beaconed to the glistening man.

Doug Warren looked up and smiled. He waved a weary arm to the attractive Congolese woman. *What a fortunate man I am*, he thought in response.

They had been married almost two years but his heart still quickened each time she reached out to him. Perhaps it was the years of rejection and distain he had endured with Patty. Maybe it was just the warmth and genuine affection she had showered on him that accounted for his joy at each new encounter. *You'd think the delight would have faded by now.* It hadn't.

Sarah Nkumu was a striking, reserved Congolese woman of 35. She had a small, slender frame, carefully groomed hair and was always meticulously dressed and fresh, even in the Congo heat. Those qualities she had acquired from her years as a foster child living with missionary *mundeles* in Litoko, her home community.

Orphaned as a young child, she was taken in by a succession of missionary families, raised in their homes and schooled on the mission. Sarah was fluent in the *mundeles'* language as well as the languages of her native Congo. She was also well acquainted with western ways and understood white people to an extent equaled by few, if any, of her fellow citizens.

Her present happiness belied the challenge of her earlier years. Sarah had lost her entire family to a warring tribe when she was six. She too had been raped and left for dead. It had been difficult to heal from the wounds and the trauma, but the missionary doctor's family had taken her in until they finished their term of service and returned to America. She had been passed from one missionary family to another through childhood. She had lived between cultures, neither regarded as a *mundele* by the Europeans nor a full Congolese by the villagers. It was like she belonged nowhere.

When Sarah graduated from secondary school, she had been spoken for and wed to a classmate from Litoko village. Her missionary host family at the time, the Ellis's, had waived the high bride price for her suitor. An educated woman like Sarah could expect a village feast, cloth for her foster mother, four goats and 2,000 francs.

After two years of marriage and no pregnancy, however, her husband wanted to visit a shaman for a powerful fertility fetish. Sarah asked if they could first consult the *mundele munganga* (doctor). He ran tests, examined Sarah and informed the young couple that she would never be able to conceive. The rape she had endured as a young girl had scarred her permanently.

Sarah's husband barely spoke as they left the clinic. Sarah felt crushed beneath a boulder. There was nothing she could say or do; her husband was now free to marry another young prospect from the village. *"If only I'd been killed with my family"* ran over and over in her thoughts. Despite her education and beauty, Sarah was no longer a prize for any man.

Of all the Protestant missionaries whose company she enjoyed growing up, only Douglas Warren remained friendly and helpful. He, in fact, arranged with Fr. DuBois to hire her as a bookkeeper after her husband sent her away.

And then Independence came. All the Protestant *mundeles* left; everyone, that is, except her friend Douglas Warren. His angry and unhappy wife Patty went away with the others, taking the children with her. In a few months, word came that she had divorced him.

Sarah was privately happy to hear this, but Douglas had been just miserable. Then Fr. DuBois told her that Warren had left CEM, moved to Orientale Provence far to the northeast and purchased a coffee plantation from a Belgian friend. Sarah sometimes worried about him.

One day Douglas Warren unexpectedly returned. He came to see her. *Her!* They spent a long day walking along cool, shadowy forest trails and talking about their lives. He loved Congo. He didn't miss the torment he had endured from Patty. He would stay and build a new life in Congo. Sarah warmed to him as he poured out his anguish.

Over the next months, Douglas Warren's visits became regular stops and more and more Sarah had found herself looking forward to them. He listened wide-eyed to her description of her former spouse's rejection and its impact. Finally, one day he held her close, told her of his love for her and proposed marriage. Shortly thereafter Fr. DuBois performed the ceremony and the two of them began a new life together at the plantation.

It was a lot of hard work and very isolated but she loved her life and she loved Douglas Warren. He was a remarkable man. He felt the same about her.

*****

Their first clue to trouble came in the crash of a food tray dropped in the kitchen. Both Doug and Sarah jumped to their feet. The next clue came from the sour odor of sweat and filth as a skinny, grimy figure in soiled green fatigues and a maroon beret appeared in the kitchen doorway. He entered the room pushing their terrified cook before him. The boy soldier wielded a machete. A rifle dangled over one shoulder.

The ANC had arrived.

Right behind the first soldier appeared a second, every bit as disheveled and dirty. His uniform sleeves were rolled up and his baggy pants were tucked into mud-caked boots. He was so emaciated he too looked like a teenager, though he may have been older.

The soldiers and the startled couple just stood there, staring at one another. Doug finally broke the impasse with a disarming bilingual welcome and invitation to dine: *"Mboté na bino. Bienvenue. Fanda. Bokolea epai na biso."* Greetings. Welcome. Sit and eat with us.

At this, both of the two scrawny soldiers relaxed and nodded. The first soldier barked a command and the second turned on his heel and returned with three more tired, dirty and sweaty ANC soldiers shuffling up the steps onto the porch and into the dining area. They appeared exhausted and stressed, smelling even worse than they looked.

Taking her cue from Doug, Sarah grabbed their cook, Thomas, by the arm and half pushing, half pulling, directed the trembling, wide-eyed fellow back into the kitchen as she told him what to prepare for their new guests.

Doug greeted the five soldiers and pulled out empty chairs at their table. Rifles and machetes clattered to the floor as the five strange visitors slumped into the seats. Sarah had managed to corral their second house worker, Emilie, to assist. She was every bit as fearful and reluctant as Thomas.

Soon fresh bread, fruit and water were carried to the table. Warm, sticky balls of fufu, the Congo manioc staple, followed shortly, accompanied by a large bowl of makayabo mwamba (salted fish in palm oil gravy). Bowls full of boiled manioc greens completed the feast.

Doug watched in detached amazement as the five haggard troops filled mouths and bellies as fast and furiously as they could manage. The only sounds came from the grunts and moans of their eating. There was no conversation, only the evidence that the warriors had not had a meal for some time. Nzaza Pierre, the first soldier and group leader, confirmed this when at last they finished eating.

As his companions slowly drifted out of the dining room, Nzaza answered Doug's patient questions. The others, dragging their rifles each found a place to stretch out on the porch or on wicker chairs in the living room. There they collapsed and slept, their bodies aching from the effort of eating and digesting.

"The five of us are all that is left of a dozen men. We were stationed four days drive to the east. The Simbas surprised us. We fled through the forest for seven days. We are trying to get to the Army base at Yakoma on the Uele River. That is still two days distance, more than twice that by foot. I fear we are not yet safely ahead of our pursuers. If we lose this race it is certain death, *'Tokokufa ya solo!'*"

They were running for their lives. That fact brought Nzaza to the point of his story. He looked Doug directly in the eyes. "*Tokai epai na voiture na yo!*" *We will go with your vehicle.*

My vehicle? I have little choice here. Doug had already concluded that it was futile and dangerous to question the demands of these frightened, armed Congolese soldiers. He stood and pointed toward his Land Rover parked outside. "*D'accord. Kasi, biso tokokenda noki.*" *Okay. Quickly. We must leave quickly.*

Doug was loathe to leave Sarah at the plantation without his protection. He wondered how many more demands the rag-tag soldiers would make. *But what options do I have? Perhaps my absence will be helpful to Sarah should the Simbas actually show up here.*

Whatever the outcome, I'd better get a move on if I hope to raise the odds of our survival, of my survival.

"Oh, no Doug. Must you?" was Sarah's response to his quiet pronouncement.

"There really is no choice here. Surely you can see that, Sarah. Hopefully, we are remote enough here that the Simbas will not show up. Nevertheless, I think you should contact Brandon Ellis by radio just as soon as I leave and let him know what's taking place. Tell him I am headed for Yakoma. Then hide the radio. Hide it well. It could take me some time to get back, especially if the ANC decide to take my Land Rover. And that seems likely."

Sarah nodded quietly, tears streaming down her cheeks. She then threw herself into her husband's arms, clinging tightly to him. They prolonged the moment, Sarah shaking with silent sobs. At last she quieted and the couple parted without further discussion. Doug headed for the Land Rover, Sarah for the radio.

CHAPTER 23
Litoko, August 1964

The next two days, the Litoko Catholic mission was filled with Congolese friends and well-wishers. They began arriving at first light. Tata Rafael came with his wife, several of his children and a basket of papaya, mangoes, bananas and a pineapple. Ellie's former cook and house helper appeared carrying a chicken, a rabbit and some eggs. She emerged from the guesthouse wearing a scarf pulled low. It only partly covered her swollen face and black eyes.

Then, Pastor Gaston from the Protestant church, elders and other church leaders, both men and women, arrived to welcome the past members of their community. Nick and Ellie were the first former CEM children to visit since the station's evacuation at Independence. The smiling Congolese clung to the young adults as though they would never let them go again.

"You have come home. You must stay. We need you here with us." At first Nick tried to pull away, but their former neighbors clung even harder. Finally he realized he simply had to hug them back just as hard until they let go.

To Nick and Ellie's great delight, several of their village peers also came to greet them. Their former childhood playmates were grown now, married with children. But briefly, they were all young again. One of the visitor's children had made a ball of wastepaper, wrapped with string and the adults tossed it back and forth, laughing as the giggling child chased first from one and then to another.

They sat together and talked about the previous day's landing. Some expressed concern that the plane had crashed on the rough landing strip because it had not been well maintained since Independence. Others declared that it was God who saved their lives, not permitting them to fall into the trap until they were safely on the ground.

Nick's six-foot height and Ellie's grown woman looks, despite her bruised face were referenced repeatedly. The two MKs quickly fell back into familiar childhood speech patterns, a combination of Lingala and French, as they reminisced with their childhood Congolese friends.

"*Kiuta! Mboté!*" The words boomed across the room as a familiar, smiling face appeared at the door.

Nick leapt to his feet and rushed to greet Masemba with a giant hug. When he finally released his grip they shifted to the soccer team's special handshake, fist-bump, finger snap.

"Hello, how are you? What's new? How's it going?" Masemba repeated the English phrases Nick had taught him.

Nick answered in the Lingala Masemba had taught him when they were boys exploring the forest, village and station. The friends had been separated during Nick's middle and high school years when he was at the Academy. But the highlight of his vacations at home was time spent together with Masemba.

Masemba grinned as he waited for a nun to pass by in her nurse's whites, and then slipped Nick a Fanta soda bottle filled with palm wine. "I brought you a gift, *Ndecko*." Nick pulled the cork and sipped the cloudy, sour fizz and burped, the polite way to compliment the brew master. That brought a laugh from his friend.

Masemba, still smiling, nudged him about Ellie, willowy in her blue and green African wrap-around, long blonde hair sticking out from her scarf. She was holding an ice pack to her face with one hand, balancing a baby on her knee with the other, while talking to a friend.

"You doctor her, yes?"

Nick laughed. "No way. *Ayeba trop* knows how to take care of herself. Just ask her! I expected to see you yesterday. *Lobi, ozali wapi?*" *Where were you yesterday?*

Masemba's smile faded. "Yesterday I was at school. I am the assistant teacher now. I will take over the class one day. I'm sorry I was not there to welcome you. Especially, since you had trouble. I am glad you are safe. And the others too."

Masemba noticed Nick's bruised arms and frowned as Nick responded. "Fortunately, we're all okay. It was a near disaster, however. Ellie brought a friend along. His name is Aaron. He's still recovering in the clinic."

The two young men continued their reunion, exchanging stories, quips about girls, and updates on Nick's sister and brother. They spoke of school and sports. Nick teased Masemba that he would soon be the school director.

"*Ah, molakisi na mayeli! Malamu pensa.* You will be a wise teacher." Masemba, smiling, puffed out his chest, mocking a prideful response.

Finally, after a brief lull in the conversation, Masemba volunteered a somber revelation, about Nick's parents' divorce. "Everyone knows. *Bato nyonso, bayebi.* Maybe it is better, *comme ça,*" he concluded in a trilingual statement of acceptance. Nick grimaced and shrugged.

Masemba wondered how much more he should say to Nick. His friend didn't seem to know how things had changed in Congo. He decided the time wasn't right. Maybe it shouldn't come from him.

Leaning forward, Nick lowered his tone as he prepared to disclose the reason for his return to Congo. Rev. Ellis's cautions came to mind. Across the dining room, several Congolese friends surrounding Ellie were in deep conversation with her.

"I'm worried about Dad's safety. I'm determined to find out what had become of him. That's what brings me back here now. Why did Dad choose to stay in Congo? What is he doing on a plantation? Why has he chosen to be separated from us, from me, Todd and Lizzy? What is going to happen to him if the rebellion is successful?"

As Nick quietly poured out his questions and worries, Masemba's face darkened. He struggled with what to say, with how much to share with his friend. He finally responded, affirming Nick's father's character. *"Tata na yo azali moto malamu."* *Your father is a good man.* After a thoughtful pause, he continued, "I think...the time of white *patrons* in Congo is over, finished, *esili. Peut-être*, even good-hearted *mundeles* like Doug Warren need to see this and find their way back home."

In Nick's single-minded focus on his father's troubles and his intent to be reunited with him, the significance of his friend's words passed by unnoticed.

"I plan to head off for Dad's plantation in the next couple of days. Commercial truck. How about coming with me – I could use your help," he said quietly in English. "Do you understand what I'm asking? *Oyebi yongo?*" he asked.

Masemba nodded. He was quiet for a long time, thinking. "Okay" he said at last. "Okay, I will come."

CHAPTER 24
Litoko, August 1964

The goose egg on Aaron's head took several days to subside and nurses kept his forehead bandaged. His head ached and he was dizzy from his concussion as well. However, in two days he was up and moving slowly to meals.

Norm's injuries were more serious, keeping him in the infirmary under the careful attention of the nuns. Three MAF personnel were scheduled to arrive by the end of the week to work on the downed plane. Fr. DuBois had placed a twenty-four hour watch on the airstrip to prevent any further sabotage.

By the afternoon of their third day in Litoko, Aaron had recovered well enough to join Ellie, Nick and their host, Fr. DuBois in the Land Rover for a short drive to the former CEM mission station.

Ellie's eyes brimmed as the priest's Land Rover neared her former home. Nick's pulse increased. The priest's vehicle turned into the familiar clearing where he had spent the majority of his childhood. The jungle had reclaimed much of it after just four years. Only the Warren house was still standing, occupied by a Congolese family unfamiliar to the MKs; the other houses, including the Ellis residence were burned out shells overgrown with vegetation.

Ellie burst into tears, burying her face in Aaron's chest. "It's just so sad." Her boyfriend tried to comfort her, despite his own stiff neck and bandaged head. "All those memories...lost forever."

Nick swallowed hard. His house, the sole remaining structure, did not resemble the home he and his family left four years previously. A section of the roof had collapsed and was covered with thatch; fires had been lit on the porch leaving the walls and ceiling charred and black; all the grass had been scraped from the yard and it had been carefully swept in the Congolese practice, to detect evening snake trails or footprints of intruders; none of the glass windows remained intact.

Nick sighed deeply.

"Pas de choses a voir," not much to see, commented the stocky priest, shaking his head slowly.

"No, Father DuBois, there's actually a lot to see. A lot of *memories.*" Nick hopped out of the vehicle, hands on hips and looked around.

Ellie's quiet sobbing ended in a deep sigh as she exited the vehicle. The small group then briefly toured the grounds. The two MKs pointed out favorite trees, former garden plots, shared reflections and told stories from what seemed another lifetime.

"I remember Masemba and I setting our goal posts over there too close to the house. Our missed kicks kept knocking over Tata Rafael's baskets of laundry. That's where I learned my first Lingala swear words."

"I remember we had a rabbit hutch back there. We kids each chose one of the baby rabbits for a pet. I was so shocked when Kyle informed us right in the middle of a Sunday meal that we were eating Mr. Wiggles, my pet. He thought it was funny. I was outraged."

Their smiles and tears marked it as a bittersweet visit. Ellie and Aaron walked arm in arm. Finally, all four climbed back into the Land Rover and headed back to the Catholic mission.

On the way back, Nick shared with Ellie and Aaron his thoughts about continuing the search for his father. "My plan is to depart as soon as I can find a commercial truck traveling east. I now have a couple places to stay and even some potential help along the way."

"Really? How in the world did you manage that?" Ellie's eyes widened in surprise.

"A gift from your father. He's not exactly excited about me continuing on, but in our last radio conversation he gave me a couple of good contacts for my travel route."

It was Aaron who made the suggestion. "Ellie, why don't we go with Nick? We've got nearly ten days to spare and I'd like to meet his father. He sounds like quite a guy...running a plantation on his own in the middle of nowhere. Nick has a mystery to solve. It'd be a great adventure. We could be there and back by the time the MAF mechanics fix the plane."

Ellie was not impressed with the idea. "There's trouble in that direction, Aaron. Who knows if it'll get worse? Besides, do you have any idea how rough it could be to ride for several days on the top of a loaded truck?" They batted the idea back and forth for several minutes before Nick interrupted.

"Hey, you two. Maybe I don't want more company. Masemba's agreed to join me already."

Ever the optimist, Aaron was undeterred by either Ellie's protests or Nick's hesitation, "That's all the better. Masemba'll be a huge help. The four of us will make a great team. I think it'll actually be safer traveling together in case of trouble. C'mon, let's do it."

"But...but what about my dad's objections? Maybe I should ask him first." Ellie's face bore an anguished expression.

"C'mon Ellie, you're old enough to decide for yourself. Besides, you know your dad will automatically say no since it's in the father's handbook to be protective and cautious of daughters. You'll have three able-bodied escorts to protect you. This is a once-in-a-lifetime adventure. Let's go with Nick and Masemba."

Caught up in her boyfriend's positive enthusiasm, Ellie's resistance melted. She reluctantly agreed to join the quest for Doug Warren. "Okay, Aaron, but you have to promise to take a medical kit along. Remember, you have spent the last two days in an infirmary."

"Yes, mother." Aaron smiled and gave Ellie a hug.

Nick smiled at the exchange he had just witnessed. He was secretly relieved to have more company. *Aaron and Masemba will be good travel companions. They can help me figure stuff out. It will be safer.* This trip was surrounded with uncertainty, filled with unknowns.

Given Ellie's initial resistance and vulnerability, however, Nick was *not* thrilled to have her included. *I have this bad feeling she might be more trouble than help.*

PART II

The Downpour

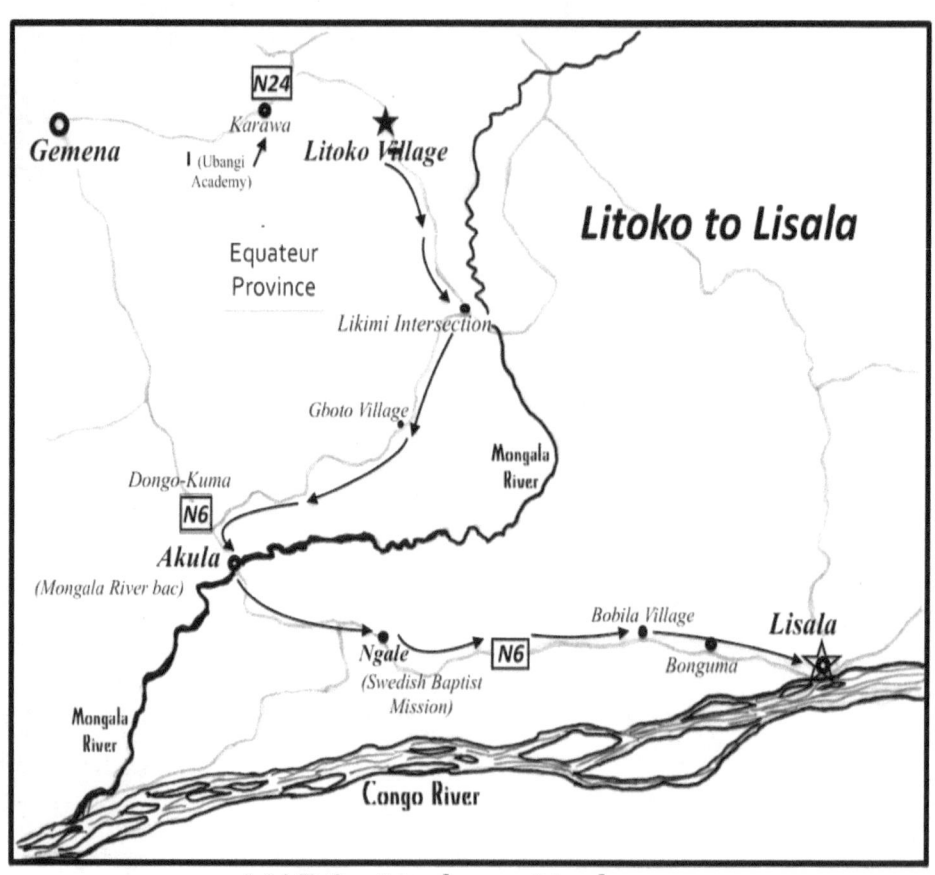

MAP 3 - Litoko to Lisala

CHAPTER 25
Akula, August 1964

Caught up in the novelty and challenge of their anticipated voyage, Nick and his companions failed to take into account the opposition they would face when others learned of their plans.

First, Fr. DuBois put his foot down: *"Absolument pas! Impossible. Il est interdit. Je ne peux pas vous permettre d'aller."* *No, impossible. I cannot permit you to go.* His comments forbidding them to proceed were directed primarily towards Ellie, but he included Aaron and Nick in his proscriptions as well. He was not persuaded by their assurances that they'd find help along the way. *"Trop dangereux!"* *Too dangerous,* was his final word on the matter.

Masemba's father showed up accompanied by his younger brother and pastor Gaston. They all attempted dissuade him from joining Nick and the others on the trip. Masemba listened respectfully. In the end, after all the reasons had been listed and objections explained, he responded.

"I honor your concern for my safety. Thank you. But in this matter I must follow my heart. I intend to accompany my friend on his important journey. It is something I have to do. It is more than a duty; it has a higher purpose." That's what he told his father and pastor, anyway.

Norm Bowerman, the injured MAF pilot also voiced objections to the group's plan. "Recent reports on BBC and on Fr. DuBois' short wave radio indicate Simba rebel activity has not yet been stalled. Their successes have put the ANC into full flight. Woe to anyone who gets in their way. Not wise, folks. I'd advise against it."

Unfazed by the objections, Nick proceeded to make inquiries at the nearby plantation regarding commercial vehicles coming through or heading out. He finally received the report he was looking for: a truckload of manioc was being transported to the Congo River port town of Lisala. He quickly purchased passage for all four. They would have to find another vehicle at that destination to continue on their journey.

The uncertainty of their travel and possibility of danger added up to just the kind of gamble that energized adventurous young adults. Spirits were high as the quartet hoisted their bags up onto the sacks of manioc and climbed aboard the ten ton Mercedes diesel truck.

Aaron found a foothold and reached down to give Ellie a hand while both Nick and Masemba scrambled up the other side. They joined a small group of eight other paying passengers sitting astride the pile of strong, sour smelling burlap sacks filled with dried manioc roots. Their traveling companions also included a goat and a small pig, both with their feet tied, adding squeals to the cacophony of noise from the embarking travelers.

As they settled in, Masemba pointed to the front center area. "Sit there," he directed with an experienced voice, "not so much *pousière*."

"Dust?" questioned Aaron.

All three of his companions answered at the same time: *"Yes!"* They were smiling broadly.

"This is going to be an unbelievable adventure," Aaron declared, his understatement directed to no one in particular.

The Congolese passengers accompanying them were quite curious about their traveling companions. The huge diesel engine fired up and the mound of goods and people on its backside bounced out onto the main road. Its dozen passengers engaged in loud exchanges in at least three languages, struggling to be heard and understood over the engine and road noise. Destinations and introductions were exchanged.

Aaron received occasional shouted translations from Ellie and Nick, since his Léopoldville Lingala was not nearly up to the task of deciphering the rapid and humor-laced exchanges taking place around him.

One fellow told a story of a new *mundele* missionary pastor who couldn't understand why so many people kept telling him *"Nakueyaki."* (I have fallen) He finally asked his cook, "What is the reason that so many Congolese fall? Is it the bad roads?" The reply? *"Te, mpo na basi kitoko."* No, because of the pretty women. From that point on, periodic cautions about bad roads or about falling brought an inevitable chuckle from both white and black companions.

Aaron took note that Nick was carefully vague in his explanation of where they were headed. *He must not want the other to know where we are going.* He also observed that Masemba stayed quiet during the discussion about rebel threats and Simbas. *Is he worried and not saying so?* Aaron resolved to ask both about his observations, later.

The huge truck bucked and swayed over the deeply rutted track that served as the main road south from Litoko. The territory was relatively open shrub land punctuated with small groupings of low trees. Occasional deep ruts slowed them down to a crawl. *These "mini-gorges" were undoubtedly dug by truck traffic during the rainy season*, Aaron concluded.

The fissures were brittle and dry. The monster truck powered through them in first gear. The size of the vehicle and the piles of manioc sacs provided some cushion from jarring but when the truck stopped at a small village after a couple of hours, Aaron was relieved to get his feet on solid ground once again. The driver and his partner bargained with villagers for stalks of bananas while several of the passengers took a nature break.

"We've got another hour or so to the Likimi intersection," noted Nick to the others. "One branch of the road heads east from there to Likimi village and a river crossing, but we are continuing south. We'll cross the Mongala River at Akula where they have a *bac* (ferry) big enough for our truck."

Masemba, who had been standing by quietly addressed his companions with a serious warning: *"Attention tout le monde. Il y a un barrage au Likimi....probablement. Pasi mingi!"* Watch out, there's probably a road block at Likimi. Trouble.

"A probable roadblock? A difficult one?" Ellie turned to Nick, "Do you think so, as well? How should we handle it?" She was concerned but not alarmed.

Nick nodded. "The ANC often sets up roadblocks at intersections. They will ask for our papers and likely try to get a little something from us, but we should be okay. Masemba can help. Forget the okay, however, if they are all drunk. Then we just wing it...and pray," he added as a grim afterthought.

This was sobering news for Aaron. He hadn't spent much time thinking about the risks of this adventure. He wanted to ask the others what they'd do if and when they were to run into rebels, but he couldn't bring himself to raise the question.

They got back underway as the warm Congo morning stretched out and heated up. The jerky, swaying ride was mostly an exposed one for the dusty passengers since large trees only occasionally shaded the track. By this time Nick and Aaron had dug baseball caps out of their bags. Nick had one for Masemba as well. Ellie found the floppy hat her mom had pressed on her at the last minute. She was glad to pull it over her blond tresses. That African sun was intense.

An hour and a half later the Mercedes truck rounded a bend and its passengers caught sight of a barrier ahead. Two oil drums were positioned in the roadway with a pole resting on top of them. There were a number of large trees by the edge of the road offering some shade for the growing heat of the day. A small thatched roof hut stood to one side of the roadblock and there appeared to be a handful of people moving about, some in uniform, others in civilian clothes.

As the truck slowed, a uniformed soldier moved into its path, right hand up, left hand loosely holding a rifle by the barrel. He approached the truck ignoring the commotion taking place in front of the hut.

As the truck drew closer the travelers could see a woman lying on the ground, screaming and crying, with her blue and yellow pagne pulled up to her waist. A young soldier was crawling between her legs with his pants down to his ankles, attempting to mount her. A laughing companion held onto a second woman who was wailing and struggling. Three tiny, wide-eyed children stood by watching, clutching one another. Slumped against the hut, beer bottle in hand was yet another soldier. He was drunk.

"Oh, no!" exclaimed Ellie, and she buried her face in Aaron's chest. He and the others around him seemed immobilized. They stared at the unfolding spectacle, aghast. Their attention was interrupted by a hostile figure in uniform who stumbled around the back of the truck, waving his rifle up at the stunned passengers.

"Descendre, Yaka na nse!" Get down! barked the bleary-eyed ANC officer as the travelers, Congolese and American, obediently slid off the truck in response to his command. *"Papiers!"*

The dozen truck riders scrambled to pull out their identity and travel papers. The scowling man leaned his rifle against the truck. He collected the handful of documents from his trembling subjects and half pretended to examine them. It was clear his eyes were not focusing on the task; less evident was whether he even knew how to read. Some of the papers were upside down.

When he came to the American passports and examined the pictures the fatigue-clad official had a minor revelation. For the first time he realized that there was a young woman before him. A *mundele!* He looked up.

He glanced around, head jerking from one person to another until he spied the young American woman. With a crooked grin he stumbled toward her, dropping the wad of papers to the ground as he reached out. In one drunken motion the soldier grasped Ellie's shirt at the neck and pulled. She screamed as shirt and bra broke loose, briefly exposing her left shoulder and breast, before she spun and bent over, clutching the torn garments tightly to her chest.

Ellie's scream seemed to electrify Aaron. In one fluid motion, he charged and slammed his adrenalin-powered right fist, full force, into the side of the attacker's face. Crack! Bones had broken. The soldier flew backwards, his head thumping into the metal side of the truck with a dull clang. He lay crumpled in a heap, unmoving.

The screams and wailing of the struggling Congolese women grew louder. "We can't just stand by and watch this happen," he yelled over his shoulder and he dashed off in the direction of the hut. Nick turned to check on Ellie as Masemba followed the big American who was deadly intent on rescue.

Aaron grabbed the young rapist by the waist. The ANC teen was well into his sexual enterprise - nearly finished in fact - but the size and strength of the American made quick work of a surprise ending. The young soldier, pants still at his ankles, went sailing against the trunk of a tree. He thumped and collapsed, unmoving.

A loud "pop" that sounded like a coconut on a rock, caused Aaron to spin around. Masemba was holding a large stone standing over a second unconscious soldier. The man's rifle lay just in front of him. He had obviously been going for it when knocked senseless. The final member of the hapless ANC unit was either asleep or unconscious; sprawled awkwardly, he lay, eyes closed, bottle in hand next to the hut.

Three ANC soldiers lay sprawled, unmoving by the hut. The fourth had been dragged, unconscious, to the roadside from the truck. The women and children, victims only a moment earlier, were nowhere to be seen. They had fled into the forest.

Aaron turned and rushed to Ellie, sobbing as Nick stood awkwardly by, one hand on her shoulder. She hugged Aaron for a long minute as the others drifted over.

"What now?" asked a very subdued Aaron.

"Well, we didn't kill anyone, but I'd say some serious damage was inflicted," replied Nick soberly. "The simplest summary is that we're in *deep doo-doo*. Do I need to translate that for you, Masemba?" The latter just shook his head.

"Don't cuss, Nick," chided a shaken Ellie, more out of habit than conviction.

Nick ignored her. "I just talked to our driver and several of our fellow passengers. A couple of them have already headed back for Litoko on foot. Most think that the soldiers were so drunk they will never identify any of *them*. They think we *mundeles* should get a move on before the word gets out. ANC may think the soldiers' injuries were from rebels.

Incidentally, they all thought the soldiers got what they deserved. Let's move. Quick."

Without further deliberation they climbed back onto the truck, located their manioc-padded seats and continued on in a smoky cloud of dust and diesel.

Aaron's bruised knuckles throbbed with the distinct memory of cracking bone and crushing tissue. *Some pacifist I am. What have I done?"*

CHAPTER 26
Stanleyville, August 1964

It was a hot, humid midafternoon Wednesday, August 5, 1964, in Stanleyville, a town of nearly 150,000 just 40 miles south of the Equator. The air was still; no breeze tickled the spiky palm leaves lining quiet streets. It was the time of day when locals took a siesta or found respite from the intense tropical sun in the shade of a porch or broad mango tree.

The door of a small auto parts shop stood open and inside a pair of lumbering ceiling fans circulated the dense air filling the dark room. A Congolese worker slowly, absent-mindedly flicked a broom at non-existent dust. A second worker lounged on a stool at one end of the counter that ran the width of the room, dozing with his head resting on one arm.

Behind the same counter, leaning back on a wooden chair, arms crossed, feet resting on a shelf, lounged a subdued young olive-skinned man, deep in thought. He was the shop owner's son, Amin Rahman, recently returned from university in Belgium. His father had left him in charge that afternoon while he checked inventory at the family's second business, in another part of the city.

Amin's quiet demeanor masked the grinding anxiety that gripped his guts. The situation was every bit as bad as he had feared. Word had come two days ago from the honorary British consul, Peter Rombaut, that the Simbas were only a scant dozen miles away. Last night there had been several extended episodes of gunfire heard on the outskirts of town. Four hundred or so ANC troops were stationed at Camp Ketele, the military base guarding the road from the south. No one was confident that they would be able to defend the city.

It was too late to leave: the last evacuation planes had departed the night before. Besides, Amin's family had decided to wait out this crisis, much as they had the turmoil following Independence four years before. While some expatriates had been roughed up and several businesses looted, no one had been killed in that earlier event.

The Rahmans were not alone in their reasoning. Mr. Roubaut had informed them that there were still 400 Indian and Pakistani merchants remaining in Stanleyville along with 500 Belgians and 700 other European nationalities. Perhaps there was safety in numbers. These, however, were perilous days. Amin took small comfort in the facts.

Like a glass falling on tile, the stillness of the afternoon was shattered by gunfire. It started as a series of irregular "pops" and grew as the staccato of automatic weapons sounded, first one volley and then another. The noise grew louder as the frequency and intensity of shooting increased.

Amin was on his feet and at the door in an instant. The two Congolese workers followed right at his shoulder. Reaching the doorway, the three peered down the street towards the shooting.

Two blocks away, olive green clad ANC troops bent over, dashing between buildings and trees, discharging their weapons down the street. It was unclear whether any shots were being directed towards them. What *was* clear was the huge salvo of bullets they were losing in the opposite direction.

"Kenda na ndako!" Go home! Amin quietly directed his anxious co-workers, assuring them that he would close the store. *"Nakokanga magazini."* As the two African men headed off at a run, Amin pulled the steel accordion security gates across the front of the business and padlocked them. He closed and locked the metal door to his father's shop from the inside. Scooping up the cash from the till, Amin pressed a hidden button under the counter and placed the money in a metal box that opened in the floor. Finally, he locked the steel-barred back door and departed.

I think I'll stick around close by and see what happens. Amin was more curious than frightened. He settled down behind a low cement wall to watch the street and the family business.

The cacophony of weapon fire ended as abruptly as it had begun. Amin could no longer make out any movement down the street. *Where have the ANC gone? What were they shooting at? Were they successful?* He waited and watched. Nothing moved.

Amin was almost ready to leave when far down the street a movement caught his eye. A single bare-chested Congolese man with feathers in his hair walked slowly down the center of the broad street, waving a palm branch as he advanced. At first he seemed to be alone. But shortly, six or seven others appeared following one another at a distance. They were similarly attired, carrying no weapons, only waving single palm branches, staring straight ahead and chanting *"Mai, mai"* in unison as they walked.

Simba sorcerers, thought Amin. Their chant proclaimed their *dawa*: the barrage of ANC bullets had not touched them.

As he watched, Amin observed that a longer column of Simba warriors followed the sorcerers. Fifty or more somber young men, also looking neither left nor right, walked by echoing their leaders' *"Mai, mai."* Some carried automatic rifles but many were armed only with spears, machetes, arrows and clubs.

The procession's attire was mixed. Tattered shorts and military fatigue pants hung loosely on most. All were naked to the waist. Their assorted headgear made it seem almost a comical parade: some sported ANC caps, cowboy hats, discarded UN helmets and even women's hats looted from European residences. Their mission, however, was far from comical and Amin shuddered as he realized how quickly, how effectively they had terrorized and routed the government troops.

The strange chanting spectacle passed by and continued on into the city. Thoroughly shaken, Amin hurried off to his family home with an ominous message. "Stanleyville has fallen to the Simbas."

CHAPTER 27
Stanleyville, August 1964

For the next few days the city was quiet. Amin's father kept his stores shuttered and locked, however, apprehensive about what might develop. The rumors and speculation circulating in the Asian business community offered plenty of incentive for caution.

Finally, word came that General Olenga was planning to meet with the city's business and diplomatic leaders in the afternoon at the Chamber of Commerce offices in the *Immoquateur*, an elegant apartment building and commercial facility downtown. Amin joined his father and over a hundred other so-called Europeans in responding to the summons.

Bright chandeliers lit the ornate *Immoquateur* ballroom, crowded with consuls, businessmen, physicians and others. The room buzzed with warm, heart-felt greetings and interaction as worried friends and colleagues found one another, relieved at discovering their friends unharmed, clearly pleased to be together.

A few minutes after 4 pm the side door banged open and General Olenga strode into the room. White and brown faces went silent as all eyes were turned his way. His entourage included several muscled, bearded aides and assistants, dressed in bits and pieces of military attire.

The General himself wore an elaborate Belgian general's uniform, with sword and pistol at each side. The line-up of somber-faced assistants accompanying him included two Nationalist Women, a paramilitary unit. This group had re-surfaced with the Simba take over, dormant since the regional rebellion following Independence. The two women bore ferocious expressions on their faces. They were dressed in trousers, wore feathers in their hair and, to appear properly military, sported blue UN helmets and pistols at their hips: toy pistols.

Amin stifled a smile. *I don't think they'd take kindly to laughter.*

General Olenga began the meeting with a short speech. "I want all Europeans to go about their work in a normal fashion. The current conflict is an internal one between Congolese. It does not concern you. You will be protected."

The spokesman for the business community, José Romnée, well-known manager of a petroleum company, responded: "Sir, several Europeans have been beaten by the Simbas in the past few days. We don't feel protected."

The general appeared upset with this information. His nostrils flared as he boomed a reply. "I assure you any Simba abusing Europeans will be severely punished."

The gathered group was not reassured with this statement, however. "Will we be allowed to leave Stanleyville, and will we be allowed to communicate with our friends and family in Léopoldville?"

The General scowled. "No! Not until we have resolved this conflict." With this declaration Olenga made it clear that the gathered Europeans were going to be held hostage, isolated from the outside world.

As if that were not enough, he further declared that in the four years since Congo's Independence, the country had been subject to the pressures of inflation. To remedy this, "All prices in Stanleyville will be rolled back to pre-1960 levels, but wages will be kept the same." To that, he added, "All taxes will be cancelled as well."

A loud murmur arose from the crowd cutting off Olenga's grim edicts. Spokesman Romnée voiced a strong protest over the agitated audience's loud dissent, "That is ruinous for business. We strongly object." After the crescendo peaked, the so-called Lord of the Simbas quieted the room with a furrowed brow and raised hand. "Only Congolese are excused from taxes," he retorted, "not others. It is, after all *a people's revolution.*" His decision was final.

General Olenga stood. *"J'ui fini. Nous avons terminé, ici."* I'm done here. Pointing to one side, he indicated that he would now address all consular corps in the adjacent room. With that, he and his menacing escorts marched out.

Amin and his father were aghast. Like other shop owners in Stanleyville their shelves were at the moment well stocked. The announced policies would be a disaster, ruinous! In short order, the city would lack a functioning economy. Further, no imagination was required to conclude that their carefully managed assets were about to disappear.

As his thoughts turned to escape and the challenges surrounding that goal, Amin remembered Nick Warren. *Is Nick's father currently somewhere in Stanleyville? Is he attempting to head this way even as we are hoping to escape?*

The elder Rahman voiced their shared concern. "I fear it's going to get a lot worse before it gets better. We'd better prepare ourselves for trouble."

CHAPTER 28
Yakoma, August 1964

The afternoon rain showers had ceased and patches of blue sky were beginning to show. Steam rose where shafts of sun lit wet vegetation. The air was thick with humidity. It seemed impossible to rush.

Doug Warren filled the gas tank and loaded two huge jerry cans of gasoline onto the racks behind his Land Rover. He was in a hurry to depart with his five unwelcome passengers. *Self-preservation is a good motivator,* he thought as he muscled the fuel cans up. Their 120-mile journey to the military base at Yakoma on the Uele River was going to be a challenge. He rushed to throw in blankets and other gear, sweat running down his face and soaking his open safari shirt.

If Nzaza Pierre was right, the Simbas were hot on their trail. To gain some distance they clearly needed to make the Baku ferry crossing before dark. They had less than three hours of light left and ten miles of rugged forest road to traverse before they even reached the main N4 highway heading northwest. It was then another three or four miles to the river crossing. If the bac was backed up with traffic or broken down, they could be in serious trouble. The bacs did not operate at night. They'd be sitting ducks.

Sarah came running from the house with a basket heaped with leaf-wrapped chikwanga bricks, bread, grilled chicken meat, pili-pili peppers, mangos and bananas. It would have to do. They needed to leave...now!

The couple shared a last long embrace as the five soldiers piled into Doug's Land Rover. *When will we see one another again? Will we ever see each other again?* Heavy thoughts marked a hasty, heart-wrenching parting for the couple.

The drive through dense forest and onto the main road, with its deeply rutted tracks, was difficult and time-consuming. On several occasions, all five passengers had to get out and push the mired vehicle free of deep mud that halted their progress in spite of all-wheel drive. Then, there were the stream crossings. One stop required a foray into the forest to cut branches to repair a primitive bridge over a narrow but deep watercourse. Filled with its cargo of tired, muddy ANC soldiers, the Land Rover finally reached the Baku ferry with minutes to spare.

The bac was a floating platform that held one large truck or two smaller vehicles. It had thick wire cables that stretched across the deep, swiftly flowing Likati River onto a pulley system attached to logs buried upright on either side of the river. When the operator released the ferry, the current's push against its angled bow pulled it across. By repositioning the bac, the current moved it on the cables back across the water to complete a return voyage. It was a clever system that functioned well without the use of engines or fuel.

The bac was on its way back across the river as Warren and the five ANC troops pulled up. Waiting at the river's edge was a lineup of seven large transport trucks piled with goods and passengers, an overloaded pickup with broken springs and a Land Rover. Quickly assessing the situation, Nzaza strode up to the front of the line and leveled his rifle at the lead chauffeur. *"Dèplacer! Longola yango!"* Move it!

The other drivers and onlookers in the queue protested at this order, but the weary military man simply waived their complaints away with a flick of his hand. He looked intensely at the lead driver and slowly chambered a shell in his rifle. At that, the protests stopped and the small crowd stepped back as if on command. The frowning, grumbling driver reluctantly climbed up into the cab of his truck, fired up its engine and backed out of line. Doug drove his Land Rover onto the bac that had by that time returned to its mooring on their side of the river.

When they had safely crossed, Nzaza had a long talk with the bac operator. Doug heard the word *"Simbas"* and *"boma"* (kill) mentioned, but could not make out the rest. When they finally drove off, he asked Soldier Number One what he had said.

Nzaza's report to the operator: "The Simbas are coming. When they discover you have transported us ANC soldiers across the river to escape from them you will surely be killed and dismembered, not in that order. Therefore," he proposed, "you should leave the bac on this the opposite side of the river and head for the forest to hide out for a few days until the rebels leave the area."

The frightened operator had quickly agreed to follow the sergeant's suggestion. Nzaza smiled. "Simbas are not good swimmers. That should buy us extra time."

Doug smiled for the first time that day.

They drove hard into the darkening shadows. It was a new moon and the lights of the Land Rover sent eerie shadows on the overhanging trees as the vehicle bounced and jostled along the road.

The odd team of travelers stopped briefly to eat but covered over 40 miles before reaching the village of Ngai. It was well after dark.

Doug was weary, having trouble keeping his eyes open. Since there was a Catholic mission located nearby, he proposed that they stop for the night. His passengers agreed.

The four regular troops disappeared off into the village to locate lodging while Doug and Sgt. Nzaza contacted the Belgian Rector at the mission for a place to spend the night. They were shown to a small guest room. While his roommate settled in, Doug excused himself and strode brusquely to the head priest's quarters. After reporting the alarming progress of the Simbas, the details of their hasty exit from Biala and the Baku bac crossing, he asked if the priest had a shortwave radio he could use.

The two *mundeles* first checked to see their movements were not being noted, then cautiously slipped across the courtyard to the radio room. Any radio use was suspect.

It was a fortunate night for Doug Warren. In spite of the late hour, he was able to reach Brandon Ellis on the first try. Rev. Ellis was pleased and surprised to hear from him. "Where are you and where are the Simbas?"

Doug offered his former colleague a short version describing the very long day he had put in. His first question to Ellis concerned the safety of his wife: "Have you heard from Sarah yet? I asked her to contact you."

"So sorry to report no, Doug."

"Ahh, that's not good! Not good at all. I fear for her safety."

"Yes, she could be in real danger. Be assured, we'll be praying for her protection. And expecting her call."

Doug then relayed the story of his military passengers, survivors of a major slaughter by the advancing rebels. He described how they had left Biala in haste at the urging of the frightened soldiers who were on the run. "Left up to the national army, I believe that Congo might well fall to the Simbas – in short order. I've heard that Tshombe hired mercenaries. What is the likelihood they will be sent to assist the army in the north and west?" he asked.

"I'd guess it is probable," Ellis declared, "...if the Simbas continue their advance. Équateur is General Mobutu's home territory. He has obligations." After a pause, he continued: "Frankly, I'm quite concerned with this news, Doug. You need to know that your son Nick is back in the Congo. He's looking for you. Ellie and her boyfriend Aaron are with him. They didn't ask for our permission to go. We would have told them all not to go. I don't know where they are by now but they are headed your way...into trouble. We're very concerned."

"Whaaa...*Nick?* What's this all about, Brandon? What's *he* doing here, now...in the middle of this crisis?" Doug's voice was strained.

"Looking for you, Doug. Worried about you. Anxious to see his father after four years." Ellis's voice was steady but non-accusatory.

A loud pounding at the door interrupted Doug. In one quick motion the priest jumped up. *"Moment!"* he called out as he turned off the radio switch and pushed the cart back into the closet. He locked the closet door while Doug moved to a chair at the opposite side of the room. His host then opened the door.

It was Nzaza. "What are you *mundeles* doing?" he demanded.

"Your chauffeur has been telling me about your great escape from the Simbas," replied the Belgian cleric, coolly. "We are going to have to consider leaving this mission. This is very important information for us."

This reply seemed to placate the suspicious soldier. "I don't want you out of my sight, *mundele*," he growled. He summoned Doug, *"Yaka epai ngai,"* Come with me, turned on his heel and headed out the door. Warren offered a hasty backward thanks to the priest and accompanied his army guard back to their room for the night.

As tired as he was, both physically and mentally, sleep did not come quickly to Doug Warren that evening. *What happened to Sarah after we left the plantation? Did the Simbas arrive? What is Nick doing in Congo? Seeking me out? What should I say to him? How much should I tell him? Could he become another casualty of this chaos?*

Finally, exhausted, he drifted off.

CHAPTER 29
Akula, August 1964

The diesel truck piled high with manioc sacks and passengers flew down the main road away from the Likimi junction and an inert squad of injured and unconscious soldiers. Gradually the distance lengthened between the frightened travelers and their disastrous ANC encounter.

The jarring, swaying, jolting vehicle and loud engine noises from frequent shifts did not lend itself to passenger interaction. The rattled young people didn't feel much like talking anyhow. A very somber mood had settled on the group, Congolese and Americans alike. They mostly stared out, glassy-eyed through the clouds of dust at the roadside foliage and forest beyond.

At one point, Nick turned and shouted to Ellie: "Based on what just happened, I think you should become a little, ah...less conspicuous. How about wearing one of my long sleeved shirts and maybe wrapping your hair with a scarf? It's one thing to be seen as a bunch of *mundeles*, but quite another to be so easily identified as a young, blonde *mundele* woman."

Ellie was about to protest, but had second thoughts. "Okay. Let's see about that shirt. I'll wrap my hair in a scarf, Congolese style." Aaron remained quiet, deep in thought.

After nearly two hours of hard driving they came to the small village of Gboto where they made a brief stop. Hearing the truck's approach, the local mamas in their multicolored wraps, babies on their backs, lined up along the road with wares for sale.

Big enamel pans were mounded with fat, moist, white grubs from the heart of palm trees; piles of caterpillars with protruding eyes wriggled their hairy orange-striped bodies. Leaf cones filled with honey colored peanuts, stacks of mottled-yellow oranges and hands of bananas were neatly arranged. Squares of pungent chikwanga rounded out the choices of fast food to go.

After making their purchases, the truck and passengers then continued on their way. Shortly, they entered a dense forest. It was sparsely populated. They passed few dwellings, sighting but a single village each hour. They made only brief stops for quick business deals that looked profitable to the driver. Several stocks of bananas and a sack of mangos were added to their load. They made steady progress.

The late afternoon shadows were long when the weary travelers at last approached the village of Dongo-Kuma, an intersection with the main east-west N6 highway. A small sentry hut stood near a roadblock.

The chauffeur downshifted and the dusty brakes squealed as the vehicle stopped. *Oh-oh.* Aaron tensed along with everyone on the truck. *Has our assault on the soldiers at Likimi been reported? Will there be some sort of trouble?*

Two ANC soldiers rose from their chairs. One slowly approached the vehicle. After a short discussion, the driver left the truck, came around to the back and motioned for one of the Congolese passengers to hand down a stalk of bananas. He placed the bananas in front of the hut. The second soldier, as if in slow motion, picked up the large bamboo pole blocking the road, lifted and dropped it to one side. He signaled for the truck to proceed.

No check of papers, no long delay, no arrest. The four young travelers breathed a deep sigh of relief as their Mercedes transport turned onto the main road and headed east. Masemba pointed to Moombo, the owner of the truck. *"Moombo, ye azali mayele mingi"*

"What was that?" Aaron asked.

"He said that Moombo is very wise."

"And clever," added Aaron in agreement. "Will we make the Mongala River bac by dark?"

"We're going to be cutting it pretty close," replied Nick after a pause. "The Akula bac is only another 6 or 7 miles from here but take a look at the road."

The so-called main highway, subject to more frequent truck traffic, had become a deeply rutted, narrow track. Some mud pits reached nearly to the top of the truck, dug by overloaded transport vehicles grinding away in mud softened by small streams that crossed the road. At each successive mud hole, the truck stopped, passengers descended, its engine revved and Moombo raced forward into the mire. They had been fortunate in making it through each time, but it had proved to be a time-consuming process.

The truck did not make the last ferry run of the evening at the Akula crossing. The narrow equatorial twilight had fully fled as the big diesel transport pulled into line for the next day's crossing. Darkness descended. The distant sound of the bac's engines could just be heard completing its last run of the day across the deep, black waters of the Mongala River. This particular bac accommodated two large trucks at a time and was powered by a pair of diesel engines. It did not, however, run at night.

That evening the four young people rented a nearby hut and sat around a small fire. As they sipped tea, they reflected on the events of the day. "How long do you think it will take for the ANC to report the incident?" Ellie asked.

"Who knows?" Nick stared into the fire. "I just hope we get a lot further away before word gets out."

After a long pause in the conversation, Aaron spoke. "I need to apologize to everyone." He reached forward to put another stick on the fire. "I claim to be a pacifist but here I am knocking people out and using violence to respond to threats. That's not being a pacifist. In fact, it's the very thing Jesus told his disciples *not* to do."

"Wait a minute, Aaron," Nick blew the fire to flame. "You reacted to save Ellie and that Congolese woman. You responded to a real threat with action. Doesn't the Bible teach believers to 'act justly'? That was 'just action' in my book."

"Aaron, I sure don't blame you." Ellie chimed in as she set her tea down and reached for his hand. "You were a hero today. You were my rescuer. I don't know what that drunk soldier would have done if you hadn't stopped him. It took courage to do that."

"It took *force*, physical violence. "Aaron squeezed Ellie's hand, deeply troubled. "If God's people have to resort to the same methods as the rest of the world, how does that demonstrate any difference? Jesus himself could have called down legions of angels but he chose suffering. Do we have a different calling?"

"So, what *should* you have done? Just stand by and watch Ellie and that Congolese lady get raped? Let the guy beat or shoot you without protest?" Nick was getting really annoyed. *This guy is not being realistic.*

"I...I don't know." Aaron's glistening eyes reflected the orange flame. "I just know that I feel badly about what I did."

Masemba shook his head. "You did right, Aaron."

"I respect your beliefs, Aaron, but I sure don't see it that way." Nick stirred the fire once more.

Aaron wasn't quite finished. "So, if Jesus is the center of our faith, Nick, where in the Bible do we *ever* see him teaching that His followers should respond to enemies with force or violence? Doesn't He instead teach about loving enemies and 'turning the other cheek'?"

"You raise good questions," Nick paused, reflecting quietly. "I just think things are not that simple in the real world."

CHAPTER 30
Ngale, August 1964

The four young people stretched out on bamboo beds in their rented hut, but halfway through the night they moved to lounge chairs on the porch. Huge cockroaches crawled about everywhere. Some made a whirring sound as they flew across the pitch-dark room. It was hot and scratchy under their netting, the chairs were hard and mosquitos were thick. Morning couldn't come soon enough.

After a quick breakfast of tea, bananas and fresh bread, they and their Congolese travel companions clambered back aboard the big Mercedes at first light. The truckload of manioc and passengers made it onto the bac on its fourth trip across the Mongala that morning.

"It is good to go forward again." Masemba tried his English out on the three others.

"I agree," Nick responded. "Perhaps we are now moving away from trouble."

"Perhaps not," was his friend's solemn reply.

The morning's journey took them through dense, sparsely populated forest tracks. The truck's loud, pulsing diesel engine broke the deep green stillness. It was only occasionally accompanied by the protesting shriek of monkeys or squawk of red tailed African gray parrots disturbed in passing. The shady forest air was cool and the roadway was firm, keeping dust to a minimum. It was almost pleasant, deceptively so. The sleep-deprived passengers dozed as they swayed and bounced along. Because of the smooth track they made steady progress for nearly three hours.

The sudden squeal of the huge vehicle's brakes broke the rhythmic ride. The Mercedes came to an abrupt stop, engine idling with throbbing pulses. All necks turned and eyes scanned forward. A line of oil drums blocked the road some 300 yards ahead. Yet, there was no sign of movement.

Masemba stated the obvious: "Army barrier."

Moombo jumped from the cab. Striding to the rear of the truck, he summoned Masemba down with a hand motion, as if practicing a one-handed swim stroke in the air. They spoke in rapid and earnest exchanges, before the older man, worry spread across his face, climbed back into the cab.

Masemba addressed his companions: "Nick, Ellie, Aaron come quick. *Yaka noki!* Bring your things. I explain later. Come now!"

The other three scrambled down off their mounded perch, bags in hand and headed after Masemba who had disappeared rapidly into the forest foliage. "*Likambo nini?* asked Ellie as they stopped out of sight of the big truck. It had once again started up and was moving away from them down the road.

Masemba explained. "Moombo says '*Likambo monene,*' big trouble is likely for *mundeles* at this stop. It is often difficult – for everyone. Why test trouble? He sends us around the barrier through the forest. He will meet us on the other side of Ngale village at the Swedish mission."

Nick placed a hand on Masemba's shoulder. "*Merci*, friend. That was close. Ellie, your dad told me about the Swedish Protestant mission here at Ngale. It's located just a short distance off the main road. It's one of his recommended stops."

Masemba nodded. "Moombo will meet us there. Then we continue together once again to Lisala."

All four looked at one another and without further discussion headed off at a good pace, with Masemba leading the way.

Aaron marveled at how skillfully his new Congolese friend moved through the thick vegetation, navigating roots and vines as if they weren't there. In a very short time, the American farm boy was breathing heavily, sweat soaking his collar and shirt. Not so, Masemba, who appeared to glide effortlessly along in the mottled light of the rainforest.

They marched wordlessly through the forest, sometimes on faint game trails and other times through gaps in vegetation their leader identified. After an hour and a half a clearing opened up. Masemba stopped and motioned for the others to do the same. It was a manioc field; a thatched hut could be seen on the far side.

"I think we're getting close to Ngale," said Nick quietly to the others.

"That way." Masemba led the group, skirting the rows of manioc plants and continued, keeping to the protective foliage surrounding other garden plots. Another forty minutes of hiking brought them to a large grassy soccer field. A bell-towered church was at the opposite end, flanked by low cement block, tin-roofed buildings.

"Mission Ngale!" Masemba smiled. His navigation had been perfect. As they stepped onto the field, a cluster of chattering, smiling ragtag children surrounded them. Someone ran to notify the missionary.

They had arrived just in time for lunch. Surprised but gracious, the resident Swedish Baptist missionary, Sven Anderson, met them as they and their noisy escorts rounded the corner of the church.

They greeted him and explained how they'd circumvented the ANC roadblock.

"Wisely done!" Sven invited them to wash up and join him at a long table in the dining area. The *mwamba* stew, *fufu*, fried plantains and fruit were the best ever, they agreed, having worked up an appetite on their forced march.

All afternoon they sat on the porch, listening for the diesel Mercedes. As the midafternoon shadows lengthened, Aaron frowned. "You don't suppose he just took off and left us stranded, do you? It's still nearly 80 miles to Lisala."

Nick shook his head. "He seemed genuinely concerned for our welfare and Fr. DuBois spoke very highly of him. I think it's more likely that he ran into trouble."

It was nearly dark when the deep rumble of an engine grew louder on the side road to the mission. The travelers gathered in front of the church by its circular turnaround as their familiar transport rolled to a squeaky stop.

Something was not right. No one moved. Slowly a door opened and Moombo descended, carefully, painfully.

He was barely recognizable. Moombo's eyes were puffy, nearly swollen shut and his shirt was splattered with blood. His assistant tumbled out the other side, looking nearly as thrashed as his boss. A half dozen Congolese - all the remaining passengers who had traveled with the four to this point - lay still on top of a diminished pile of manioc sacks. The goat and pig were gone as were the mangos and bananas.

"Herregud!" declared the shocked cleric as he rushed to the injured men.

He called for other helpers and soon all of the occupants of the truck were seated or stretched out in the dining room. Food and drink were summoned. Resident Congolese nurses cleaned and bandaged their battered guests' wounds.

It was well after dark when the concerned Rev. Anderson finally asked the injured chauffeur what had happened, *"Qu'est-ce que s'est passé?"*

Moombo had correctly assessed the threat. The soldiers at the roadblock were well lubricated with beer and hemp. They had learned by radio that a truck was moving through the region carrying three young *mundeles* who had attacked fellow army soldiers at an outpost the day before. The roadblock soldiers had questioned the stubborn driver and his passengers at length, employing repeated blows. None had admitted seeing the fugitives. Not a single one! And now, here they were, as promised, to continue their journey.

Ellie was in tears as the story unfolded. She moved over to hug Moombo. He winced at her embrace and with a sly smile, responded: *"Il n'y a rien, mademoiselle." It is nothing.*

"No, it's a *very* big deal," asserted Aaron. "To think what they did for us, *mundele* strangers, no less. Protected us, suffered for us. I am impressed with the heart Congolese have for kindness and caring. It counters the kind of awfulness we have recently witnessed by soldiers. Love trumps violence."

Nick turned. "Might I speak with you privately, Rev. Anderson?"

When they had stepped out of hearing of the others he asked, "Does your mission have a shortwave radio?" Sven Anderson nodded. "Might I send a message through to the girl's father in Léopoldville?" he inquired, nodding toward Ellie. "He is undoubtedly quite worried."

Looking both ways to see they weren't followed, the Swedish missionary led Nick through the dining area and around to a small room at the back. He unlocked the door and turned on the transmitter.

Brandon Ellis was both surprised and relieved to hear Nick's voice on the shortwave receiver. "I'm so glad to hear from you, Nick. I'll admit I had hoped you would reconsider your quest and return to Léo. We were shocked and alarmed to learn that Ellie and Aaron decided to accompany you. We're not happy with that decision. So you're already at Ngale. How have things gone so far?"

"This will have to be a very short contact, Rev. Ellis. We've had some trouble. We're all OK, but we're pretty shaken by what happened yesterday."

"We were stopped at a roadblock. Aaron and Masemba ended up knocking out some soldiers while protecting Ellie. We're now in trouble with the ANC. We snuck through the forest to avoid a second roadblock near here but the soldiers beat up our chauffeurs trying to find us. It's too late and too dangerous to return to Litoko. I'm sorry you're upset. You have good reason. It appears we all misjudged the danger."

"What are you thinking you'll do next, Nick?"

"We plan to continue on to Dad's plantation. We have heard rumors about Simbas but have seen no sign of any yet."

When Nick paused, Rev. Ellis jumped in. "I was afraid something like what you just described might happen. It's just a relief none of you were harmed. Returning to Litoko may be out for now, but going forward is not much better of an idea. I'd insist that you four stay on with Rev. Anderson but it sounds like the area is crawling with ANC. They are much too close. Besides, my sources indicate the Simbas may be headed west on that main route."

"I still want to reach Dad. He'll know what to do."

"Nick, I just heard from your father. He's not at the plantation. A squad of ANC soldiers on the run from Simbas commandeered him to drive them to the military base at Yakoma. If you can somehow find transport in Lisala, your best bet may be heading north in that direction as soon as possible, rather than traveling further east."

"Got it. Thanks for the warning. Didn't you give me a radio contact along the route to Yakoma?" Nick had to think fast.

"Yes, I'll try to reach them after we finish this call. Our contacts indicate that the Simbas are at or near Bumba on the Congo River, headed west in the direction of Lisala. That's why you should leave the area...now. The nearest contact I have is a Pakistani merchant with the same last name as that young man you met on the plane. Nasir Rahman. He's at the Yandongi crossroads about 90 miles north of Lisala. That's a long hard day's journey, maybe two."

The short wave exchange ended with a message of love sent to Ellie, strong words of caution and assurances of prayer for all four travelers.

Nick rose as Sven turned off the radio and relocked the door. *My adventure is quickly turning into a nightmare*, he thought.

CHAPTER 31
Lisala, August 1964

There was movement in the Ngale Mission before the first dark outlines of palm trees appeared in the gray pre-dawn sky. Coffee, bread and fruit were set out, the chauffeur's dressings changed and cool cloths applied to his squinting eyes. Still moving slowly, Moombo roused his battered band and they gathered in the dining area. Rev. Anderson blessed the food and prayed for safety on the journey. Nick wondered what would become of him after they left.

The first orange and golden rays of morning sun touched a thin cloud of fog hovering at the tree line. The travelers thanked the missionary and his staff with hugs and handshakes. They scrambled up the familiar pungent sacks of manioc, and the big diesel roared to life; truck, cargo and passengers bumped onto the main road toward Lisala.

A short distance into their drive, when the truck shifted down through some hairpin turns, Nick beaconed for the others to lean in. "I have some important news to share. I deliberately waited until now to tell you. Last night I spoke with Ellie's father, Rev. Ellis by short wave radio."

"What? Why didn't you tell me you were going to talk with him?" Ellie blurted in exasperation. "You *had* to know how much I've wanted to talk with my parents! I just can't believe you, Nicholas!" Frowning, arms crossed, she sat back hard into a lumpy manioc sack.

Nick replied in English, not wanting the Congolese passengers to understand. "I had to keep it quiet that Rev. Anderson had a radio and that we used it to contact Léopoldville. It could cost him his life. Sorry for being secretive. Frankly, I waited until now to tell you so that *no one* would pressure him." He glanced quickly at Ellie.

"I can keep a secret!" Ellie harrumphed. "When is the *next time* we'll be able to contact Dad?"

"I don't know," Nick paused not wanting to give away the radio network. "Maybe a few days from now? He sends his love, Ellie, and says to tell you they are very worried and praying urgently for our safety."

"Knowing Dad, I'll just bet he had something to say about Aaron and me joining you on this journey." Ellie looked at Nick for some signal she was correct, but he did not respond. Instead, he looked at Masemba. After a quick confirming check to see if he understood the conversation, *"Oyebi yonso?" Understand everything?* he continued.

"Rev. Ellis informed me that my father has left his plantation with a squad of ANC soldiers on the run from Simba rebels who slaughtered the rest of their unit. They are headed for an army camp at Yakoma north on the Uele River. He also reported that the Simbas are rapidly advancing west, heading in the direction we're going: Lisala. Ellis advised us to go north as soon as possible. No place is safe but that's a better direction than the one we're on."

"That's bad news, Nick." Aaron frowned. "We're on a collision course with the rebels?"

Nick nodded somberly before continuing. "Since Lisala is a port city I'm thinking that we will be able find commercial trucks heading north. That's our next step, anyhow. We do need to move fast, though."

The road was rutted but it skirted the forest for nearly 30 miles and the sun helped dry up the mud bogs. They were therefore able to make steady, but rugged progress. There were few villages in the area, a fact that pleased the cautious voyagers: they were not anxious to come upon another military roadblock.

As they drove along, however, two pickups crowded with noisy soldiers passed them headed in the opposite direction. The soldiers yelled as the vehicles passed, but Moombo did not slow or stop. His bruises were still far too fresh to take a chance. Two hours later another troop-filled transport truck passed them. It also was piled with ANC soldiers. Nick and the others looked at one another and grimaced: this could be a bad sign.

It was early afternoon when they reached the small hamlet of Bobila on the edge of a dense section of rainforest. Moombo pulled over, as was his pattern and chatted with the elders. His weary passengers descended and stretched their legs or made a quick detour to the foliage in the nearby forest. When he returned, Moombo walked straight to Masemba and spoke at length before calling and motioning for the scattered riders to load up.

"What did he say?" Nick asked Masemba once they had settled back into their perches on the truck.

"The army is leaving Lisala. Simbas are coming soon. The Chief is not sure if they are in the town yet," Masemba reported. "We are still 40 kilometers from the city."

Masemba removed the baseball cap and handed it back to Nick. "This may be trouble for me."

"Do you guys think we should continue in that direction?" asked Ellie, her forehead lined. Her crash bruises had faded to yellow.

"I don't see that we have any choice. We're gambling that we beat the Simbas to Lisala." Nick was somber as the truck started up once again, settling the matter.

The afternoon shadows darkened the dim corridor as the track entered the forest canopy. The growing gloom matched the spirits of the passengers, both *mundeles* and Congolese alike. They were on a slippery slope. The lack of conversation among the passengers showed they all knew it.

The squeal of the huge Mercedes' brakes threw the travelers forward, then back. They craned to see the reason for their abrupt halt. Parked crosswise in the narrow road was a dented green pickup. Ragged looking, shirtless boys hung onto a metal frame welded onto the truck bed. Each held an automatic rifle pointed directly at the idling truck.

One of the armed group, a tall skinny fellow with a sparse stubble at his chin, stepped forward and motioned for Moombo to kill the engine and come his way. Moombo did as ordered. The gunman's companions hopped down off the back and moved slowly toward the big vehicle in front of them. They bore angry expressions.

"Simbas," Nick murmured the obvious. "Do exactly as they say. Let's not test their patience."

The Simba leader had a scowling exchange with Moombo that Nick and the others could not make out. He then swung his rifle, violently, catching the driver on the side of the head, sending him crashing to the ground in a heap. He snapped a question at his prone victim and without waiting for an answer shot him in the face. The four looked on in horror as the back of their chauffeur's head exploded and he crumpled into an expanding pool of blood.

"Américains! Allez au camion." The Simba leader barked, motioning toward the pickup.

The three pale-skinned Americans crept down from their perch still in shock. The ragged Simba gunmen pushed and prodded them into the green pickup. Two of them climbed in behind to guard the captives. Three more scampered up on top of the manioc sacks, weapons pointed at the remaining passengers, including Masemba. He remained seated, motionless with his fellow Congolese. Not a good time to identify with *mundeles*.

One young rebel jumped into the pickup, fired up its engine and backed around heading up the road, tires spinning a cloud of red dust in his wake. The squad leader climbed into the cab of the big Mercedes, started its diesel motor and with much grinding of gears, caravanned behind the pickup, heading for Lisala.

Nick could hardly think. The sound of the gun blast still rang in his ears. The image of Moombo's head blown in pieces...*what chance do we have of getting out of this alive?*

"Pasi mingi!" Huge disaster! Nick mumbled as they drove away from the body of their slain friend and chauffeur.

CHAPTER 32
Léopoldville, August 1964

Brandon and Nathalie sat at the table, heads bowed, holding hands. Tears streamed down Nathalie's cheeks; the mission administrator's eyes also brimmed. Their prayer session had ended mid-sentence in choked sobs. "Oh, what have we done, Brandon?" moaned his distraught wife. "We sent our daughter and those dear young people to their deaths!" More sobs racked her heaving shoulders.

Brandon released his wife's hands and, moving closer, encircled her in his arms, rocking her gray tresses against his chest. "We don't know that for sure, Nattie." He stroked her hair, struggling to believe his own words. "We have to trust their welfare to the Lord. Life has many risks."

While he voiced the right sentiment, the knot in his guts conveyed a different truth: Ellis was eaten up with worry about his daughter. It had been three days and not a word. *What was I thinking to allow those kids to head up country at a time like this?* The Simbas had become far more successful and dangerous than he or his CIA collaborators had guessed. *I've made a serious miscalculation.*

At that moment, a loud crackling noise came from the next room. It was followed by the sound of a heavily accented voice. *An incoming call!* Ellis jumped up and dashed to the radio, snatching up the mike. Nathalie followed close behind, leaning over his shoulder as he sat at the desk.

The caller was Rev. Sven Anderson from the Swedish Baptist mission at Ngale, the same helpful cleric who had allowed Nick to report in three nights earlier. His was not an easy report to receive.

After initial greetings were exchanged he got right to the point. "I am afraid I am the bearer of bad news. A village youth from our parish who joined the Simbas is still friendly with us. He stopped by today to report that three young Americans are being held in Lisala, along with the others they were traveling with. Their chauffeur was killed and they were captured the same day they left Ngale, three days ago".

Rev. Ellis' heart sank. "Did he tell you anything else? What's to become of them?"

"He told us that he believed the three *mundeles* were going to be sent to Stanleyville with some others, either to serve as hostages or to be..." he paused, "publically executed. The fate of their Congolese traveling companions has yet to be determined but our young rebel friend made it sound as if it was not likely they would be spared since they had befriended the enemy...*les Américains.*"

The worried father signed off, expressing deep gratitude for the Swedish cleric's risky report. *What a courageous, man. I wonder if I'd be willing to take the same risks were our positions reversed.*

Brandon and Nathalie Ellis silently held one another for a long time. What could they say? Fear and anxiety pulsed through their extended embrace.

Finally, as if his torment had moved him to a decision, Rev. Ellis stood and released his wife's hands. He turned and with a determined look on his face, marched into the next room, reaching for the phone. He dialed the U.S. Embassy.

"May I speak with Consul Loren Durban, please? It's an emergency."

CHAPTER 33
Kamina, August 1964

Two planeloads of recruits totaling nearly 500 aspiring mercenaries, landed at the Kamina Base (aka BAKA) in mid-August, 1964. Gary 'Crash' Wilson was among them.

Located in a remote area of Congo's Katanga Plateau, the facility had once been considered a military marvel. The Belgians constructed it prior to Independence at enormous cost, intending for BAKA to serve as a strategic NATO base. It was a garrison town designed to house thousands of troops with their families, complete with schools, cinemas, swimming pools, passenger jet runways and rows upon rows of housing. It was here the motley group of aspiring soldiers of fortune began their Congo mission.

Heat waves smelling of creosote and jet fuel radiated off the tarmac as Crash and his fellow recruits exited the chartered plane and gathered in small groups. A murmur arose. It began first as astonished chatter and then grew in volume to angry alarm as the tough-looking recruits surveyed their surroundings.

What lay before them was a hideous monument to neglect, a haunting shell of its former self. The entire BAKA facility had been thoroughly looted and gutted. There was no electricity or running water; all bulbs, fixtures, wiring, windows, doors and plumbing were gone. The stench of urine and excrement adorned the rooms of nearly every building. It was a shocking sight and an assault to the senses.

"What the hell?"

"I didn't sign up for this shit!"

"This must be some sort of bad joke."

"No way...I'm outa here!"

"Who's in charge of this mess?" The angry protests grew louder.

At that moment, a trim, confident, steel-eyed, uniformed officer strode onto the scene. He looked every sense the quintessential stiff-upper-lipped British officer. In a firm no-nonsense voice he took command: *"Everyone. To the football field. Now!"*

It was *The Man*, Major "Mad Mike" Hoare, himself. He stood, eyes penetrating the mob and slowly pointed toward the adjacent field. There was no doubt who was in charge of this facility.

Aspiring leaders among the recruits echoed his directions in staccato commands and the entire group moved toward the open field. As one of the few with prior military training, Wilson stepped forward and began to line the men up for inspection.

Observing this, Hoare smiled ever so slightly and mused, *"Maybe there's hope yet to make a fighting force out of this rabble."*

Maj. Hoare strolled along each line of the assembled men looking closely into their eyes as one by one they called out their names. Occasionally, he paused to acknowledge a former volunteer from the Katanga war or to ask someone to remove their sunglasses. He steadily worked through the ranks until he had mentally recorded the name and face of each man. He then gathered the entire assemblage in a semi-circle and addressed them in a calm and confident voice.

Hoare explained their mission. "Men, we have been employed to quell the upstart rebellions that are threatening the security of this country. And quell them we will!" A small chorus of cheers answered his proclamation.

"We have a larger purpose, however. Ours is a noble and worthwhile task, one that will change the face of the Congo and alter the course of history." He continued, "Our actions are intended to prevent the spread of Communism. That's a cause of particular interest to you lads from Rhodesia and South Africa. If the Commies get a foothold here, all of Africa falls."

Hoare assured his recruits that the deplorable conditions that had greeted them at BAKA were only temporary and that he would personally travel to Léopoldville to improve supplies and to straighten out pay and contract questions. He promised that they would not fight without being paid. *"No ticket, no laundry."* The men laughed.

Finally, the charismatic leader concluded his remarks. "Those who aren't up to the rigor and risk of combat...must say so now. You will be sent home on the same plane that brought you here."

Maj. Hoare sought out those with previous military experience. He appointed leaders, organizing the mercenaries into several commando units of 40 or so, led by one or two officers. Finding leaders was difficult, however, since few volunteers had had any military experience. His recruits included far too many drunks, derelicts, addicts, unemployed bums and pursuers of easy money. The ranks needed thinning. Within days, nearly 200 departed either by choice or directive.

Crash was one of only six men whom the infamous mercenary found capable of taking on leadership. Hoare appointed him to the rank of Lieutenant, separated 40 men to serve under him and announced they would be called *"51 Commando."* Wilson, in turn, found two no-nonsense sergeants, a Brit and a Rhodesian, to help him lead.

The first combat group was in place. 51 Commando led by Crash began training as a fighting unit the very next day, though it took fully three weeks for the first uniforms and used semi-automatic FN rifles and ammunition to arrive. Untrained and ill equipped, they appeared far from ready for action. Their call to duty, however, did not wait.

On the first of September, BBC reported that the Simba advance into Equatéur Province had reached Igende, 60 miles east of Coquilhatville and that another column was headed for Gemena in the north. With over half of the Congo now in rebel hands, Commander-in-Chief Mobutu was greatly distressed. Additional reports indicated that whole garrisons of ANC were fleeing before the enemy without a shot being fired. This was Mobutu's home territory. It was time for mercenary intervention.

The call for assistance came to Maj. Hoare as a command rather than a request. Both Mobutu and the CIA ordered mercenary forces to the rescue. Hoare, Wilson and 51 Commando flew to Léopoldville to receive CIA weapons, equipment and further briefing.

When Crash and his unit arrived at N'djili Airport the next morning some of his men were still in jeans and tee shirts. Maj. Hoare himself checked and counted the CIA supplied weapons and equipment: crates of ammunition, automatic rifles, mortars, bazookas, grenades and five machinegun-equipped vehicles. Ready or not, they were headed to Gemena for battle.

51 Commando's plane dropped munitions in Coquilhatville to frightened ANC troops stationed there, before continuing to Gemena 250 miles further north.

Col. Bokala, a rotund officer with a huge smile, met them at the airport. Sweat ran down his face, dripping off his nose and chin, soaking the shirt that strained to contain his huge gut.

"Bienvenue" Bokala beamed to Lt. Wilson as he stepped off the plane. *"Nous sommes heureux que vous êtes arrivé avant les Simbas."*

"He's glad you beat the Simbas here," quipped Wilson's translator, French Canadian volunteer Denis Gagñon.

Crash Wilson shook the ANC leader's hand. "Tell him thanks for the welcome. I'll meet with him later this evening for a briefing on the rebels' advance. Where do my men go to bunk for the night?"

The warriors didn't notice a small, wiry man standing near the airport terminal. The man known as Kasongo carefully counted the new arrivals, took note of their weapons and slipped away.

Lt. Wilson discovered that he had more accurate information on the Simba advance than did Bokala thanks to the briefing in Léo from the CIA. His was about to be one of the first real tests of Hoare's Commandos.

The briefing contained a surprising added incentive: the rescue of three American youth being held captive in Lisala.

CHAPTER 34
Yakoma, August 1964

The luminous dials on his watch told him it was nearly 5 a.m. but the dark African night had yet to see the first hints of dawn. His bladder alarm had gone off some time ago but he had put off rising from his cot, clawing out from under the mosquito netting and slipping outside. As his mother used to say, "My bridgework is floating." That's what roused him.

Doug Warren had not slept well. In fact, he doubted he had slept at all, since the soothing nocturnal sounds of the rainforest – cricket chirps, mango bat creaks and wood owl whistles – were intermittently shattered by nearby gunfire. It had persisted throughout the night. Sometimes it was an isolated "pop, pop!" Other times the staccato "brrraap!" of automatic weapons startled him into full consciousness. The threat was real and it was close at hand.

Doug had arrived at the Yakoma army base with his five ANC passengers nearly a week ago. The soldiers were relieved to have escaped the clutches of their pursuers. Their report to the garrison officials likely accounted for his positive reception.

I suppose I can call it "positive," Doug thought, *since they did give me a place to sleep out of the elements and they are feeding me...the same meager fare served to the soldiers. On the negative side, my hosts have confiscated my Land Rover.* They had not provided him with any other means of transport home. He was stranded.

Meanwhile, the Popular Army of Liberation, the Simbas, had arrived and were testing the ANC garrison's strength and resolve. Doug had some questions about that issue himself since he had witnessed scores of frightened soldiers shedding their uniforms and slipping into the dense forest to flee the dreaded *dawa* of their attackers.

The camp's headman, Col. Gebanga, told him that an urgent request had been sent for *mundele* mercenaries to assist in repelling the rebels. He hoped they'd arrive *soon* before he was left to greet the enemy...alone.

Doug had no sooner stepped back into his tiny room than the sound of shooting and loud voices rose right outside his door. He heard scuffling, running footsteps and loud voices yelling *"Pota! Kima!" Run!* People were fleeing in panic. He slumped down into the corner, hiding in the darkness of the room, waiting. The shooting and shouting receded.

Sunrise lit the treetops in the camp when Doug at last opened the door and looked out, regretting it in the next instant. Walking between the buildings was an irregular line of shirtless, young warriors. Each carried a rifle; some also had knives or machetes at their waists. As they came to each building one threw open the door while another raked the inside with a burst of bullets, sometimes met with shrieks from within.

He was spotted immediately. *"Mundele!"* someone called out. All nearby gun barrels pointed his way. Doug froze. He did not breathe.

"Kanga ye!" Grab him! Several sets of hands grasped Doug and threw him to the ground. He took a blow to the side of his head; a rifle stock pounded into his kidneys producing a sharp pain that took his breath away. His hands were securely bound.

Wrenched to his feet, still seeing stars from the blows, Doug was half-dragged, half-carried to a central area where other captives sat and lay in a group, hands bound. Most were hapless ANC regulars; a few were officers. The main body of the national army had pulled back just in time. These prisoners were the unlucky ones.

The next few minutes were a nightmare that would plague Doug for the rest of his days. One by one the captives were dragged from the group and without comment, stabbed or hacked to death, screaming and pleading for mercy. Some were disemboweled alive; others had hands, ears, eyes or genitals lopped off. It was a gruesome, hellish ritual, one that typified Simba battle success throughout Congo.

Doug was too alarmed to pray, other than to mumble *"Oh, God; Oh God; Please...Oh God."*

When the Simba leader finally came to Doug, the one non-Congolese prisoner, he pointed at him with a bloody, dripping machete: *"Ye wana, mundele Américain, akei na Buta. Otage."* That one there, the white American goes to Buta. Hostage.

I'm to be sent to Buta as a hostage? His relief at not being a part of the post battle entertainment was mixed with alarm. *Is it delaying the inevitable?* Doug wondered about his fate as a grinning adolescent roughly pulled him away.

*****

It was late afternoon as the aircraft flew low over the Ubangi and Uele Rivers on a final approach to the landing strip outside of Yakoma. Weary, slightly nauseated, ears ringing, 2nd Lieutenant Forsbrey and the forty men comprising his mercenary unit, *54 Commando* had just endured a daylong flight of over 1,200 miles. They had taken off from Kamina mercenary headquarters before dawn, winging 750 miles to Coquilhatville, another 250 to Gemena to refuel and then the last 200 to this remote military outpost in the far northwest corner of Congo.

Their fearless leader, Maj. Hoare, had been at the airstrip in person to see them off. "I will accept nothing short of victory no matter how brutal the price," was his parting charge. Their mission was clear: join beleaguered ANC forces in defending the Yakoma garrison and defeat the attacking Simbas. To accomplish this, they had a full load of mortars, machine guns and ammunition for their automatic weapons. It was going to be a loud and lethal encounter.

The "safe to land" flare had been fired, the fly-over checked out: the Yakoma runway was clear. Excitement filled the loud, sparse interior of the four-engine DC4 as its tricycle landing gear came down, nearly clipping the trees on the approach to the unpaved landing strip.

The big airplane bounced once, twice. On the third bounce, the pilot slammed on the brakes, reversing the engines with a loud roar. But the plane kept on moving down the field. It was going far too fast. The lack of gripping pavement, the heavy load of men and equipment, the short landing strip...a bad combination.

Tires skidded, engines roared, men screamed and the great silver bird overshot the runway, plowing forward. Its front wheel sank into soft earth and, as if in slow motion, the great plane's tail lifted slowly at first and then picking up speed, crashed to the earth, upside down.

Only the creaking and popping of hot, stressed metal mingled with the low moans of mercenaries could be heard for a long minute. All *had* survived. Some were bruised but there was not a single broken bone or gash among the mercenary men.

When Lt. Forsbrey and his comrades in arms slowly exited the plane they were surrounded by friendly forces: the ANC had created a wide parameter around the airstrip. They could safely exit. Col. Gebanga was the first to greet them. Soon, equipment, ammunition and supplies were unloaded from the overturned aircraft and plans were drawn up for a counter attack.

The battle for Yakoma was on, even louder and more brutal than Hoare had predicted in 54's early morning briefing. The mercenaries discovered that their enemy actually believed in their own magic: eyes straight ahead, chanting *"Mai, Mai,"* they marched directly into the line of fire and were slaughtered like some kind of bizarre amusement park game. In this case, however, the blood and shattered body parts were reminders of its gruesome reality.

After three hours of non-stop shooting, 54 Commando forces advancing from building to building, the Simbas began to run. It turned into a rout. They fled in disarray. The fortunate ones found keys in vehicles, and escaped at full speed.

Revenge-crazed army soldiers chased the unfortunate rebels who were on foot. The pursuit went well into the daylight hours of the following morning. The fate of any apprehended rebels was no better than those they had dispatched the day before.

2nd Lt. Forsbrey reported on 54 Commando's battle success by radio in an evening call to Maj. Hoare. After describing their disastrous landing, the absence of mercenary casualties and the quick collapse of the enemy, he offered one other noteworthy fact.

"Simbas overran a small Swedish Covenant Hospital just south of here in the tiny village of Wasolo. It was ugly. They killed all the staff, pillaged the hospital and captured its resident missionary doctor. He is an American, Doctor Paul Carlson."

"We found out they also captured a second American, an ex-missionary living in the region. He had recently transported some soldiers to the base. His name is Douglas Warren."

"Unfortunately, the rebels managed to escape with both American prisoners, Carlson and Warren. According to surviving Simba captives, they are being taken to Aketi."

CHAPTER 35
Lisala, August 1964

Nick, Ellie and Aaron sat together on the floor, backs against the wall in a narrow storage room lit only by a high barred window. The humid, pungent air smelled of mold and urine, including their own at the far end of the room, over the two days they had spent locked inside. That morning a plastic jug of water, some bananas and a bowl of cold rice had been placed inside the door, before it quickly banged shut. They were parched and famished; the meager provisions were welcome.

Hungry, frightened, sore and confused, Ellie had been praying practically non-stop since the teeth jarring ride in the back of the pickup delivered them to Lisala. They were roughly dragged from the vehicle by a milling crowd of young, wild-looking Simba warriors, their greeting party. The three were taunted and punched by the agitated throng.

According to Nick, "in spite of our bruises, we were very fortunate it wasn't worse." A large bearded man wearing an odd combination of military gear, a rebel leader, had appeared on the scene. Scowling and shouting orders, he ordered the three to be locked in their present despicable cell. "Otherwise," Nick shook his head slowly, "our jubilant captors, who just occupied the city, might have used us - our bodies anyhow - to celebrate their takeover."

Even Nick, who was typically not very vocal about his faith, attributed this deliverance to answered prayer. *But,* Ellie thought, *we're going to need a whole lot more prayers answered to ever make it out of this mess alive.*

"So, what's going to happen to us?" Ellie finger-combed her greasy hair and pulled her scarf back over her head and bruised arms.

Ignoring her question, Nick voiced the thoughts he had obviously been turning over in his mind: "I think we ought to try to escape. It doesn't sound like there is a guard outside. A best-case outcome is that they plan use us as hostages, maybe send us to Stanleyville. Worse case? We could end up being tortured for retaliation or sport. Simbas are infamous for gruesome violence. I'd frankly prefer not to stick around and chance what they decide to do."

"But we're *mundeles*, easily spotted. We're a long way from any help, surrounded by crazed rebels. What possible chance could we have if we escape from here?" Aaron sounded exasperated.

"Masemba's out there somewhere, for one thing. Your dad, Ellie, knows we were headed here. He will probably find out what's happened. Perhaps he will send help. Then...well, there's always prayer." Nick looked up at both companions when he said this. He wasn't being cynical, but no one responded.

There came a soft tapping at the door. Ellie jumped up and leaned her head close to the door handle. "*Oui? Nani wana?*" *Who's there?* she asked.

"*Ngai...Masemba*" came the whispered reply. "I have a key. Same key works all the old doors here. Come now." The two guys scrambled to their feet at a clicking sound. The heavy wooden door creaked open.

Masemba, scanning carefully in all directions, motioned for the others to follow. They slipped carefully around buildings, crouching behind bushes, following their leader's hand signals. By stealth, they made their way from the edge of town heading down toward the river, the mighty Congo.

When they paused a moment after crossing a street, Masemba finally briefed them. "The Simbas beat all of us from the truck. They asked us many questions. No one had anything to tell them. When the ANC started shooting nearby they lost interest. We just walked away. I finally found you after two days of looking. I watched: there was no guard at your door. I think we must head for the river, find a pirogue and escape. We will travel at night."

"Do you *have* a pirogue?" asked Ellie.

"Not yet," Masemba admitted. "I found a place for you to hide while I look for one. Big baobab tree is down that way, next to the river, thick brush on one side. Go under the roots and wait until I come. After dark."

They found the tree, cleared a hiding place under its massive roots with a good view of the river and settled down to wait for nightfall and Masemba's return.

Ellie tucked herself deep under the tree. "It's not going to go well for us if we're caught." No one replied.

It was late afternoon when they heard twigs cracking and leaves rustling. From the deep shadows of their hideout they saw three rebel soldiers working their way along the river's edge, climbing over slick rocks and across slimy, downed tree trunks, rifles in hand. They were headed directly for the trio's baobab refuge.

"Quiet. Don't move," whispered Nick.

A startled cry and splash. One of the young Simbas, a skinny boy barely in his teens, thrashed about in the deep green waters swirling near the shoreline. He sank and bobbed. His two young, wide-eyed comrades called and reached out, not daring to go in after him. The struggling and choking cries became ever more desperate, echoing in the watery jungle.

Aaron started to move, but Nick grabbed his arm. "No, no, stop...you'll give us away. They were headed straight here."

Aaron continued to climb through the baobab roots. "It's not right. We're not supposed to destroy our enemies, or watch them die. That kid is drowning. I can't do nothing."

Without further comment Aaron burst from their hiding spot and dove into the river, surfacing right next to the futilely thrashing rebel. A few brief strokes later he was at the edge, dragging a sputtering and gasping youth onto dry ground. Back from the very edge of death, the fellow continued coughing and gagging as his companions knelt beside him, expressing their relief.

As if noticing for the first time, one of the two suddenly looked up at the panting, muscular rescuer and exclaimed, *"Mundele!"* Collecting his wits, he demanded to know where the others were, *"Wapi mibale mosusu?"* Resigned to their being discovered, Nick and Ellie had by then emerged from hiding. They were already headed toward the men at the river's edge.

One of the Simbas snatched up his rifle and pointed it at the two. Ellie rushed the last few steps to Aaron's side. "Are you OK?" She hugged his dripping form.

Aaron returned the embrace, nodding. Nick shook his head in disgust. "I can't believe he did that. We've really *had* it now!"

After a few more minutes, one of the two dry Simbas motioned up the bank toward the town with his rifle. *"Mindele! Kenda."*

Ellie began to weep.

CHAPTER 36
Gemena, September 1964

The Lieutenant awoke from a sweaty and restless night spent on a hard cot under a stifling mosquito net.

"Hey Crash!" A voice called through the open door. "Coffee is on."

Still groggy in the first light of day, the leader of 51 Commando sat up and held his throbbing head. It had been a long flight the day before and it was true that he hadn't had his caffeine fix yet, but that wasn't what was giving him a headache. As his thoughts cleared Wilson realized that it was the reality facing him that triggered the head pain.

His briefing with the Gemena garrison's leader, the rotund Col. Bokala, had convinced him that they could not sit there and wait for the Simbas to arrive. Not if they wanted to survive, anyhow.

First of all, the ANC were losing soldiers to desertion like water through a sieve. *Discipline and command are a serious problem*, he thought. Second, while the army possessed decent weaponry and supplies, it lacked any sort of basic battle savvy and strategy to employ their resources. *The Colonel seems more interested in stuffing his face than commanding his troops. Ouch...*the headache.

As he shaved from a shallow pan – Mad Mike had insisted his soldiers be clean-shaven – Crash thought of one more reason to take the fight to the rebels instead of waiting in Gemena: *we've got to rescue the hostages!*

In the CIA's briefing the previous morning, the agent, Loren Durban, explained. "Not only is General Mobutu insisting on a Gemena victory, but the U.S. government is also very concerned with the fate of three young adults, American missionary types I understand, who are currently being held captive in Lisala. They need prompt military intervention. The Simbas are not known to treat prisoners well or for that matter even to keep them alive for very long. Make haste."

After he had consumed his first cup of strong, black coffee along with fresh bread, salami and fruit, the uneasy mercenary leader expected to feel refreshed. Instead, Lt. Wilson received yet another reason for a headache: overnight trouble with his troops.

Two of his men had been caught by an army patrol, looting a shop near the base. Three more were being held at gunpoint after engaging in a drunken midnight brawl with army soldiers at a local bar. Finally, he had another five men in his unit asking to be sent home. The approach of battle - real shooting, real bullets - had sunken in and they simply wanted out.

Crash assembled his men and in short order put things on the line. His authoritative tone invited no questions. "I am sending ten of the 42 in this unit back to Léo on the same plane that brought us here. Sending you cowardly idiots home. You have broken your contracts. Does anyone else want out?" Two more raised their hands.

"OK. Out. Get out of my sight...now!" He growled in disgust. "As for the rest of us, we are going on a lion hunt, starting today. We're going to haul-tail as fast and loud as we can to Lisala, shooting Simbas all the way. You're going to have plenty of target practice. If you follow my lead, my orders, you're not only going to survive but you'll have stories to tell the grandkids and a nice payday at the end. If not, we'll likely send your rotting carcass home in a bag. No more stupid moves like brawling and looting, got it?"

The remaining men looked at each other and mumbled their assent.

Wilson then marched with his interpreter, Denis, to Col. Bokala's headquarters. He had a head of steam on by then. The colonel wasn't as full of smiles in this day's encounter, especially when he heard the mercenary's plans. Bokala objected to moving an attack force toward Lisala, but Crash looked him right in the eye.

"We're going, all my men and all five of our vehicles. If you stay, I'll report to General Mobutu *today* that Gemena's ANC commander refused to fight the enemy and is unwilling to back us up. He sent us here, personally. How do you think he'll like *that merde*?"

He turned to Denis, "Translate it *exactly* as I said it."

The oversized Colonel took no time to contemplate the question. *"OK. D'accord."*

He turned and gave instructions to his assistants to follow Wilson's directions and prepare a convoy for immediate departure...under the mercenary leader's command.

CHAPTER 37
Akula, September 1964

51's five mercenary vehicles headed the convoy, a strike force with fearsome mobile firepower. An armored truck led the way. It was mounted with a 50 mm machine gun turret behind two thick steel plates. Two more trucks equipped with 50 mm machine gun turrets followed, with two cage-framed, open-bed pickups between them. The sides of the pickups were lined with 18-inch high steel plates, offering cover to the occupants, each armed with an automatic weapon. The unit was also equipped with mortars and grenade launchers for pitched battles.

Trailing behind the last pickup was a convoy of a dozen huge Mercedes transports. They carried supporting ammunition and supplies plus the 250 ANC troops who would be serving under Lt. Crash's command. He was apprehensive. Would they be an asset or a liability? He needed their firepower, especially when they engaged the Simba army.

In the end, he insisted that the ANC vehicles maintain a distance of 300 yards from the mercenary pickups. When fighting began in earnest, he did not want to risk being shot by his poorly trained allies. Friendly fire or enemy bullets, dead is still dead.

The early morning mist was a pastel pink and orange in the rays of the rising tropical sun. It had just begun to lift from the tops of the trees at the edge of town when the caravan of soldiers – Congolese and mercenaries – headed out.

Crash's orders were to make haste for Lisala. The challenging 180-mile trek was sure to be a jarring and fatiguing ordeal. Would it prove a fatal one? They were about to find out.

*****

Meanwhile, Kasongo the shadowy recruiter of Simbas, had also been busy. 51 Commando's arrival gave him a unique opportunity, or at least that's what he considered it to be.

Kasongo rounded up the nearly two-dozen local insurgent recruits, including several army deserters who possessed rifles. Most, however, had only spears and arrows. They were much too small a force to present any serious military challenge to the departing army convoy but his plan was to harass its departure by ambush, to perhaps kill a few *mundele* mercenaries in the process and then to disappear into the forest.

It was a naïve and fatal miscalculation.

The determined novice rebels found a narrow stretch of road near the small village of Bozagba 20 miles east of Gemena. Dense foliage lined both sides of the track. There, they felled a large tree across the road and set up their ambush.

Not even an hour from their departure point, the road passed through a small deserted village before entering a section of rainforest. Crash was positioned in the lead truck. He had no sooner spotted the tree blocking the way than the first sniper shots pinged off the metal plates of his armored vehicle.

"Ambush," he yelled, crouching low. "Fire! Open up!" he directed his gunner. "Pull the tree," he shouted to the following truck.

His words were unnecessary. Men were already piling out of the pickup firing steadily with their automatic weapons as they moved toward the roadblock.

Neutral observers of this scene would notice several things: first, the roar of weapons and engines, shouting and cursing of mercenaries. Then, as if by magic, they would see the foliage on either side of the road disintegrate, leaves and sticks flying into the air, creating an illusion of the forest passage widening under its own power. The steady fire of formidable machine guns was like a high-powered mower. Finally, if they listened carefully they might hear high-pitched screams coming from the chopped up roadside foliage.

In no time at all, Crash and his five-vehicle force were beyond the ambush. They pulled up in a clearing. In the distance they could hear random shots and one last prolonged scream.

"That's what a mopping up operation sounds like," the young leader quipped to the smiling group of wide-eyed, adrenalin-stoked warriors surrounding him.

"Good work, fellows. That's just the way we'll do it: open up at the first sign of trouble and move forward as fast as we can, leaving the ANC to do any follow-up that's needed. Now let's get a move on."

The main route east, the N6, was in reality a single rutted track. Since this was the dry season, the road surface was mostly firm. As a result, 51 Commando made good progress though the line of trucks created huge clouds of dust as they raced along.

The convoy occasionally reached 30 mph, their maximum possible speed. From time to time, streams crossed the road, creating marshy bogs that slowed their progress. On those occasions they slid and ground their way through the mini-canyons created by previous transport traffic before resuming at full throttle.

The five lead vehicles reached the busy river town of Akula by mid-morning. Dogs barked, children stared wide-eyed, mamas with burdens on their heads and babies on their backs scurried off the road; men dove into doorways. The grim looking warriors of 51 Commando had arrived at the river crossing more than an hour ahead of their ANC allies, lumbering along in the larger vehicles.

Predictably, the entire company of hot, dusty and parched mercenaries disappeared into local waterfront bars to quench their thirst and rest their travel-weary bones. Some soon discovered additional pleasures awaiting them in the local brothels.

The first of the army trucks finally pulled into Akula, alerting Crash to begin to round up his soldiers. He wanted as minimal a delay as possible. He cursed his lack of forethought in allowing the men to scatter. Few of the motley mercenary troops were motivated to leave the modest comforts of shade and cool beer they had located.

After nearly forty minutes of searching, threatening and cussing, the usually cool-tempered lieutenant had had it. Nine of his men were still missing. "Screw it, and those bastards as well. We'll go with what we've got. Let them find their own way back from this godforsaken place."

And with that, he signaled the drivers to fire up their engines. The convoy roared to the front of a long queue of trucks waiting to cross the mighty Mongala River. Not surprisingly, no one among the commercial truck drivers voiced a protest as the newcomers cut the line to the bac and crossed the river ahead of them: too many fearsome warriors, too many guns.

As the convoy crossed the river all attention focused on the menacing mercenaries and the loading and lining up of the huge army trucks. Had Crash surveyed the scene more carefully, he might have noticed the two young motorcyclists at the crest of the hill overlooking the dock. They absorbed every detail. As the last two trucks drove off the bac the two riders sped away...in the direction of Lisala.

51 Commando would have no surprise-factor advantage on this mission.

CHAPTER 38
Lisala, September 1964

The afternoon shadows crept across a crowded courtyard filled with rough looking Congolese clad in shorts, army fatigues, well-worn slacks and large tee shirts with faded sports logos. They sat around tables and on the ground. Some were bare-chested. Most sipped at oversized bottles of Primus beer. Nearly all were young and fully armed: rifles, machetes, knives and clubs. An aura of menace filled the place like river fog at daybreak.

The courtyard mood was serious, restless, an unusual atmosphere for a plaza filled with young African drinkers. Word had arrived earlier that afternoon that a mercenary-led army force had crossed the Mongala and was headed their way. Ever since that time, apprehension and excitement enveloped the hundreds of Simba warriors occupying Lisala.

Their call to action would come soon. This was the first time thus far in the rebels' westerly campaign that ANC forces were actually headed *toward* them to engage in battle. The Simbas, the lions, had always been the invaders, the aggressors before whom the army fled, leaving behind weapons, ammunition, vehicles and supplies.

But a new element had entered the equation: *mundele* mercenaries. This would be the true test of their power, of their *dawa*. Would the enemy's bullets turn to water as their leaders proclaimed?

Masemba sat in the shade of the bar staring hard at the ground, cheeks resting on the heels of his hands, elbows on his knees. He was feeling sick at heart. The phrase, *"I betrayed my friends"* kept looping again and again in his mind.

From somewhere else came the thought, *"You had no choice...it was them or you."*

"I betrayed my friends."

"They are mundeles. Congo for Congolese; you are a Simba recruit. Your loyalties are to the new Congo."

"I betrayed my friends."

The events that afternoon had reversed Masemba's fortunes and those of his – could he still say it..."*friends?*"

He had finally found a pirogue and was searching for supplies when a young Simba in a passing group recognized him. "You were with the escaped *mundeles*" the fellow called out, pointing a finger at him.

"You are mistaken, brother." He had responded lightly with a forced smile. He moved along quickly before the distracted companions of his accuser paid attention.

However, no sooner had he turned the next corner than another voice called out. "There. That one was on the truck we stopped with the escaped *mundeles*." This time he couldn't deny it. He had to think fast.

"I heard that the *mundeles* have escaped." He blurted. "On the truck I overheard them talk about fleeing down river. The big baobab tree next to the river...have you looked there yet?"

"Who can believe this stranger?" one scoffed.

"He was with them on the truck, he heard them" another argued. "I say we look by the river and the tree."

"And I say we cut this one and see if he changes his story."

Finally, they decided to dispatch three of their number to check out the nearby riverbank and baobab tree.

"You wait with us. If you have lied and our brothers fail to find the missing *mundeles*, it is you who will be missing a body part very soon." And so he waited.

"*I betrayed my friends.*"

Without warning, a commotion began at the far side of the courtyard. It grew louder as more of the rebel soldiers jumped to their feet, craned their necks and moved to see what was happening. Masemba stood as well. He observed a small cluster of individuals making their way slowly to the center of the courtyard, quickly surrounded by a circle of increasingly agitated bystanders.

It was Nick, Ellie and Aaron moving at gunpoint prodded on by three young rebel guards!

Someone rushed from the crowd as Aaron passed and smashed him in the back with the butt of a rifle. The tall white man fell hard, groaning. Others pulled and punched at Nick and Ellie, screaming insults in several languages.

In the midst of this chaos one of the three Americans' young captors, still wet from his plunge in the Congo River, shouted for the attackers to stop. "You will not beat the *mundeles*," he declared at full voice. "This one saved me from the river."

Others contended loudly until the young rebel's two companions stepped up. They chambered rounds in their rifles. The crowd instantly fell back from the captives. All three were by then sprawled on the ground.

At that moment, a loud explosion echoed across the courtyard above the agitated jumble of voices. The noise of sustained gunfire accompanied a roar of engines and shouting. A cry went up, "They're here!"

The Simba war chant *"Mai Mulele! Mai Mulele!"* quickly filled the space as with one voice, scores of young rebel warriors grabbed their weapons and rushed toward the sound of battle, tables overturning and chairs flying.

Nick turned to Aaron on the ground beside him and with some urgency insisted: "Now's our chance, Aaron. In this chaos, it may be our only chance. I say we jump our captors, grab a gun and go."

The courtyard was quickly emptying. The *mundeles* had been forgotten by all but their three young captors.

Masemba appeared from nowhere. Holding a knife to the throat of one of the young guards, he grabbed the fellow's rifle. At the same instant, Nick tackled the second of the three snatching his weapon as the young man fell. The third appeared stunned by this sudden action and reacted slowly. As he brought his rifle up, a shot rang out.

Ellie screamed. The young man flew backward, landing in a motionless heap, his weapon clattering beside him. Blood oozed from a fatal chest wound. Masemba shoved his captive to the ground. Smoke still wafted from the gun in his hand.

"Run. We go now!" he called to the others.

Nick bellowed to Aaron, who scrambled to his feet. "Grab the rifle, let's go!"

Aaron, instead grabbed Ellie's hand and they headed off in the opposite direction of the gunfire and explosions sounding from the main road into Lisala.

Nick seized the third rifle and running alongside Aaron, thrust it toward him. "Take it, Aaron. It's life and death."

Aaron shook his head vigorously, holding up one hand as he ran. "No. It's not right. I won't do it, Nick." Ellie's eyes bulged as she stumbled along after him.

First one shot and then several zinged over their heads as they arrived at the edge of the courtyard. Nick spun and fired back in the direction of the volley. More bullets shattered the cement walls as they rounded the corner and sprinted up the next block. They had been spotted.

*****

51 Commando stormed into Lisala that late Tuesday afternoon in the middle of September. The lead vehicles reached speeds of 50 mph racing through the streets of the city as mercenary bullets raked every moving thing. Grenades and bazooka rockets were launched toward any enemy troops spotted from the speeding vehicles.

Meanwhile, the Simbas quickly formed long lines of *"Mai, Mai"* chanting warriors, marching slowly toward the rapidly advancing enemy. *Dawa* would surely turn their adversaries' lethal bullets to water. It didn't happen. As the speeding mercenary vehicles passed, machine guns and automatic weapons blazing, chanting rebels fell in heaps.

It was a slaughter.

The rebels shot back, but their enemy's fast moving trucks made elusive targets. Only one mercenary was injured in the entire afternoon's mêlée, a grazing wound.

It wasn't long before the lethal mercenary shooting and deafening noise stirred panic in the ranks of the previously undefeated Simbas. First in small groups of twos and threes, then in large numbers, they turned and fled.

By that time, the convoy of ANC soldiers had arrived in the city. They worked their way through the streets, showering bullets on hapless rebels. It became a rout. Lisala was liberated in record time with just a handful of mercenaries and a small force of regular Congolese army troops.

Working their way from building to building, the four young people headed toward the edge of town. Nick voiced the plan. "Let's escape into the forest. We can hide there and return when and if the fighting is decided in favor of the right side."

Their last dash to the forest sanctuary, however, was their undoing. Shots rang out as they sprinted toward the tree line. In the lead, Masamba and Nick both made it safely to their forest refuge.

Aaron and Ellie, however, did not. Zinging bullets turned them back to the shelter of the nearest building. There, they were quickly surrounded by armed rebels and whisked away as they fled the city.

CHAPTER 39
Stanleyville, August 1964

The brooding Simba strongman leaned back in his squeaky chair and put his feet up on a cluttered wooden desk. General Olenga had retreated to his sparse office at Camp Ketele, just outside Stanleyville. A deep frown creased his sweaty brow as he sipped from a glass half-filled with Scotch.

It was only 10:30 a.m. and he already had a buzz on, but who could blame him? The weight of leadership was a heavy one. He had a score of things to figure out. The "People's Republic" he was launching was proving a greater challenge than anticipated.

Chief among his unexpected troubles were the uncontrollable local *jeunesse*. These fearless youth were looting businesses, taking over white folks' homes and cars without permission and shaking down the local citizens for MNC (*Mouvement National Congolais*) party membership cards.

Olenga had broadcast stern warnings threatening severe punishment for offenders, but they were being largely ignored.

Then, there was the matter of Bukavu.

In the Simba's virtually unopposed sweep north from Albertville to Stanleyville they had left unconquered one major government controlled city on the far southeast border: Bukavu, the capital of Kivu Province. This former resort town was now an isolated port city on Lake Kivu. It was held by the ANC, being supplied by the Léopoldville government with the assistance of American planes. This was a great annoyance to the Big Man. *It is a humiliation that cannot not be ignored.*

Taking a big gulp of the amber liquid, Olenga resolved, *I will take this campaign under my personal command and eliminate once and for all the stubborn resistance. It will happen in the next few days.*

Those problems aside, General Olenga found himself exhilarated by the first weeks of occupying Stanleyville. It was the end of August, 1964. *No longer are the white and Asian foreigners in charge of this lovely city, lording it over my Congolese colleagues and me, making us feel like strangers in our own land. Now, at last Africans are in charge!* He smiled to himself. *This is a good time to be alive, to be a strong African man.*

Even as the wheels turned to prepare for the assault on Bukavu, Olenga reflected on the meeting with the *mundele* business and diplomatic leaders in Stanleyville. *It went well, except that they demanded protection.* They didn't seem at all pleased with his appointed charge of their safety, the new president of the People's Republic: Alphonse Kinghis.

Kinghis was an imposing figure, a heavily bearded man, well over six feet and exceeding 230 pounds, a Captain in Olenga's army. He was well known by the local European expatriates, infamous as the "bishop" of the Stanleyville Kitawalists, a religious sect, incorporating elements of Jehovah's Witnesses and animist spirituality.

The Simbas had only recently released him from prison where he and several of his followers had been incarcerated, caught in the very act of crucifying an opponent. Among his strange ideas, Kinghis claimed that Americans had bewitched the Congolese twenty-five franc note, making it radioactive, thereby killing anyone who kept one overnight. In their zeal, he and his followers had torn down monuments to explorers, colonists and even religious figures in Stanleyville.

In short, Stanleyville expatriates considered Kinghis unstable and dangerous. That fact made him exactly the kind of man Olenga wanted in charge. People would fear him and therefore be unwilling to openly rebel. The only problem was that this charismatic appointee was also treacherous and unpredictable.

The General took another long swallow from his glass, emptying it. *I will just have to take this risk.*

In the next days, General Olenga prepared for the assault on Bukavu. Radio messages were sent to troops in Kindu and other towns telling them to move east and rendezvous outside the port city. At the same time he took over communications in Stanleyville. Nicolas Olenga's voice rang over the city and into the surrounding jungle from the local radio station, vowing that he would surely conquer Léopoldville and all of Congo. The one-time clerk also acquired control of the local newspaper, *Le Martyr*, proclaiming in writing that total victory was now in sight.

In the evening of August 13 a convoy of requisitioned autos and trucks pulled out of Stanleyville and headed south down the Kindu road and east to Bukavu. General Olenga was at the front, accompanied by handpicked officers and his favorite sorcerers.

After collecting additional forces along the way, the Simba column arrived at their destination. They began their attack on the defending ANC garrison in the afternoon of the 19th.

At first the invading rebels were successful, pushing the government troops back as they entered the heart of Bukavu. But then, under the command of the ANC's most famous officer, Colonel Léonard Mulamba, they were stopped. He called in air support, and two Cuban-piloted T-28 planes strafed the rebels with machine gun and rocket fire, killing scores.

The next day three American C-130Es dropped 150 Katanga gendarmes with additional ammunition and supplies in nearby Rwanda. They soon linked up with Mulamba's forces...with deadly effect. The Simbas were pushed back and finally driven completely out of the city by the end of that day.

Mopping up operations continued for several days more but the result was a resounding defeat that left over 300 Simba bodies sprawled and lifeless in the streets of the mile-high city.

The Bukavu loss resulted not from superior numbers, but from American-supplied reinforcements and aircraft, a fact not lost on General Olenga.

CHAPTER 40
Stanleyville, August 1964

General Olenga had no sooner departed Stanleyville for the Bukavu campaign than his newly appointed president and guardian of the European community, Alphonse Kinghis, seized the opportunity to demonstrate his sadistic power.

Kinghis quickly rounded up a score of former government officials, brought them to the Lumumba Monument in the center of the city and cut them to pieces. His Simba soldiers shot, stabbed and hacked their victims to death in bloody executions that went on for five days. Over 120 Congolese were slaughtered at the blood-soaked monument.

The Olenga-appointee only agreed to halt his public executions after a delegation of revolted and incensed Congolese women marched into his headquarters and demanded it. Even he, the president, dared not risk the fury of determined Congolese mamas. Under Kinghis' watch, however, the executions continued unabated. They just no longer took place in the public park.

Meanwhile, throughout the city, lootings, home invasions, confiscation of vehicles and beatings of Europeans became commonplace. Darkness had descended on the confined residents of Stanleyville. The city had become more dangerous for both Congolese and expatriates.

*****

In the immediate aftermath of the Bukavu campaign, excited radio reports from Léopoldville reported that General Olenga had met his end in the fighting. The reports were in error. In the chaos following his resounding defeat, the infamous general fled west to his former hometown of Kindu. Ironically, the wily leader's escape was interpreted by the local populace as further evidence of his personal *dawa*; evidence he had turned the enemy's bullets to water. Or so it was contended.

Nicolas Olenga was not flattered by these sentiments. He was not even grateful to be alive. He was in a rage. Bukavu was his first taste of defeat. More than being shocked and distressed, he was humiliated. *Who is to blame? The Americans! They furnished the T-28s that cut down my forces. They supplied the ANC with their big planes and brought in reinforcements. They need to be eliminated.* Revenge was on his mind.

Olenga's first edict, fired off by radio Stanleyville, ordered the arrest of all Americans. There were to be "court martialed for judgment without pity." He principally had in mind Michael Hoyt, the city's U. S. counsel and his staff of diplomats. On Kinghis's orders, the Americans were quickly rounded up, beaten and thrown into a filthy cell at the airport.

Upon his return to Stanleyville, the irate general discovered his worst fears were realized. His newly appointed president had not kept the peace but instead had engaged in presumptuous and systematic terror and atrocity. Suspecting Kinghis of scheming against his rule, Olenga abruptly removed the bearded sadist from office. He was placed under house arrest, a reluctant concession to the huge man's powerful Kitawalist following.

The general then brought in two well-known local Congolese politicians, Christophe Gbenye and Gaston Soumialot to lead his reborn "People's Republic of the Congo." Appointed president and defense minister respectively, everyone knew the real power rested not with them. It remained with Nicholas Olenga, himself.

Olenga's rants against the Americans continued in the following weeks. He claimed to have captured over a hundred U.S. citizens near Bukavu. His ministers repeatedly lectured the incarcerated American diplomats regarding their country's "imperialist aggression" in the Congo.

One day, nearly a month later, the opportunity to make good on repeated claims of having American soldiers in custody fell directly into General Olenga's lap. President Christophe Gbenye informed him that he had discovered there were two Americans being held under house arrest in his hometown of Buta. Both had been captured a month earlier near the fighting at Yakoma. Olenga was delighted with this news. He ordered the two men brought to Stanleyville. Here was the proof he needed to validate his claims that U.S. soldiers were fighting in Congo.

The two Americans were identified in *Le Martyr* as "Major" Paul Carlson and "Captain" Douglas Warren.

CHAPTER 41
Lisala, September 1964

Nick and Masemba looked back in horror and disbelief to see their companions pulled out of sight by a squad of pursuing Simbas. The shots Nick and Masemba fired at their pursuers with the captured weapons had discouraged the rebels' further interest in coming after them.

Soon it was quiet in their immediate surroundings, though volleys of gunfire and occasional explosions continued in the distance. Lisala was falling to its liberators. The rebels were fleeing; Ellie and Aaron had disappeared with them.

"Now what?"

Nick's mind raced almost as fast as his heart. Before he could say anything further, Masemba voiced their common thought: "Shall we go after them?"

They stared at each other, anguish clouding their faces. Long exchanges of gunfire continued in the distance.

After a protracted pause, Nick spoke. "I think we'd better see if we can safely link up with the mercenaries retaking the city. There's *no way* the two of us can find and rescue Ellie and Aaron on our own. This place is crawling with Simbas. Besides, we're going to have trouble ourselves with the ANC if we don't make contact with the mercenaries soon."

Pointing at their weapons he added, "These rifles could prove to be a dangerous liability."

Masemba nodded and paused. "I worry about our friends."

Nick and Masemba carefully worked their way back into the heart of the city. Turning a corner, they came upon a mercenary truck stopped in a side street. A soldier had hoisted a large jerry can and was filling the gas tank while others stood by smoking.

Thinking quickly, Nick leaned his rifle against a building and stepped out so he could clearly be seen. He called out loudly in

English...*"Hey guys, help!"* Instantly, a half dozen guns pointed his way as the tough-looking smokers went into full alert mode.

"We escaped the Simbas. Help!" Nick called out again as Masemba now stepped around the corner, joining him, hands in the air.

"C'm 'ere," growled one of the mercenaries, motioning to Nick. "Let's take a looka you." Pointing to Masemba, he inquired "An who's 'e supposed ta be?"

Nick introduced himself and Masemba to the circle of menacing warriors. One of the men, a flat nosed fellow with thick eyebrows that nearly met, commented "He must be one of them damn Americans we were supposed to find." Eyebrows turned to Nick. "So where are the others?"

"The Simbas took them." The two young men both pointed in the direction they had come. "Can you help us go after them?"

"Not 'til we get the OK from Lt. Wilson" said the growly voiced leader of the squad. "We gotta make sure we don't get cut down by our own army escort. They're comin' this way firin' at anything that moves."

*****

By the time the shooting died down in the city it was fully dark. The blackness of the African night descended abruptly, blanketing all but small circles of light from spotty cooking fires and lanterns scattered here and there across the city. Guards were posted, a safe parameter was established and the small mercenary force finally relaxed in the smoky interior of a dimly lit bar.

Nick and Masemba were the center of attention as they told their story to Lt. Wilson and his circle of interested comrades. Darkness prohibited any follow up chase after Ellie, Aaron and their captors, but Crash Wilson assured the two anxious friends that it would be 51 Commando's top priority at first light to do so.

The captured rifles were returned to Nick and Masemba. "You'll need these," was Wilson's succinct comment.

Crash Wilson found himself intrigued with the story Nick shared that evening. It was a compelling tale. Perhaps he identified with the young man's desire to reconcile with his father, since the pensive lieutenant had long been estranged from his own. Perhaps it was the courage the young man had shown in the horror of war. At any rate, by the end of the evening, Wilson had determined that he would extend himself and his resources to help Nick.

Lt. Wilson brought out a map and unfolded it on a table in the bar. "At first light we will start our chase of the Simbas and our push toward

Bumba. That's likely where their main force has retreated to." He pointed out the easterly location of the Congo River port town and continued.

"If we catch up to your captured friends we'll do our best to set them free. About half way, maybe 60 miles from here at the village of Modjamboli, there's an intersection. The main R6 heads southeast toward Bumba, but the other fork heads north toward Yakoma where your father was last seen. If we haven't caught up to your friends by the time we reach that intersection, you and your young Congolese friend should leave us. I'm willing to send you on with a patrol as far north as Yandongi where you indicated having a contact. We want to find out if any of the rebel forces have turned north; you need to find your father. Agreed?"

When there was no immediate answer from Nick, Wilson added: "Look, I know you are worried about your friends. You two simply cannot help them at this point. You must leave that to us. We're the professionals. Their safe return is one of our mission goals."

"You go find your father!"

CHAPTER 42
Yandongi, September 1964

Just as promised, a well-armed mobile patrol assembled and departed the next morning even before the rising sun, in candle-like fashion, lit the tips of the Lisala palm trees.

A dozen mercenaries in two lead vehicles led another 45 Congo army troops packed into three Mercedes trucks. The soldiers, to a man, were at full alert. As a further ambush deterrent, they headed off as fast as the rutted road conditions would permit. Nick and Masemba rode in the back of the second pickup along with a machine gunner at the turret and four heavily armed mercenaries.

About an hour into their drive, the vehicles passed the tiny village of Liwea and entered a dense rainforest. The first shots rang out. Nick was startled by a zinging noise near one ear; then, the metal plate on the side of his careening transport pinged sharply twice as bullets hit but did not penetrate its thick protective metal. Their driver accelerated. The quiet morning erupted in sound as soldiers discharged their weapons in a deafening barrage, spraying both sides of the road.

Five minutes later it was all over. The pickup pulled over at a clearing. Its adrenalin-filled occupants waited for the rest of the vehicles to catch up. No casualties.

The five vehicle patrol had two water crossings on that morning's voyage: the first, an hour further on, utilized a mechanical bac; the second, at the 40 mile mark required crossing over a small bridge.

The bac crossing was uneventful, but as the small convoy slowed in their approach to the bridge, once again bullets zinged and pinged. Nick and Masemba could see the enemy this time: a line of shirtless rebels, weapons in hand, marching slowly across the bridge in their direction, chanting *"Mai, mai."* At the first shot, the trucks stopped. The men streamed out at a run, weapons firing in fully automatic mode.

In a short time, the shooting was over. Rebel bodies lay sprawled at awkward angles, bloody and crumpled in front of the bridge. Two wounded Simbas were dragged over to the trucks by ANC troops for questioning. The captives confirmed that the *mundele* man and woman from Lisala were with their main forces, headed for Bumba. The squad at the bridge was merely a rear guard. The two Simbas' cooperation did not spare them, however; this was a "take no prisoners" mission.

When the small convoy finally arrived at the Modjamboli intersection it was late morning. They stopped briefly to purchase bananas and peanuts from roadside vendors before turning north towards their destination: Yandongi. No sign of Ellie and Aaron. It was time to leave their fate to others, to God.

As they proceeded north, Nick was deeply distressed. Masemba also remained silent. Both had hoped against hope that somehow they might overtake Ellie and Aaron. It wasn't at all clear what would happen to them now. Whatever the outcome, it would be dangerous, possibly deadly.

Nick was sick at heart. *I was the one who proposed this trip; it was my quest to find Dad, not Ellie's or Aaron's. They are innocent victims in this mess. Who knows what they have seen, or worse, what they are being subject to right now at the hands of bloodthirsty Simbas. I'd kill them all if I could. And I could, all right, with this trusty rifle.*

As soon as that thought entered his mind, however, Aaron's admonition echoed in his head: *"That's not what Jesus would do with enemies."* Aaron would never approve.

"Well, just look where that notion has gotten you, big fella," exclaimed Nick out loud in exasperation.

"Nini?" responded Masemba with a quizzical look on his face.

"Rien," sighed Nick in French. *"Rien de tout."*

The long afternoon shadows were beginning to creep across the road when five truckloads of hot, dusty, parched soldiers finally rolled into the crossroads village of Yandongi. It had been a long day of hard travel. Bouncing and swaying on the rutted roads was one thing; maintaining a high alert for snipers and ambushes was quite another. No doubt the entire contingent - Congolese troops and mercenaries alike – was relieved that they had had no further attacks or incidents after the morning bridge crossing.

The mercenaries pulled over at the edge of town to ask a terrified local resident for directions to the Pakistani merchant's shop. They then made a beeline for the place. They were anxious to use the proprietor's short wave radio to report back on the day's experience and to drop off Nick and Masemba before hitting the bars.

The three Congolese army trucks turned off at a small military garrison located at the far edge of town. They planned to join their surprised ANC comrades for an evening of alcohol-lubricated fellowship.

Nasir Rahman greeted the two pickup loads of mercenaries like long lost relatives. He rushed out to the street, taking the leader's hands in both of his. "Welcome, welcome to my modest place of business." He motioned them towards the tables and chairs in the shade along the single-story cement store and bar. The previous customers at the tables hurried away with worried backward glances as the squad of hardened *mundele* mercenaries, weapons on shoulders, made their way to the tables.

The smiling merchant's warmest greeting was reserved for Nick and Masemba. "Ah Monsieur Nick and friend. I have been looking for you. Rev. Ellis has been asking for you regularly in his radio contacts. Welcome, welcome."

He hugged the two young men and then suddenly stepped back in alarm. "But where is Mlle. Ellie and her friend? Has something happened to them?"

Nick's face dropped. Masemba responded in Lingala to the question Nasir Rahman had posed in English, *"BaSimba na Lisala bamemaki baninga na biso epai na bango."* (Simbas in Lisala carried our friends away with them).

"Oh no." That was all the somber Asian merchant could muster, hand to mouth.

*****

That evening, after a sumptuous meal of bread, fresh fruit salad and goat stew, the two former Litoko residents got acquainted with their host. He turned out to be a cousin of Nick's former seatmate on the flight from Brussels. The affable Pakistani had already heard of Nick's quest to reunite with his father, both from his Stanleyville cousin and from Rev. Ellis.

He shared a troubling disclosure of his own: "My wife and two small children are presently in Stanleyville, themselves. They traveled there weeks ago to visit the family and to enjoy a short respite from our isolated life here. It was intended to be a taste of the pleasures of civilization. The Simba occupation has now blocked their return home. I am quite concerned. All radio contact has ceased since the rebels occupied the city."

Nasir was sympathetic with his guests' story, responding warmly with questions and encouragement as they told of their travels and harrowing adventures. The Asian merchant voiced repeated concern about the welfare of Ellie and Aaron. "A mercenary-led force is the best one could hope for, in terms of rescue," he concluded in a hopeful tone.

They spoke at length of the rigors and dangers of travel during the present unrest. Rahman observed that even though the rebel forces had not advanced as far as Yandongi, "one never knows for sure who the Simba sympathizers are. These are dangerous times."

Masemba stared at the floor, silent, deep in thought.

As the evening conversation came to an end, Nasir Rahman had two important revelations to share. First, he informed Nick and Masemba word had just arrived that the Simbas had been driven out of Yakomo. "Therefore," he concluded, "your best chance to locate Mr. Warren, your father, would appear to be at his plantation." His next comment, however, was the shocker: "I intend to take you there."

Nick was astonished and delighted with this pronouncement. "I...I don't know what to say," he managed to stammer. "We'd be so grateful. It's more than I could expect." Masemba smiled, sharing the same thought.

The second piece of news was less encouraging. "As I told you, we've had only sporadic contact with Stanleyville since it fell to Olenga's forces weeks ago. Finally, just in the last few days I heard from my family through a courier. Things are deteriorating rapidly. It's very troubling. There are many Asians and Europeans being held in the city. More are being brought there daily. Your friends Ellie and Aaron, if they survive, will likely end up in Stanleyville."

The "if they survive" comment sent a cold chill down Nick's spine. As exhausted as he was, sleep would elude him that night as a deep heartache set in. *Sooner or later, one way or another*, he concluded, *I will likely find myself in Stanleyville as well.*

CHAPTER 43
Bumba, September 1964

Ellie huddled close to Aaron in the darkness, shaking. It wasn't from the cold: the night was warm and humid. After all, the town of Bumba was located right on the Congo River. They were not alone in the pitch black, confined space. The whimpers of several other occupants came from across the room filtering out of the shadows.

The young American couple sat close together, backs against the wall on the dirt floor of a cement block structure. Its small windows high above them sent a dim shadow through the embedded metal bars installed to keep intruders out...presently keeping captives in.

Their captors' panicked flight from Lisala had been a harrowing, difficult experience for Ellie and Aaron. The frightened and angry Simba soldiers had dragged the two into the back of a pickup in a hail of bullets. They sped away from Lisala into the rapidly descending darkness, intent on getting as much distance as possible from pursuing ANC forces.

A brief stop two hours into the journey to relieve themselves in the darkness was their only respite from the relentless pounding and pitching of the vehicle over the uneven road. They were bruised and exhausted and above all else, mortally afraid.

Their arrival in the port town of Bumba in the middle of the night ended one ordeal for the young couple and began a second. They were shoved into their present quarters with a hail of blows and a final, sprawling push. A bar dropped onto metal holders with a "clunk" confirming their secure confinement.

"Aaron...are you awake?" Ellie whispered in a shaky voice after they had been sitting quietly for some time, too dazed and tired to speak.

"Who could sleep? Yeah, I'm exhausted, Ellie, but plenty awake. How're you doing by now?" He put his arm around her and gave a gentle squeeze.

"Not so good, I'm afraid" Ellie replied. "I'm really scared, Aaron. They're probably going to kill us aren't they?"

"Not necessarily." His reply lacked conviction. "The fact they've brought us here could mean that we still have some value as hostages." After a pause he confessed in a quiet, apologetic tone, "I'm trying to think positively, here."

"How could God allow this to happen?" Ellie blurted out. "I've been a good Christian all my life. So have you, Aaron. We don't deserve to die some horrible death at the hands of these evil people."

"I don't think that's how it works, Ellie" Aaron replied.

"Well, how *does* it work, then?" she fired back with an edge.

"Is God just not aware of us, busy listening to someone *else's* prayers? We're in big trouble. I've been praying non-stop. Why doesn't He rescue us?" Hot tears streamed down Ellie's cheeks in the darkness.

"Do you feel like God is somehow obligated to free us? Obligated because we have lived such good lives?"

Ellie sat up, straining to see Aaron in the darkness. "Not...not exactly, when you put it that way. I just feel so helpless, vulnerable. I've always understood that God was my protector and defender. I need...we need his protection now like never before."

Aaron was quiet for some time before he spoke again. "I agree with you, Ellie. I do. But what if God has a different view of suffering and death than we do? This is hard to put into words."

After another long pause he continued, "What do we do with the fact that God didn't spare Jesus from suffering or death? And what about the list of martyrs in the book of Hebrews or in *Martyrs Mirror?* Sometimes He does rescue us from harm. We've already experienced a bit of that. But sometimes...sometimes He chooses not to."

"That's *not* reassuring, Aaron. I prefer the rescuing God a whole lot better than the 'let's let them be martyrs' God."

"There you go again. I agree with you completely!" Aaron wrapped both arms around her. "I suppose we are forced to conclude that His purposes and ways are not ours."

"Now I'm the one in agreement. Reluctant agreement," Ellie admitted softly. "He may not guarantee deliverance or long life, but He *did* promise to be with us always, in the good and the bad, didn't He? I'm not wrong about that, am I?"

"No that's true. And so is His promise that death is not the end. Ellie, God *is* here. He's with us tonight, in these dark shadows."

He could feel Ellie's shoulders shaking as she wept, her head against his chest. When she spoke again her question was more a quiet accusation. "Why didn't you take that rifle from Nick and use it to keep us from being captured?"

"I owe you an explanation since it seems that decision put you in danger." Aaron sighed before continuing.

"Here's the deal. I do believe that God is able to deliver us. But I also believe that our actions in this world should not violate His commands. Jesus put His life into God's hands. I'm convinced we're supposed to do the same."

"You mean we're just supposed to let people get away with doing horrible things to us?" Ellie sat up once again.

"No, not at all. I don't think that means we stand by passively when evil happens – Jesus didn't – but I do not believe taking action against enemies includes killing them. That's not consistent with His teaching or example. It takes more courage to be willing to *suffer* harm rather than *do* harm."

They both sat silently for several long minutes. Aaron's quiet voice broke as he next spoke. "The fact that my beliefs may have put you in danger, however, bothers me greatly."

Ellie put both arms around her companion's waist and hugged him tightly. "You're right, Aaron. I love you for those beliefs. But I don't know if I can summon up that kind of faith. I'm so scared."

"I am too," Aaron admitted. "I just hope I have the courage of my convictions if they get put to the test in the next days. Now, let's pray together."

And they did.

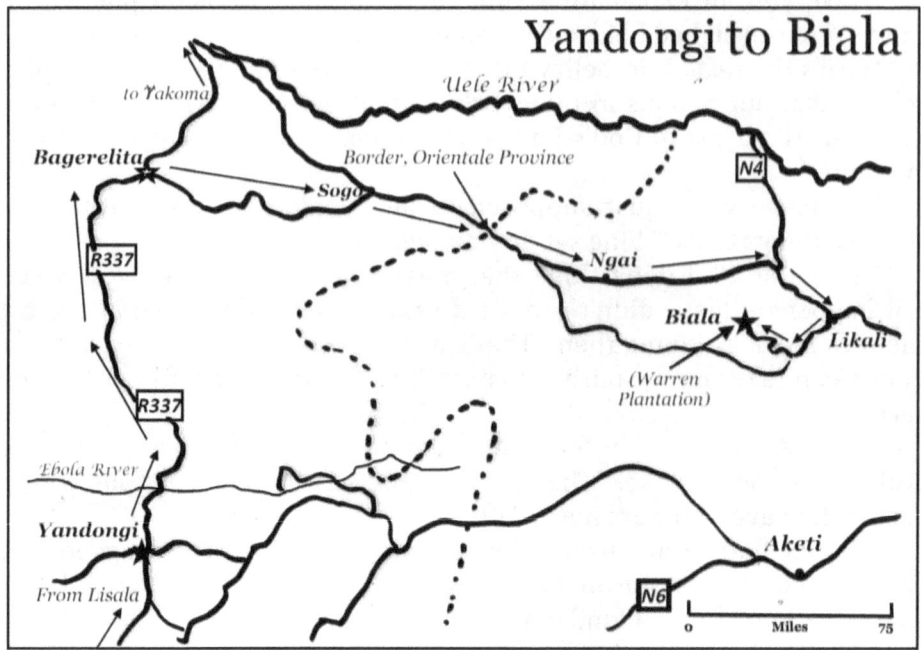

MAP 4 - Yandongi to Biala

CHAPTER 44
Biala, October 1964

It was mid-morning before Nick and Masemba were up, bathed, breakfasted and ready to head out. With a measure of optimism they departed in the Rahman fellow's Land Rover, headed for Douglas Warren's plantation.

The day's travel objective was the crossroads village of Bagerelita, 80 miles away. They planned to spend the night there with yet another Pakistani merchant, a friend of Nasir's, before taking on the longest leg of their voyage: a 140 mile marathon to Warren's remote plantation near the community of Biala in Orientale Province.

After just thirteen miles they came to the Ebola River bac. This was technically their second crossing of this river, headwaters to the mighty Mongala. Nasir explained that Ebola was a name derived from its local Ngbandi language origins, meaning "white water." It was a fitting moniker for the fast flowing river.

Nick noted with mixed feelings the long queue of trucks waiting to cross. The news that the Simbas had been driven out of Yakoma had resulted in more commercial traffic heading away from trouble and toward marketing outlets on the Uele and Ubangi Rivers. On the down side: the trio had to endure a three-hour wait to board the mechanical bac and a sluggish push across the cables by the swift flowing current.

Afternoon stretched into evening before Nasir's Land Rover passed through thick sections of isolated rainforest and into the dusty crossroads village of Bagerelita. The main road, R337, continued on north another 30 miles to Yakoma. Nick, Masemba and their genial chauffer planned to head east the next morning.

Flickering cooking fires lit a line of thatched roofed huts as they arrived at their destination. Only a handful of permanent structures clustered at the village center. Faded letters identified the largest as a combination store, bar, hotel and café. It was the establishment owned by Rahman's Pakistani friend, Malik. The tired travelers stopped there for the evening.

Malik's gracious wife greeted them, delighted at this rare opportunity to host English-speaking guests. She served them a simple meal of fruit, mwamba, rice and greens. Malik produced a rare but welcome bottle of wine to enhance the spread. The crossroads gossip over dinner was mostly positive: no Simba activity had been reported nearby nor on their proposed route. They slept well.

The next day found the Land Rover following a rutted track that headed east. It skirted the rainforest for 50 miles. Occasional mud bogs and small streams slowed their progress, but this was not a heavily traveled road, so they were able to make good progress. At Sogo village, the road joined the main route. The ruts were deeper, now, and the going was much slower. This road was more likely to be traveled by rebel forces so tension and vigilance built inside the jarring vehicle.

Nick found Nasir to be good company on the long drive, personable, interested and generous in his comments. He was encouraging and positive regarding Ellie and Aaron's status, though Nick was not reassured.

Nasir described growing up in rural Congo. "I remember standing on a box to run the cash register at my father's store. I could barely see over the counter. I loved serving the café and store guests. They always smiled and were so friendly to me. I thought they came just for me." He laughed. "Maybe they did."

"Our family occasionally vacationed in the rugged mountains of Pakistan, but my mother's father was an Imam and my father despised his strict religious rules." Nick nodded. *Perhaps that was one reason Dad stayed in Congo.*

Nick shared some of his favorite memories of growing up in Litoko. "I loved the jungle sounds at night, the cool and colorful mornings, and the quiet, soothing pace of life. Of course, Masemba and I had many adventures together. We'll have to tell you about the *ngando* later. My best memories also include my friends on the soccer team and hunting with Dad. But Dad's absence over the past four years has left a hole in my heart like nothing else."

Masemba listened from the back seat, engrossed, but only occasionally contributing to the exchanges. Like Nick, his thoughts were consumed with worry for their two friends who were likely suffering at the hands of the Simbas.

Nick disclosed to Nasir the questions that surrounded his father's choice to stay in Congo after Independence. "I don't understand why Dad chose to stay. Why didn't he keep in touch with us? I wonder what kind of a life he has built in the last four years." *I wonder, will there be any space for me, his eldest son, in Dad's life?* That was the unspoken issue behind each unanswered question. But it was not one Nick voiced out loud.

Nick's questions stirred Masemba's heart. *Should I tell Nick more about his father's life in Congo? We've come this far. I think it's better I let him find out for himself.*

The vigilant travelers crossed into Orientale Province without passing a single military roadblock. Nasir was philosophical. "I view it as a positive consequence of the Simbas having circulated through the area. As is evident, the ANC troops are long gone. Normally, all travelers' paperwork is subject to careful scrutiny, especially that of passing *mundeles.*" They were relieved to see an open and abandoned province barrier.

Their relief was short lived, however, when they finally reached the city of Likali, near the end of their long day's journey. An unwelcome roadblock appeared at the edge of town. It was guarded by a handful of scruffy looking young men. They surrounded the Land Rover, automatic weapons raised.

Nasir appeared calm and relaxed. He greeted the menacing *jeunesse* rebels in fluent Lingala. *"Mboté na bino yonso."* Greetings to you all. He handed several packs of cigarettes to the men. After exchanging further small talk, the barrier was removed. The vehicle was waved on without inspection. Nick took a breath. Beads of sweat coursed down Masemba's relieved face. Their savvy chauffer just smiled confidently.

"That went well," was his wry comment.

It was only a short distance further, about 12 miles, to Douglas Warren's coffee plantation. The route, however, coursed through dense rainforest over a rough, narrow track. It was slow going. The closer they came to his father's place the more nervous Nick Warren became.

Perhaps my quest will soon be over, my questions answered. But will Dad be glad to see me, or angry? Will he seem a stranger? What should I say to him? Nick's back tightened and his legs cramped. He tried to shake them out by shifting around, talking to Masemba, gazing into the forest, but nothing helped.

After nearly three quarters of an hour of careful winding through the forest, the Land Rover crept past a small collection of thatched roof houses of sticks and mud, the tiny village of Biala. The track continued on into the forest, but a path ran off to one side. Through the trees the three exhausted travel companions could see a large house.

"Let's check here to see if this is your father's place." Nasir turned up the drive.

From the cluster of curious workers who soon surrounded their vehicle, Nick and his companions discovered that this plantation belonged to a Belgian named Wouters. The Warren plantation was located further down this same road. As they prepared to leave, one of the workers added an afterthought: *"Madame Warren azali kuna na ndako te. Azali awa epai na Madame Wouters."*

"Madame Warren is not at her home but here with the lady of the house?" Nasir puzzled out loud.

Nick was dumbfounded. *"Madame* Warren? Who was that?"

Even as he pondered the question, an attractive Congolese woman came out onto the porch. She looked very familiar. Her worried face suddenly broke into a warm smile and she called out in English, *"Nick, is that really you?"*

In a flash he knew. *Sarah*!

CHAPTER 45
Biala, October 1964

Nick turned toward the willowy, familiar figure of Sarah who had flown down the porch steps and was now rushing toward their Land Rover, arms out in greeting. Sarah warmly hugged first the startled young *mundele* standing with an open mouth, and then proceeded to greet his two companions in a similar fashion.

"I can't believe it's really you!" she exclaimed. "And Masemba, how wonderful to see you again. I've missed you. It's a Litoko homecoming!"

She turned to Nasir, "I'm happy to finally meet you in person. I feel like we're already acquainted through Rev. Ellis's radio messages. Douglas says you have been very helpful. And now I see with my own eyes why he speaks so highly of you. Thank you for bringing these boys all the way here...safely," she added, smiling graciously.

"My pleasure, Madame Warren." Nasir returned her smile.

"Madame Warren?" echoed Nick. "No one told me. You and Dad? How? When? Where is he, anyhow?" The questions spilled out in a stream. "Why are you here and not at your home? Hasn't Dad made it back from Yakoma yet? When can I see him?"

Sarah held up a hand halting further queries just as Nick ran out of breath. "OK, Nick. There's plenty to catch up on. Come in now to my friends' home. I'm staying with them; it's safer for us to be together. We can cover all of your questions over dinner. You must be hungry and exhausted; we were just about to eat."

She herded the three surprise guests up the steps just as Monsieur and Madame Wouters appeared on the porch. *"Bienvenue á tous,"* offered the lady of the house with a warm smile, adding in English with a strong accent, "Your timing is good. We shall have dinner together just now."

Sarah was right on both counts: the travelers were famished and tired. Nick, however, was far hungrier to take in the revelations offered that evening than to consume the delicious meal. One fact followed another! It was overwhelming, painful, gratifying and life changing all at the same time. He drank it all in like a parched desert wanderer.

Sarah reported that Nick's father had made it safely to Yakoma with his ANC passengers. Shortly after he arrived, however, the Simbas had attacked the army garrison where he was staying. While a mercenary-led counterattack later drove them out, Rev. Ellis had informed her by radio that Douglas was captured and taken hostage by the rebels, possibly taken to the town of Buta. She had no further word about him.

Tears streaked her cheeks as Sarah paused to regain her composure. She recounted the invasion of their property by the ANC soldiers, and Nick and Masemba told of their harrowing journey and escape from rebel captivity. But when they got to the part about their friends being taken away, Nick was the one whose composure was shaken.

Madame Wouters served a fine upside-down pineapple cake, but the attention was not on food that evening.

Sarah addressed the group. "I don't want to offend anyone, but I need to speak with Nick privately. May we please be excused?"

"Bien sûr!" Monsieur Wouters nodded.

She and her perplexed stepson rose and moved to another room. "What's this all about, Sarah?" Nick's expression conveyed both curiosity and apprehension.

"I need to tell you how your father and I got together. It involves some of my own story and pain that I'd rather not share with the whole group. I also need to tell you some other things about your family that are not for others to hear."

Though she was more than a decade older than he, Nick had known Sarah from childhood, since she had been an adopted member of the Litoko missionary community. He was, however, unaware of her disastrous first marriage, her rejection, banishment and subsequent recovery at the Catholic mission. Nick had been in middle school at the time and had simply lost track of her. He also did not know that his father had kindly orchestrated her rescue with the help of Fr. DuBois.

Sarah stressed, "It was only well after your parents' divorce was final that Douglas and I formed a serious relationship. By now we have been happily married for nearly two years." Her eyes smiled.

The soft-spoken, articulate Congolese woman then shifted the topic to Nick's parents' difficult marriage. "Nick, your father was truly devastated at being separated from his family following your evacuation at Independence. It was just a short time later that your mother declared in writing she would never, under any circumstances return to the Congo. She insisted that it was Douglas' calling, his dream and obsession, not hers! She was done with Africa. He was not."

"Your father wrote to Patty pleading for her to reconsider. Letters, letters. Douglas also sent letters to you, Todd and Lizzie in the first year or so following your evacuation." She continued, with a slow shake of her head. "Sadly, your mother mailed a sharp reply telling him to stop sending letters. She told Doug that she had destroyed all of his letters, unopened, including his notes to you children. She demanded a divorce. Patty insisted it was best for her and you kids to just forget about him. She advised that he do the same."

Nick stared straight ahead, shocked. It was especially painful to find out his mother had thrown away his father's letters and discouraged any contact. *How could she do that to us kids? But how could Dad let it happen?*

He ran a hand through his hair and took a deep breath. "I know my mother is a little crazy, but why did *Dad* give up on her and on us kids? Isn't marriage supposed to last a lifetime, for better and for worse? What about *our* wishes and needs?" Nick's face showed the painful strain of the long simmering questions.

"Nick, you don't know the whole story," replied his newly discovered stepmother. "He did *not* give up on his marriage, at least not for many years."

She sighed. "I believe after having come all this way and at such a great effort, you deserve to know the truth. I just hope Douglas will not resent me for telling you."

"What are you talking about?" Nick asked, his voice going quiet. He braced himself for difficult news. It was a wise move.

Sarah's reply softened, "In your parents' first years at Litoko when you were just a toddler, your mother had an affair with the manager of our local palm oil plantation. He was a suave Belgian who gave her a lot of attention at a time when your father was away on mission trips to outlying villages. She was flattered, tempted and eventually gave in."

"Your father found out and confronted Patty but there was a pregnancy...your brother Todd. Your mother expressed remorse and they reconciled for a time, but she continued to struggle with being in Congo, with her role as a missionary wife and with Doug's strong sense of calling. Things remained strained between them. When she eventually became pregnant with your sister Elizabeth, he had doubts she was his child though Patty insisted she was his."

"Your father was deeply hurt by Patty's deception and infidelity but he chose to forgive her, again and again; to claim all you children as his own and to hold their marriage together. It was a frustrating battle. Eventually, it was a losing one."

Nick, in shock, listened with rapt attention. He finally managed to stammer a question, "Who...who else knew about this?"

Sarah sighed deeply before answering. "Well, most of the Litoko community was aware of the whole thing. It's nearly impossible to keep such secrets in a village."

"But what about the missionary community? Did everyone know but us kids?" Nick tried to absorb this appalling information. He was feeling embarrassed and humiliated.

"Well, I'm pretty sure Rev. and Mrs. Ellis were aware," Sarah replied. "They helped mediate things between your parents many times over the years. I don't think any of the others knew about the affair and its results. They just knew that your parents had a very difficult relationship."

"What about Dad?" Nick asked. "How did all this affect him?"

Sarah's face softened as she considered the question. "It was painful and shameful. He felt unloved and unworthy, a failure as a husband and father. It seemed nothing he said or did made any difference to Patty. Her guilt and resentment of him only deepened her bitterness. She, no doubt, felt trapped. She blamed Douglas for her moral failures and hated him because of them."

There was more to tell, much more, but Nick was feeling both exhausted and overwhelmed. Sarah noticed this.

"That's plenty for now, Nick. We can talk more later. Just be assured that I believe in your father. He is a kind, wonderful and loving man who has endured terrible rejection. I know about rejection as well. He may have made mistakes but his heart is pure. He never stopped loving you kids and grieving at being apart from you."

Sarah's last words echoed as he retired for the night to one of the Woulter's guest rooms. *Can I trust Dad's love? Should I? I'll never be able to look at any of my family members in the same way again. How should I feel about Mom? And what about Todd and Lizzie?*

Nick drifted into a troubled and restless sleep.

CHAPTER 46
Bumba, October 1964

The loud chattering of squirrel monkeys and noisy chirping of weaverbirds in the trees just outside their room roused Ellie from exhausted sleep. For a brief moment the familiar sounds of Africa awakening to dawn stirred pleasant feelings inside. Then, almost in a spasm she remembered they were locked up, Simba captives. A deep sinking feeling gripped her guts.

She found herself sprawled out with her head resting on Aaron's chest. He was still slumped against the wall, breathing deeply in sleep. In the dim pre-dawn light she saw seven other sleeping forms, sharing their space. They wore the long white garments and habits of nuns. One sister sat on the floor, leaning against the wall, her arms draped over two others, like a mother hen protecting her chicks. The others in the room were stretched out, still sleeping.

Mother Hen looked directly at Ellie. *"Bon jour"* she mouthed with a weary smile. Surprised, Ellie returned the greeting and stirred. *I need to find a bathroom. A bathroom!* Glancing around their confined space, it was almost an amusing thought, were the reality of her circumstances not so distressing. Feeling ready to explode, she carefully moved to the far corner of the room and relieved herself. *How awful. Dear God, help us.*

Ellie's careful movement had been enough to rouse Aaron who stood and found the same corner of the room Ellie had just left, and with his back turned, accomplished the same goal. He returned to hug a morning greeting to his girlfriend. Fear filled her eyes.

"Oh, Aaron...we're still here, it's not just a bad dream."

Others in the room began to wake. In a few minutes the young American couple greeted and introduced themselves to their companions and exchanged stories of their capture.

The Simbas' raid of a nearby Catholic mission two days earlier had resulted in the gruesome deaths of the priests and the transport of the nuns to this location. Their abductors had sexually assaulted two of their number the night before. They huddled under the comforting wings of their Mother Superior. The whole group was terrified, traumatized by what they had witnessed and experienced.

Ellie searched for words of condolence, though she simply could not think of anything encouraging to say. The room lapsed into silence, broken only by the periodic "Hail Marys" murmured by the nuns.

Midmorning, the door to their narrow space opened briefly and a jug of water, a hand of bananas and a large bowl of rice were placed on the ground. The captives gathered to nibble at the modest fare. No one was in the mood for small talk.

By mid-afternoon voices and movement approached outside. Ellie grabbed Aaron's arm and ducked. The door flew open and a fierce looking Simba in baggy pants and feathers in his hair stepped inside and in a loud voice, summoned them. *"Yaka!"*

Ellie looked at Aaron with wide eyes. "Oh, dear God" was all she managed to say.

A crowd of menacing rebels milled around a central area between buildings as the small line of captives emerged with dreadful apprehension. Several of the nuns held each other's hands as, eyes downcast and shoulders slumped, they shuffled into the courtyard. Shouts of *"Boma! Bula! Violer!"* echoed all about as the crowd fired itself up for an afternoon of entertainment torturing their captives.

As if to match the darkening mood, black afternoon thunderheads piled up, blocking the sun. A sudden chilling wind swirled dust around the milling mob.

One young Simba dashed up to a terrified Congolese nun and seizing the top of her robe wrenched it half off of her back. She instinctively clutched the torn garment to her chest even as he grabbed for a final tug. The elderly Mother Superior stepped forward to intervene but was thrown to the ground by another grinning young warrior. He crashed the butt of his rifle into her temple and she lay still.

Encouraged by the dramatic actions of the two, the crowd surged forward, snatching and grasping at the group of female captives. Ellie was pulled to the ground by several men. Reacting instinctively, Aaron lunged into the mêlée, flinging several attackers away from his fallen companion. He stood over her, presenting an imposing defense as the attackers regrouped. Gun barrels quickly swung in his direction.

Several shots rang out penetrating Aaron's chest with such force they threw him upward and backward off his feet. But before his lifeless body could reach the ground a loud CRACK and flash exploded in the very center of the crowd, filling the courtyard with an eruption of thunder and light. A huge dark, smoking hole was left surrounded by charred bodies and shattered eardrums. Not a single person was left standing in the area.

It took some time for the survivors to rouse themselves. It took even longer for any of them to regain their hearing.

The facts were unsettling to the rebels. The Mother Superior had been killed attempting to protect a young nun; a young male *mundele* had been shot also protecting his partner. A powerful force from the heavens had instantly fried a dozen or more Simba soldiers. Twice that number had been gravely injured or burned, all in the flash that followed. Even more remarkable: not a single female prisoner had been burned by the blast from above.

When the Simba leaders finally surveyed the scene, recorded the carnage and assessed its meaning, the first thing they did was move Ellie and the nuns to a residence in the town. There, the women were able to use the bathrooms, sleep in beds, drink water and eat decent food. Simbas had high regard for *dawa*. These captives had demonstrated that they possessed dangerous amounts of it. The pronouncement? No one was to harm *any* of them...at the peril of their life.

Second, the Simba leaders concluded that they did not need any further demonstrations of such awesome power. They quickly passed a report of the day's events to their superiors along with the urgent request that this group of prisoners be immediately transferred to Stanleyville. Let General Olenga harness such power; it was far too dangerous for them!

Ellie sat on the bed, head in hands. She was crushed, too heartbroken to cry. She was also still in shock from the traumatic events of the afternoon, culminating in the loss of Aaron. *Dear, sweet Aaron. What did he ever do but try to protect me and others in distress? Why did he have to die? Couldn't God have sent that lightning bolt a minute, an instant earlier?*

As she turned these things over in her troubled mind, too grief-stricken even to pray, Aaron's words returned to her.

"Sometimes He saves us...sometime He chooses not to. God's ways are not ours. He promises death is not the end. He is with us."

"Dear Aaron," she said out loud, "you *did* have the courage of your convictions. Right to the end."

And *then* she wept.

CHAPTER 47
Buta, October 1964

The last vestiges of morning fog had long since disappeared from the scene, driven off by the intense and relentless arrival of the tropical sun. A small group of young African soldiers lounged in the shade of a huge mango tree, laughing, drinking beer and watching the *mundeles* work. Periodically they called out insults, made jokes and threw things at them. "Hey long noses, *zolo mulayi*. Work faster, *sala noki!*" It was great sport. The tables had turned. Who were the *patrons* and who were the workers, now?

Bent over, sweat soaking their shirts, running down their uncovered heads and arms, Doug Warren and Paul Carlson labored in the sweltering midday sun, chopping at a field of tall grass with machete blades lacking handles. Their hands were blistered and bleeding, especially the highly skilled digits of Dr. Carlson, the surgeon. Hard labor on Doug Warren's coffee plantation had toughened his hands, but by the end of the morning they too were a raw and bloody mess.

Several of the onlookers drifted off to nearby houses, having became bored with their entertainment, run out of beer or both. The Simbas had taken over a section of former Belgian residences for their headquarters in the town of Aketi after fleeing from the Yakoma calamity. The large shaded porches of the European homes provided a good retreat for their midday siestas.

One of the remaining guards casually picked up his rifle by the barrel. Dragging the stock along the ground, he slowly headed for the nearest building.

"*Mindele!*" he called to the weary pair, guesturing toward the house. "*Kenda kuna.*"

"Finally!" whispered Carlson to his companion as they turned to obey the guard's command. "I didn't think I'd last this long." Doug just nodded, perspiration dripping off of his nose and chin.

Lunch consisted of tepid water, cold, buggy rice and an over-ripe papaya. It was followed by a grim afternoon assignment: cleaning the prison gutters.

After two days of hard labor, Paul Carlson and Doug Warren were exhausted. "I'm afraid I don't have much left," confessed the doctor as they roused themselves in their tiny cell the next day. He examined his blistered and swollen hands in the gray morning light, scratching mosquito and flea bites that covered his body. His bones ached from another night spent on the hard ground.

"Yes, I'd say we're both pretty much in survival mode by now." Doug started to rub his sore arms, but it just made the insect bites itch. "Let's see what those prayers last night will bring us in this new day." His tone was hopeful.

The two men had discovered common ground in the few days they had been together. The soft spoken *Munganga Paul* was clearly the initiator, however Doug had readily joined him in a time of prayer each evening before they attempted to sleep. He had shared very little of his story, but did alert his cell mate to his missionary past. To Doug's great relief, Carlson's response was gentle and accepting. "I hope to hear your story when you are ready to tell me."

Later that morning, without explanation, the two American hostages were hauled from their quarters, placed in the caged bed of a pickup and driven 80 jarring miles to the town of Buta. They were delivered to a Catholic mission and placed under house arrest.

Their Buta accommodations were a huge improvement over the Aketi prison. The men were puzzled at this development but greatly encouraged. "I think God has heard our prayers, Paul. I had expected the worse." Carlson nodded and managed a rare smile.

The mission's welcoming priest and nuns diligently attended to the wounds of their new residents who settled in for a lengthy stay. "Now here's an irony for you, Douglas. I'm actually hoping we remain here for some time. At least until the rebellion ends."

September turned into October and the two men's daily tasks became routines. Carlson's medical talents were well used by a steady line of patients seeking the healing touch of the *munganga*. His cheerful, low-key manner and competent medical skills won over both his hosts and their Simba guards. The mission residents took advantage of Douglas' tactile talents in facility maintenance. Plumbing was repaired, a generator fixed and broken chairs, tables and doors were rebuilt. His easy, friendly manner and fluent Lingala endeared him to the locals as well.

Doug was impressed with his fellow detainee. Authentic, upbeat and unpretentious, Paul Carlson was the kind of man one could trust and call "friend." Like Doug, he was passionate about the Congo and its people and often said so. He loved living there despite the unpleasant things they had endured.

One evening the two of them sat together enjoying a cup of tea along with some quiet conversation. Paul turned to his new friend and inquired, "Doug, after getting to know you a bit, it has become obvious to me that you possess a genuine faith. That being so, I'm curious: what made you decide to leave missionary service?"

Doug had long anticipated the question, but hadn't fully figured out how he wanted to respond. *How candid should I be?* He had never really spoken to anyone about this topic. Well, he had spoken to Sarah about leaving CEM, but even with her he had guarded his deepest emotions.

"Okaaay," Doug replied slowly stretching out the word, "I think I'm going to tell you, tell you the whole thing."

With that, he started his narrative, beginning with his early devotion to God, his sense of calling, and his delight in establishing a life in Africa. Doug struggled to describe Patty's difficulty in adjusting to Congo living and her persistent opposition to being there. Even more difficult, was disclosing her infidelity and eventual betrayal of him and their marriage.

"I was determined to reconcile, to love and accept the child I had not sired and to win back Patty's affections. Perhaps I was too determined to stay here, too insensitive to my wife's complaints, too slow in acknowledging the problem, in making the effort." He stared at the cement floor and ran his fingers through his hair. "I guess the results speak for themselves."

The two men sat in silence for several minutes. Finally, the kindhearted doctor posed a gentle question. "So, Doug, what kind of toll has this taken...how has all this impacted you?"

Tears ran down Doug's deeply tanned cheeks. "Truthfully? I feel like a failure. I failed my calling, failed my marriage and I've failed my children. I've felt unworthy to be a father, unworthy to represent God. I suppose I've failed *Him* most of all."

Doug's voice had choked almost to a whisper and the tears were flowing steadily. He buried his face in his hands and wept.

Paul Carlson placed a comforting hand on Doug's shoulder and did not comment for some time. Finally, the spasms slowed.

"Friend, God knows we humans are frail, flawed creatures. But He made us with noble character, "a little lower than the angels." You have made mistakes – I acknowledge that – but the virtue of your motives comes through clearly in your story. You made impressive efforts to do the right thing, to love and restore brokenness in your life. There's more to be done, however. You must continue by forgiving yourself."

After a pause Carlson added, "And then, reconcile with your children. I think Patty has healing and forgiveness of her own to seek but in my judgment that's no longer *your* business."

In spite of the unsettled circumstances that surrounded Doug Warren at the moment. Paul's words brought a deep, inexplicable sense of peace.

Forgiveness and reconciliation...gifts and goals, Doug thought as he drifted off to a rare, restful sleep.

CHAPTER 48
Biala, October 1964

Masemba and his traveling partners felt like new men the morning after their surprise arrival in Biala. A much-needed night's sleep on clean linens, coffee and a hearty Belgian breakfast of fruit, eggs and fresh banana bread did wonders for both body and spirit.

Nick and Nasir discussed with M. Wouters the challenges of coffee plantation management during political turmoil. They planned to tour the Warren plantation later in the morning.

Masemba got up from the breakfast table at the same time Sarah rose to leave. "Come take a walk with me and let's speak more of Litoko, Masemba," said Sarah with an inviting smile. "I could use an update."

He nodded, following her out the door and down the steps. The morning was still fresh and cool and the lively sounds of whydah birds and swifts and the chatter of jungle creatures in the rainforest canopy were familiar and comforting.

They spoke mostly in Lingala, with occasional French and English phrases thrown in, a natural rhythm that needed neither explanation nor translation. Theirs was a unique and comfortable exchange few Congolese could replicate or perhaps even appreciate.

Sarah was curious about her friends both in the village and at the Catholic mission. She asked about Nick and Ellie's tour of their burned home station. "Was it a sad homecoming? Were they shocked to see how things looked? Were many happy memories stirred?" Then, she asked about Masemba's family, his experience in the classroom and his future plans for career and marriage.

As she posed these questions in succession, the young man's responses became increasingly abbreviated and tentative. When the topic finally shifted to how he happened to accompany Nick on his quest to find his father, Masemba's demeanor abruptly changed. He sighed deeply, frowning and became quiet, staring at the ground.

Sarah easily recognized this change in mood. She turned to him, and stretching out a hand to his arm, gently asked, *"Likambo nini, ndeko? What's wrong, brother?"*

Turmoil was written all over Masemba's face as he struggled to find words. Finally, after another deep sigh he answered. "I have a couple of things I need to confess. They are weighing heavily on my heart and I need to release them, to tell someone...to tell *you.*"

He continued, "I...I became a Simba. I was recruited from Litoko village and have secretly trained with others in the forest for some months. I was convinced at the time that we've had enough of *mundeles* ruling in our land. Independence was supposed to change that, but it didn't. Growing up, my father used to tell us: *'Milk and honey have different colors but they can share the same house peacefully.'* I rejected his words, defied his prohibitions and despised his moderate views."

Masemba's comments then took on a sinister tone. "I became aware of other things. I discovered that Rev. Ellis created a network of government supporters throughout Èquateur Province. They are informers, spies. I thought that I could help our cause by traveling with Nick, identifying Ellis' contacts."

Sarah looked startled. "So you were not actually traveling as Nick's friend, but rather as a secret enemy?"

"I know it looks bad," he replied, "and I felt guilty about deceiving my good friend and the others, but a free Congo seemed like a much more important goal at the time."

"At the time?" Sarah noted. "Did something change?"

"Yes. Much happened on our voyage. My father's sayings keep echoing in my mind: *'You can tell ripe corn by its look; you must judge a man by the work of his hands.'* I was not prepared for the hate and violence that accompany my Simba brothers. They act like vicious, devouring beasts, not liberators, saviors. In contrast, the genuine friendship and love shown to me by Nick, Ellie and her friend Aaron has shamed me. I want to be more like them, not the others. My father's words return to condemn me: *'If you don't stand for something you will fall for something.'* I stood for the wrong thing and fell for it."

By now, Masemba's eyes were brimming with tears. He continued, "But there's more. When Nick, Ellie and Aaron first escaped and went into hiding in Lisala, I was accused of being with them. I denied it. To save myself I informed the rebels where they were hiding. I was afraid for my life and I gave up my friends. I betrayed them." Tears were now flowing steadily down his cheeks.

"I later tried to make up for this by helping them to escape a second time. I even shot a Simba guard. I killed him. But that doesn't change the fact that it was I who turned them in."

"What have you said to Nick and the others about this, Masemba?" asked Sarah.

"Nothing. I think they suspect it was me but no one has accused me and I did not tell them myself," Deep sadness filled his voice.

They walked slowly along the garden path, dappled light filtering through the canopy high above.

After several minutes, Sarah broke the silence. "You're a young man, Masemba, who can blame you for wanting a better future for our beautiful land? I do not. I want that too. I do, however, think you misjudged the best way to bring this about. Sometimes we suffer from the smoke of fires we ourselves have created. God has provided you with powerful experiences that make it clear who your real friends are and how you should balance your loyalties in the future."

"But...but should I tell them?" Masemba turned and looked directly at Sarah. "Should I let them know I've had a change of heart, that my actions almost got them killed and that I feel really badly about this? Do I need to ask for their forgiveness?"

"I think whether you tell them your secret and ask forgiveness is between you and God...and your three friends, Masemba," Sarah responded thoughtfully. "You have to live with *yourself*, first of all, *mon ami*, so you shall be the one to decide your next step. In the words of our village elders, *'not until we have fallen do we know how to rearrange our burden.'*"

And with that, Sarah leaned over and encircled her former Litoko friend in a warm hug. He returned the gesture. Several quiet minutes passed before they turned and retraced their steps to the big house.

CHAPTER 49
Biala, October 1964

That warm October day proved to be memorable to Nick, Masemba and Nasir. First, Sarah guided the small group on a tour of the Warren coffee plantation. In addition to the three visitors, *M. et Mme.* Wouters came along for an excursion to the Warren property located just two miles down the road.

The plantation was well organized and efficiently laid out, much as Nick had imagined it to be. What was even more impressive to him, however, was its scope and beauty. Rows and rows of healthy, green and groomed trees, heavy with clusters of pink *Robusta* coffee beans stretched in neat lines far over the adjacent rolling hills.

The main house and cluster of sheds, storage buildings and workers' residences sat on a knoll under mature mango and palm trees. Afternoon convection currents provided relief from the humid tropical heat as raptors soared high above. The wide shaded veranda of the main house was inviting and that's just where the group finally settled at the end of their warm tour. Sarah's smiling house-helper Emilie served lemonade, tea and biscuits, as they processed all they had just witnessed.

"It's wonderful," exclaimed Nick. "What you and Dad have done in this beautiful place...I'm really impressed. I couldn't have imagined it any more, well...beautiful!"

"It is a lovely setting," Sarah agreed. "Our trees are approaching their seven-year prime and if we are able to market our crop this year and next, we will actually pay off what we owe." Then with a sigh she added, "But with all the trouble that's about it remains a big gamble."

"But what a lot of work," observed Nasir. "It appears to be very labor intensive." He motioned to a line of workers who were arriving with large baskets of raw "cherries." They emptied their burdens into big bins across the grassy yard from where the group sat.

"Coffee operations do require lots of manual labor." M. Wouters helped himself and passed the biscuits. "But because of it, they also provide a key source of employment and a livelihood for any willing, able-bodied villager in this whole rural region. It's a craftsman's job with over thirty steps. Beans are picked manually when ripe. Over there are the drying trays. They must be regularly raked and any fermented beans, removed by hand. When the plants are producing fruit, you treat them with more respect, just as if each were a mother."

He drained his lemonade and looked from Nick to Masemba to Nasir. "Douglas Warren and I have combined our operations so we can both make a go of it. We jointly purchased a hulling machine and sorter. It's at my place. Our biggest challenge, however, is transport from this remote location both because of the bad roads and now, as Sarah indicated, because of war."

After further conversation, *M. et Mme.* Wouters excused themselves and headed back home to their duties, while the others helped gather up the plates and glasses, stacking them on a tray to be returned to the kitchen. As the Belgians' Land Rover rounded the bend at the end of the drive, Sarah thanked her staff and dismissed them for the rest of the day. Then, she turned to the others.

"It's now time to contact Rev. Ellis by radio. I've buried ours in a trunk behind the house. If we were to get any unwelcome visitors," she explained, "I wanted to make sure they wouldn't find it. I need help digging it up. Also, we need to take care none of my workers see what we're doing. The Simbas have their ways of extracting information."

In a short time the radio was out of its hiding place, assembled and warming up in Sarah and Doug's office, surrounded by an anxious circle of faces.

When Rev. Ellis's familiar voice crackled a response on the speaker there was a definite note of excitement in his first words. "Sarah! How good to hear from you again. Did you say that Nick, Masemba and Nasir are there with you? What a relief to know that they made it safely."

Sarah reported that all were in good health at her location but that they were, to a person, very anxious to hear what Rev. Ellis might have to report. "Do you have any further word of Douglas? Of Ellie and Aaron? What are the reports from Stanleyville?"

"I'm afraid I don't have much good news to report. First, your mercenary rescuer, Lt. Wilson and his 51 Commando unit have successfully pushed as far as Bumba. However, they reported that Ellie and some nuns were sent away to Stanleyville before they reached the city."

"What about Aaron? Was he with them?"

"Their sources did not mention Aaron."

All four listeners had risen out of their chairs and were leaning forward, ears straining to take in every word.

Ellis continued, "Also, just yesterday we picked up a claim via Radio Stanleyville, that the Simbas now have two American officers in custody: a "Major" Paul Carlson and a "Captain" Douglas Warren. I believe we can correctly conclude that those two individuals are now in Stanleyville. The General has distorted their identities to fit his needs. He obviously intends to make an example of them. Many are praying for their safety on both sides of the Pond."

"But what's being done about freeing the hundreds of expatriates held in Stanleyville? Isn't the U.S. or Belgium doing anything? What about the mercenaries?" Sarah's voice was breaking as her composure crumbled. Tears streamed down her cheeks.

At that point, an idea occurred to Nick. He pulled the microphone towards him. "Rev. Ellis, it's Nick here. Can you confirm whether 51 Commando is to be part of a Stanleyville rescue attempt?"

After a long pause, Rev. Ellis offered several nonsense sentences that Nick identified as code language he had been briefed on. He quickly jotted down the phrases before returning some of his own. Following firm directions to keep their transmissions short, Sarah and Rev. Ellis then signed off.

The small group was somber as they repacked the radio equipment into its trunk and, with a watchful eye, reburied it behind Sarah's house.

CHAPTER 50
Biala, October 1964

By the time the guys had returned from re-burying the radio equipment, Sarah had fully regained her composure and placed a fresh tray of fruit and drinks out for all to consume. The group nibbled at the provisions and sat in silent reflection for several minutes.

Nick was the first to speak. All eyes turned to him. "OK, everyone. Here's what I understood Rev. Ellis to say in code."

"This is not a perfect translation but I think I got most of it right. A major effort is underway to capture Stanleyville. A large column of mercenary and Congolese army forces are already working their way north. Within the next two weeks, they expect to occupy the major Simba stronghold of Kindu, and at that location, assemble an even larger column to push on into Stanleyville."

"Ellis believes that 51 Commando is being replaced and will be flown into Kindu to reinforce the main Stanleyville column."

Nick sat forward to offer his next thoughts. "Since it now appears likely that my father as well as Ellie and Aaron are being held in Stanleyville, that's where I intend to go next. When they are rescued, I want to be there, to be a part of it if I can." He was deliberate in his emphasis on "when" rather than "if."

"But how..." Sarah began, when understanding flashed across her face. "No, Nick...it's way too dangerous. Too many lives are already at stake. We...I don't want to chance losing you, too."

Nick continued, shifting his gaze toward Nasir and Masemba. "If you, Nasir are willing to drive us down to Bumba before Lt. Wilson and his troops are replaced, perhaps we can convince our former liberators to include us with their unit. We can offer to be translators or maybe just additional manpower." He grasped for ideas. "I figure that's pretty much the *only* way we're going to be able to get to Stanleyville."

"I admit I am uncomfortable with the mercenary shooting-killing thing, but saving Dad and our friends is what I *have* to do; it's the right thing to do."

Sarah again voiced caution. "The right thing? Nick, mercenaries are brutal. They're killers. Do you *really* intend to join them on their bloody mission? Who knows what you'd be expected to do! In our village there is a saying, *'If the cockroach wants to rule over the chicken, then it must hire the fox as a body-guard.'* You'd be joining the foxes."

Turning to his two companions, her voice rising sharply, she implored them, "*Please* don't help him do this. Don't go along with it. You've all been through plenty. You've seen enough death and suffering already, haven't you?"

Nasir reached out, laying a reassuring hand on her arm as he spoke. "Madame Sarah, as you know very well, this world of ours is a dangerous place. Sometimes...sometimes we have to take big risks for those we love."

Addressing Nick, he continued in a firm voice, "I am with you, friend. I too feel I must try to reach my wife and children in Stanleyville. If harm should come to them...well, I don't think my life would be worth much." His voice trailed off.

Masemba had been quiet during these exchanges. Thoughtful and reflective, he spoke. All attention turned to him.

"*Ndecko* Nick," he said softly, "do you remember the time when we were young boys and we became lost deep in the forest as night fell? Your young brother and sister were with us and we were all very frightened. We did not know how to find our way. Todd and Lizzie were too tired to walk and too heavy to carry. You wanted to keep going, to search out the way home, but someone had to stay with the children. We reluctantly parted and I went on ahead...alone. I was full of fear but I kept going. I knew I *had* to find the way out. Not just for me but also for you, my friends. And somehow, I did find the way. Help came."

Nick's eyes had filled with tears as he sensed the direction of his friend's story.

Masemba paused before carefully continuing. "I believe a time has come in our journey when we must once again part. But this time it is *you* who must go forward into the shadows to find the way. Your going, much as mine years ago, is not only for you. It is also for the others you love. I will remain here to guard and assist Sarah until you return...just as you once did with your family."

The two friends hugged each other in silence.

*****

With gas tanks and jerry cans topped off from the Warren plantation's fuel supply, Nick and Nasir said their good-byes early the next morning. In the pre-dawn darkness, they turned down the narrow forest track towards the main highway. They planned to retrace their previous course, the same looping circuit that brought them to Biala. A more direct route to Bumba existed to the south, but since it passed through the Simba controlled town of Aketi and other occupied territory, they opted for the longer (170 mile) course.

Almost as soon as Nasir's Land Rover turned onto the main road, the town of Likali appeared and with it, came the same military roadblock they had faced two days earlier. This time, however, the guards at the barrier were older men and not about to be deterred by an offer of mere cigarettes.

Nasir and Nick were ordered out of their vehicle at gunpoint. Their ID papers were demanded and they were roughly shoved aside, sprawling to the side of the road.

Nick observed that the soldiers' eyes were blood-shot and their gestures were exaggerated. They had likely spent the night drinking, smoking hemp or both. An argument ensued among them as to whether they should just beat these new strangers or shoot them.

"What are you *mundeles* doing in our land driving at night?" the leader demanded. "Your papers show you are not from this region."

Nasir began to explain, but his captors were not the least interested in listening. It looked like this encounter would turn into a painful shakedown or worse.

Nick suddenly remembered. *"Tala papier na nsima na passeport,"* he requested of the lead thug. His papers were contained in a plastic folder, and the *Laissez-passer* given to him at the Njili airport – it seemed a lifetime ago – by Amin, Nasir's cousin, was included.

The blurry-eyed sergeant scanned the document in the dim light, holding it close, next to his nose. Recognizing its official *Orientale Province* stamps at last, he slowly refolded the paper and stuffed it back into the plastic folder.

The other soldiers were still arguing among themselves as the lead man handed back the travelers' papers and, yelling something to his comrades, motioned Nick and Nasir on past the barrier. They jumped into their vehicle and roared off.

"I now owe the Rahman family, double," Nick said to his smiling travel companion. "That was way too close!"

It was once again a long day of travel and well past dark when the two weary travelers finally pulled into Yandongi, for a short night's stay at Nasir's home. Both were relieved that their drive had been unmarred by additional encounters with either breakdowns or roadblocks.

By noon the following day, Nasir and Nick turned onto the muddy main street of Bumba and were directed to the tin roofed, cement block residence where Lt. Crash Wilson had his headquarters. They had rehearsed their approach to the tough mercenary leader on their drive, but were nervous about its reception. They were only going to get one shot at this request.

Crash Wilson appeared pleased and surprised to see the former Lisala hostage. "Well, look here...I figured we'd never see *you* again." Still looking for your father? What brings you back here, and who've you got with you?"

Nick introduced Nasir, informing the mercenary leader that Nasir was the merchant the patrol had delivered him to in Yandongi several days earlier. Hoping to impress him, he also pointed out that Nasir had graciously fed and hosted the patrol's overnight stay at his home.

"A radio message received at my father's plantation informed us that Dad has been moved to Stanleyville where he is being held hostage. Nasir's wife and children, visiting Stanleyville, are also among the large number of expatriates unable to leave."

Crash lit a cigarette, blew a plume of smoke toward the ceiling and leaned forward. "What else did you learn?"

"We found out that a major rescue operation is presently underway, led by 5 Commando forces."

Crash was impressed with Nick's CIA contacts, though the information wasn't new to him; he was already aware of the military action taking place. They would soon be a part of it. The intensity of Nick's desire to locate his father and friends did move him, however.

"What is it you want from me?" he asked at last when Nick finished his story.

"Nasir and I want to join up with 51 Commando for the assault on Stanleyville. We have a personal stake in the outcome. We're both able to translate; we are familiar with guns and how to use them. We'll be help, not a liability. I realize we're not trained soldiers, but I'll bet that's also the case for half of your men as well. We're fast learners."

Crash smiled, blowing another cloud of smoke in the air before responding. "This kid has guts all right," he said as though to himself. He took another deep drag, exhaled and replied.

"What we do is no walk in the park. Do you fellas have the balls to follow orders, to shoot first and ask questions later? Our work is not for the weak-willed!"

Without waiting for an answer Crash scrunched up his face. "On second thought, I think I'd better run this one past Mad Mike. Let him decide."

His eyes then clouded. "You've got another little problem, however, my young friend. Americans are forbidden to become mercenaries in this godforsaken land; they can lose their citizenship if they join up." Wryly smiling, he quipped, "How'd you feel about being Canadian for a while?"

It was only a tentative agreement to take on Nick and Nasir, but a timely one. It was enough to get them a seat on the DC-4 that arrived to transport 51 Commando to Kamina headquarters...the very next day.

PART III

The Aftermath

CHAPTER 51
Stanleyville, October 1964

Ellie sat in a small circle of women, holding hands in prayer at a Stanleyville Catholic mission. The others were all nuns, evenly divided between Congolese and Europeans. Their voices rose, soft and soothing, worshipful. It was the *"none"* or ninth hour after dawn, the mid-afternoon prayers. Ellie's mind was far away from the mission, however, and her spirit was troubled, not peacefully communing with God in the third of the Three Daily Prayers. She had not yet been able to pray.

It had been over two weeks since she and the captive nuns were dumped off here after a rugged two-day, 400-mile transport from Bumba in the back of a dusty Simba pickup. *"Tika awa!" Stay here!* they were ordered: house arrest.

The new arrivals were warmly welcomed by the resident sisters, given fresh clothes and food and introduced to the order's routines. The structure helped distract its followers from the perpetual menace that surrounded them.

As the women softly sang and chanted the familiar liturgy, Ellie's thoughts were again of Aaron. She had dreamed of him regularly since that terrible afternoon. Her nightly visions were of Aaron walking beside her, his strong arm around her waist, looking down at her and smiling. Such moving, comforting and vivid images! Upon waking she found herself in tears, desperately desiring to prolong his presence, however improbable. He seemed so real in those dreams. How was it possible that he was gone?

The nuns' liturgical chants reminded Ellie of her final evening with Aaron, the shared intimacy of their anxious prayers. His words echoed: *"Lord, we beg you to help us, protect us and rescue us. If You intend for our journey to end here, however, in Your mercy and kindness let it happen quickly; deliver us from suffering at the hands of our captors. May Your will be done."*

Ellie remembered Aaron's words as a desperate appeal, but also a practical one, an indelible one. His prayer was a statement of deep trust and reliance. But was it misplaced faith? *Was God's will really done? How could it be His will to take such a fine person away...away from me?* She pondered the thought for the umpteenth time.

As she reflected on these things, a new insight came to her as if audibly spoken: *"Yes. Those prayers of Aaron's were answered. You were delivered. His end came quickly, without suffering."*

Ellie released the hands she had been holding and abruptly stood up, startling the circle of worshippers. *"Pardon,"* she blurted in French before rushing out through the doorway and down the hall to her room. She threw herself on her bed and wept.

A short while later, Sister Beatrice slipped into the room and sat on the bed beside Ellie. A kind, middle-aged woman from the Netherlands, she had served the church in the Congo for many years. She spoke flawless English and had been one of the first at the mission to welcome and orient the young American girl.

She raised Ellie up to sitting and hugged her, a gesture eagerly returned. "Would you like to talk with me about what happened?" the nun invited. Ellie nodded and slowly, hesitantly, bit-by-bit told her story.

She first described her background as an MK in Litoko, her delight in returning to Congo for summer service, and her blossoming friendship with Aaron. She then told of Nick's arrival, his quest to find his father, and the four friends' travels and troubles leading to their capture. Finally, with a shaky voice and brimming eyes she detailed Aaron's death and the miraculous delivery of her and the other nuns from harm or death in Bumba.

Sister Beatrice listened carefully, interjecting only short questions or acclamations: "What happened, then? My, that must have been frightening!"

When Ellie finished, nearly two hours had passed. Everyone else had moved on to dinner. The two women sat quietly, side by side on the bed. The late afternoon shadows had by then reached the barred windows high above. The dim light in the room added to the privacy and intimacy of their conversation.

The older woman turned to the younger and lifted the sad, downturned face to look fully into her eyes. "My dear Mademoiselle Ellie, your story is filled with the touch of God's hand. He is obviously not finished with you yet, maybe just begun."

"That sounds like something Aaron would say," Ellie murmured. "But how can a loving God allow such bad things to happen?" She was still troubled. "I don't understand...how could He *allow* Aaron to die?"

Beatrice sighed, shaking her head slowly. "Yes, it is impossible to answer such heart-wrenching questions. How could the same God so clearly and dramatically deliver you and the others from sure ravaging by the Simbas, but yet not prevent the two sweet novices from being raped the night before?"

The Sister's voice dropped as an edge of pain crept into her eyes and words: "And I have often questioned how God could have allowed my rape as well, all those years ago."

She looked up with a gentle smile, "But, my young friend, that was not the end of my story. You see, it also has the touch of God's hand on it. The Scriptures teach that we are to *'comfort those who are in any trouble with the comfort we have received from God.'* That has indeed been my experience. I have had many opportunities to comfort the women of this land. Most have suffered far greater harm than have I."

"Are you saying that God allows tragedy so He can somehow use us in service?" Ellie was skeptical. She had heard that explanation before, but it never made sense to her.

"No." Sister Beatrice's voice was firm. "But I *am* saying that in times like these it is important that we do not hold onto a distorted view of God. We must not imagine we can control Him or determine His purposes. God is not obliged to do our bidding, to keep us safe and comfortable in this fallen world of ours. Our Savior Himself, suffered at the hands of evil men; yet, through that sacrifice, He redeemed us. That is our belief."

"So, my dear," concluded the kindhearted nun, "I have learned that what others may intend for evil, God is able to use for good. Even the real adversity we experience can be redeemed. Mine has. He has promised to be with us to the end. He will keep His promise. He did so to your dear Aaron and He will do so for you as well."

Ellie wrapped her arms around the now tearful nun. "Thank you," was all she could say.

"Now, let's see if they left anything for us to eat," said Sister Beatrice, rising from the bed.

CHAPTER 52
Stanleyville, October 1964

The Simba guards loaded up their two prize captives, Doug Warren and Paul Carlson in the gray pre-dawn shadows. A concerned cluster of priests and nuns from the Buta mission was gathered to send them off. Their parting gifts were food, water and tearful prayers of blessing. Someone also scrounged up a pith helmet, once worn against the tropical sun and snakes dropping from dense jungle vines, but rarely seen in post-Independence Congo. It was filled with bananas and handed to Dr. Paul. Theirs was going to be a hot and bruising drive and they would be exposed in the back of the open bed pickup. Even an outdated head covering was welcome.

The hot and dusty 200-mile drive from Buta to Stanleyville was an exhausting one for the two men. They had been filled with foreboding ever since learning that Olenga's devious president, Gbenye, had declared them to be captured American military officers. That declaration had prompted their transfer to Simba headquarters. Just what Gbenye had in store for them there was not yet clear. Nothing positive came to mind.

The N4 highway stretched south from Buta to Stanleyville traversing two rivers along its course: the Aruwimi and the Lindi. Sixty miles separated the two crossings. In both cases, thanks to prominently displayed weapons, the Simba's pickup with its hostage cargo drove straight to the front of long lines at the bacs. Their progress was thus only slightly slowed. The guards had been directed to complete this prisoner transfer in one day and they were determined to fulfill that order.

As color faded from the short African twilight, the dusty Simba vehicle finally pulled up in front of a large structure identified by letters on the cement block wall as Stanleyville's *Central Prison*. Did this arrival bring the men one step closer to rescue and freedom, or only one step closer to death? Neither Doug nor his well-regarded medical friend knew the answer.

For two weeks five Americans from the U. S. Embassy had been held in cell number eight. It was fairly spacious as Central Prison cells went, fifteen by thirty feet, but incredibly filthy. Vermin crawled the planks that rested on low ledges that the men sat and slept on. At night hideous wails came from mentally ill prisoners nearby and huge rats scurried about in the filth underfoot. A bare light bulb lit the room all night, inhibiting sleep and adding to the prisoners' torment.

The cell's occupants included Stanleyville's U.S. Consul, Michael Hoyt, Assistant-Consul David Grinwis and three other members of the American consular staff assigned to that city.

On the evening of October 23, 1964, as the prisoners dozed on their planks, the cell door squeaked open and two thin white men were shoved in, staggering to remain upright as they entered. Both flinched as the door clanged shut behind them.

The paler one was clad in a white shirt and khaki pants. He was in his late 30s and carried a medical bag and pith helmet filled with bananas. His dark-complected companion wore shorts, a safari shirt with sleeves rolled up and was in his mid-40s. His hands held a small bundle of clothing.

Since they looked like Belgians, Michael Hoyt extended his hand, greeting them in French, *"Bonjour, messieurs."*

"My name is Paul Carlson. I'm an American...a missionary too. Gee, it's great to meet some Americans again," blurted the younger newcomer, grasping Hoyt's hand.

"Douglas Warren," offered his companion as the others in cell eight gathered around. "American also. I run a coffee plantation over 200 miles from here...northwest of Buta, in the rainforest."

"U. S. Consul for Stanleyville, Michael Hoyt. Welcome to our palace." Turning to Doug, he said, "I've heard of you, Warren. Since you're living in Orientale Province you're on our embassy's list of American citizens. If I remember correctly, pre-Independence you were a missionary somewhere in Équateur Province."

Doug just nodded. "So how long have you fellows been in here, anyway?" He was anxious to change the subject.

Hoyt held up a hand to signal he'd get to the question later. "And you, Dr. Carlson...or should I say, *Major* Carlson?" he added with a slight smile. "Your reputation precedes you. A couple days ago Radio Stanleyville announced your capture as well as that of your partner here, *Captain* Warren. We have speculated about the timing of your arrival."

The two newcomers looked at one another. "It's not getting any better, is it Doug?" Carlson quipped to his friend, with a worried glance.

In his practiced leadership role, Michael Hoyt then set about clearing space for the new arrivals, cleaning and spraying down sleeping planks with insecticide their outside contacts had supplied, and finding extra blankets. He offered a short explanation of the schedule and logistics of their imprisonment: latrine breaks, food deliveries, avoiding trouble from guards and other inmates and additional survival details.

After they were settled, the small circle of hostages began sharing stories. Doug and Paul told of leaving wives and work and of their capture in the battle of Yakoma. Hoyt, Grinwis and the others told of the Simba's takeover of Stanleyville and their illegal detention and mistreatment by their dangerous captors.

Hoyt shared from his sources that in recent days the Simba army had been regularly losing ground to mercenary-led ANC forces throughout the region. All agreed that they were in grave danger of being on the wrong end of a wholesale slaughter, if liberating forces were not able to pull off a quick victory. American hostages throughout Stanleyville could not expect mercy from their captors once they had lost their value as bargaining chips in a losing war.

One morning several days later, Hoyt called his cellmates to gather. Their morning food delivery had included the latest edition of *Le Martyr* newspaper. In it was an article that, with chilling effect, featured their latest arrivals: Doug Warren and his companion Paul Carlson.

Hoyt translated the lead story from French. It repeated the claim that two American military officers had been captured: *Major* Paul Carlson and *Captain* Douglas Warren. The article noted that they had been taken during the battle for Yakoma on September 20. The two were reported to be in good health. A military tribunal was studying their dossiers in advance of the prisoners' appearance before a court of justice.

"Well, it looks like Gebenye's lie has now become public information. Military tribunal? Court of justice? I'd say that pretty well seals our fate." Carlson was downhearted.

"It's not over 'til it's over, Paul." Doug's reassurance lacked conviction. He had lived in Congo long enough to know that harsh rhetoric and threats did not always translate to outcomes. However, this time the threat was close and real.

Consul Hoyt added his attempt at reassurance. "What's true, Dr. Carlson, is that you and Mr. Warren here are Gbenye's last trump card. I'd say he is not likely to play it any time soon."

No one responded. His listeners shifted on their boards and did not meet each other's eyes.

CHAPTER 53
Stanleyville, October 1964

Amin bounded up the broad porch steps of his family home taking two at a time. He startled Bernard the house worker who was setting the table for the noon meal, as he flung open the front door and strode across the room. "Father, take a look at this," he called out.

His startled father looked up over his spectacles from his bookkeeping work. "What in the world, Amin?" he puzzled, pushing away from his desk.

"Look," his son pointed to the paper he carried, "It's Nick's father. They've got his father in Central Prison! The Simbas are calling him an American military officer, but he's no soldier. He's a businessman, a former missionary. They're using him as a convenient scapegoat for their losses."

"What's this about a 'Nick'?" his father asked in confusion. "What are you talking about?"

Amin began again, reminding his father of the contact he had had with Nick Warren on the plane from Brussels where he learned of his seatmate's quest to find the parent he had not seen for over four years. "I'm almost positive that this is the same man. It's Nick's missing father. I intend to find out for sure."

"Think carefully before you do something you'll wish you hadn't." His father grimaced as though knowing his advice was futile. "If you go to Central Prison, Amin, you may not return."

"I'll be careful. I think I'll just accompany the Jenkinson and Barlovatz's food delivery to the American prisoners. We've been taking them to the Hôtel des Chutes for the Belgians, so maybe they'll just think 'it's one of those Pakistanis again.'"

Deliveries arranged by the British missionaries Herbert and Alice Jenkinson, managers of the LECO bookstore, along with well-known Hungarian physician Alexander Barlovatz and his wife Lucy, had supplied the American prisoners with regular food, blankets, books and even insecticides. They were a true lifeline for the imprisoned Americans.

Later that day, Amin arranged to assist with the food deliveries to Central Prison. He accompanied the Jenkinson's worker carrying a box of food and water for the hostages. His first move was to introduce himself to the Americans – in English – and ask for Douglas Warren. One of the U. S. consular staff members pointed him out.

"Mr. Warren?" he began, "I'm Amin Rahman, a friend of your son Nick. I sat with him on the plane from Brussels and learned about his plans to find you. My family operates businesses in Stanleyville. I just learned of your being here and decided I had to come check on you."

Doug was stunned by this unexpected contact. "Yes...Nick is my son. What do you know of his whereabouts?" he managed to stammer, feeling both surprised and skeptical.

"I'm afraid I don't have any recent news for you," Amin replied, "other than the fact that I was told Nick and his friends began their search for you from your former residence of Litoko."

"That much I know as well." Doug nodded. "I've been most concerned for Nick's safety and that of his friends, too. Obviously," he gestured toward his cellmates, "these are dangerous times for Americans in Congo."

At that point, the prison guard, shifting on his feet at the door, frowned and motioned Amin to leave.

"I'll be back in the morning." Amin edged for the door. "Perhaps you'll have questions for me. I understand it's been some time since you saw Nick."

Doug thanked Amin with a wave of his hand. He stood staring at the door long after the visitors left and the door had closed and clicked shut behind them. The contact triggered his realization that he knew little of his son as a young adult. *What have the last four years been like for Nick? Where is he by now? Is he still alive?*

CHAPTER 54
Stanleyville, November 1964

As the days turned into weeks, Amin became a regular visitor to the Americans in Central Prison. He brought news of unfolding events in the city and provided a barometer of conditions outside the four walls of the prison cell.

Circumstances were not going well for General Olenga and his ragtag army. In contrast to their early advances throughout the country, the Simbas were now being subject to regular setbacks in their clashes with mercenary-led ANC forces. In Stanleyville, the tension was increasing. Lacking the skills of a diplomat, Gbenye had failed to persuade *any* of the surrounding African heads of state to recognize the People's Republic of Congo.

By the end of October, anti-American rhetoric by Gbenye and Olenga had increased, as had their actions against Belgians in the city. Following a major defeat near the town of Beni on the eastern border of the Congo, Gbenye declared a mythical invading Belgian army to be responsible for their loss. He rounded up scores of Belgian citizens – men, women and children – and sent them to the Hôtel des Chutes. The town's Indian, Pakistani and Greek residents increased their efforts to supply food to the detainees whose number had ballooned to more than 350.

On one of his visits to Doug Warren and his cellmates, Amin delivered a hand-drawn map of Stanleyville, showing the location of Central Prison, the main streets in town, and the hotels where other expatriates were being held. A star marked the location of the Rahman family's residence.

"If you ever find yourself free of guards and in need of sanctuary in the city, memorize this map so you can find your way to our place." "You'll be safe there."

He paused and looked at them all intensely. "My father insisted that I share this with you. Memorize and destroy it."

Over time, Amin became impressed with Doug Warren's character and with his calm demeanor. They appeared to have a stabilizing effect on the morale of his companions. With each new demand by the jailors, Doug was the first to step forward to negotiate in Lingala or French. Often, however, that resulted in him taking insults or blows intended for the group.

One evening, several soldiers, well lubricated with beer, entered cell number eight loudly proclaiming their intent to beat the prisoners, *"Tokobula les Américains." We shall beat the Americans.* When Doug blocked their way and questioned their actions, the lead soldier raised the butt of his rifle and brought it down hard on his back. The slender *mundele* was driven to his knees with the force of the blow, but as it hit him, the wooden rifle stock cracked and broke apart. The Simba soldiers quickly backed away in alarm at his indication of mystical power. *"Mundele wana azali na dawa makasi!" That white man has strong power!* They fled the cell.

Amin took note of both the courage and good fortune Doug possessed. *Nick's father is both capable and brave. That's some legacy he's passing on.*

With regular visits, Amin finally won over the confidence of Warren. He began to ask about his son, Nick. "What did you learn of my family in your airplane conversation?" he inquired of the young Pakistani one muggy afternoon. "Did Nick tell you anything about his life in Illinois? You may not know...his mother and I divorced soon after Independence. She has now remarried. So have I."

"Yes," Amin replied somberly, "he talked a good deal about his life in the States. Unfortunately, he did not have much positive to say about it nor about his mother and her new husband. He told me that his brother and sister were unhappy with their new life, as well."

Taking a risk, Amin concluded, "Apparently all three of them have a lot of questions about why you and their mother divorced and why they had not heard from you. Does he know about your new wife?"

"They did not hear from me because their mother wouldn't allow it; she destroyed my letters!" Doug shook his head in disgust.

He continued, frowning. "My divorce is a complicated thing, with many layers...it's difficult to describe, let alone defend. What is clear, however, is that Patty, my former wife, hated her life in Congo and eventually blamed me for being the source of her unhappiness. I disagree, but I will always feel badly about how it all turned out." Pausing, he volunteered, "For my part, I did not handle things well."

Doug Warren sighed deeply. "Frankly, I don't know if Nick knows about my remarriage. He must have learned of it by now. I'm sorry to admit that he did not learn of it from me. I have a lot of explaining to do when and if Nick and I ever see one another face-to-face."

Doug stared down at the plank on which he had placed one foot, leaning a bent elbow on his knee. A single drop of sweat coursed down his cheek. *The hot, humid prison cell...or is it the topic?* "I probably should have expected the divorce but it came as a surprise."

Doug paused to collect his thoughts before continuing his disclosures. "Following the chaos at Independence and the end of my marriage to Patty, I determined to begin again in the Congo, to set down roots here. An unexpected opportunity came about when a Belgian friend offered to sell me his coffee plantation."

The path that led to his marriage to Sarah was a bit more challenging to explain. "About that same time I renewed an acquaintance with Sarah. She grew up in the Litoko missionary community as a foster child. She was a bright, sweet and lovely young girl. She's as close to bicultural as a Congolese can be. Her marriage dissolved about the same time mine did. Our paths crossed and we found a lot of common ground. After a year or so our friendship became something more. We married two years ago. It's a good marriage but I have struggled with how to tell the kids. And Patty."

Amin listened carefully. He withheld commenting on Doug's disclosures. "Here are a few more things that might interest you from my conversation with Nick." He then shared what he had learned about Nick's college years, his summer work and how he had managed to arrange his travel to Congo. The few facts Amin had to reveal from his brief acquaintance with Nick were all new information to Doug.

As he listened to the descriptions of his eldest son's struggles to adapt in the U. S. and the efforts he had extended to meet with an absent father, with *him*, Doug's eyes brimmed with tears. They eventually overflowed, tears streaking down his anguished face.

Amin stopped mid-sentence, finally recognizing the obvious grief of the tormented father. He did not know what to say, so he just stopped talking.

Doug finally spoke. "I need to thank you, Amin. Thanks for coming here and talking with me about Nick. I can see now that my own pain clouded my judgment concerning my children. My absence from their lives was a grave error on my part. I abandoned them, left my children to deal their unhappy mother. What was I thinking? And Nick...his efforts to reach me...well, they are simply remarkable, courageous. Frankly...I'm feeling a bit overwhelmed just now."

The guard signaled for Amin to leave. As the door opened for his exit, Doug caught a brief glimpse past the gray prison walls; a bright orange-red frangipani tree was framed by the blue sky. Long after the cell door clanged shut his gaze remained focused beyond it.

CHAPTER 55
Kamina, November 1964

The 775-mile flight from Bumba to the BAKA base at Kamina was noisy and freezing for 51 Commando. Noses ran, fingers turned numb and men hunkered into their shoulders in the cold, bare fuselage. It took fully three-and-a-half hours to reach their destination since their flight path required several diversions by the Cuban pilots to avoid dangerous wind shear that accompanied billowing thunderheads. Such flight conditions were typical during the rainy season in Congo and by early November they were well into it. The small band of tough warriors were, to a man, relieved when the wheels of the DC4 finally touched down.

Nick Warren and Nasir Rahman were the last to climb down the aircraft steps and onto the unfamiliar tarmac. Strong smelling blacktop fumes and steam from the recent rain radiated from its surface. Lt. Wilson pointed toward the dorms where they would stay. The others had already headed in that direction.

"For now, you two stick with the men in our unit." Wilson stopped to light a smoke, taking a deep, satisfying drag. "I'm quite sure you'll be visited by Maj. Hoare soon. He likes to meet and approve all mercenary recruits, personally."

Nick and Nasir looked at one another. What kind of scrutiny were they in for?

The two new recruits threw their bags onto adjacent cots in the dorm and followed the others to the mess hall for lunch. Nick was still a bit nauseated from the bumpy flight so he only nibbled at his beans and gravy-covered rice.

The others in their unit appeared to be in fine spirits. Loud story-telling, joking and coarse laughter filled the large room. While 51 Commando's numbers had dwindled to twenty, Nick estimated that more than a hundred other men were seated around the long tables.

When they had nearly finished their meal, two huge muscled mercenaries appeared at the entrance to the mess hall. One called out in a deep, resonant voice: "Attention! Major Mike Hoare!"

The laughing and raucous noise ceased; only the scraping of feet and benches echoed across the huge room as the men scrambled to their feet and stood at attention. Nick and Nasir followed their lead. This immediate and respectful response by the otherwise undisciplined men surprised Nick.

Legendary mercenary leader, "Mad Mike" Hoare strode, shoulders back, chest out and jaw set, into the room between his beefy escorts. For a long moment he gazed around the room, as if taking in each individual, before he finally called out a firm, authoritative, *"At ease!"*

Hoare welcomed 51 Commando back from their successful campaign in the northwest.

"You bloody bastards really put it to the Simbas," His face beamed and eyes shone with pride. "You exceeded expectations. Only two of our company were lost, though I believe a few more from the other side went down."

This comment brought a murmur of laughter and smiles to his audience.

The Major then began listing the next assignments of the various Commando groups who were present. The only one that Nick focused on was Hoare's announcement that 51 Commando would be resupplied and expanded in number before being flown to Kindu. There, "Lima One," the Stanleyville column of nearly 200 vehicles was massing for a final push toward the Simba's capital and their principal objective: hostage rescue.

As Nick and Nasir exited the mess hall, a gravelly voice called out from behind, "You two! Hold up a minute. I'd like to have a word with you."

Startled, they spun around to see *The Man* himself, accompanied by the same two burly companions from the mess hall.

"Lt. Wilson tells me you are interested in signing on for the Stanleyville campaign. He informs me that you both speak Lingala and French and that each of you have a personal interest in joining us…to liberate family members being held in the city."

"Yes sir," Nick replied. "My father and Nasir's wife and children are among those being held in Stanleyville."

"How do I know you've got it in you to help us and not hinder our efforts?" The mercenary looked directly at them, hands on hips. "This is no picnic we're on. We can always use translators but what I really need on this march is *soldiers*, not tourists. How am I going to decide which you are?"

Major Hoare then glanced up at the group of soldiers standing nearby watching them. His face lit with a sudden inspiration.

"Clark and McClellen," he called to two gnarly looking hoodlums in the crowd. "Get your sorry asses over here on the double. I've got a little job for you."

Turning to Nick and his companion, he continued, with a wry smile, "Let's see if you can hold your own with these two in a little bare fisted street fight. That ought to serve as a good *toughness test* for you fellows."

With those words, a roar went up from the men standing nearby. *"Fight!"* The energy level spiked as the word spread. Quickly a large group formed around the four men facing off at the center.

"I wasn't expecting this," Nick muttered to Nasir.

"Me neither," Nasir crouched beside Nick, fists raised. "I guess we just give it our best shot."

Clark and McClellen charged their two opponents. Clark reached for Nick, but he dropped flat on the ground. His action was so swift that the first man's momentum carried him right into the young man's prone body. Unable to recover, Clark flew over him, sprawling face-first. Nick sprang up and leapt onto the mercenary's back wrapping his right arm around the man's thick neck.

Nasir was not as successful in dodging his opponent. He stepped to one side of the brawny warrior's charge but not fast enough. A glancing blow from McClellen's shoulder knocked the lighter Pakistani man off of his feet. As Nasir rose, the mercenary spun and kicked him, full force in the side of the face. Head snapping to one side, Nasir dropped like a sack of grain. He lay in an unconscious heap, blood trickling from his nose.

McClellen then turned to his partner, red faced and gagging from Nick's firm chokehold. One solid blow to the young man's head released his grip and put him down and out. Clark rubbed his neck. McClellen massaged his fist. He turned to Hoare with a smug smile.

"Anything else you want fixed, Major?" he quipped.

"Nah, that's good enough." Mad Mike reached down to help up a stunned Nick Warren, who was by then just beginning to regain his senses. Nasir remained still, lights out. Others reached down to pick him up. With this action he moaned, eyes not yet focused. Nasir's face was bleeding and beginning to swell. Someone found a wet cloth for Nick to place over a puffy eye that was nearly shut.

"Okay," the mercenary leader said with a wry smile, "I'd say you fellows showed us you can take punishment. And I see you're at least willing to try dishing it out as well, though that was a pathetic effort.

Get yourselves cleaned up and report to the quartermaster. He'll fix you up with what you need: uniforms and weapons. You'll have about 10 days to train with 51 Commando before you ship out."

As an afterthought Hoare added, "And you both had better make damn good use of it."

With that, Maj. Hoare turned on his heel and strode off without a backward glance.

"Welcome to our war, mates!" called out a cheerful McClellen over his shoulder as he headed off with his friends.

In some ways, the next ten days at BAKA felt more like ten months to Nick. He and his Pakistani comrade engaged in long hours of training. It was painful at first because of the membership test they had been subjected to and later, because of the unusually intense physical demands placed on them. Theirs was a crash course in combat strategy, teaching them how to become effective killers and how to avoid being killed.

Both of the new recruits could dissemble, clean and reassemble their weapons with their eyes closed. Well, not really...but that was the legendary goal they heard in the Sergeant's daily harangues. Nasir demonstrated surprising sharpshooting prowess during target practice drills. Nick was far less accurate but had still mastered the automatic firing features of his weapon. They each acquired hand-to-hand combat tricks and techniques.

"Clark and McClellen wouldn't have such an easy a time of it now," mused Nick, dusty and sweaty after wrestling commandos all morning.

One evening, Lts. Hogan and Wilson sat on their cots, chatting and cleaning their handguns. Wilson had inadvertently failed to clear the last live cartridge from the chamber of his pistol. While absentmindedly clicking the trigger the gun fired, severing a finger from his right hand. He was shipped out to Léo. Word soon arrived that he had headed home to South Africa.

According to Lt. Hogan, Wilson's parting words were: "So long, buddy. I'm done with bloodbaths. I've had plenty enough killing for one lifetime,"

Nick shuttered at that final statement by the professional soldier. *If that's his reaction, what am I getting into?*

The change of leadership in 51 Commando was significant. Lt. Hogan was a good friend of Crash Wilson, but since he had not been present at Lisala or Bumba, he was less familiar and less impressed with Nick and Nasir. His leadership style was distant, demanding and unsympathetic. This change was unsettling for both Nick and Nasir who were now expected to produce just as any other recruit.

CHAPTER 56
Kindu, November 1964

Nick, Nasir and their fellow 51 Commando colleagues, slung rifles and bags over their shoulders and climbed out of the DC4 that had ferried them from Kamina to Kindu. It was Wednesday the 17th of November, 1964. A large Mercedes truck waited to take these latest reinforcements to the staging area for Lima One. Their arrival supplied a last missing piece for the big push to Stanleyville.

As Nick rode into Kindu with his unit, there was something attractive, satisfying, even alluring about being part of a Band of Brothers, jostling along shoulder-to-shoulder with loaded weapons in hand, preparing to face a deadly threat together. The enemy would be intent on killing them but they would prevent that, saving each other's lives with the pull of a trigger, release of a grenade pin or thrust of a blade.

On the other hand, saving lives – his own as well as his comrades – would require *taking lives.* Killing someone had always seemed like the worst sin to Nick the missionary kid, the biggest violation of the Ten Commandments. Yet, in this setting, to Nick the mercenary, it seemed almost natural. Killing was *required* of him. In the heat of battle there would be no time to figure out whether an enemy's death was deserved or justified. *"Kill or be killed"* was the Congo mercenary mantra.

Then, there was the example and words of Ellie's friend, Aaron: *"Where do you get the idea, Nick, that we Christians are to kill our enemies?"*...or something like that. *Why does Aaron have to be such an idealist, anyhow?* Nick thought of himself as a Christian believer, but what exactly did he believe in? The horrors of Simba violence seemed to contradict Jesus's words, to neutralize the power of Divine authority over evil. *How should I put it all together? Can a person ever reconcile such things?*

*****

When they arrived at base camp, the mercenaries, who had just captured Kindu told of racing full-speed through the streets under heavy enemy fire ahead of the lumbering ANC trucks with machine guns blazing. Lima One forces had surprised the Simbas.

The rebels had fled in terror. Scores of them had clambered onto the bac near the Lualaba to escape across the river, but when its motor failed midstream, they had become sitting ducks. The mercenary guns onshore killed so many that the muddy brown waters flowed red with their blood.

General Olenga's own Mercedes had been discovered parked by the bac at the riverfront. Discovered and captured in the vehicle was his personal chauffer, dressed in his commander's uniform. Olenga was said to have escaped alive by exchanging clothes and hanging onto the side of the bac while the exposed soldiers on the deck were slaughtered.

There were other tales of dramatic hostage rescues, harrowing ambushes, firefights and numerous near disasters all on the road to Kindu. The combat veterans relished the opportunity to embellish their tales to entertain and impress the 51 Commando newcomers.

The story telling continued uninterrupted until a sudden shout went up from ANC soldiers across the field. It was dark by then but a bright blaze of fire had erupted from the back of a big truck, lighting up the area. One of the troops had poured petrol on a cooking fire and this had set the truck's canvas canopy ablaze. An alarm arose because the bed of the truck was filled with ammunition.

BOOM! The vehicle was destroyed in a huge explosion accompanied by fireworks. It served as an unintended warning shot for enemy forces anywhere within 20-miles.

By the time the fire and excitement had died down, the two novice mercenaries were more than ready to turn in for the night. As they opened their bedrolls Nasir flicked a glance at his partner, brow deeply furrowed. "Are you ready for all this, Nick? I'm not so sure I am."

Nick's head was spinning. *How many innocent bystanders were stacked at the side of the road? How many rebels lay slaughtered at the bottom of the river? Are we supposed to applaud this, to join in on this?*

"Me neither" was all he could murmur out loud.

*****

At first light the next morning a seventy-vehicle Lima One caravan – more to follow later – departed Kindu in a cloud of diesel and fine red Maniema dust, heading for their next objective, the town of Punia 135 miles away. Just 20 miles beyond lay the last major obstacle before their final charge into Stanleyville: the Lowa River crossing.

The road surface was good, but periodic showers and the long line of churning vehicles created deep mud bogs that slowed their progress. Winches were employed to extract the trucks and jeeps mired in the deep, clinging muck.

There were few villages along the thickly forested route and it was just as well for any inhabitants. Any parked vehicle, suspicious clump of grass or mud hut too close to the road triggered the caravan's merciless machine guns. They blazed away, shooting first, checking later. Occasional village dwellings the nervous column came upon were deserted. In some cases cooking fires were still smoking and in others, freshly gunned residents lay in pools of their own blood. Lima One was not a spectator-welcoming parade.

The column finally stopped for the night, some 20 miles shy of Punia. Lt. Hogan decided to take a fighting patrol out in search of an enemy truck to replace the one lost the previous night. Nick was among the select few who were "volunteered" to join him.

The jeepload of mercenaries returned an hour's drive back to a sharp curve in the road. It was there they set up their ambush.

Not long after midnight, the lights of a big Mercedes Benz truck flickered through the trees approaching the mercenaries' position. As it slowed for the curve, Lt. Hogan stepped into the middle of the road directly into the truck's headlights, holding one hand up. Its brakes squealing, the huge vehicle slid to a stop. When the driver jumped out, Hogan raised his pistol and shot him. The truck's surprised and alarmed passengers scrambled, jumping out of the back, as the mercenary leader yelled, *"Now! Let 'em have it, mates."*

Hidden patrol members opened up with their automatic weapons and the quiet forest roared with gunfire. It lasted no more than a minute. Then, all was silent. All except for a low moan near the tailgate of the truck. One last BANG and then...total silence. The four members of the patrol cautiously emerged from their hiding places to view the results.

Eight rebel soldiers lay crumpled and still in the truck's headlights. Nick's heart was racing. He had taken down two, maybe three of the enemy. They were his first kills. He was now official, a full-fledged soldier, a success.

Or *was* he?

Lt. Hogan was exuberant. Back-slapping his fellow patrol members, he praised their success. "Wait 'til the Major sees this prize," he declared. Then, "Okay, let's head back to the column, men. Morning comes early."

With that, Hogan climbed up into the cab of the big Mercedes truck and fired up its diesel engine. In the dark no one noticed the hot tears that streamed down Nick's cheeks.

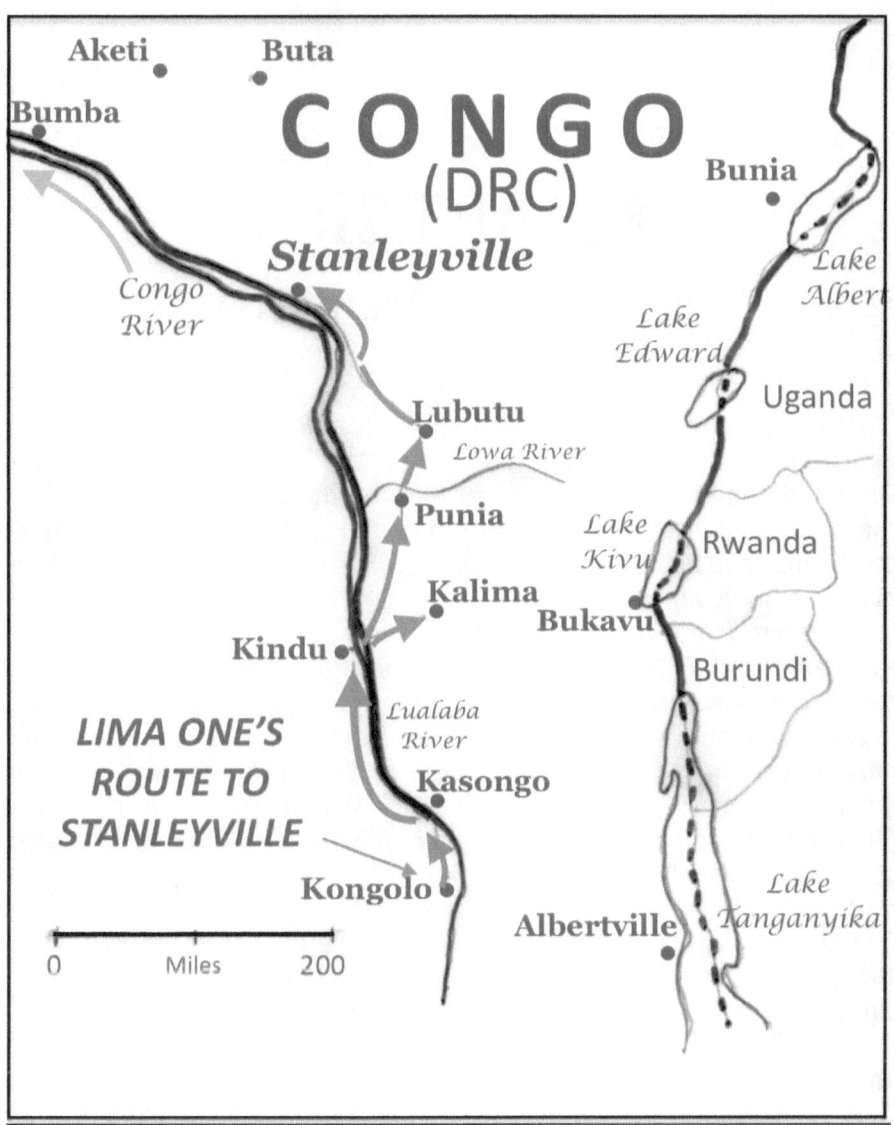

MAP 5 - Lima One's Route to Stanleyville

CHAPTER 57
Stanleyville, November 1964

Time seemed to stand as still as the humid air in the confines of Central Prison's cell number eight. It was the first of November, 1964. Doug Warren leaned back, elbows out and hands behind his head on the hard plank that served as both bed and seat. He rested, staring at the beams and rusty tin roof far above. His mind was not as inert as his body, however.

Jumping from present discomforts to past distresses, for the thousandth time, Doug reflected on his first marriage: the unrelenting frustrations, conflicts and eventual betrayals leading to divorce and separation from his family. *How could I have been so slow to recognize impending disaster? Why didn't I aggressively seek help for Patty, for our marriage? What should I have done? Why had I passively allowed Patty to dictate the final outcome? Why hadn't I considered the children's needs? What should I do now? Will there even be a future for me?* He could barely breathe in the jail cell's sweltering heat.

Footsteps approached in the hallway. The cell door creaked open, two young white men entered and the door clanged shut behind them. Doug was up and on his feet before any of his cellmates.

"Well, whom do I have the pleasure of welcoming to our humble abode?" he quipped in a mock formal greeting.

The two newcomers looked scared and confused, glancing around the filthy cell and appraising its seven scruffy looking occupants. Finally, the younger man, who appeared to be about the age of Doug's son, spoke up.

"My name is Gene Bergman and this is Jon Snyder. I'm from California and he is from Oregon. We are both Mennonite CO's doing alternate service at the Protestant University. I'm a builder and Jon is the university's bookkeeper."

The others in the cell introduced themselves and helped their new roommates find places to settle in. Two planks were swept off with dried palm leaf brooms, sprayed with insecticide and repositioned. Blankets were found and distributed.

"How many more Americans are still out there?" wondered Doug out loud to no one in particular.

*****

Four days later, Nov. 5, 1964, the town of Kindu, 250 miles south of Stanleyville fell to the combined forces of Lima One. It was a substantial victory, one that both encouraged and frightened the residents of cell eight. Kindu was General Olenga's hometown. That fact explained his special interest in its defense. The level of threat in the rhetoric echoing from Radio Stanleyville escalated through the hallways of Central Prison. The broadcasts condemned the mercenaries, the *mundele* allies of the ANC forces. America was singled out as the primary source of the Simbas' humiliating defeat.

While news of approaching friendly forces gave hope to the worried captives, the increasing agitation of their jailers raised the likelihood they would not be allowed to survive to be rescued.

What the nine prisoners could not know was that key decisions addressing this matter – their survival – were underway half a world away. U.S. Undersecretary of State, W. Averell Harriman met with Belgian's Foreign Minister, Paul-Henri Spaak, and by November 8 the two had agreed to launch a joint rescue effort to free the hundreds of foreign nationals being held by the rebels in Stanleyville.

By November 13 a military conference had convened and plans were firmed up for a complex operation, code-named *"Dragon Rouge."* Belgian Colonel Charles Laurent, a veteran of Congo operations, including dramatic rescue missions following the nation's independence in 1960, would lead the expedition. Twelve U.S. aircraft would transport 320 Special Forces, Belgian paratroopers lightly but lethally armed, to conduct a lightning fast raid and rescue the hostages. Mercenary-led Lima One forces would simultaneously strike and secure control of the city. That was the plan.

The 6 p.m. Radio Stanleyville broadcast on Saturday, November 14, carried chilling news for Central Prison's American detainees and a deadly serious announcement for two in particular: Dr. Paul Carlson and Doug Warren. The report said that lawyers had represented the two before a "war council tribunal" and that they had been officially sentenced to death as spies and war criminals. U.S. consul Michael Holt was named to negotiate their fate.

This announcement came as a surprise to the key subjects who had had no lawyer consultation and no such trial.

The next day, the newspaper *Le Martyr*, in a follow up piece, indicated that all Belgians and Americans being held would be "slaughtered" at the first sign of any bombardment of the city by outside forces. It was clear that Stanleyville's expatriate hostages were a last trump card, one presently being turned.

On Wednesday November 18, the nine Americans were marched out of their cell in the Central Prison and packed into two vehicles: a canvas covered jeep and a VW. To their questions about where they were being taken, the driver simply answered with a deadly smile. "I'm taking you to the Lumumba Monument to be killed."

Gene Bergman's response to the others was a practical one: "I sure hope if this is the end, that it comes fast. I don't want to have to first lose a hand or foot."

When the two vehicles crowded with *mundeles* reached their destination the men discovered a huge, unruly crowd had gathered. A roar went up as the mob caught sight of the white faces. Those near the Americans shouted insults and tried to hit, stab or burn them with cigarettes.

Looking out of the vehicles, the tightly packed Americans saw General Olenga himself pushing his way through the crowd. When he finally arrived at the front, Olenga immediately became engaged in a heated exchange with the Simba officer in charge of the prisoners. A serious difference of opinion ended with the enigmatic General felling the contentious officer with a huge right-handed blow. He then gave orders to the downed leader's subordinates that they should return the *mundeles* to their cell.

Michael Hoyt leaned forward and in a low voice – in English – offered an interpretation to his relieved companions: "My best guess is that this last minute reprieve was all about self interest not mercy. Olenga no doubt determined that appeasing the crowd by executing us would also remove the last restraint from the forces closing in on him. He's hedging his bet."

Paul Carlson closed his eyes. "Thank you, God!"

General Nicolas Olenga's action halting the execution of the Americans was the last time he was seen in Stanleyville. Some thought he had left to lead his troops against the advance of Lima One. There were other indications, however, that calculating defeat, he fled the country.

On Friday, November 20, Doug and his cellmates along with 35 Belgians held in Central Prison were summoned by their captors and lined up outside the walls. "Now what?" they wondered. The line of *mundeles* was marched the three blocks through the city to the

Victoria Residence where other Belgians and Americans were being assembled. The mood of the growing numbers of whites was dark.

The next morning, Saturday, November 21, yet another puzzling development faced the captives. President Gbenye was in a rage at the fall of Punia, a town on Lima One's march to Stanleyville. "The American spies will die," he declared again and again on local radio.

Two vehicles, a bus and a truck, were backed up to the hotel. Roughly half, 110, of the 200 men present were packed into the transports to be taken outside the city, blocking any hostage rescue effort. Wives and children wailed, husbands and fathers called out with tearful eyes last "I love yous" as the vehicles chugged away from the hotel to an unknown location and fate.

The men were packed into the bus so tightly they could hardly breathe. Paul Carlson managed to mutter into Doug Warren's ear. "From the proverbial lions' den to the fire. How many more tests? How is this going to end?"

"Keep praying, Paul. We're not in control here."

A short way out of town, however, one of the vehicles broke down. The Simbas located a Belgian prisoner who was a mechanic and ordered him to repair it. He agreed, but instead, managed to permanently disable the engine. After nearly 12 hours, plans were reversed. Other trucks returned the men to the hotel.

Tension was mounting in Stanleyville. Safety or suffering...which would it be?

CHAPTER 58
Stanleyville, November 1964

It was the morning of November 24, 1964 and Amin was once again the first of his family to rise. He had given up on sleep, finding comfort in a fresh pot of coffee he had brewed as the gray of predawn gave way to the pastel colors of sunrise.

The news reports from Radio Stanleyville's daily rants as well as those from whispered rumors coincided: the mercenary-led ANC was on its way, rapidly approaching. *Something* life-changing was descending on the city and its inhabitants. Would it lead to rescue and relief or death and destruction? That question was the source of Amin's present insomnia.

He leaned on the porch pillar, sipping the steaming drink, calming his troubled thoughts under a chorus of twittering, chirping, warbling birds in the nearby trees. Down the street a neighbor's rooster crowed, familiar and comforting morning sounds, all.

The humming began as a low sound that slid beneath the chattering and crowing of the waking city. It grew until Amin stood up straight and cocked his head to better take it in. It was coming right in his direction!

He set down his coffee cup and ran to the middle of the yard where the big mango trees did not block his view. The humming grew to a roar as a huge four-engine plane thundered overhead. It was flying low, emitting a din that scattered the panicked birds. Then a second, third and two more followed: five planes roared by in the direction of the airport.

"It's begun!" said Amin out loud. He looked at his watch. It was just past six a.m.

Reacting more by instinct than plan, Amin headed off in the direction of the airport over a mile to the west. At the time, he couldn't have explained why he took this action; it was a dangerous move and it had no clear purpose other than to satisfy his curiosity.

He avoided the main streets frequented by the Simbas and ran through familiar back yards and alleys, alert to any others moving about in the early morning light. As Amin hurried past the former homes of the city's expatriates, the five-plane armada roared back overhead. By now, most of the city was awake; dogs barked, parrots shrieked and then he heard it clearly...the sound of weapons firing!

Ratta-tat-tat, whump, whump! Those sounds brought Amin to an abrupt stop. *What was I thinking?* He quickly turned on his heel and headed back for home, the sounds of shooting closing in behind him.

*****

What Amin heard but could not see was the launch of operation *Dragon Rouge*. Within 80 seconds all 320 Belgian Special Forces paratroopers had jumped from five U.S. piloted C-130E aircraft flying low at just 700 feet so that the soldiers' drop time would be minimal, and so they would not be scattered too widely in landing. The paratroopers touched the ground after just 40 seconds hang time. They were spread over slightly more than a mile onto the city's airport runway and adjacent golf course. It was a textbook precise drop, no casualties.

The five C-130Es then made a second pass to airdrop weapons, ammunition and two armored Land Rovers affixed with three machine guns each. The paratroopers secured and cleared the airfield of rebel resistance and of obstacles that had littered the runway to prevent landings. As the first of the soldiers began working their way towards the city under fire, street-by-street, the next wave of four C-130Es landed with still more troops and equipment. Only 45 minutes had lapsed.

One of the Belgian paratroopers charged with clearing the airport control tower came upon a constantly ringing phone. Hesitantly, he picked it up. A frantic Belgian resident from the central city was on the other end. "Hurry," he blurted to the astonished soldier, "the Simbas have assembled all the white people outside of the Victoria Residence. Come quickly!"

By the time Amin neared home more than an hour had passed since the planes first roared overhead. As he approached his neighborhood, he could see between the trees and houses that the next street over, *Avenue Sargent Ketele*, was filled with people. This street ran past the Victoria Residence where most of the Belgian and American hostages had been held. Amin crouched between two thick poinsettia bushes to watch.

Seated in the middle of the street, three abreast, were 250 Europeans, in columns that wound around the corner of the intersection. They included men, women and children, some just infants. A dozen or more

Simbas armed with automatic weapons stood along the line. Both fear and menace were reflected in their faces.

Amin recognized his friends, the Americans, sitting in the middle of the line: Warren, Carlson, Hoyt, Grinwis and the others from cell number eight. The short, portly Simba Colonel Joseph Opepe stood at the front of the column. He was arguing with other rebels. The sound of intense bursts of automatic gunfire grew ever louder, and closer.

Without warning, one of the teenage Simbas near Opepe turned and began firing into the assembled group. As if by signal, his fellow guards began spraying the seated crowd with gunfire as well. A score of victims fell, dead or mortally wounded. Others moaned in pain, blood pooling or spurting from their wounds.

A small pause in the shooting triggered some sort of flight instinct among the hostages. Scrambling to their feet, they began running in all directions. Amin saw Jon Snyder and two other men dash across the street in the direction of a small yellow house. Paul Carlson followed close behind them.

The confusion, gunfire, screams and chaos continued. The young Asian man watched in shock, frozen to his hiding spot, the sounds, sights and smells of horror overwhelming his senses.

The three Americans crossed the street, leapt over a low wall, one after the other and ran into the yellow residence. Dr. Carlson hesitated at first and then turned, starting after them over the wall. A young Simba, spying the doctor, directed a hail of gunfire his way. Paul Carlson managed one leg up on the wall; it slid off and he crumpled in a heap, dead.

Hoyt, Grinwis and Warren dashed to the opposite side of the street in the direction of Amin. Simbas were yelling, shooting and beginning to flee. Paratroopers had appeared at the far end of the street and escape, rather than slaughter, became the rebels' top priority.

A Belgian man fell, shot in the back between the three fleeing Americans. They split, Hoyt ducking behind a wall, Grinwis diving into an open door, a servant's toilet at the rear of a house. Warren fled at full speed past the abandoned residence beside Amin's vantage point.

It took the young Pakistani almost three blocks of adrenalin-fueled chasing to draw close enough to Doug Warren's frantic flight, calling out his name to catch up to him. "Amin? What in the..." was all Doug got out.

"Follow me. You'll be safe at my house," Amin gasped. Breathless, he pointed in the direction of his home and signaled for Doug to follow.

Sporadic gunfire burst around them as the two men ducked beneath windows, dashed through back yards and around empty residences, finally arriving at the Rahman family home.

Amin's father, watching for any sign of his missing son, was relieved at his approach. He unlocked and opened the front door for the two men, before banging the sturdy metal barrier shut behind them. It would be no easy task for Simbas to break into this house, guns or not.

"Welcome to our home." The elder Rahman's smile a hint of irony. "It seems you have brought a bit of excitement into our dull lives, Mr. Warren."

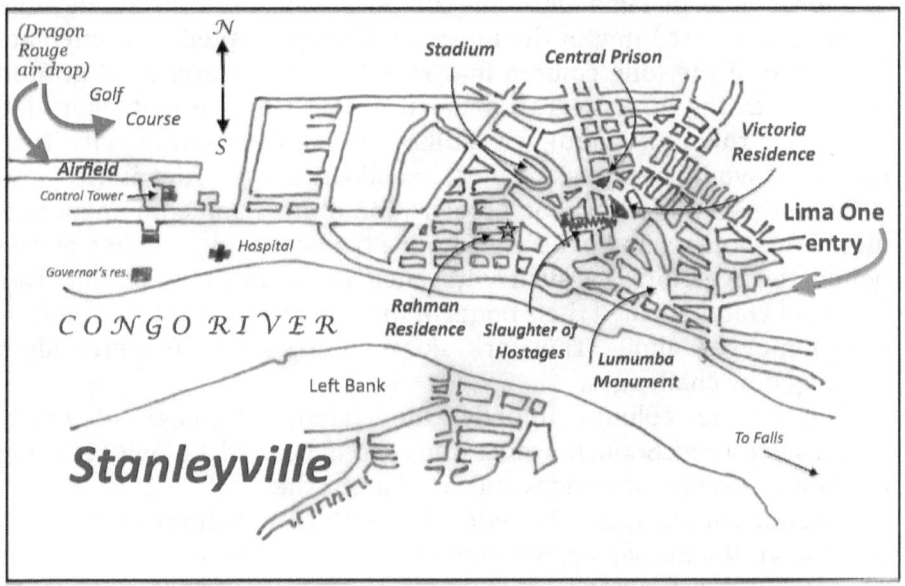

MAP 6 - Stanleyville City Map

CHAPTER 59
Stanleyville, November 1964

Word came to Lima One that the paratroop drop on Stanleyville would begin first thing in the morning. That prompted an immediate departure of the long column in a race to link the arrival of ground troops with the airdrop. The departure point for the mercenary-led forces, the town of Lubutu, was still 60 long miles from the city. Nick realized it would be a push, at best, to make that 6 a.m. deadline.

Lima One's mid-afternoon acceleration of men and equipment was met with another kind of acceleration: a tropical deluge. Sheets of rain pelted the warriors' caravan with such force and torrent that two inches of water sloshed their boots in the open jeeps and truck beds as they lumbered along. The dark skies soon closed fully into night creating new challenges.

The rescue column initially sped along stretches of newly constructed road. Soon, however, the road narrowed and with it, came the first of a series of villages and rebel ambushes.

An ammunition-filled Mercedes blocked the road at the first spot. It was blown up. Sniper fire greeted them at the second village. It was silenced with a furious machinegun barrage from the lead armored truck. At the third village, the armored vehicles were allowed to pass before heavy gunfire rained down on the thin-skinned trucks filled with soldiers. The village was nearly leveled by return fire from Lima One vehicles up and down the line.

It was at that point that Maj. Hoare and the other convoy leaders called a halt to wait for daylight. Further progress in the pitch black driving rain was far too risky. They burned the village to the ground and remained parked in the road to wait for morning light. It was by then 3:30 a.m. They still had another 20 miles to go. The dawn deadline would not be met.

It was the most miserable night of Nick Warren's young life. He and Nasir sat hunched under the bed of a huge Mercedes Benz truck, wet, tired and hungry. *This is just unbelievably awful*, Nick thought. Just beyond the edge of the truck, waves of soft roaring sounded from sheets of rain. Rivers of mud flowed around them. The two friends leaned against a four-foot high tire, resting, soaking, waiting for morning. The wetness, discomfort, and intermittent crashes of thunder combined with their keyed-up emotions, to drive away any real prospect of sleep.

Since his first armed encounter, Nick had gained full peer recognition as a mercenary combatant. He had lost count in the past few days how many times they had taken fire, how many rounds he had loosed in return. He had no idea what the exact body count was, how many Simbas had been killed on this deadly journey. The mercenaries' practice of spraying foliage, huts, grass clumps and fleeing people obscured such specifics.

But Nick had demonstrated he could be counted on to do his part. He was no cowering outsider now. What *did* haunt his fitful dreams, however, during any rare moments of sleep were images of the individuals he knew he had killed. He knew it because he had watched each one fall and die.

In moments like this when Nick's thoughts returned to the grim role he had embraced, a deep sinking feeling came over him. Sometimes he became so nauseated he had to turn aside and retch. "Just a touch of malaria," he would assure his comrades.

Most often, at times like those, Nick thought of Aaron. What would he eventually say to him? He could never tell him about all of this. Yet, still...it was bringing them closer; it was part of rescuing him and Ellie; it was necessary action.

He sighed deeply. *Aaron would never buy that.*

A sickening thought rose ever so quickly to mind: *I'm not so sure I buy it, either.*

A cold shiver shook Nick as he interrupted these troubling thoughts and turned his attention to Nasir. "It shouldn't be long now," he offered. "Stanley in the morning! You know the city. Is our approach going to bring us anywhere near your uncle's home?"

"Actually, it is, Nick," returned his companion, rousing slightly. "We'll be entering the city from the east. Our first test will come from Olenga's headquarters, Camp Ketele, at the very edge of town. The Rahman home is less than a mile further on, near the city center. It's close to the Victoria hotel where the radio said the hostages are being held. I'm anxious to get going, but truthfully I'm more than just a little scared, too. This could turn out *bad*, bloody bad. I just hope my family is safe."

"I know what you mean," confessed Nick, "and I just hope we get there in time."

It was close to 11 a.m. when Lima One rolled into Stanleyville. Bracing for a huge battle, they were astounded to find Camp Katele abandoned. The first vehicles rolling up to the gate discovered a Belgian paratrooper casually resting in the grass. He waved a friendly greeting and pointed toward the camp, *"Ils sont partis, mes amis."* They have departed, my friends.

While the main column continued west through the city towards the airport, Maj. Hoare sent his mercenary squads in various directions. Nick and Nasir's unit, on foot, followed a machinegun-mounted jeep heading toward the Victoria Residence. Almost immediately, they came under fire from fleeing Simbas.

Automatic weapons blasted at them from several directions. The heaviest fire came from a vacant whitewashed bungalow beside the street. Crouching low, Nasir dashed for the cover of a huge mango tree in front of the house. Nick followed close behind.

As they scouted out their next move, two loud "thunks" shattered the bark close to their heads. Nick spun in time to see a young rebel slip from behind a tree, kneel and take aim again.

The shots fired simultaneously.

The young rebel spun, flinging his weapon into the air as Nick's bullet caught him in the chest. Nick let out a loud groan. The Simba's bullet slammed him back against the tree trunk. Nasir fired a blast at their enemy but his bullets only caused the lifeless body to shudder at impact.

"Nick! How bad is it?" cried his anxious friend, bending over him. Bullets continued to zing past their cover from the bungalow.

Nick groaned, grasping his shoulder. Blood ran through his fingers and down his right arm. His left arm hung limp, shoulder sloping at a strange angle. He gasped. "It's my shoulder. I think it broke my shoulder blade."

Nasir looked around. The rest of their squad had moved on past the bungalow and were advancing down the street. They were out of earshot. He quickly came to a decision.

"Two blocks, Nick. Can you make it that far? We are only two blocks from my uncle's place. We'll be safe there while we wait for help."

Nick nodded. "Let's do it."

Nasir first took off his belt and, securing Nick's arm across his chest, cinched it down. He then emptied his bullet clip in the direction of the house as the two men stumbled from cover to cover: tree trunk to wall to vacant house. Half supporting him, Nasir guided his wounded friend down the street, as they worked their way through the familiar neighborhood.

"There! That's it," he said at last. They hastened across a final yard and up to the porch of the big house. Nick, pale and fading, stumbled up the steps, nearly unconscious from the pain and loss of blood. Nasir pounded on the door. "Help! Quickly, Uncle."

Amin Rahman peered around the edges of the porch window. The *click* of the lock followed.

"Nasir...it's you! And Nick!" he called out in surprise as he flung open the heavy metal door.

From behind Amin came a familiar voice, one that Nick had not heard in four years.

"Nick?"

But he still did not hear it. Nick had collapsed, unconscious.

CHAPTER 60
Stanleyville, November 1964

Nick was carried to a back bedroom; his shirt was cut away and clean water, alcohol and bandages were collected. Doug Warren bent over his unconscious son, worry and anguish clouding his eyes, while Amin's mother worked quickly and expertly to clean the young man's raw, oozing wound.

"It appears the bullet passed all the way through," Mrs. Rahman observed quietly, "but your son's collarbone is shattered. It will need to be repaired. Thankfully, no major arteries were severed." She carefully bandaged the open wound and secured Nick's arm so it would not move.

"That's a relief, for sure," Doug murmured. "I wonder how soon we can get help. We have nothing for his pain. We've got to get him to a doctor."

Doug remained focused on his son, as if he might somehow disappear if he looked away. He still couldn't fully grasp Nick's unexpected arrival; he was actually *here*, he could touch him!

In the next room another kind of reunion was taking place, but it was every bit as joyous as the Warren's meeting was worrisome. Nasir was trying to hug his wife while both of his young children's arms were wrapped around his neck, feet dangling in the air. They had burst into the room upon hearing their father's voice for the first time in months. They had leaped onto him and were not about to let go.

Tears streamed down Nasir's cheeks. He was weeping and laughing at the same time. His wife had buried her head in his chest, arms encircling both the children and her beloved husband. It was certainly *their* special moment and no one present had any desire to interrupt it.

The interruption came, however, not from within but from outside the house. Loud pounding resonated from the front door.

A booming male voice called out at full volume. *"Attention, dans la maison. Sortir vite. Forces spéciales belges ici."*

A red bereted head appeared at the porch window. Amin unlocked the door and quick evacuation negotiations took place between the huge, thick-necked Belgian soldier and the occupants of the house. He spoke rapidly into a portable radio carried by a comrade before heading off for the next house, leaving one of his team behind to guard the occupants.

Amin's father calmly but firmly addressed the anxious circle of faces. "I told him we have a wounded person in need of transport. He sent for a vehicle. We have just five minutes to gather a few things: one bag only per person. We are being taken to the airport under guard and will be flown on to Léopoldville. Let's say farewell to our Stanleyville home. We must hurry."

Within five minutes, two vehicles skidded to a stop in front of the Rahman's porch. Soldiers rushed in with a stretcher and whisked Nick out and into the back of a covered pickup. The lead Minerva Land Rover was armored and equipped with three medium class machineguns. Doug, unwilling to leave his son's side, sat close to his head while the rest of the Rahman clan, children and adults, scrambled into the back of the vehicle.

"Tenir fermement, nous allons rapidement!" The driver urged his passengers to hang on tight as they roared off towards the airport. The machineguns' intermittent chatter and the roar of the engines drowned out most conversation on the short but hazardous drive. The stunned passengers kept silent, heads down.

The roaring motor and gunshots roused the half-conscious Nick Warren. He groaned in pain and struggled to look around. His father's face appeared before him.

"Dad!" he croaked in surprise. "It's you! I've finally found you. Or, wait...did you find me?" He puzzled, glancing about in confusion.

Overjoyed at his son's first conscious words, Doug hugged him before a wince and moan that reminded him not to.

"Nick, my boy...I'm so relieved. I'm...I'm so glad, I..." words failed him as emotions took over. For a long minute he just held onto Nick's outstretched arm, both of them tearful. When he finally regained some control, Doug held his son's head and shoulder still on the swaying canvas litter.

"We have much to say to one another, Nick." Doug spoke into his son's ear over the road noise. "I have a lot to atone for and also a lot of catching up to do. But let's first get you healed up, okay, son?"

Nick just nodded, the pain and emotion robbing any further reply.

*****

When the two-vehicle caravan reached the airfield the scene was chaotic. Three C-130Es sat on the runway, engines turning. More planes circled overhead waiting to land. Columns of Europeans and Asians escorted by paratroopers arrived in groups of fifty to a hundred or more. Jeeps and Land Rovers such as the Warren and Rahman's transport, roared in with wounded hostages, then headed back to the city. Medical personnel triaged the wounded while others positioned the dead into rows. Crying, moaning, rejoicing at discovering friends and family mixed with shouted orders, a cacophony of sound.

Over all the noise and motion was the ratta-tat-tat of machinegun fire from Simba rebels still hidden in the surrounding forest and the steady pulse of heavy return fire from the Belgian Special Forces, now reinforced by ANC from Lima One.

By the time the Warrens and Rahmans arrived, the first planes had already filled and departed. The most severely wounded from the Victoria slaughter were among the first to leave. Nick was given morphine to ease his pain. He and his father waited in the shade of the hanger with other wounded to be summoned for the next flight.

Doug watched a group of fifty nuns and priests, both Europeans and Congolese, walk slowly towards one of the idling planes. There was something familiar about one of the nuns in the group. They were all dressed alike in white habits, but one in particular caught his eye. *What is it about that one? Is it the way she carries herself? Is it her blonde hair – the only blonde in the group?*

Doug turned to a Belgian lady next to him. "Who are those priests and nuns?" He pointed toward the receding group. "Where did they come from?"

"Ils sont de la mission du Sacré-Cœur ici à Stanleyville," she replied. *From Stanleyville?* Recognition suddenly flashed across his face.

"Ellie!" he shouted, starting off at once in the direction of the line. "Ellie...is that you? *Ellie!"*

Doug was by then running at full stride toward the shuffling line of nuns and priests. At the sound of his father's shout, Nick sat up. He rose to his feet on wobbly legs, eyes fixed on the column of evacuees.

As the line approached the plane, one of them – the young blonde – stopped, her face turned toward the man heading for her, yelling.

Ellie gasped. Both hands flew open wide and with a squeal of delight, sandals flopping and robe flapping, she ran straight into Doug's outstretched arms. Catching her in the air, he spun her around and the two hugged one another tightly until it seemed they would burst.

Meanwhile, Nick's heart had nearly stopped as he recognized his missing friend. Could it really be *Ellie*? It now felt like his heart would explode in his chest. Nick stumbled forward, but in doing so his legs gave out. He dropped to his knees.

The joyous delight on Ellie's face quickly turned to dismay as she looked past Doug to see Nick stumble and fall.

"*Nick!*" she screamed, tearing from Doug's welcome arms to dash toward her fallen friend.

"Nick, you're hurt. What's happened? I told myself I just couldn't bear it if something happened to *you* as well," she blurted out. Falling to her knees she wrapped her arms about him.

Weak from blood loss and groggy from morphine-dulled pain, Nick managed a weak smile and a question: "*As well?* ...What's happened to Aaron?"

"Oh, Nick," Ellie replied.

And he knew.

CHAPTER 61
Léopoldville, November 1964

Nick's morphine-slurred demand to know about Aaron's death was interrupted by the sudden appearance of Major Mike Hoare. As Nick and Nasir's commander, his orders dictated what would happen next in their lives. The Major's combat-hardened eyes softened in recognition as he strode up to Nick, lying prone on the cot.

"Well, young man, it appears you got all you bargained for and more, on that enlistment request of yours." He patted Nick's healthy shoulder.

"You must be the elusive father he was searching for, the famous 'Captain Warren' we heard about on Radio Stanley." He shook Doug's hand. "Your son proved himself to be quite the soldier on our march from Kindu. You can be proud of him."

Doug replied, respectfully, a bit in awe of the famous warrior, "The 'Captain' thing was just a Simba lie. I'm no soldier, that's for sure." He continued, "I have always been proud of Nick but never more than now. What he went through to reach me no son should ever attempt...no father should ever expect. I'm amazed, overwhelmed, grateful."

Hoare appeared a bit uncomfortable with the emotional tone of the exchange. He proceeded in a more authoritative voice. "I've decided to release your son and his friend Nasir from their service obligation to 51 Commando. His medical needs will still be covered, however," he added.

"The two young men fulfilled their duties very nicely. I believe some charity is warranted here in light of what each of their families have been through, what *you've* been through, Mr. Warren."

Maj. Hoare had been addressing Doug, but he shifted his attention to Ellie who was singularly focused on Nick, leaning over him with a distressed expression on her face.

"And you must be the young friend I heard about... the girl from Lisala."

Ellie flicked a glance and a nod at Hoare, returning her worried gaze to the blurry-eyed Nick, who at that point appeared to be fading in and out of consciousness.

"I was sorry to hear of the loss of your other companion, young lady, and for all you've had to endure. But I'm pleased to see you here together with your friends once again."

He turned to leave, adding, "Safe travels to Léo and beyond." With that, Maj. Hoare strode off, escorted by two of his aides.

One of the priests from *Mission Sacré-Cœur*, hurried up to them from the plane, intending to summon Ellie. Sister Beatrice accompanied him, but when they recognized the reunion taking place the two quickly shifted purpose, extending their blessings to the young woman they had come to love and respect.

"You must stay with your friends and accompany them to Léo," the sister said after being introduced to Nick and his father, "But know that we will all miss you greatly, dear girl. Don't forget us, will you?"

Ellie embraced them both warmly. "Forgetting all of you would be impossible. Impossible! I promise I'll search you out in Léopoldville when things get settled."

*****

The loud roar of the four turboprop engines reverberating in the cavernous interior of the C-130 made conversation difficult, though not impossible during the three-hour flight to Léopoldville.

Shortly after they were airborne, a nurse stopped by Nick's cot and, finding him in considerable agony, administered another dose of morphine. With that, he slipped into a painless sleep.

Doug and Ellie had been sitting across from one another, she kneeling by Nick's head and he sitting on the bench that ran along the wall. He patted the space beside him, inviting her to move to a more comfortable spot now that Nick was asleep.

In addition to being noisy, the plane's rear section where the wounded were situated was also chilly and drafty. Doug wrapped a spare blanket and a comforting arm around Ellie. She leaned into him, savoring the sense of security and familiarity.

"Would you like to tell me about Aaron and what happened with you...how you came to be with the Sacred Heart nuns?" Doug asked after a while. "These are not easy things to talk about, I realize, so if now is not the right time or if you are not up to it, that's OK, too, Ellie," he added in a gentle tone.

Beginning with their rough MAF landing at Litoko, Ellie highlighted the events of the previous months' journey and their impact on her. Once the adventure had begun, she underscored, there was no turning back.

The ANC roadblocks and Simba capture were terrifying, she contended. "I found myself questioning God. How could this be happening and why didn't He answer our prayers for rescue? Aaron was perhaps the most consistent in trusting God during our trials."

"What about Nick?" Doug asked.

"Well, he was more about planning our escape, though he called for prayer on several occasions."

"It was when the four of us escaped our captors at Lisala and when Aaron and I were recaptured," Ellie noted, "that I became the most overwhelmed. I felt so helpless. I wondered where God was and why He had abandoned me, abandoned us."

"What was Aaron's reaction? You said he seemed most consistent in his faith."

"Aaron kept insisting that God is not some department store Santa. He is sovereign. His ways are not ours and His view of adversity differs from ours. I didn't grasp these ideas at the time, but later the truth of his words became real to me."

"How did you and Aaron get separated from Nick and Masemba in the first place?" Doug shifted his seat and repositioned the blanket on Ellie's shoulders.

"I suppose that question highlights a difference between the guys. Being action oriented, Nick grabbed a gun and used it to keep the Simbas away. Aaron adamantly refused to follow his lead. With no weapons, the Simbas were able to capture us. This confused me at first, but he was convinced that God had other ways to deliver us from our enemies besides us having to shoot or kill them. In my case, he was proved right, but in his...well, *he* would say God had a different purpose for him than deliverance."

Ellie explained her dramatic delivery from almost certain harm and how it lead to the safety and healing refuge of Sacred Heart Mission under Sister Beatrice's wise care and counsel. Doug listened intently, only occasionally asking for clarification of a detail or location.

After nearly ninety minutes of disclosure, Ellie turned the conversation to Nick and his well-being. "Mr. Warren, I've had a lot of time to think about what happened. Until today, Nick didn't know Aaron had died. That happened over a month ago. He has a lot to sort through. I think he might even feel guilty about it, like he should have prevented it somehow. He has to heal from his bullet wound. That comes first. But I also wonder – what deeper wounds might he have acquired before the one that brought him down?"

She paused and then added in a sympathetic voice, "And then there's the matter of your relationship. Finding you after all this time and effort...it's a big deal. He's got to find answers to whatever questions your extended absence created for him."

Doug was quick to respond. "Ellie, there's even more in our family story that Nick and I need to resolve, things that you don't yet know about. You're right, though. He's got a lot of big issues to tackle in the coming days."

"Well, if I've learned anything from Sister Beatrice and the nuns at Sacred Heart," Ellie offered quietly, "it's that life has many mysteries. They insist that our most important response should be to pray, rather than to despair. So that's what I'd like to do."

Doug did not join Ellie's prayer, except in spirit, but he marveled at her perspective and authentic demeanor. *Could this be the same superficial know-it-all that grew up next door,* he wondered?

CHAPTER 62
Léopoldville, November 1964

Nick sat propped up in a crisp white-sheeted bed in the U.S. Embassy infirmary in Léopoldville. The intense mid-morning sun streamed through the windows brightening an otherwise drab room, colored only by a bouquet of bougainvillea on the table in the corner. Ellie was standing near the head of the bed talking quietly with him. Nick looked up with a smile as his father entered the room.

"Hi kids," The elder Warren exchanged a hug with Ellie. "The doctor says you came through the surgery in fine shape, Nick. How're you feeling by now?"

"Hi Dad. I'm not yet ready to take on a left-handed arm wrestle, but I'm doing much better, feeling stronger. Maybe it's that blood of yours they put in me."

"Yes, your wound required some work, all right. Extra blood, a metal plate and screws and some fancy stitching."

Doug turned to Ellie. "It was very gracious of your folks to take Nick and me in for the next several weeks while he recovers. I'm not sure what sort of arrangements we would have been able to come up with otherwise. Now, I've got to see what I can do about getting in touch with Sarah."

"And Masemba," added Nick. "Don't forget about Masemba. I just hope they're both safe."

Ellie placed a hand on Nick's arm and leaning over, kissed him lightly on the cheek before turning to go. "I'm going to leave the two of you alone, now. You need some time together. See you later, Nick; bye Mr. Warren."

Father and son watched as she quietly slipped out of the room. "That's not the same Ellie I remember," Doug commented at last. "She's always been very attractive but now she seems, well…"

"Mature?" Nick finished his father's sentence. "They say if trouble doesn't kill you, it makes you grow," he added. "And we've just been through plenty of the killer kind of trouble recently, that's for sure."

Doug smiled. "I prefer to apply the familiar Litoko village proverb. A rough translation: *'Struggle is required to turn a caterpillar into a butterfly.'* That's a better image for Ellie."

Nick decided he wanted no more of this particular line of discussion, so he changed the subject. His next words came out in a stream of pent-up thoughts, an emotional dam burst.

"Dad, Sarah told me about you and mom; about her affair with that Vermeulen guy in Litoko and about Todd and Lizzy. She told me how difficult all that was for you: that you put up with a lot, maybe too much before our evacuation permanently split the two of you up. Is it true?"

Nick's eyes were brimming. He continued without waiting for an answer. "And why did you let her take us kids off to America without a fight? Why didn't you tell us what had happened? Why didn't you ever come to see us, Dad? We didn't know what to think. We always knew Mom was sour on Congo and harsh in caring for us. We counted on your love and strength. After Independence we mostly felt...*abandoned* by you."

Tears were streaking Doug's face by then as well. On it were written pain and anguish. He paused to regain some composure before replying.

"Nick, as a man you are presently able to take in many things that would have simply been too confusing and overwhelming to learn about as a youth. To be frank, some of my history with Patty, with your Mom, I still don't fully understand, myself. Why did I do what I did and fail to do what I should have...I don't have an adequate explanation to offer to you, nor to myself for that matter." He was silent, pensive for a moment.

"Above all else I need to ask your forgiveness, son. I was just so focused on my own pain and so preoccupied with the disruptions of Independence that I neglected the needs of you kids. There's no excuse for that failing." His voice broke into sobs.

"Oh, Dad...I forgive you. I just missed you so much." Nick managed, as he reached out with his good arm.

The two clasped each other in a long embrace. For an extended period the only sounds in the room were quiet weeping as the souls of the long separated father and son touched one another at last.

When they finally released their grasp, Nick and his father began a new chapter in their relationship.

"Tell me about Sarah, Dad. How did that come about?" Doug sat back in his chair, and crossed his legs. With one hand at his elbow and the other at his chin, he began.

"I suppose our friendship grew out of the shared disasters of our marriages that neither Sarah nor I believed were primarily our doing. We long enjoyed a friendly relationship; one that dated back to the days

Sarah was a teenage foster child with the Ellis's. Neither of us ever entertained thoughts of any romantic interest, however."

Nick sat up fully as he listened to his father, soaking up every word.

"Patty and you kids evacuated and she filed for divorce. Around the same time, Sarah's husband rejected her and ended their marriage. She is unable to conceive. It's from wounds she suffered in childhood. I arranged for her to work for Fr. DuBois, but she was quite alone. We were both lonely and wounded. I suppose we found solace in each other's company. We shared with one another and found mutual support. Our friendship became interest and eventually, love."

"Sarah is a bright, remarkably kind and loving person, Nick. We are completely committed to one another. We are also aware that we face opposition. There are many who distain our marriage, both in the missionary and Congolese communities.   And probably from my family as well." He looked Nick squarely in the eyes.

"Not from me, Dad," Nick countered. "I think Sarah is one fine lady. She's gentle and loving, a good match for you. Besides, Mom has already remarried. I frankly don't see her being able to even grasp the damage she did in the past, let alone to ever resolve things with you in the present."

"Interesting," Doug replied. "That's just what Paul Carlson thought as well, God rest his soul. He urged me to make my first order of business reconciling with you and your brother and sister, not Patty."

"Are you planning to tell them who their real father is?" Nick's forehead wrinkled in a quizzical grimace as he sat back into the pillow behind him. He was unsure of how this question would be received.

"I'm their real father, Nick. I claim that role. But to answer your question, no, I'm not sure what I should tell them." Doug stroked his chin, gazing at his son. "It's something that requires more reflection and prayer. At this point *whatever* steps I take need to be based on what is in *their* best interests, not just what fulfills mine."

He added, "I do want to see them, however, and soon. We can discuss later whether I should go to the States to do that or have them come here. Sarah needs to be a part of that reunion."

Nick shifted the conversation one more time as he repositioned himself on the bed. "Dad, I need to tell you something that's troubling me. I'm not sure how to say this, so I'll just say it...I killed some people."

Doug remained quiet, listening, observing the torment that had filled his son's eyes.

"I felt like I had to. It was like the price of a ticket to Stanleyville, expected behavior among mercenaries. We did a lot of it, killing, I mean. It made me sick. It still does."

Tearful now, Nick concluded, "I wish I could take it all back, Dad, but I can't. How do I deal with this, with my nightmares?"

"Where are you with God on this issue?" Doug asked, simply.

Nick's returned an angry reply. "I was afraid you might ask that, or say something spiritual. That's too easy, 'just talk to God.' Dad, I *killed* people, shot them dead. How do I live with that? How can you or anyone else love a killer? How can *God* love a murderer?"

Laying his hand on Nick's arm, Doug smiled. "I, for one, am not going to cast the first stone, son. Neither am I going to think of you in any way other than with gratitude for all you went through to find me. It's going to take time for you to sort these things out for yourself. The dawn expels the darkness little by little, not instantly. Let's you and I agree to focus more on grace and mercy these days, than on fault and judgment. That suits my needs much better as well. Agreed?"

Nick smiled through tearful eyes. *It's so good to have a father.*

CHAPTER 63
Léopoldville, December 1964

It was a warm, muggy December afternoon in Léopoldville. The shade of the huge mango tree in the Ellis's back yard was welcome, as was the faint hint of a cooling breeze that drifted across the backyard where the two young people strolled, sharing quiet conversation in the warm day. It had been nearly two weeks since their dramatic departure from Stanleyville. Nick's shoulder, still very tender, was healing well though his left arm remained supported in a sling.

"What's going to happen next?" Ellie asked as they settled down on a bench to converse.

"Well, Dad tells me that next week the American Embassy is sending a plane and a recovery team to Bumba to see if they can locate and retrieve Aaron's body." Nick shifted on the bench to address Ellie.

"Oh yes. My father indicated that Aaron's parents made that request through the State Department," Ellie volunteered.

Nick continued, "Dad's hoping to somehow make contact with Sarah before then. If she and Masemba can make their way to Bumba they can take the plane on its return to Léo. Your dad is also trying to help contact her through his sources."

As an afterthought he added, "But Sarah may still have that shortwave radio of hers buried."

"I'll bet your Dad is glad Masemba is there with Sarah. He's such a capable fellow and a good friend."

"For sure!" Nick chimed in. "He'd like to convince our Litoko buddy to remain with them and serve as the plantation's business manager. He's hoping that maybe he could also persuade him to reopen the school in Biala village, at least on a part-time basis."

"But what about you, Nick? Are you going back to the States, returning to Wheaton for spring semester?" she asked with raised eyebrows.

"I told Dad that what I'd really like is to stay here with him and Sarah for a while longer. He, on the other hand, feels strongly that I should return to school. Dad thinks I'm too close to the end to delay things any further. Besides, we're in conversation about whether he and Sarah travel to the States to see Todd and Lizzie or whether we three kids return back here for a reunion. I told him either way, I'm for sure returning to Congo next summer...that's non-negotiable!"

Ellie just smiled, rolling her eyes as she slowly shook her head at his determination.

"And what about you, Ellie?" Nick asked quickly. "Are you back to Gordon College after the first of the year?"

"That's my plan. Mom is going to join me for a couple of months. I think she is worried that I might have some delayed freak-out reaction or something." Ellie smiled. She lifted her hand to her forehead in a mock worried expression. "But actually it'll be good to have her around for a while. I'm really okay with that."

Their conversation once more turned to Aaron's death. "Tell me again about Aaron, would you please, Ellie?" Nick asked. She complied without protest. At this retelling Nick was impressed that just prior to being shot, Aaron had moved protectively over Ellie to guard her from assault.

"That really took courage," he declared. "Aaron was sure no cowering pacifist, no passive victim. He put himself on the line for you."

"He did," agreed Ellie. "But he did so believing that God could deliver him and that he therefore had no need to defend himself or me with deadly force."

She added, "I am convinced that the lightning strike that immediately followed *was* God's deliverance for me."

"But that's what I don't get about God." Nick paused, perplexed. "How could He allow a good guy like Aaron to be killed and then allow someone...someone like *me* who chose to join in killing others, to escape scot-free with my life...well, with a non-lethal wound, anyhow?"

"Aaron would say something like: 'That's another one of those mysteries of life we'll have to ask God about some day.'" Ellie, smiled lightly. Then, with a more serious expression, she leaned forward.

"Here's how I've come to understand it, Nick," she continued carefully. "It takes light to reveal shadows and dispel darkness. The darkness and evil of the Simbas was fully revealed by the light of good people like Aaron, Dr. Carlson and other righteous and innocent victims who died at the rebels' hands."

"But, Ellie...they all *died!* How is *that* a positive, enduring message?" argued Nick, exasperated.

"I suppose that's where faith comes into it," Ellie replied. "The Apostle John wrote, *'The light* – referring to Jesus – *shines in the darkness and the darkness has not overcome it.*" Don't you think that applies to our situation, to how God intends for us to live on this planet?"

Nick frowned and scratched his head. "That seems like a pretty high standard, to live like Jesus did."

Ellie continued, her voice rising in intensity. "Nick, dispelling the darkness and revealing the shadows of Congo *requires light* – people living and dying in the Jesus way. I believe *that* is Aaron's lingering message to us. In fact, I believe he had a kind of premonition about doing this in a dream he once shared with me."

She sighed.

They sat together wordlessly for some time, absorbing Ellie's poignant reflections. Finally, Nick broke the silence. His voice trembled as he spoke.

"In view of your comments, I'm afraid I have to accept the fact that I made my way to Stanleyville joining in with the 'darkness and shadows,' as you put it. The things I did, the actions we took, were not ones I *ever* want exposed to light. I...I suppose my motives were good but my methods, well..." His voice faded, shoulders slumped. Nick stared down at his feet.

Ellie reached over and took his free hand in both of hers as she forced Nick to look into her eyes. She studied him carefully.

"You traveled a ways in the darkness, Nick, it's true. That close an exposure to evil is costly. It cost your victims their lives. It cost you a high price in guilt and ghastly memories. I believe, however, that your regret says much about the light that still lives inside you."

"I'm reminded of the verse that says, *'I am the light of the world. Whoever follows me will never walk in darkness, but will have the light of life.'*"

Pausing to give him time to take in her words, she concluded, "I'm expecting you Nick, to go forward in life dispelling darkness rather than lingering in shadows, even in your memories."

Nick smiled at Ellie. He raised his hand to shield his eyes, as a sunray pierced the thick mango leaves above him.

Author's Note

This is a work of fiction. Its principal characters, with the exception of key historical figures, are imagined and bear no relation to any real persons as far as I know. The Warrens – Brandon, Nathalie, Ellie and siblings – are fictional. So are Aaron Krehbiel, Masemba and Sarah Nkumu. All of the Warren family – Nick, Todd, Lizzie, Patty and Doug – are imagined, as are Amin and Nasir Rahman and their families. CIA Station Chief Loren Durban is fictional as well. All Congolese family members, minor military and government officials' names are my inventions.

The historical figures and events included in this novel, however, are real. I have drawn my descriptions of them from published accounts and as carefully as I am able, have attempted to depict their interaction with my story's characters in a manner entirely consistent with those reports. The timing of events in which they participated closely follows the historical record. This applies to the time lines of Nicholas Olenga and members of his leadership team, including Kinghis, Gbenye and Soumialot. It also pertains to the much-revered missionary doctor, Paul Carlson, and the much-maligned mercenary, Col. "Mad Mike" Hoare. Lt. Gary Wilson was a real person who won impressive but gristly victories over the rebels before he abruptly departed. I invented his nickname, "Crash" from facts in his actual history.

The major events that animate the story – the Simba Rebellion and the Stanleyville rescue – are very real. In one sense, this novel represents an attempt to retell a dramatic tale of suffering, survival and rescue from fifty years ago to a generation who has never previously heard of it. Unfortunately, many of the story's darkest shadows persist to the present day in that beautiful but troubled country.

Litoko is a fictional village in Congo's Équateur Province. The Warren children were said to attend a missionary children's boarding school in Karawa. The Ubangi Academy actually existed there until 1991 when it was closed because of an evacuation of missionaries. The Congo Evangelical Mission is a fictional organization. The CIA did indeed have a presence in Congo in the early 1960s. However, the depiction of its covert recruitment and use of missionaries is fiction, imagined in service of my story line. I know of no such collaboration during that period or later. The era's missionaries are likely to consider even the idea of such a partnership, repugnant.

Nick's choice to respond to mortal threats with violence is an echo of present day calls to do the same coming from within the Christian community. Some advocate the expansion of concealed weapons, the arming of public school teachers and the prompt shooting of gun-carrying enemies all in defense of American freedoms. Aaron's pacifist response represents a quiet contrasting voice within the Christian community, one largely overwhelmed by loud and emotional patriotic declarations from god-and-country advocates. Nick's struggle with his actions as a mercenary comes from my personal observations during the Viet Nam War while completing a yearlong psychiatric social work internship in a 1,000-bed VA hospital. It was impressed on me that in real life, killing enemies leaves an indelible scar on young men. Others will have to resolve the theological rationale for Christians to kill rather than, as Jesus taught, to love their enemies.

I was aided in my writing by a variety of resources. Primary among them were David Van Reybrouck's *Congo: A history of a people* and Jim Bertsche's huge chronicle, *CIM/AIMM: A story of vision, commitment and grace*. These two books provided rich background information and detailed the many competing forces swirling about at Congo's Independence. They also described the evacuation of expatriates both from the perspective of non-Africans as well as Congolese. Larry Devlin's *Chief of Station, Congo* added background to the CIA's interests and illuminated the influence of the era's political personalities. V. S. Napaul's novel, *A bend in the river*, depicted life in Stanleyville during the early '60s from the POV of a South Asian expatriate much like my characters. Mike Hoare's memoirs, *Congo Mercenary* and *Congo Warrior*, provided important details regarding mercenary life, the military campaigns of the Simba Rebellion and the infamous Lima One march to liberate Stanleyville. Finally, David Reed's *111 Days of Stanleyville* served as my primary source of background material depicting the details, conditions and persons comprising the *Dragon Rouge* rescue event.

I accessed numerous Internet references to identify cultural issues, maps, geographic information and facts regarding real personalities of the era such as Paul Carlson, Nicholas Olenga and Mike Hoare. My writing, however, was shaped most significantly by my personal experience. I resided in Kinshasa, DRC (ex-Léopoldville) for four years and traveled about in the Congo. I learned to speak Lingala. I continue to have contact with others who live and work there, such as missionary Glen Chapman, a helpful source of Lingala phrases and nicknames. Other former MKs and alumni from the American School of Kinshasa have supplied valuable stories, images and sensory memories of life in Congo via their FaceBook reminiscing. Former Congo MK Faith Eidse provided wise editing suggestions.

Finally, I want to recognize that this novel presents a filtered view of Congo in general and its volatile early years in particular. It offers a non-African perspective, a snapshot from a different era. Private ownership of rural plantations in the Congo, like the fanciful enterprise acquired by Doug Warren is rare or non-existent these days. The intervention of white mercenaries, a salvation for Stanleyville's 1,600 expatriates, was and is considered by most Africans a shameful invasion, an abuse of power. It was certainly experienced as a horror by the innocent Congolese whose lives were subject to the white soldiers' brutal and amoral actions at the time. So while I am conflicted in my story telling, I remain convinced it is an account worth sharing.

John B. Franz
Clovis, CA
October 2016

www.ingramcontent.com/pod-product-compliance
Lightning Source LLC
Chambersburg PA
CBHW021645260626
47154CB00017BA/2455